PRAISE FOR VIVIAN AREND

"If you've never read a Vivian Arend book you are missing out on one of the best contemporary authors writing today."
~ *Book Reading Gals*

"A Rancher's Heart was a spectacular start to this new series and I am very excited to see what comes next for the rest of the Heart Falls crew."
~ *Guilty Pleasures Book Review*

"Brilliant, raw, imaginative, irresistible!!"
~ *Avon Romance*

"This story will keep you reading from the first page to the last one. There is never a dull moment..."
~ *Landy Jimenez*

"Arend became a favorite author of mine because not only does she write about sexy cowboys, she gives us families who love and take care of each other."
~ *SmexyBooks*

"This was my first Vivian Arend story, and I know I want more!"
~ *Red Hot Plus Blue Reads*

ALSO BY VIVIAN AREND

The Stones of Heart Falls

A Rancher's Heart

A Rancher's Song

A Rancher's Bride

A Rancher's Love

A Rancher's Vow

Holidays in Heart Falls

A Firefighter's Christmas Gift

A Soldier's Christmas Wish

A Hero's Christmas Hope

A Cowboy's Christmas List

A Rancher's Christmas Kiss

The Colemans of Heart Falls

The Cowgirl's Forever Love

The Cowgirl's Secret Love

The Cowgirl's Chosen Love

A full list of Vivian's print titles is available on her website:
www.vivianarend.com

A RANCHER'S VOW

THE STONES OF HEART FALLS
BOOK 5

VIVIAN AREND

A Rancher's Vow
Copyright © 2023 by Arend Publishing Inc.
ISBN: 9781990674631
Edited by Angie Ramey
Cover Design © Damonza
Proofed by Linda Levy

1

June, Silver Stone ranch

His fishing line stretched taut as the bobber resurfaced then floated gently toward the middle of the lake. Contented as only a man can be with a rod in his hand and an afternoon off from work stretching before him, Dustin Stone laid back on the shore and covered his face with his cowboy hat.

Sunshine had warmed the grass, and the scent of early summer filled his senses. Peacefulness wrapped him up in an embrace, and he reveled in it. Moments like this truly highlighted that he lived in a spot that was heaven on earth.

Didn't mean he wasn't also looking for excitement. Hell, he'd only turned twenty-four this past December...

The same age Caleb had been when he'd become responsible for the entire family.

For a moment the warmth of the day cooled a little, and

something inside tightened as it always did when Dustin was reminded of his missing mom and dad. He was only eight when they'd died in a car accident, so it wasn't memories of them that struck.

It was the fact his oldest brother, Caleb, had given up so much to always be there for them.

Dustin would be the first to admit he had a serious case of hero worship. Especially over the past years as Caleb had worked to rally the Stone clan into the tight-knit unit it was today. A successful ranch, a thriving family—

Yeah, Dustin would do anything for Caleb, and that pretty much carried down the line to the rest of his siblings. As the youngest of five, plus a foster sister, he'd gotten parented by all of them. Could have been hell, but it hadn't been.

It simply was.

They were good people, his family. They'd been through a lot and come out the other side with a variety of skills that made them shine individually and as a group.

Made it difficult to stand out in the crowd, though. Dustin wasn't one to crave the spotlight, but it would be nice to be the center of attention once in a while.

The wind *whooshed* over the lake hard enough that the warning bell attached to the tip of his fishing rod shook once. The light peal of sound faded instantly, but he sat up and checked his line anyway.

The bobber floated easily, the bait untouched.

Dustin's phone pinged with an incoming message. During the workday, only a very short list of people could contact him. The Silver Stone foreman, Tucker Stewart, was a hard ass when it came to concentrating on the task at hand. Didn't matter that Tucker was also Dustin's brother-in-law, there would still be hell to pay if Dustin fucked with the rules.

But now that his shift was over, his phone was back on, and

that sound was linked to his best friend, Shim. Another ping sounded, and Dustin dragged the phone from his pocket.

Shim: *You never told me. Holy crap, seriously?*
Shim: *In case you need it. Here:* [*link*]

Dustin stared at the message, confused. He hit the link Shim had included, only to end up on one of those scroll-through-the-bullshit clickbait articles. The title alone made him blink.

Ten billionaire cowboy bachelors you need to meet!

His phone pinged, and then pinged again. This time, one was the tone he'd assigned a different friend, as well as a third message from Shim. Dustin ignored them both and kept reading, not sure what the hell kind of joke Shim was playing.

The fourth clicked-through page made the hair on the back of Dustin's neck stand up.

The article opened with a couple of pictures.

The first showed Dustin with his second-oldest brother, Luke, and Luke's wife, Kelli, at a horse sale this past February. The two of them stood side by side, laughing. A good-looking couple, dark haired Luke's arm was looped around Kelli's waist as he held her to his side. Her brown hair hung in the two braids she usually wore while working, but the joy on her face made her as bright and shiny as a glamorous front-page model.

Dustin stood beside them with his hands shoved into his front pockets as he grinned toward the ground. For the first time, Dustin realized he stood taller than Luke. And maybe it was a trick of the camera angle, but his shoulders looked broader as well.

Huh. When had that happened?

The second image was just him. Dustin remembered the moment it had happened. He'd been walking beside Kelli, who was leading a new purchase they'd made. Some fool set off a firecracker, and the horse had spooked.

Kelli had the reins and shifted to haul the beast to a stop instantly—she was rock solid when it came to controlling even the unruliest animal. But the horse was big enough he'd reared skyward, jerking her petite frame off the ground.

There'd been no time to think, only react. Dustin had caught the animal around the head, corralling him to a standstill even as he spoke softly to gentle him.

Dustin had looked that horse in the eye and told him to mind his manners, and damn if the creature hadn't listened. He'd shivered for a moment, as if chasing a fly off his withers. Then he'd breathed out a huge sigh and relaxed his head against Dustin's shoulder.

When it was over, Kelli had kissed Dustin's cheek. Luke had patted him on the shoulder with an older-brother approval that meant the world to Dustin.

Meanwhile, out in the crowd, someone had used that moment to take a picture of Dustin looking all serious and had now plastered it all over social media.

Dustin rolled his eyes. Stupid what people wanted to waste their time on. His gaze leapt to the words of the article, already wondering how much worse it could get.

Plenty.

Set your sights on this #SilverStoneStud

He might be young, but as part of the newly minted Silver Stone success story, twenty-four-year-old Dustin Stone is one very eligible bachelor. The ranch seems to have found the pot of gold at the end of the rainbow after a tragic beginning. This second-

generation family operation is gaining ground in a huge way in the horse breeding community. Plus—we've heard there's now oil rights added to the story, and well, there's only one unmarried Stone who still needs to find his perfect match. You can all see that in the physical area, he's got what it takes to make anyone sit up and take notice.

Who's going to be the lucky woman to strike Silver?

Dustin flopped back on the ground, hands flung to the sides as he stared into the sky and groaned. Hell, he was in for such a razzing. His friends and brothers were never going to let him live this down. Cheesiest thing he'd ever read. Strike Silver? God. It wasn't even a good pun.

And that hashtag? Gross.

His phone rang. Shim, obviously having given up on waiting for a response to his messages, had gone to the method of last resort.

Dustin hit accept and pressed speaker. "What?"

"Oh good. You are still speaking to the little people in your life." Shim snickered then cleared his throat. "What the hell, Stone?"

"No idea, Choi. I'm busy minding my own business like usual. Hauled cattle this morning, and now I'm sitting here looking for some fish."

"Well, you should consider looking for a hiding spot. *Billionaire?* They might as well have painted a red target on your back and shoved you onto a shooting range."

Dustin snorted. "I'm not a billionaire. Whoever wrote that article has a great imagination. I mean, yes, Silver Stone is doing great. That doesn't mean *I* have more in my wallet than most of the hands."

His friend clicked his tongue. "I know that, and you know

that. But the people who read this are going to think differently."

"They'll find out the truth damn quick. Couple of questions in the right places, and they'll know the only thing that article nailed was that I'm single." Which was okay by him. Eventually, he'd find a life-partner. Too many examples surrounded him of people doing marriage well to not want to dive in at some point.

But now? Hell no.

"Ignoring the article, after asking how you ended up reading such bull, when do you get here?" Dustin asked.

"The article was my mom's fault. She spotted the nonsense about fifteen minutes ago while researching something. She forwarded it with a note that said ranching obviously paid better than technology, so maybe my past summers spent working with you wouldn't be a total loss." Shim snickered along with Dustin, then added the more important details. "I handed in my final project today. I'll be arriving on Monday if that still works."

"Of course, it works. I'll be damn glad to see you again." This was one area where Dustin knew exactly what was going on. "Congrats on finishing school. You're back in your same room in the bunkhouse. Shoot me your details, and I'll come grab you at the airport."

"No need. I've got a truck this time."

Well damn, more good news. "You bought it?"

"I did. I can't wait to show her off when I get there." Shim cleared his throat. "Of course, my fourth-hand Chevy, as pretty as she is, won't get a second look next to whatever fashionable billionaires are driving this week."

"Fuck off," Dustin said lightly.

"Just saying."

"You're an ass. *That's* what you're saying?" Dustin considered. "Sure, I agree with you."

Shim laughed. "Okay, I'll give you a break. But seriously, the article could be nothing or nothing but trouble. I hope it's the first."

"Not much I can do about it. It's already out there in the world." The tip of Dustin's fishing rod dipped, the warning bell dancing merrily as a fish finally found his bait. "Got one. Gotta run."

"Have fun."

Dustin dropped the phone and grabbed his rod from the holder. He enjoyed a sweet little battle with a rainbow trout before carefully releasing the fish back into Big Sky Lake.

That's when he noticed his phone was still making noises where it lay in the grass.

Dustin picked it up and glanced at the screen. "The fuck?"

The alert warned 37 MESSAGES. Even as he stared at the number in shock it went up as another *buzz* sounded.

What the ever-loving hell?

"And that cupboard is where we keep the extra office supplies. After you've been here for a few days, if you want to reorganize to make your life easier, feel free." Tucker Stewart gestured around the room. "I think that's it in terms of the office tour. Any questions?"

Charity Gruzing linked her fingers together on the back of the office chair in front of her to keep from bouncing with delight. "I'm good for now. If I think of anything, I'll make a list so I can ask them all at once."

Tucker grabbed his hat from the rack and replaced the black Stetson on his head. A quiet smile curled his lips as he offered her a wink. "I'm all about efficiency, but if you need to interrupt, go ahead. Don't worry about saving up the questions to dump them all at once. I'm just delighted to have you take over some of my least favourite tasks."

"We all have our strengths," she said politely. She waited until he was no longer visible before closing the sturdy wooden door firmly.

After checking the window that faced into the barn was covered by its privacy curtain, and the window to outside showed an empty green pasture, Charity shot her hands into the air and did a happy dance right there in the middle of the Silver Stone office.

Finally.

She turned eagerly toward the stacks of projects Tucker had laid out for her. With her first day falling on a Friday, she wanted to work fast to familiarize herself with everything so she could dive in full force on Monday.

Her phone rang. She answered it quickly, chatting with her friend Fern Fields even as she organized the first pile of paper according to the dates on the invoices. "Silver Stone ranch. Charity Gruzing speaking. How can I help you?"

A delighted squeal echoed across the line. "Tee! You must be quivering with excitement. First day at the new job. I'm so pumped for you."

"I'm beyond quivering. Somewhere between vibrating and earthquake, which is going to make it tough when I get on the computer later."

"Your nerves will settle down soon enough, but I foresee you staying thrilled for quite a while," Fern said, laughter in her voice. "So?"

Charity paused in the middle of her sorting. "So... What's the rest of the sentence?"

Fern lowered her voice. "I didn't want to say anyone's name in case you're on speakerphone."

Oh. *That* topic. The office seemed pretty soundproof, but just in case, Charity picked up her phone and put it to her ear. "I did not get this job in the hopes of ogling Dustin Stone."

"But it is a sweet side benefit. Besides, he's a good guy. You're my best friend. I like it when people who I like also like each other."

And that was where this conversation needed to get redirected, PDQ. "We do like each other, Little Miss Busybody. Dustin and I are good friends, and that's that. Do not try any matchmaking."

"I would never dream of such a thing." Fern attempted a tone of astonished dismay. Failed miserably.

"You're such a lying liar, but I love you anyway." Charity glanced at the clock on the wall. "In the meantime, I am now gainfully employed at a wonderful new position. Which means I'm going to say goodbye to you until tomorrow so I can focus on impressing my new bosses."

"Sounds like a plan. You're going to rock that job," Fern assured her. "Meet you at seven?"

"You bet."

Charity dove into the paperwork. Her new position as office manager would utilize skills she'd picked up during the four years since graduating from high school. After two years of college on a scholarship, and follow up on-the-job training, she had the basics down pat—simple accounting, organizing, and calendar management.

Some of the new work was a lot more technical, though. Silver Stone had several online booking systems in place that she needed to go over in more detail to make sure she absolutely knew how they worked.

The idea of screwing up something important was enough

to make her focus on her tasks and ignore most of the happy distractions floating through her brain.

It wasn't only that her new job was at a highly respected place like Silver Stone, although that was a huge part of it. Having a consistent salary above minimum wage was the biggest improvement. Charity was tired of living from paycheck to paycheck.

It's not always easy to do what's right, but we do it anyway.

Her grandmother's voice echoed in Charity's head. The woman had passed on now, but she had been the biggest influence during Charity's teenage years. Grandma Lily had raised Charity and her sister Chelsea after their parents had gone from pretending to be the perfect family to everything blowing apart.

One result of the mess meant Charity hadn't had much financial support past high school. The past four years had been a struggle.

A knock sounded on the office door a second before it swung open. "Tucker, I wanted to talk to you about—" Tamara Coleman jerked to a stop. "Charity. Well, damn. He actually went and did it."

"Excuse me?" Charity rocketed to her feet when the older woman entered the room. She'd taught Tamara's daughters ballet lessons in the past. Married to Caleb, the oldest brother and head of Silver Stone, Tamara was one of those people who had a quiet way of seeming to look into your soul with just a glance.

Charity had no desire to tangle with the woman or get on her wrong side.

Tamara strolled all the way into the room and sat, waving Charity back to her chair. "Tucker. Caleb and I have been telling him to hire somebody for ages. He kept saying he would. I assume that's why you're here?"

"Just started," Charity agreed, eager to be helpful. "If you want to know where he is, I can find out pretty quickly."

"No, that's okay. It can wait."

Charity already had the *Finder* app open on the desktop. She'd spent the past thirty minutes making sure she could work it properly. "He's with Ashton Stewart and Caleb in arena four."

A long low whistle escaped Tamara. "Damn. Can I see?"

Charity rolled her chair back slightly and gestured to the computer screen. "It's handy, but the data tracing also makes my skin crawl."

Tamara stood behind her, leaning closer to examine the little icons that showed up on the overlaid map of the ranch. "Oh, look. Dustin's riding his favourite trail again." She pointed to his icon near the farthest north boundary of the ranch before stepping back and shaking her head. "Yeah, I hear you. I'm equally amazed and horrified by technology. Knowing someone could find me that quickly is kind of creepy."

"Leave your phone behind." Charity forgot who she was talking to as the impulse to joke kicked hard. "Tucker said they hadn't quite got to the point of embedding trackers in everyone who works at Silver Stone. It's on the schedule for next month."

Tamara's head jerked up, her eyes sharp behind her hot-pink framed glasses. A moment later, a grin bloomed. "You know, I've always liked you. I think you'll be a good addition to Silver Stone."

"I like you, too," Charity said honestly. "I plan to do a great job."

With a final glance at the screen and a shake of her head, Tamara returned to the other side of the desk. "I suppose I should ask you this question before getting in Tucker's way. Do you have access to the work roster for the next few weeks?

We all had timing issues with girls' night out last month. I want to make sure Kelli is free before we nail down a new date."

"I think I can do that. One minute." Charity opened another section of the computer. She grabbed the pile of paper on the desk Tucker had indicated was scheduling data to be amalgamated. After flipping through a few pages and peeking at the calendar, she hesitated. "I'm going to have to get back to you. According to one source, Kelli works different times than the other. Either I'm not reading it right, or they have her double-booked."

"It's probably the double-booked option," Tamara said dryly. "If you could find out and let me know on Monday, I'd appreciate it."

"Sure."

Tamara dipped her chin. "Welcome to Silver Stone. Thanks for dealing with the chaos. And trust me, I know intimately how wild and woolly the paperwork can get around here."

"You're welcome. I'm looking forward to the challenge," Charity said brightly.

With Tamara gone, the rest of the afternoon passed quickly. Charity made her way through piles of data, filed a million papers, and had another impromptu lesson in Silver Stone bookkeeping when Stone brother number two, Luke, blasted into the office with a sheepish expression and a fistful of unfiled receipts.

With a sense of accomplishment, Charity finished tidying the desk.

She was in the middle of pulling on her coat when the third brother of the Stone family stopped in.

Walker Stone was a lean, muscular cowboy. He was softer spoken than Luke and had spent time on the circuit as a bull rider. Just the thought of the danger he'd faced made Charity queasy.

He spoke as he rounded the corner into the office. "I wanted to ask you a question."

Probably expected to find Tucker, not her. "I can leave a note for Tucker," Charity offered. "Or if it's an emergency, I can get a hold of him right away."

Walker smiled. "Nope, I was actually talking to you."

"Oh. Of course. What's up?" Charity settled her purse strap over her shoulder and waited expectantly.

"I know you're wrangling things around here now." Walker twirled a finger in the air as he indicated the office. "Thank God, if I might add."

She laughed.

"Ivy and I were wondering, does this mean you won't be teaching ballet anymore?" Walker frowned. "Wait. The summer camps sponsored by the Boys and Girls Club include dance. What's happening with that now that you've started work here?"

"The summer camps are still on," Charity assured him. "I set my calendar at Silver Stone so the days I teach during the summer can still happen."

Walker nodded, his expression thoughtful.

"As for the fall, I haven't set my plans that far out, but I have no intention of giving up the after-school dance lessons. I love teaching them, and I think they're a good thing for the community."

Working two jobs meant she would have nearly zero days off over the summer, even after giving up her volunteer position with the fire department.

Her schedule was manageable.

Barely.

Walker eyed her, but his expression brightened. "All three

of my kids are interested in dance. I'm glad to hear that it'll still happen."

"If things change in the fall, I could give them private lessons."

Damn it. She really needed to think harder before she spoke. Because if she wasn't teaching through the community run program, it wouldn't be financially feasible to do something for just a few kids.

Oh, well. If she ended up donating some hours, but the kids had fun, it would be worth it in the end. Staying on the Stone family good side was a priority.

Walker held out his hand. "Appreciate it."

Accepting his hand, she shook it firmly. "No problem."

Locking the office behind her, Charity put her head down and beelined for her car.

A relaxing evening was followed by a late sleep in. Saturday was her usual cleanup of her tiny one-bedroom apartment including catching up on dishes—a once a week marathon event.

The day passed quick enough that it was soon time to get ready to meet Fern. Charity pulled on a jean skirt and a button-down, blue-checked shirt over a pretty yellow tank.

She left her hair natural. Her spiral-like curls hung to the top of her shoulders, a glorious wreath of dark brown, as her grandmother used to say. She felt pretty and was still buzzing inside from the great first day on the job.

Fern stood on the wooden boardwalk outside Rough Cut pub, waving as Charity crossed the street from her apartment.

"Hey, girlfriend." Fern offered her a high five, then curled her arm with the prosthetic hand around Charity's elbow. "Ready to trip the light fantastic?"

"Dear Lord. Someday you're going to say one of these

phrases around someone who thinks you're poking fun at them."

"If they used to trip the light fantastic, I doubt they'd be that hung up on semantics." Fern tugged her forward. "Come on. There's been a huge number of people coming in tonight. Let me reboot that— There's been a huge number of *women* coming in tonight. I checked to see if there's a special *all you can drink ladies' night* or something, but nothing. We might end up having to dance with each other."

"Not the worst punishment," Charity pointed out. "You don't have two left feet."

"True that." Fern grabbed the door and pulled it open, pressing Charity ahead of her into the dimmer light as country music swelled in volume.

Jostled by the bodies around her, Charity struggled to keep her feet. She'd been at Rough Cut when the place was full, but this was beyond anything she'd seen before.

Shoulder to shoulder with the people around her, she was pushed forward as if caught in a wave. And when the pressure broke momentarily, it spat her forward, hard, into the back of a cowboy.

He teetered, tilted. Charity fought for balance, but another bump against her rear simply sent her harder into the man. Even as she apologized, they were falling to the ground, twisting in midair.

He caught her by the arms, and when they landed, he was under her, his back to the dance floor. She bounced against his torso, air rushing from their lungs as she stared into the face of the man she'd been daydreaming about getting horizontal with. Not this way, but still...

Her cheeks heated to boiling as her focus narrowed to the small space on the dance floor where Dustin Stone lay under her in all his muscular glory.

2

It had been one hell of a weekend. It looked as if it was going to be one hell of a night, as well.

Laying on the dance floor wasn't a good idea in the first place, and tonight it was downright dangerous. Which meant instead of taking a second to appreciate that his fancy gymnastic-like move had worked—

Don't lie. You're appreciating the soft curves tucked up against you, not your superhero moves...

Shit. Not a place his thoughts were allowed to go.

Dustin rose to his feet, lifting Charity with his hands around her waist. Even once they reached vertical, he kept her close because the crowd at Rough Cut was outrageous. "You okay?"

"I think?" Charity wavered, slapping a hand against his chest to catch her balance. "Sorry. Again."

"Not your fault," he insisted, letting his gaze dance over her. She didn't look as if she'd been injured, but a shove forceful enough to tip him over could have hurt.

Fern Fields stepped forward, her wide-eyed gaze darting over the crowd around them. "This place is out of control."

Charity ducked, narrowly avoiding being punched as someone enthusiastically threw their arms in the air and shouted *Yee Haw*.

Enough.

"Come on." Dustin tilted his head toward the side of the dance floor, tugging Charity along for the ride.

After a quick glance proved Fern had followed, Dustin focused on keeping his feet as they wove through the crowd to the small alcove tucked to the right of the stage.

The thankfully empty alcove blocked a portion of the high-volume music and rowdy voices. The moment of relative calm was a welcome relief.

Dustin put his back to the wall and took a deep breath. "Jeez. Fucking chaos."

"What's going on?" Charity asked, peeking back into the mayhem. "I haven't seen a crowd like this since the night the country singer your brother Walker did backup vocals for showed up in town and did an impromptu set."

"I remember that night." Fern punched Dustin in the shoulder. "You were enjoying his backup singer's gyrations so much you stepped on my feet a dozen times while we were dancing."

"Thanks, Fern. Of course you remember me doing something embarrassing."

Fern patted his cheek fondly. "You can always count on your best gal pals to keep it real."

Charity didn't say anything, but a hint of a smile twisted her lips.

It was too tempting. Dustin rolled his eyes. "You're thinking something terrible about me as well. I can't catch a break with you two, can I?"

She outright grinned. "I didn't say a word."

"You were thinking really loud," Dustin complained, but he offered a wink with the words. He took another glance toward the dance floor and shook his head. "I don't know about you guys, but I'm not a big enough glutton for punishment to stick around for this."

Fern wrinkled her nose. "There's more milling about than dancing going on."

"Still wonder why," Charity muttered. "It's like a puzzle to solve."

"Except this puzzle means stomped-on toes and bruised hips." Fern shrugged. "Maybe it's just a weekend thing, but I agree we should do something else for fun tonight."

Charity looked disappointed but dipped her chin in agreement. "I've got the fixings for nachos." Her gaze flicked to Dustin. "You're welcome to join us."

He certainly wasn't staying here. No reason for him to head back to his room at the bunkhouse—he was trying to spend more time away from Silver Stone ranch rather than sticking around even during his nights off.

Besides, the girls were easy company. It was a simple decision to nod his agreement. "Want me to grab anything?"

"We're good," Fern informed him even as she pulled him off the wall and turned him toward the crowd. "We'll use you as a defensive linebacker. Straight through, Stone. Get us to freedom in one piece, and I'll let you put jalapeños on the nachos."

Laughter bubbled from Charity's lips. "Forget about running the gauntlet. Follow me." She guided them away from the crowd. Slipping behind the stage, the volume of music swelled to deafening. Charity didn't bother to speak, just pointed up at the illuminated *exit* sign tucked behind the massive speakers.

A moment later they stood in the back alley behind Rough Cut. The warm spring air was a refreshing change after the closed-in atmosphere of the pub.

Charity's expression turned to pure contentment. "Freedom, as requested. Which also means we'll skip the jalapeños. At least on my portion of the tray."

Fern offered a high five. "Well done, bestie. New plan for the evening activated. Come on. Nacho time. We'll find something to watch."

"You are not getting me to watch that horror flick you were raving about," Charity warned as they formed a line three across, striding down the alley away from the noise of the pub.

"It's not horror, it's a psychological thriller."

"Oh goodie, that makes it so much better—*not*. It's a mind fuck," Charity complained. "That's not relaxing and entertaining. It's stressful."

"Adrenaline is good for the system."

"Ha."

Dustin paced beside them, enjoying their quiet banter after the noise, not just of the pub, but his past two days.

While he still had his phone on him, Dustin had shoved the device in his back pocket. He'd muted the ringer and every type of notification possible. Right now, the only people who could get a hold of him were Caleb and Tucker.

Damn social media.

A soft nudge hit his shoulder, and he glanced over to see Charity eyeing him with curiosity. "You're awfully quiet tonight."

Dustin shrugged. "Just thinking."

Fern tucked her arm around his. "A dangerous thing to do."

Charity snickered.

Time with these two was comfortable. Easy.

As Fern had said, they were pals. The Fields and Stone

families had been friends forever, which meant he and Fern had spent a lot of time together off and on over the years. When Charity had moved to Heart Falls a few years ago, she'd slipped right into that comfortable space as well.

Which reminded him. He squeezed Fern's hand. "Shim will be here on Monday."

"I know."

It was tempting to roll his eyes again. "I should have guessed you'd already heard."

Fern waved a hand. "Considering we've talked to each other on a weekly basis the entire time he's been gone, of course I'm up to date on his schedule."

Well, damn. "I had no idea you guys were—" Dustin stopped, literally. Right there on the sidewalk outside Charity's apartment. Shim hadn't said a word about Fern. "Come to think of it, I have no idea *what* you two are up to. Did you really manage a long-term relationship all this time?"

A chorus of laughter danced between Fern and Charity.

Fern shook a finger in his direction. "No. There's nothing like that between me and Shim. He's been mentoring me online in some tech skills I need for my job at the gallery."

"So you're *not* dating?" Dustin was confused. Although Shim had never come right out and admitted anything, Dustin had his suspicions. "I always thought you guys were interested in each other."

He followed Charity into her first-floor apartment.

"Of course not. Shim knows that. I have my eye on someone else," Fern offered with a bright smile.

Interesting. "Well, that's an open invitation to ask for more."

Charity transferred ingredients from the fridge to the counter. She paused to shake her head firmly at Dustin. "You'd think so, but the woman is a steel-trap when it comes to details. She drops just enough to tease the hell out of me. I pride myself on being observant, so I have no idea why I can't figure out who she's pining for."

Fern placed two cookie sheets on the table and pointed to the cupboard over the refrigerator. "Not that I'm changing the subject, but I'm totally changing the subject. Dustin, your turn, please."

He chuckled even as he stretched up to grab two bags of chips. "I've never asked. Why do you put your chips in the tallest cupboard? If I'm not here, you have to haul a chair over to get at them."

"Exactly. It's either put them out of easy reach or not have them in the house, and I'd prefer to have them around for when I really want them." Charity pointed to the grater and block of cheese on the counter. Dustin obediently got to work. "When I put them on the top shelf, I can't access them without making a deliberate choice. Ergo, I don't grab them as often as I would otherwise."

It was brilliant, in a twisted sort of way. "Good idea, I guess."

"Thanks for the enthusiastic endorsement." Charity grabbed a couple of ripe avocados off the counter and began making guacamole. "Since Fern doesn't want us poking into her business, let's go back to my original question. What deep thoughts were you pondering? Or were you just sad you didn't get to trip the light fantastic all night?"

Really? "Who the hell says things like *trip the light fantastic?*"

For some reason that made Fern snicker.

Charity paused in the middle of crushing the avocado and shook her fork at him. "Deep thoughts?"

"Social media."

"*Ohhhhhh*." Fern alternated the nacho chips with cheese as he completed grating handfuls. "The evils of this modern reality or the amazing pros?"

"The annoyance factor at the moment." He didn't want to look at his phone to see how many messages he was currently ignoring. "It appears my name was mentioned in some clickbait article, and now anyone who's ever been in contact with me has to find out what I thought of the article and if it's true."

He wasn't going to tell them about the *friends* who had already tried hitting him up for a loan.

"Damn. That is annoying," Charity agreed. "I had something go viral once. It wasn't pleasant."

Fern frowned. "Is that why you have zero social media accounts? To get away from it?"

"Pretty much. I can talk to everyone I want to in other ways." Charity shrugged. "Just my thing."

Exactly. Dustin looked her in the eye and nodded. "I like being able to keep in touch with friends. When I want mindless entertainment, people doing wild shit is right there for a short-term, no-commitment kick. I don't like so called friends who only seem interested in my three minutes of glory."

"All hail the power of connection—five miles wide and half an inch deep." Fern popped the loaded trays into the oven. "Sorry you're having to deal with that." She hauled out her phone. "Which clickbait site? Oh, never mind. I'll google you."

"*Fern*," Charity scolded as she poked in the fridge. "Give him a break."

"Give him a beer," Fern suggested, eyes glued to her phone screen. "*Ohhhh*. You're a rich man, are you? Shall I put some caviar on your nachos?"

Dustin blew a raspberry as he took the beer Charity

pressed into his hands. "Careful, Fields. The urge to actively investigate your love life is growing..."

"I'm all aquiver." Fern popped a jalapeño in her mouth and hummed happily before patting his arm sympathetically. "Sorry, bud. That *hashtag* is rude."

"Being called a stud makes me feel like one of our horses."

Fern's eyes widened. "Oops, yeah, that isn't the bad one."

Damn it. "Show me," he demanded.

She held out her phone. Some comedian had added on *#OneCockyCowboy* to the article, and now that and *#SilverStoneStud* were both being sent around with the clickbait.

Dustin sighed. "Fuck it."

Fern grimaced. "Again, sorry. Fingers crossed it's over and wiped away by tomorrow's next Big Deal. Okay—next on the agenda. Distraction by movie selection. Tee, you and Dustin go arm wrestle to decide what's up first."

It was comfortable having them in her space. Fern and Dustin.

Fern made sense. After all, they hung out together whenever possible.

Dustin, however— They were friendly. They were friends, absolutely.

Damn it all anyway.

Charity sighed even as she counted her blessings. She might like the way he looked, and she might physically have the hots for him, but she was not in the position to acquire a full-time boyfriend. Not even one like Dustin.

Maybe *especially* not one like Dustin. The distance between them financially had always been a lot, and now it was a gaping chasm. Not because of that stupid article, but because she knew the actual family.

A single woman without any family support except an equally broke but well-loved sibling was not the equal to a man who belonged to a family dynasty.

Ergo, being friends was the best and only solution. Having a support network of both sexes was wonderful and, for now, exactly what she needed.

She just wished there was some way of telling her body that as she sat on the couch next to him, their thighs touching.

Fern had taken control of one corner of the couch, and Dustin the other, leaving Charity as the stuffing in the middle. Every time her elbow bumped his as one or the other adjusted position, a little buzzing sensation slid up her spine. It was a cheap thrill, admittedly, but did she move further away from him?

She did not.

Which meant she was not only blissfully ignoring her own excellent advice, but she was also asking for potential trouble.

Her phone rang, and she jumped to answer it, waving off Fern's suggestion to pause the movie. "It's my sister. This shouldn't take long."

She slipped into her bedroom and closed the door. "Hey, Chelsea. How's it going?"

"Over here? Excellent. More importantly, how was your first day yesterday?"

"Wonderful and scary all at the same time," Charity admitted. "Most of that was first day jitters, but also a little of *am I in over my head?*"

"From what you've told me about Silver Stone, as long as you're trying your best, they'll help you over any bumps in the road."

"You're right. Just nervous."

"Makes sense, but you've got this," Chelsea assured her.

Which was exactly what she needed to hear. "Thanks."

"It's true."

Charity took a deep breath. "You are awesome, and I love you, but I can't talk for long because I've got friends over."

"I only have a minute, myself. Suz and I are headed dancing, but I ran out of time last night and I wanted to touch base with my little sis before too many days passed."

Which was how Chelsea operated, which was part of the reason why Charity loved her so much. They didn't live in each other's pockets, but they made sure they kept in touch. "I'm glad you called, and things are great. Give Suz a kiss for me, and you guys have a wonderful time tonight. I'll be in touch next week with my final schedule so we can plan our summer holiday get-together, as short as it will have to be."

"Perfect. Love you."

"Back atcha."

Solid warmth flooded her heart. Charity might not have her Grandma Lily anymore, but a rock-solid sister and sister-in-law in her corner was enough. Still smiling, she headed back to the main room to rejoin her friends.

The front door was just closing, a soft chuckle escaping Dustin as he turned back into the living room.

He spotted her and grinned, poking a thumb over his shoulder. "Fern got a call. Something about her brother-in-law needs her to deal with a computer gone crazy at the gallery, and it can't wait until the morning or his paints will melt."

Charity attempted to keep her suspicions off her face. It was entirely possible the story was true. It was also possible that Fern was, once again, being a *good friend* and leaving Charity alone with Dustin.

Nothing to do but push through. No reason they couldn't enjoy the rest of the movie together.

"More nachos for us." She winked as she went to grab more ice for her drink. She turned to discover Dustin frowning over her shoulder, peering past her into the fridge. "Need something?"

He glanced at the coffee table where the nacho plate and his and Fern's beers sat.

He met Charity's gaze evenly. "Why are you drinking water?"

Her cheeks heated. She wasn't about to admit there had only been two beers left in the fridge. Shopping for treats was reserved for the start of the month. "Hydration is important."

Dustin's expression tightened. "We could have shared."

She snorted. "It's fine. Drinking water for a night isn't going to kill me."

"No. But neither would have pouring two beers into three glasses." He grinned. "I'd have lifted my pinkie in the air like I was fancy. Fern would have loved it."

Embarrassment fading as he joked, Charity nudged him back to the couch. "Okay, next time I forget to buy beer, I'll insist we share."

He didn't say anything, and he was a few steps behind her when she settled on the couch.

Dustin sat, picked up his beer, and began pouring into the glass he must have grabbed from the cupboard. "There we go. Just like we tell my nieces and nephews. Sharing is caring."

Good lord. "You did not just do that."

He paused with the glass held out. "Pour without spilling?"

"Pour from the bottle you were already drinking from." Charity gestured at it. "Germs, dude."

A snort escaped him. "Really?"

"Really."

He calmly put the glass on the table then turned toward her. He leaned in.

She leaned back. "What are you doing?"

"Trying to figure out if you're serious." He was right there in her face, expression somewhere between amusement and concern. "I'm healthy. I brushed my teeth recently. Any germs in your beer are less than you'd get from a kiss."

A shiver raced up her spine as if a finger had trailed over sensitive skin. How did she get out of this situation without doing what she wanted, which was to grab him by the lapels and kiss his brains out?

She went for an easy shrug. "Yeah, but we don't kiss."

"We could." Dustin planted a hand on the armrest of the couch which meant he was now leaning over her, smile in full force as he teased. "Then you'd be able to drink the beer I so gallantly acquired for you."

"That's how it works? Like a pre-germ load up makes them not exist anymore?"

"Exactly." He was close enough to lean his forehead against hers. "It's science. It's..."

His words trailed off. His smile slipped, gaze dropping to her mouth.

Curse words flew through her brain, but none escaped her lips. She was too busy trying to find the one solution that would fix—

"Tee—Damn it, tell me *no* if you don't want this." His voice was dark chocolate, raspy and deep.

"Want...*what?*" The words were a whisper. He remained over her, and despite what she knew she needed to do, her hands rose to capture his torso. Sliding over his waist and up until she had rock-solid biceps under her fingers.

He groaned at her touch. His eyes closed briefly before meeting hers again. "I'm going to kiss you, and it's not for any reason other than I fucking want to. Okay?"

She could have sworn she nodded. Her head bobbled—it must have.

But he didn't move. Waiting, motionless.

Damn it. He wanted her to say it. "Yes. Kis—"

His mouth was on hers, sweeping away the rest of the words. She wrapped her hands around his shoulders and pulled him closer.

Their lips made contact with just the right amount of pressure to make her skin prickle in a million places. She opened her mouth and his tongue teased in, stroking over hers then retreating as a flash of heat rolled through her and made her moan.

Tongues still tangling, he adjusted his weight until she lay under him. His hard body pressed her to the couch cushions. One thick thigh settled between hers, and she gasped as he nudged upward against her sex. He pressed a hand to her belly and then higher, groaning as he cupped her breast over her shirt and bra.

It was everything she'd dreamed of. It was exactly where she shouldn't be, only it was too late to turn back the clock. Too late for regrets.

Kissing had happened. She may as well enjoy herself and face the consequences later.

She dragged her fingers through his hair, tilting her head as he kissed a path down her jaw to her neck. "That feels so good."

He rocked his hips, the thick length of his erection pressing to her hip. "It feels too good." The words soft, deep. "Damn it, Tee. We shouldn't be doing this."

"Nope, we shouldn't." She caught his face in her hands and turned him back so she could kiss him again. The pressure on her clit was not nearly enough to make her come, but it still felt amazing. And the kissing—more than she'd ever imagined.

And she'd imagined it a lot.

His body weight on hers was perfect. His lips on hers. His hand, opening her button on her skirt and slipping into her underwear—the only thing that would make right now better was to be naked and in her bed.

Dustin groaned, rolling to the side as he broke the contact between their lips. "Let me..."

He stroked a finger over her folds. Charity closed her eyes and let pleasure become her focus.

His mouth returned to hers, soft kisses now. Teeth nibbled on her lower lip. The heated air of his breath washed over her cheek. His tongue darted out to ease against hers.

The entire time, he stroked between her legs, edging over her clit as it swelled to his touch. "So wet," he whispered. "You like this?"

"Yes."

"What about this?" He pushed a finger into her, the back of his hand trapped against her skirt, and she hated clothes with a passion at that moment.

"It feels good, but I need more pressure on my clit—oh, my God, yes. *There*."

He laughed softly as he continued to stroke his finger into her. His thumb had found her clit again, though, and the combination was deadly. The sensation of her rising orgasm tingled through her core.

"Look at me," he ordered.

Charity forced her lids up, half expecting the room to be filled with flames, she was so hot.

"God, you're beautiful." His gaze danced over her face. "Enjoy. I know I will."

He leaned in and kissed her again. Between her legs, the demand on her clit increased as he stroked faster, hitting all the right spots. Pleasure rushed in with a vengeance.

"*Dustin*." She called out his name, back arching as the

orgasm took her. Body pressed to his, her core pulsed around his finger.

His lips curved against hers into a smile. "That was fun."

"It was." An enormous, satisfied sigh escaped her.

Regrets? They arrived a second later.

3

———————

*D*ustin felt the change. One moment she was all loose and happy under him, and the next, Charity tightened up as if ready to bolt.

She sighed heavily a second time, only this one had more to do with frustration than satisfaction.

Dustin pulled his hand from between her legs. "That's not the sound a man likes to hear after he's helped with an orgasm."

"No, I suppose not." Her gaze met his, worry furrowing her brow. "We shouldn't have done that."

"I don't know. It seemed like the right thing at the time." He leaned in and kissed her once more. Lingering on her lips, teasing out a final willing response. Once he had that sweet surrender, Dustin slipped back to his side of the couch. Far enough to give her a small circle of personal space, close enough that if she wanted to touch him, she could.

Choices. He'd learned a lot about them in the past years. And right now, Charity needed to know that as fun as this had been, she still had all the choices she needed.

Which started with getting her shoulders to relax away

from her ears. "You needed that germ-proof layer, remember?"

Thankfully, laughter broke through her serious expression. "Absolutely. But now I need to know if you go around kissing all the girls so you can prove *sharing is caring*."

She had no idea, which was good. Meant what he'd done over the years had somehow stayed out of the gossip mill. Not that he'd been up to anything too wild, but still, some things were supposed to stay private.

"You see me hound dogging around town?" He paused. "Not that hound dogging would be a bad thing, as long as whoever I was with was willing and enjoying themselves."

Charity hesitated then shook her head. "No. Most comments are that you're a fun dance partner and most likely to be the designated driver instead of the partier." She smoothed her shirt over her chest. Straightened her skirt. Obviously getting herself back under control.

Thankfully when she met his gaze again, a real smile danced on her lips. "Unexpected as it was, I did enjoy myself." Her gaze trailed over him. "What about you?"

"I enjoyed myself, too." Absolute truth.

Her lips twitched. "My sister insists that if I'm old enough to do the things, I can say the things. Therefore, straight up. You didn't come. You want some help with that hard-on?"

He shook his head. "No. I don't have any germ phobias to deal with."

She laughed out loud. "That's not an answer."

Dustin shrugged. "Straight up then. Just because you came doesn't mean I have to as well. It won't set the universe spinning out of whack if there isn't cosmic balance in climaxes."

A soft hand landed on his knee. "I don't mind."

He covered her fingers with his and squeezed. "I know, and I'm interested on one level. But I'd actually like to finish watching the movie with you more than jerking one off right now."

Her eyes lost some of their brightness. "Oh. Okay."

Damn it. Seemed he needed to deal with one other issue. He caught her chin in his fingers and kissed her again, hard and needy. As he kissed, he slid their joint hands to his cock. The damn thing was a steel-rod against the front of his jeans.

Her fingers tightened over the ridge, and her small gasp escaped between their joined lips.

Dustin forced himself to speak softly instead of growling the words. "In case you were wondering, I'm not saying no because I don't find you attractive. If you don't believe the words, believe my cock."

She pressed her palm to him, rubbing lightly. "Okay. So—you don't want to get off?"

"Don't need to right now. Having a hard-on doesn't mean I have to come. They aren't dangerous, no matter what some guys might have told you."

A snort escaped her. She slid her hand up to cup his face, staring at him as if seeing him for the first time. "Okay. Tonight —whatever this was tonight—we're okay?"

"We're okay," he agreed. "We're friends, yes?"

She nodded, easing back on the couch. She curled her legs partially under her, though, which left her feet pressed to his thigh.

Dustin considered his words carefully. "I don't fool around with all my friends, in case that question hits your brain. I'm not interested in kissing Fern."

"What about Shim?"

He checked carefully, but since she wasn't joking, he answered the question seriously. "He's a great guy, but nothing about him makes me want to kiss him. Kick his butt, absolutely."

"Okay." Her hair was tousled wildly around her shoulders, and with her expression, she looked as if she were about to embark on a dangerous mission.

"Straight up, I didn't expect this to happen. I had fun touching you. Kissing you. But I'm not looking for this to change anything between us."

Worry slid away, and her expression brightened. "Thank God."

He chuckled.

"Oh, damn." She made a face. "I didn't mean that to come across as if I don't find *you* attractive. It's just with the new job at Silver Stone, I really can't afford to mess anything up."

Valid point. "I'm just a lowly ranch hand, so that's not really an issue. But we didn't fool around tonight to start dating, am I right? And that doesn't offend either of us."

She nodded firmly.

Dustin lifted his shoulders easily. "To friends.

She picked up the glass off the table and raised it to him. "To friends."

He laughed, grabbed his beer bottle, and clicked it against her drink. "Now where the hell is the remote, Tee? And these nachos aren't going to eat themselves."

They found the remote between the seat cushions, which triggered another round of laughter. They settled into a comfortable silence as time passed and the movie rolled to the final epic conclusion.

Dustin helped clean up, gave her a quick around-the-shoulder hug, and left before midnight.

With the truck windows wide open, the scent of the June night filled his cab. Yeah, the night had been unexpected, but he thought they were in a solid place right now, despite the surprise factor.

She was gorgeous. That part was undeniable. He just

wasn't ready yet for more than casual. And he was pretty sure Charity wasn't a good choice for repetitive casual—she cared too deeply. He'd seen that in the way she was around her ballet kids.

Heck, she'd been part of the motivating factor for a huge fund raiser a few years ago, mainly because she'd wanted a way for the kids to perform during the holidays.

Nope, Dustin thought as he pulled into his parking space and headed into his quarters. Charity was a good friend. The moment of pleasure would just have to stay that—a moment.

His head hit the pillow and he was out like a light.

Minutes later? Hours? He wasn't sure, but suddenly it wasn't only him in the bed.

Charity was there, a twisted smile on her face that meant mischief. "Don't mind me."

Mind? Why the hell should he mind when there were soft hands caressing his chest. Kisses being pressed along his jaw.

Fingers curling around his cock and stroking him exactly right.

Christ, it was good. Dustin pumped his hips, driving harder into her grasp. "Just like that. Fucking perfect."

Her breasts were right there, so he palmed one, teasing the tip until it was hard against his palm. He needed to come. Needed to taste her even worse. He dipped his head to lick the tight brown nipple—

Loud banging against his door broke him from the dream. Dustin blinked hard, cursing as he discovered his own hand curled around his rock-hard cock.

"*Dustin.*"

"Keep your shirt on. I'm coming."

Dustin snorted. Or he *would* have been coming if he hadn't been interrupted.

He found his feet and peered out the peephole. "Tucker?"

"Get up and get dressed. I want to see you in the office in ten minutes." Tucker turned and strode away, vanishing into the distance rapidly.

Shit. Dustin scrambled for his clothes and hurried into the washroom to deal with cleaning up.

Nine minutes and thirty seconds later—he'd had to run to make it—Dustin stepped into the office. "I'm not on shift until eight."

"You're not late," Tucker reassured him from his seat behind what was now Charity's desk. "But this is getting out of hand, and I wanted to talk to you before I made any executive decisions."

With no idea what was going on, Dustin sat in the chair Tucker pointed at and kept his mouth shut.

"One second. I want to be sure I have the full picture." Tucker's frown deepened the longer he stared at the computer screen. "By the way, do you have your phone on you?"

"Yeah, but I haven't checked it since yesterday afternoon." Because he wasn't a glutton for punishment.

"Check it. Emails first."

Dustin reluctantly pulled out his phone. "Anything in particular I'm looking for?"

"You'll know it when you—"

"What the fuck?"

"Yeah, I figured."

Dustin hadn't cursed out loud on purpose, but shock loosened his tongue. He had over fifty unread emails when he'd usually have five to ten max overnight.

"What the hell is going on?" He checked the titles and this time cursed with real feeling. "Interview requests? This can't be real."

Tucker leaned back in the chair and folded his arms over his chest. "There are at least twenty that came to the Silver

Stone email address that only horse buyers should know. And there's over eighty to the ranch email. Some are legit queries into Silver Stone services, but a lot seem to be asking about you specifically. Any ideas why?"

Dustin's frustration rose even as he apologized. "I'm sorry. It must be that stupid article."

Tucker frowned. "What article?"

Embarrassment really did hit like a wave. "Clickbait nonsense about me being a billionaire bachelor."

His brother-in-law snorted. "Good one. Ginny is going to love this. Send her the link."

"My sister has a twisted sense of humour," Dustin said dryly. "And I've been informed you can simply google me and get all the dirt you need."

With an enormous sigh, Tucker closed his eyes. "Just great."

"Can we please update the website and add a secured contact page?" Dustin begged. "It won't help get rid of the people who already know how to contact us, but it'll mean a buffer for the future. Shim will be here on Monday, and he could update it first thing."

"Good idea." Tucker shook his head. "A little like closing the barn doors after the cows are already out, but a good idea nevertheless."

"It'll stop the skunks from sneaking into the barn in the future."

A burst of laughter escaped Tucker. "Okay. I don't need to check with Ashton or Caleb to make these calls. My uncle might still be backup foreman here at Silver Stone, but he's not a tech guy."

Dustin nodded, attention on his phone. "Why on earth would people want to interview me other than for more bullshit articles?"

"You don't want to talk to any of them?"

Raising a brow, Dustin gave Tucker his best *what the fuck* expression. "Do I look the type to want to be all over social media with people wondering what I eat for breakfast, how often I ride, and what size condoms I use?"

Tucker grinned harder. "You've grown up nicely, little brother-in-law. And hell, no, I don't think being in the media eye is your thing at all. None of us, really."

"Maybe Luke—he's cocky enough to play for a crowd."

"Maybe." Tucker went thoughtful. "Fine. We go into defense mode. No interviews, no contact. We'll update the website as soon as Shim gets here, and you can delete anything that comes to your phone. Maybe it will pass."

"I hope so." Dustin checked his watch. "I need to hit the chow line if I'm going to make my shift."

"We're done," Tucker assured him, rising to his feet and coming around the desk to offer a brotherly pat on the shoulder. "Your time in the spotlight. May it be short and sweet."

"Short. That's all I ask."

First thing Monday morning, Charity propped the heavy wooden door to the office open to give herself a clear view into the barn hallway. Cats strolled along the railings of the stalls outside the office on a regular basis, going about the important business of being barn cats. While Charity was getting work done, she was also enjoying watching them.

She loved cats. Couldn't have one growing up, and couldn't have one now, so cats outside her office were like a business bonus in her books.

A rapid knock on the office door had Charity jumping in her chair. "It's open."

Literally.

The woman who floated into the office was beautiful. Jaw droppingly beautiful, in fact. Long blonde hair with perfect waves lay over her shoulder, a silver-white cowboy hat on her head. Her white skin had just enough tan she looked healthy, but not as if she truly spent tons of time outdoors.

Or tons of time using the cowboy gear she wore on her elegant frame. Her boots were also silver-white with high detail embroidery. Lucchese? Fern would know. Expensive, for sure.

Charity hoped the woman didn't plan on walking the ranch in them, though. Dust was the least of what would coat the pretty things after a round in the arena.

Pale blue cambric shirt, narrow faded blue jeans that clung to a perfect pair of long legs. Charity felt every curve on her own body protest at the idea of being in jeans that tight.

When the woman stopped in front of the desk and pulled off her aviator-style sunglasses, it was to reveal eyes of shockingly bright blue. "Marie Plassier with *Cowboy Country Living*. I have an interview with Dustin Stone. Let him know I'm here."

Ah. Now it made sense.

Charity rose to her feet. She'd been warned by Tucker about the possibility of unwanted arrivals. The slew of posts that included the hashtags about Dustin had grown when Charity had poked online that morning. "I'm sorry, but there's been a mistake. Dustin is not giving interviews at this time. If you'd like to have infor—"

The woman laughed, and it was a perfect laugh—if there was such a thing. "No, I believe you're mistaken. I have the appointment in my calendar. That's fine. You just don't worry about me."

She twisted on one elegant boot and floated out the door.

Damn it all. Charity rounded her desk. "You can't go out

there without a guide, miss. This is a working ranch, and all visitors need to—"

Charity cursed as the woman unexpectedly broke into a run and sprinted for the door that led to the arena. "For Christ's sake."

Chase her down? As tempting as it was, Charity was likely to trip the woman and then Silver Stone would end up with negative press. Nope, time to call her backup.

She whipped out her phone and hit the number. "Tucker? Sorry, but some journalist just raced from my office after demanding to do the interview she has with Dustin. She's in arena one."

"I see her. Thanks. Hey, do me a favour. Lock every building access from the parking lot, okay?"

"Got it."

Charity was back in her office in plenty of time to peer out the window and see the woman being escorted to the ranch parking lot by Tucker and Caleb.

Curious, Charity checked the *Finder* app. Dustin was safely off riding in the far northeast quarter—what Tamara had called his favourite trail. The only way someone could reach him was if they were on an actual horse.

Content with that knowledge, she finished a few more tasks then gathered a stack of invoices that needed to be signed.

She stepped out of the barn and jerked to a rapid stop. "What?"

The entire driveway and Silver Stone parking lot were full of cars.

Nearby, leaning on a railing, Kelli Stone offered a wry smile. "Careful. It's a circus out here."

In the parking lot, the semi-retired foreman Ashton Stewart was speaking sternly with a man wielding an oversized camera.

Beside him, a couple of cowboys were stopping people from exiting their cars and pointing them back up the long driveway.

"Who are these people?" Charity eased closer to Kelli. The woman was only a few years older than her, but she seemed to have a backbone of titanium. Word of Kelli's riding ability and fearlessness left Charity a touch intimidated. They'd attended a couple of girls' night out gatherings together, but Charity was still in awe.

"I think some of them are curious about Silver Stone, and the others are looking for a sugar daddy."

"A sugar—" Realization hit like a two-by-four. "*Dustin?*"

"Yup." Kelli swung onto the top rung of the railing and patted the spot next to her. "Poor kid."

"He's not a kid," Charity said without thinking, then regretted her tone. "Sorry. Didn't mean to snap."

"No, you're right," Kelli assured her. "There would be less trouble if he *was* a kid. All grown up means he's fair game for this nonsense." The other woman sighed. "I hope having this many people around doesn't mean more Stone secrets get dug up."

Damn. Like the fact that Kelli was heiress to a large horse operation in her own right. It wasn't an outright secret. People in the horse breeding community, or those who knew Kelli's grandfather, could put two and two together quickly enough. The only reason Charity knew was that Fern had found out ages ago and told her on the down low. Then, with Kelli's permission, Tucker had shared the information during Charity's office introduction under a strict NDA.

"I'll go get people cleared out," Charity offered, turning to do exactly that.

"No, stay. This is one for the guy hands to deal with. And..." Kelli tossed her a quick grimace. "I'd like you to stay close. If someone does head our way, you have my permission to run interference then."

"I can walk you home," Charity offered. Kelli's house was on the other side of the arenas and barns. Beside it, a second house that would be Tucker and Ginny's was nearing completion.

"Thanks, but for now, I'd prefer to keep an eye on things." Kelli sighed. "What if someone decides to sneak up on my house to get an exclusive?"

Charity's skin crawled with terrible memories. "We need to up security around here, big time."

"We do." Kelli considered. "Sad in a way. Silver Stone has been a welcoming place for years. Very open-door policy, but if this is the kind of thing people think is permissible?" She gestured at the unwelcome crowd.

"It's not always easy to do what's right, but we do it anyway." Charity quoted her grandmother with conviction, bracing herself to be strong enough to follow through on the motto.

"Yeah." Kelli kept watching the parking lot. "Stupid that one little article can result in this mess."

Charity arranged herself so that if anyone took a picture from the parking lot, they'd get her face and not Kelli's. Then she pulled out her phone and started searching for recent updates connecting Silver Stone and Dustin. "I wonder..."

"I thought the article was funny when I read it," Kelli admitted.

"It could have been, except for the hashtags that went too far. How on earth did—" Charity stopped. "Oh, shit."

"What? You can't just say *oh shit* when we're in the middle of a situation and not explain yourself," Kelli complained.

"He's been doxxed." A bad taste flooded Charity's mouth as memories of her own viral experience rushed in. "There are text messages turned to screen shots added to the hashtags. Dustin's email and the ranch address. His phone number."

"Crap." Kelli leaned over the phone. "Who did it?"

"Their info is scrubbed off." Charity read a little closer, and a cold chill went through her. Dustin was going to be so pissed. "It's a woman. Says she dated the *#SilverStoneStud* in the past, and here's the scoop on how good he is in bed."

Kelli swore. "That's seriously shitty. I'm calling Luke and Tucker. They'd better know why we've been invaded."

Charity kept reading and searching on her phone while Kelli connected with her husband. There were maybe four or five screen shots in total, but every one of them included some dirty detail plus a way to contact Dustin.

People online were running with it, though. Adding their own comments and increasing the viewing audience as every minute passed.

"Luke. You with the guys?" Kelli nodded at Charity. "Gather them up. You might want to find Dustin and give him an escort home. Charity found the source of the nonsense— some extra-level social media bullshit. We need a family meeting, ASAP. Meet us at Caleb and Tamara's."

"Dustin was in field thirty-seven fifteen minutes ago," Charity offered.

Kelli flashed a thumbs-up. "You hear that? Good. I'll get the guys here to finish clearing the riffraff... No, I will not go hide." Kelli rolled her eyes. "No, I will not put Charity on."

Charity's phone rang. She glanced down at the screen then back at Kelli. "It's Tucker. Do I answer it?"

Kelli laughed. "You're double teaming me," she complained to Luke. Here. Talk to Charity."

She passed her phone over.

Charity was in the middle of the Stone family up to her neck and the water was still rising. "Luke?"

"Hey. Thanks for the info on the media invasion. Can you stick with Kelli? I just got off the phone with Ashton. He's mustering extra hands to deal with the crowd, so you two can take Secret Path and meet us at the ranch house."

"Of course, I'll stay with Kelli. But I was going to do that anyway. Also, Kelli is wicked smart, and she's going to be just fine."

Damn it. Her mouth was going to get her in trouble, but seriously.

Thankfully, both Kelli and Luke laughed. "She *is* wicked smart," Luke agreed. "Thanks for being there. We'll see you at the house."

Charity passed back the phone. "What's the secret path we're supposed to take to the ranch house?"

Kelli grinned. "Brilliant idea. We'll hide in plain sight. Come back to the barn."

Charity stopped at the office to drop off the unsigned paperwork. That was a trouble for another day. "Ready if you are."

Opening the gate to a stall, Kelli patted the nose of a beautiful brown mare. "Here she is. Secret Path."

They had to be kidding. "The path is through a horse stall?"

Kelli swung herself up on the horse's back as if magic was involved. She held a hand down to Charity. "Secret Path is the *name* of a horse. Come on."

Charity stared. At the hand reaching out to her. At the horse.

The very, very tall horse.

She swallowed hard. Probably not a thing a person working at a ranch should admit, but it was too late to hide the truth.

"I can't ride."

4

The expression on Kelli's face—

"You look as if I just confessed to murder," Charity offered with reluctant amusement.

The other woman dropped her extended hand, clutching the horse's mane under her fingers instead. "I didn't know this. Why didn't I know this?"

"Because there was no reason for you to know?" Charity stepped a little farther back as Secret Path shifted on her feet.

Kelli patted the horse's neck and soothed her as she spoke softly to Charity. "You afraid of her?"

"No. Not really," Charity corrected. "Not more than being massively aware that she's bigger than me, and I don't speak horse. I don't want to do something wrong and upset her."

"Well, that's good. The *not really being afraid* part." Kelli took Charity in with a long assessing gaze then nodded firmly "If you're okay with it, how about I do the driving? It'll get us past the crowds faster than trying to scurry around the entire perimeter. Path is a sweet horse. Trust me."

Charity considered. Riding made a ton of sense. She really

45

wished she'd been a typical horse-crazy kid when she'd been younger so that this wasn't her first time, but riding had never been in the picture. "Okay."

Kelli snorted. "A very enthusiastic response." She pointed to the side of the hallway where a couple of bales rested. "Climb up on that. It'll make things easier."

It wasn't perfect—the horse still looked huge as Kelli brought the beast beside where Charity balanced on the top bale. But the hand Kelli offered steadied her as Charity followed instructions. She swung her leg over Path's butt and wiggled until she sat tucked behind Kelli.

"Arms around my waist," Kelli ordered. "And I will not break if you hold on tight."

"I have extraordinary upper body strength," Charity warned.

"I've had Luke behind me while on a bucking horse that was trying to send us both into the stratosphere. Trust me, I'll be fine."

Charity tightened her hold.

Once she had a good grip, it was easier to look around. "How do we get out of the barn? We won't fit through the regular door anymore."

Kelli twisted Path on the spot then pointed to the end of the hall. "Out through arena four. I'll keep Path walking for a bit. See how it feels. Okay?"

"So far, so good." Charity took a deep breath and allowed the experience to wash over her.

Being perched on Secret Path's back wasn't scary. It was... odd? Unusual. There was no other experience that Charity could compare the movement to.

Kelli chuckled softly, turning them into the arena through the tall open barn doors. "You just relaxed. Which means Path relaxed—good job."

"She's worried about me riding?"

"No, not in a bad way," Kelli assured Charity. "Horses like Path are people pleasers. She wants people to like riding her, so if she senses something is wrong, she wants to fix it."

"Great. Now I'm making horses develop neuroses."

A bright laugh danced over the open air as Kelli turned Path again, tighter to the right this time. "You're doing wonderfully. I'm going to speed her up a little and do some circles. Just hold onto me and pretend you're dancing with a new partner."

"Let Path lead? I can do that."

"Exactly." Kelli leaned forward slightly and clicked her tongue.

Path sped up.

Charity's fingers instinctively went into a clutch for a few breaths until she figured out the new rhythm. "It's not bad. I'm still a long way up, but this is mostly fun."

"It's one of the best things," Kelli assured her. "Okay if we make the run to the house now? I won't do anything fancy, but we will go a little faster."

Charity checked her grip. "I'm good."

Kelli brought Path beside the gate, reaching for the rope that held it closed.

"I can do the gate," Charity offered, even though she wasn't sure how she'd get back up again after crawling off Path's back. Climb on the railings?

"No need. Path is being trained for Ultimate Cowboy competitions. Opening and closing gates is one of the tasks."

Charity forgot to be nervous as Path waited patiently at the correct moments and moved obediently the next. Once the rope was free from the fence, Path backed up through the opening. A moment later, Kelli refastened the rope and the gate was once again firmly shut.

"That was amazing."

"Sasha's doing a great job training her."

"Wow. She's only fourteen."

"Turned fifteen this past March. She's a natural, though." Kelli tilted her chin toward the left. "The hands have gotten a few of the trucks to leave, but there's still a crowd. Let's go before they spot us."

Charity squeezed Kelli's waist. "I'm ready."

Kelli must have turned Path and hit the start button at the same moment because seconds later, they were skimming down the path between the barns and the main ranch house.

Movement swirled at the edge of the parking lot. People's faces turned toward them.

"They see us." Charity caught the glint of sunlight on glass. "Cameras."

Ahead of her, Kelli tucked her chin to the right. "Look toward the lake," she ordered.

"Got it." Charity pressed her cheek to Kelli's back and attempted to sway in time with the animal under her. The motion was still unnatural but growing less awkward.

It could end up being a thing she'd try again.

"Nearly there." Kelli slowed Path, sitting straighter on the horse's back. "There's a shelter off the greenhouse side of the house where we can stable her for now."

Charity glanced back over her shoulder. "Wow. The hands are out in full force. There's a line of a half dozen vehicles headed back to the highway."

"Good." Kelli patted Charity's leg. "You did well."

"You're a good teacher."

"Pick someone who loves a thing to teach you that thing. That's always been my rule." She glanced back at Charity. "Like you and your dance stuff. The fact you love it is clear in the way you talk. And the way you make even boring old repeats of the same move fun for the kids."

"Thanks. I do love it." She wasn't good enough to be a professional dancer, not after her training had come to an abrupt end as a teenager. And now it was not a thing she could afford to do much of just because. "Teaching is my way of sneaking in dance time on a regular basis," she confessed.

"Smart."

They were beside the shelter now, the crowds and worries of the day temporarily forgotten. Kelli swung her leg over Path's head and was on the ground a second later. She glanced up. "Want me to grab the stool?"

Charity didn't think, just moved. She copied Kelli the best she could, one hand resting against the horse until her feet hit the ground. Then she stood gracefully and patted Path's neck. "Thanks for the ride."

Only the fact that Kelli stood behind her kept Charity from levitating off the ground when Path tossed her head.

Kelli chuckled. "It's okay. Remember that bit about how she likes to please people? You gave her the perfect thank you. She's happy."

"Well, that's good." Charity still stepped back quickly, opening more room between her and Path.

Kelli led the horse under the shelter then tossed some grassy stuff into the trough. "Good girl. You stay here for a bit. I'm sure Sasha will be out to get you as soon as she can."

Drat. Another complication Charity hadn't thought about. "The girls. The kids—"

Kelli wiped her hands on her thighs, glancing up at Charity with a question in her eyes.

Charity twirled a finger around the ranch area. "With this many unwelcome guests on the property, the kids won't be able to do stuff like normal. Not unless Tamara wants pictures of them slapped up online."

The other woman's expression darkened. "You're right. We're going to have to deal with this quickly."

"I'll head back to the office—" Charity began.

Kelli glared. "No way. You're not going out there alone either. Wait until Luke gets here, and then he'll walk you to your car."

Inside the house, Charity slipped to one side of the room and tried to stay out of the way as the Stone family gathered.

Walker showed up with his three children—aged five, seven, and nine. Harper, Chloe, and Carter took off for the basement toy room with Emma Stone pushing her four-year-old brother Tyler after them.

The thirteen-year-old paused by her mom's side, blonde head tilted to the side as she eyed the gathering family. "I'll take care of them while you talk, but after, I want to know what happened."

"Of course, you do," Tamara agreed. "I'll catch you up on everything, because you're not a little girl anymore."

Emma grinned as she poked a thumb toward the stairs. "But they are little, so off I go to play pretend for the millionth time."

Tamara kissed her. "You're a good big sister and cousin."

"The best," Emma agreed. She swung past her own big sister, Sasha, and spoke quietly in her ear.

Sasha's eyes widened. She nodded, glancing at her mom. Tamara had turned to the kitchen and was dealing with the coffee maker.

Sasha drifted across the room. "Mom?"

"Yes?"

Sasha met Charity's gaze briefly before focusing on her mother. "Does Auntie Ginny know to come over?"

"Yes, sweetie. If she's feeling up to it, she'll be here."

Sasha nodded then joined Kelli in the living room.

The door opened again, and a couple of the men who had been out on the ranch arrived. Caleb and Tucker, and Tucker's wife Ginny.

The men headed into the laundry area to use the sink.

The only Stone sister by birth waved at Tamara's greeting. Her other hand rested on the bump of her belly that protruded from under her pale pink shirt. "I'm fine. You caught me awake and not snoozing with my beach ball."

"You have a fine beach ball and napping while you can is always a good idea," Tamara insisted. "Come. Claim your seat."

"Yes. The cozy corner is mine." Ginny rubbed her hands with glee, kicked off her shoes, and then nabbed Tamara for a hug. "How's it going?"

"Not sure," Tamara admitted. She pointed at Charity. "She knows more than we do."

Two pairs of eyes landed on her, and a shiver of worry struck. Charity pressed a hand to her chest. "I'm only here because I was a ride along with Kelli."

Ginny made a rude noise and gestured her forward. "But you know things. Spill. What's the big ruckus in ten words or less?"

"Ten? That's a challenge." Charity considered. "Clickbait article. Dustin got doxxed. Too many strangers looking for gossip."

The two of them both lost their amused expressions.

"Well, damn. That sucks." Ginny rubbed her belly absently. "I heard about the article, but if it's gone viral, Dustin will hate the attention."

Charity debated for all of three seconds before deciding it was important enough to share. "Kelli is worried as well,"

Charity said softly, "that someone will announce *she's* newsworthy, being an heiress and all."

Tamara's head snapped up. "Well, crap. I'd forgotten about that."

"Because we consider her family, and it's not anyone's business how much money she does or doesn't have." Ginny made a face. "Except people like to make news out of anything these days."

"It'll pass," Tamara insisted, pushing her glasses back into place. "But...how soon?"

Charity turned as the door opened once again and Luke and Dustin entered the room. They both wore serious expressions and a fine layer of dust, as if they'd been riding hard.

Caleb stepped forward. "Take five minutes and get washed up. We'll be waiting when you're ready."

IT SHOULD HAVE BEEN SIMPLE. A great Monday shift with the anticipation of his best friend's return to look forward to. Limited heavy lifting, a wonderful ride over his favourite fields on a beautiful summery day.

Instead, he'd been interrupted in the middle of his shift by Luke's demand to close off the field and get his ass back to the barn as fast as possible.

The terse "there's paparazzi looking for you" was enough to make Dustin's great mood turn foul.

Luke met him on the edge of the ranch line, and with an unknown ATV racing along the neighbour's gravel road, Dustin was grateful to not be alone.

Stalked at his own home? No fucking way could this be allowed to continue.

He washed up quickly in the laundry room sink, the grime from the dusty air sliding into the washbasin with a dirty swirl. He could have used a shower, but his five minutes was nearly up.

He stepped into the kitchen and blinked to discover Charity was there, pouring drinks from a pitcher. She spotted him and dipped her chin, her serious expression so out of place that he wanted to rush to her side to find out what was wrong.

Then he realized she was probably frowning over him and the nonsense he was dealing with.

He accepted the glass she held out. A momentary spark of amusement struck. "Is this germ-free?"

Her gaze snapped up, her lips twitched, and her cheeks flushed.

Damn. He glanced to the floor and whispered an apology. "Sorry. Meant to be funny."

She snorted. "You are funny, in spite of it all."

Thank God she had a sense of humour. Maybe he could borrow some, because he figured he'd need every bit of his for the next while.

He lifted the glass in thanks.

Caleb paused at Charity's side. "Stick around, please. I'll have someone walk you to your car once we're done."

"Okay." Charity glanced around as if trying to find a place to hide.

"You know what's going on, so don't feel you have to cover your ears. In fact," Caleb eyed her, "running the office, you'll need to know what we decide. Feel free to contribute if you have any suggestions."

She swallowed hard. "Okay," she repeated, sliding onto one of the tall chairs by the island counter.

Dustin offered her a wink then followed his brother into the living room. He stopped at Caleb's side. "Sorry."

He seemed stuck in apology mode.

His brother frowned. "For what? You didn't do anything."

"I feel like crap that this is happening."

Caleb laid a hand on Dustin's shoulder. "I hear you. Still, not your fault. And I don't want you to beat yourself up over it. We'll get through it."

Dustin nodded. "I'll just feel a little crappy, then."

His brother chuckled. "Okay, you do that." Caleb lifted his voice and got everyone's attention. "Sit or stand, your choice. We've got a situation."

Dustin settled on the stonework in front of the fireplace. That left the couches and easy chairs for his siblings and their partners. Caleb and Tamara settled in their usual chairs. Ginny curled up against Tucker on one couch, Luke and Kelli on the other. Walker had taken the rocker by the fire. Sasha sat beside Ginny.

Charity remained in the kitchen, looking as if she'd like to bolt.

Which made sense, but Dustin was distracted by another issue. He messaged his missing sister-in-law, Ivy.

She answered right away.

Ivy: *Hey. What's up? How's the big meeting going?*
Dustin: *Just about to start. You want to listen in or watch? I can link you in no problem.*

Ivy had severe social anxiety, even around family at times. If she wasn't here, it was because she wasn't having a good day.

Dustin: *If you're up for it.*
Ivy: *You are a darling. Turn on video. I'll cut out if I need to.*

He clicked until connected, then stood and propped his

phone on the shelf where she'd have a view of the entire room. "I've put you on the bookcase. Volume check?"

A minute later he was back in front of the fireplace, standing now so that Ivy could see him as well.

Caleb nodded his approval. "Thanks for thinking of that. Hey, Ivy. Good to see you."

Ivy waved. "What's up?"

Caleb gestured to Kelli. "You called the meeting."

Kelli rubbed her hands on her thighs. "That article about Silver Stone and Dustin. As outrageous as it was, we all know outrageous was what they were going for. Something to catch people's attention."

It made no sense. Dustin shook his head. "But this is beyond..."

"Some woman used the hashtags and posted your contact info, Dustin. Your email, your social media links, your address here at Silver Stone." Kelli glanced at Sasha then met Dustin's gaze again. "She inferred you two had a sexual history."

Dustin closed his eyes. His face had probably turned beet red. "Great."

"This is beyond the interview bullshit," Tucker complained. "That was annoying but somewhat understandable. This is now an invasion of privacy."

"Can we stop it?" Ginny worried her bottom lip with her teeth. "Or is gossip like this the same as the story of the woman with the bag of feathers she let loose?"

"We can contact the police," Tamara suggested.

"That's not helpful." The comment came from Charity of all people. "Sorry for interrupting, but sadly, I have experience with this. Complaining to the police doesn't change anything. They can't arrest anyone for gossip. There's no such thing as a cease and desist against a nameless entity like social media. You can get a restraining order placed on material sharing with a place, like a tv studio or a person. But once a story goes viral, there are no laws that apply. Not yet."

Caleb's expression went dark. "Damn."

A knot tightened in Dustin's gut. "So we just have to sit here, locked inside, to keep people from taking pictures without our permission?"

Across the room, Sasha bolted upright on the couch beside Ginny. "Wait, I can't stay inside. I need to train. I have a competition in a month. I have—"

"We have a ranch to run. None of us can stay hidden inside," Caleb reminded her. "And none of us will."

Walker's expression had gone grim. "I don't want my children exposed to the media. I had my days in the spotlight, and while there were positive moments, hell no."

Looking around the room, Dustin examined the faces of the people who meant the world to him. The people he'd long ago vowed to be there for, somehow, despite being so much younger.

And now he was the cause of this trouble. Sasha's worry, Walker and Ivy's, Caleb and Tamara's need to protect their innocent children, and rightly so.

Walker had stepped away from the spotlight.

Fuck—Kelli had never stepped into it, and she could have.

Dustin met Ginny's gaze across the room. His sister, pregnant with her first baby. No way in hell did he want anyone poking and prodding into hers and Tucker's lives. Not now, not ever.

He spoke directly to his sister. "No one will need to hide. We'll have to post something official to deal with the interview requests regarding Silver Stone herself, but the part about me? Let's make it clear that I'm not here. Then there'll be no reason for anyone to stick around Silver Stone to bother the rest of you." He forced a smile as he turned to his oldest niece. "You're right—you do need practice. Remember, I was with you the last time you worked the stop and ride task. Secret Path followed you like a puppy instead of standing in place like she should."

Sasha looked torn between crying and laughing. "You're terrible."

"Admit it, I'm your favourite dusty uncle."

Tamara broke in. "It's not a bad idea. Going away for a bit."

"Have you seen the shifts I've given him?" Tucker demanded. "No one else wants these shit jobs." He gave a loud squawk and rubbed his side. "What? I was trying to lighten the mood in here."

Ginny pulled a face as she shook out her fingers. "You have rocks for ribs." She turned her attention on Dustin. "Tamara is right. It's not a bad idea. Want me to talk to Dare? You could head up to Rocky Mountain House and work with the Colemans for a while."

"God, no." Dustin shook his head. "First off, isn't she headed this way in a week or so to be with you when your kid drops? But also, if the stupid does follow me, no way in hell am I bringing that kind of trouble to their door."

"Damn. Too many family stories to latch onto up there as well." This time it was Tamara who grimaced before offering a rueful smile. "There's more than a few skeletons in the Coleman family closet that I'd like to remain undisturbed."

"Where can he go?" Walker asked.

Caleb stood. "To Pincher Creek."

Dustin's first instinct was to deny the idea outright. Pincher Creek meant Uncle Frank, and he hated his uncle. Not an exaggeration either, just cold hard facts. Usually the idea of being anywhere near the man would get his back up and he'd find all manner of reasons to get out of it.

Now? "Perfect. I'll go."

Caleb blinked. "I expected an argument."

This was still going to absolutely suck, because Uncle Frank sucked, but there was a bonus prize to the shithole proposition. "Not that I'd try to make it happen, but if the paparazzi *happened* to follow me, I couldn't think of a nicer person to have to deal with the crap."

Luke choked on a laugh. Caleb rubbed his chin with a hand, conveniently covering his smile. Walker stared skyward and fought to keep a straight face.

Only Ginny let her grin shine out. "Damn, you adore the man, don't you?"

"Always and forever," Dustin lied smoothly, crossed fingers held high in the air.

Caleb had gotten himself under control enough to shake his head. "He's not that bad."

"He's the worst, but going to Pincher Creek is a good idea, so I'll do it."

Caleb nodded. "I'll give him a call and tell him to expect you. If you can leave right away, we'll make sure the news gets out. If they're not expecting it, some of the cameras will catch you going without having anyone available to trail you. We'll deal with the rest of them once it's clear you're unavailable."

He paused, his gaze trailing to the kitchen. Charity remained, quiet now as she sat on one of the stools at the island.

Dustin moved toward her. She'd been helpful today, more than she probably knew. A burst of sadness struck as he considered the time he'd miss with his friends. Yeah, leaving was the right thing to do, but Shim would arrive in a few hours, and Dustin would be gone. Charity and Fern would be doing things over the coming weeks—

"I think you should go with him."

Caleb's voice broke through Dustin's thoughts. Behind them, the rest of the family was talking quietly, but Caleb now stood by Dustin's side at the edge of the kitchen area.

"What?"

"Who?"

Dustin and Charity spoke at the same time.

Caleb pointed a finger at Charity. "Uncle Frank has been slow to share project information that we need on file at Silver Stone. It's the perfect opportunity, really. And the perfect excuse. Dustin will go along as your ride and escort. While you update the information we need, he'll be very polite and do the chores Uncle Frank assigns, yes?"

Dustin's brain was still spinning. "Charity is coming to Pincher Creek?"

"If she's okay with the idea." Caleb paused. "I know you've just started working for us, but this is within your job description. What do you think? Can you go? It should take no more than a week if everything goes well."

Charity's jaw snapped closed from where it had been hanging in shock. She swallowed hard then nodded. "Okay. Sure."

5

———————

Whirlwind had always been a word that evoked crystal clear images. One passed by, and the world around was left in chaos. Grasses strewn everywhere, trees bent over, clothing tossed from a laundry line and left scattered on the ground.

The only whirlwind happening right now, though, was in Charity's head. Which meant she was a mess, her thoughts dispersed like fallen leaves.

What had she been thinking? Other than how much it sucked that good people like the Stones were putting up with nonsense—and the next thing she knew, she had agreed to leave town for a week.

Chaos. Whirlwind.

After some brief strategizing, Walker followed her home in his truck. He waited until she was safely inside before heading back to the ranch.

Charity threw a gym bag on the bed and scrambled to pack. She also put her phone on speaker and got a hold of Fern.

"This is top secret." Charity grabbed jeans, shirts, runners.

Stacked her clothes in piles so she could make decisions as soon as she'd updated Fern and gotten off the phone. "You'll find out more from Ivy, I'm sure, but Dustin is leaving town to get away from the media crap."

"I heard there was a riot out at Silver Stone. Was there really?"

"Don't know about that, but a lot of people were not where they should be. And Dustin's contact info got posted on social media, so—"

"Get out. Who the hell would do that?"

"Some woman he dated, according to her posts."

Which left a sour taste in Charity's mouth. Not because Dustin had been with someone. She knew he'd dated, although he hadn't been with anyone in particular the entire time she'd lived in Heart Falls.

So annoying, her inner turmoil. Charity knew he'd had sex in the past. *She'd* had sex in the past. Sex was an agreeable pastime to share.

Assumptions continuing, Dustin and this woman had enjoyed sex at some point. For this woman to out his contact details turned that sharing gross and not fun at all.

Fern had gone silent on the other end of the line. "He's leaving town?"

"To get the press away from his family. Yes. But I need your help because I'm going with him. There's a job I can help with that makes a great excuse for him to go. It's complicated, and I need to pack, but I need a favour."

"Of course. Let me pick my jaw up off the floor first. You're running away with Dustin Stone?"

"It's not like that, and you know it. We're just friends." Charity was very glad Fern was not in the room to witness how embarrassed she was right then.

Fern laughed. "Okay, I won't tease since you're in a hurry.

What's the favour?"

"Swing by my place and make sure nothing rots in the fridge or the garbage? I'm packing and out of here in the next ten minutes."

"Done. FYI, I also plan to find the cold-hearted creature who started the nonsense. Just because."

"You do that. Gotta go. I'll text when I can."

"Stay safe."

Two pairs of pants, four shirts, an extra pair of shoes, and a bunch of socks. All of that was shoved into the bag without a second thought. Only when she pulled her underwear drawer open did bad thoughts arrive.

Whirlwind, swirling together images of her best underwear and Dustin's appreciative stare.

Screw it. She grabbed the top two layers of both bras and undies, and a pair of pyjamas, and refused to consider her choices. This was a job. A way to help a good family out of a tough situation.

It was about helping a friend.

Her stomach rumbled as she locked the door.

Cutting through a series of back alleys, Charity took her usual shortcut to the edge of town, strolling as nonchalantly as possible. While she had rarely visited Walker and Ivy's home, their house sat next to the cemetery. The quiet setting was one of Charity's favourite spots to go to reflect and remember.

Of course today, peaceful thoughts were missing entirely as she peeked over her shoulder repetitively. Probably looked more like an owl than a person out for a casual walk with their workout gear.

Still, she made it to Walker and Ivy's house relatively certain no one had followed her.

Ivy welcomed her in, the dog at her feet barking in delight. "I bet this isn't what you expected to be doing right now."

"No, but that's okay. Life is one big adventure, isn't it?" Charity greeted Faithful then gestured to the hallway. "May I use the washroom? I packed so fast I forgot the cardinal rule of road trips."

A gentle nod of permission followed. "Help yourself. I'm putting together a supper for you two. I assume Dustin came in straight off the fields?"

Damn, he was going to be starving. Plus— "I hope he has time for a shower."

"If not, you get to travel with eau de cowboy for a few hours. It's pungent, but not deadly."

They headed in different directions, both laughing.

By the time Charity joined Ivy in the kitchen, the delicately built woman was closing the lid on a large travel cooler. "I put in a few types of pop and three types of sandwiches. You take what you like first, okay? I know Dustin will demolish anything you don't want, so nothing will be wasted."

"I appreciate it."

Surprise struck as Ivy turned to wrap her arms around Charity's shoulders and hug her briefly. "I'm glad Dustin isn't leaving on his own but with a friend."

Charity offered a gentle squeeze in return. "I'm glad that I can help."

Ivy stepped back, her pale complexion and silver blue eyes making her look otherworldly. "He won't like me saying this, but Dustin loves his family. Very much."

"That's clear, not only now, but before."

Ivy nodded, but concern slid in. "He doesn't like his uncle, and from what I've heard, he has some valid reasons to feel that way. Which are not mine to share. But I will say this—Dustin needs his people. If he can't have his family right now, you'll be his only anchor. I hope you'll forgive him if he clings a little."

The idea that big, strong, independent Dustin would cling to anyone nearly made Charity laugh out loud. It was as ridiculous as Kelli calling him a boy.

Still, she held back because Ivy obviously meant well. "I think he'll be fine, but yes, I'll be there for him. Like I said, we're friends."

Ivy smiled. "I'm glad." Her gaze went to the main window, and she tilted her head toward the garage. "He's here."

The convoluted escape continued. Dustin pulled into the garage and closed the door behind him. Ivy and Charity met him there.

He took the bag from her and put it in the back seat of the truck. "This all you got?"

"I'm a micro-mini-minimalist packer," Charity shared.

"Oh, wait. One more thing," Ivy insisted, pressing the supper bag into Dustin's arms then turning. "I'll be right back."

Dustin opened the passenger door for Charity. "Up you go."

In the back seat, Dustin's dog, Patchwork Annie, thumped her tail vigorously as Charity climbed into the cab. "You brought her. Hi, Annie. Who's a good girl?" Charity reached between the seats to scratch the dog on the head. "You are. Yes, such a good girl."

Dustin chuckled as he climbed back behind the wheel. "She won't let me out of her sight. Not that I want to take her back to Pincher Creek, but leaving her behind isn't an option. She'd try to track me all the way there."

"Ah, she loves you."

"A little too much. Pain in the butt." But Dustin also ruffled Annie's head.

Ivy had returned, a pair of cowboy boots in her hand. "Here. They should fit." She passed them through the window to Charity then leaned to the side to speak to Dustin.

"Kelli said you're to give Charity riding lessons while you're gone."

"Riding lessons? Why would—" His gaze snapped up to Charity's. "You can't ride?"

"And on that note, I'm off. Drive safe, and I hope this all passes quickly." Ivy blew them both a kiss. "Charity, you might want to duck down until you guys are on the highway. Just in case."

She opened the garage door then vanished into the house.

Charity leaned her seat back and slid below window height. "This good?"

Dustin glanced at her as he backed out of the driveway then turned the truck toward the highway. "You're going to get a kink in your neck."

"Who cares? Anyone following you?"

"Not that I can see. Now let's discuss your riding lessons. As in the need for them."

"I don't need them. I don't need to ride," Charity said firmly.

"Because you don't think riding is important if you work at a ranch?"

She snorted. "No. It's really hard to do paperwork while on a horse."

"Not that you know for sure, because you don't ride."

"It's a logical conclusion." Although, she wasn't sure why she was arguing.

Dustin adjusted his grip on the wheel, turning them onto the main highway. "Well, just so you know, I'm happy to teach you if you want lessons."

Charity sighed. "I sort of do want them now. Kelli rode with me to the ranch house. It was weird, but in a good way."

"A glowing recommendation."

"Shut up, Stone."

"I mean, if riding was weird in a bad way, that would be...*bad*."

"I'm going to kick you," Charity warned.

He laughed.

Yeah, she wasn't in the right position to offer that as a threat. "Do you think I can sit up soon?" Her stomach rumbled audibly. "The food your sister-in-law packed smells wonderful."

Dustin checked his rear view. "There's no one in sight. Go ahead and unfold yourself. And hand me one of whatever. I'm starving."

Charity dug into the cooler. Chicken sandwiches, thick ham and cheese. Peanut butter and jelly. She passed him a chicken and nabbed a PB&J for herself. "How did it go at the house when you left?"

"I pulled my truck up outside the house, and everyone came out on the porch to wave me off. An appropriate send off if I was leaving on a year-long jungle expedition."

"Anyone watching?"

"Some media. Ashton had called the RCMP, so the news trucks were slowly leaving." Dustin took a bite of his sandwich and hummed happily. "I hope it's that easy. That I'm gone for a week, and everything goes back to normal."

"I hope so, too." Charity frowned. "You're going to miss Shim's arrival tomorrow."

"I know. It sucks, but he'll be around on a permanent basis. Plus, Ginny's baby is due in the next three weeks, so my foster sister, Dare, will be joining the family again. You'll like her. She's a little quieter than Ginny but still all heart."

"She sounds awesome."

"I hope the baby arrives after Canada Day. That would suck. Having to share a birthday with— Oh, *shit*."

Charity glanced around in concern to see what had upset him. "What?"

Dustin sighed. An enormous, frustrated sigh. "Canada Day."

Nope. Charity shook her head. "I don't get it."

"Canada Day in Heart Falls. All the traditional events. A picnic, a petting zoo." He met her gaze. "The bachelor auction."

OF COURSE, this couldn't be simple. Dustin swore again. "I can't believe none of us thought of it. The annual bachelor auction—I can't be involved."

Charity whistled softly. "Or you could be involved and make a shit-ton of money for the boys and girls fund." She held up her hands. "Kidding. No way should you go near the event."

Frustration seethed inside. "Which means I'll be gone for more than a week. No way things will settle down enough in time." He shrugged and motioned to the food. "Can't be helped. Feed me."

She offered him a can of pop first. "If you can't do it, someone else will have to take me back when I'm done."

"Yeah. Don't worry about the details." He put the pop can in a cupholder and accepted another sandwich. "It's damn frustrating, but I'll make the best of it." He kept his gaze mostly on the empty highway, finishing the sandwich as thoughts tumbled in his head.

Beside him, Charity was still taking neat bites from her first sandwich, staring out the window at the passing fields. She looked relaxed and competent, just like always.

"Not much fazes you, does it?" Dustin asked.

Charity blinked. "Oh, I don't know. You've seen me flustered."

"I have. It's cute." He grinned at the face she tossed him. "But you recover quickly. I like that. You feel—solid."

"That's a... Well, okay, I'll take it as a compliment."

"It is. It was meant to be." Dustin leaned back and got comfy behind the wheel. "Solid makes things work. My brother Caleb is solid, as in I'd jump off a cliff if he told me to. Tamara is solid in that she'd tell me before I got on the cliff I shouldn't be there in the first place."

Charity laughed. "She does have that 'I know things' aura."

"Exactly." Dustin nodded excitedly. "I tried to explain that to Luke once, and he looked at me as if I'd grown antenna."

"Luke seems the type to look at the facts, not the energies under them." Charity went thoughtful. "He's like...a fun uncle. But one who gets you to eat your vegetables while making a game of it."

Amusement bubbled up. "I'll need to tell that one to Kelli. She'll get a kick out of it."

"You have a great family." Charity leaned on the headrest. "You're doing a sweet thing by leaving for a while. No matter how long it ends up taking."

"They've done so much for me," Dustin explained. "It's not a chore to return the favour."

She laid her hand on his arm and squeezed. "Still, good for you. And I'll do what I can to help make the time easier."

"Thanks."

They both ate another sandwich then broke open a bag of homemade chocolate chip cookies.

Charity checked out the window. "You're not driving south."

"Fastest way to Crooked Creek ranch is off Highway 1. We go east before turning south. We'll stop for gas first and see if we have anyone on our tail. If we do, Caleb told me to drive north." Dustin shrugged. "I figure we'll head south no matter what."

Charity shook her head. "You don't like your uncle much, do you?"

"He's made it tough to like him." Dustin reached into the back seat and patted Annie lazily. "I'd prefer not to talk about him."

"I'll have to work with him," Charity pointed out. "Forewarned and all that."

"He'll be fine with you. I personally piss him off." Dustin offered her a wink. "It's my sparkling personality."

"You are shiny and bright like the sun." Charity leaned forward. "Best way to get around him?"

"You mean over? With a bulldozer." Dustin held up a hand. "Kidding. Okay, like I said, you'll probably be fine, but the best way is to mostly ignore him. Just do what you need to do. Figure out what's right and do it. He'll still probably make noise, but he won't be able to argue with the results."

"I can do that. Being right is always my plan."

They chatted about nothing important for the next hour while finishing most of the food in the basket. Grateful for the easy company, Dustin was in a better mood than usual as they arrived at the turn onto the Crooked Creek ranch.

The setting was pretty, he supposed. With the Waterton mountain range to the south, the land stretched out like a slightly wrinkled blanket. The few dips and rises were nothing compared to the rolling foothills of Silver Stone territory.

Charity leaned forward in her seat, peering around with interest. "It's not as big or impressive as Silver Stone."

"You're a wonderful person. Also, very observant."

She stuck out her tongue. "Be nice."

"I'm always nice," he insisted even as he glanced down the

lane and wondered where he could park that would piss his uncle off the most.

A sharp tug on his sleeve made him glance at Charity. "What?"

"You look evil. What are you plotting?"

He slowed his truck so he could gape at her. "Are you reading my mind now?"

"Apparently, if you were thinking evil thoughts." She pointed to the open space outside the main barn. "Park there. Your brother texted to say your uncle is expecting us, and he'll meet us by the office."

"When did you get a text? And from who?" Dustin demanded.

"Fifteen minutes ago. And Caleb told me not to tell you because, and I quote..." She pulled out her phone and clicked to her message screen. "Dustin will probably try to piss off Uncle Frank six ways to Sunday, including stupid shit like parking so he blocks Frank's truck."

"Well, damn, I never even thought of that one. It's brilliant."

"It's also off the list. Park in the spot labeled *Guest* and behave," Charity ordered again.

"Yes, ma'am," he teased. "Even though you're taking all the fun out of my evening."

"I know. I'm mean." She squeezed his arm and smiled. "But I'm also appreciating the fact there seems to be no extra media hounds in the area. That makes it worthwhile, right?"

"Yeah, I guess. And pissing off my uncle isn't going to help anyone back home, so I promise to bite my tongue. Even when he's an ass."

She laughed. "You assume he'll be one?"

"Oh, trust me on this, Tee." Dustin pulled to a stop where

she'd ordered and put the truck in Park. "It's not a matter of if, but *when*."

He hopped out and rounded the front of the truck, pulling her door open before she had a chance to get herself organized enough to do it for herself.

He held out a hand.

She blinked, then nodded her approval. "Good idea. Your truck is as high as the horse Kelli got me up on." Charity took his fingers and let him help her down.

"At least your manners have improved."

The gruff comment grated on Dustin's nerves, but he took the high road and ignored his uncle for the moment. "You good?" he asked Charity.

"I still need my bag."

"Me too. I'll get them in a minute. First, I need to deal with the most important things." He couldn't resist. He pulled open the back door of the crew cab and snapped his fingers.

Patchwork Annie jumped down and paced obediently to his side.

Then Dustin turned to face his uncle. "Uncle Frank."

The older man stood with his arms folded over his chest and a glare on his face. "You brought my dog."

"*My* dog," Dustin corrected, then stepped next to Charity. "Charity, Frank Stone. Uncle, this is Charity Gruzing. She'll be gathering the documentation the lawyers have been requesting."

Charity flicked a warning glance at Dustin as she extended her hand to his uncle. "Nice to meet you."

Frank didn't move. He was too busy glaring at Patchwork Annie and Dustin to even attempt politeness.

Charity had begun to pull her arm back when Uncle Frank shook his head and accepted her hand. "Not your fault the company you're forced to keep."

Lovely—at least Uncle Frank was living down to Dustin's expectations.

Back beside him, Charity's smile was still in place, but no longer shining bright. More strained than natural. "I'm not sure what you mean by that."

Frank ignored her and pointed to the side of the main barn. "I've set you up in the south trailer. It's a little out of sight, so you shouldn't be bothered too early in the morning by the crews. Hopefully, you'll be done in a few days."

"It'll take as long as it takes, depending on how well you've kept track of the information I need to gather. If Crooked Creek has been capably managed, it won't take too long. I'll know how competent you've been in the morning."

Dustin barely kept from reacting to the unexpected cutting tone in her voice.

Frank frowned as if trying to figure out if she had deliberately been insulting or if he'd misheard. He shrugged and turned his attention on Dustin. "Bunkhouse is full. You'll sleep in the barn."

Of course. "That's just fine—"

"Oh, that's not necessary." Charity lifted her chin. "Dustin will stay with me."

Frank snorted. "I don't know what you think you're staying in. It's a horse trailer, darling. Only one bedroom, one bed."

She linked her arm through Dustin's, tucking herself against his side. "Perfect. Because, you see, Dustin's *exactly* the type of company I damn well like to keep. Which is why he's my boyfriend. If you'll excuse us, we'll get settled. I'll meet you, or your foreman, in the office at eight a.m. as Caleb arranged."

Like a force of nature, Charity tugged Dustin with her. Away from the truck, away from their bags, and away from a gaping Uncle Frank.

6

———

*E*mbarrassment waged with fury. "I shouldn't have done that."

"Oh, no. You really should have. It was spectacular." Dustin trotted along at her side, Patchwork Annie beside him.

Charity kept marching farther from Frank Stone before she was tempted to say something that would make things worse.

She glanced at Dustin's face, only to discover him grinning from ear to ear. "You're not mad at me for losing my temper?"

"I'm feeling happily justified that he pissed you off even faster than expected." Dustin punched a fist in the air. "Sweet. I didn't curse at him first. Tamara won't give *me* shit."

"Dustin," Charity scolded. "Not what I need to hear right now."

He caught her by the arm and turned her toward him. Tucked to the side of the barn where no one could see them, he leaned over her and cupped her cheek. "You're fine. He was being a dick."

"Don't insult dicks. They have a purpose, and when wielded correctly, they don't cause aggravation."

A burst of laughter escaped him. "Noted. So, before we start stomping again—"

"Shut up, Stone."

He just grinned harder "—do you want to stay? Because I can take you back to Heart Falls."

"Of course, we're staying." She frowned at him. "You still need to be gone from the circus back home. Plus, Caleb wasn't lying about needing information. Tucker forwarded me the lists of what's needed and how long they've been waiting. Looks as though digging through the files might be the only way Silver Stone will ever get the data they need."

"Then we stay." He tilted his head toward the way they'd come. "Sneak back and grab our bags? And the leftovers, if there are any?"

"God, yes. I was so busy in stomp mode," she winked, "that getting away from that man was the only thing on my mind."

"A properly timed exit is a beautiful thing." He brushed his lips over her forehead. "Come on. Let's sneak."

The return trip to the truck for their stuff was rather anticlimactic. A few men in cowboy gear passed by, dipping their chins at Dustin and offering Charity appreciative smiles. Frank Stone was nowhere to be seen.

Charity carried the cooler. Dustin slung their bags over his shoulder then guided her to the trailer. "Frank wasn't lying when he said it's small. I don't mind sleeping in the barn."

The trailer was teeny, but squeaky clean. She dropped the food on the table and slipped around the small space to open windows and let in fresh air. "No. We can share, and what's more, I think we need to. There's a reason."

Dustin put her bag on the foot of the bed. "Go on."

She peeked into the small icebox then transferred the remaining food from their dinner into the open space. Unwelcome butterflies took flight in her belly.

Stop it. This is about being a friend. The friend who Dustin needs right now. Not about sex.

Charity twisted to face him. "You mentioned the bachelor auction and that you won't be able to go home. But Ginny's expecting right around then. Do you really want to be chased from your own home and family during a milestone like her baby's arrival?"

"Of course not, but if I have to stay away, I will. They're too important to me."

"But if you weren't expected to take part in the auction, then that's one problem off the list." Charity raised a brow.

He snorted. "The only acceptable way to get out of the auction is to be out of town or..." Dustin blinked. His expression brightened to a full grin. "Out of town or off the market. As in I already have a girlfriend, thank you, very much."

"Exactly." Charity glanced at the ceiling guiltily. "I have to confess I figured that out exactly five seconds after I'd already claimed you as my boyfriend just to piss off your uncle."

"I totally approve of your initial motivation and the following brainwave." Dustin clapped softly. "Tee, you're brilliant."

"It means we have to pretend to date."

Dustin shrugged. "No worries there. We'll go dancing a few times, like we would usually do. We can grab a pizza with Shim and Fern, like we would have anyway."

"You're right. Who knew dating would be this boring?"

He laughed. "Not boring, but simple. I'll pass this update on to the family so they can start spreading the word. The sooner the news gets out, the better."

"I'll let Fern know." Charity checked her watch. "And Shim will have arrived. You should tell him."

Setting into the U-shaped seat at the small trailer table,

Dustin looked thoughtful. "Let's brainstorm a game plan first. Details, that sort of thing. We tell everyone in Heart Falls that we're seeing each other. Our family and friends obviously know it's not true, but they won't say anything to contradict us. I doubt anyone in town will think we're pulling a fast one. It's not as if we *couldn't* date."

"The people who messaged you after the article came out— what did you tell them?" she asked.

He made a rude noise. "Nothing. I haven't responded to any of them except Shim. If the first time someone messages me in a year is to discuss the loan they'd like me to float, they don't deserve a response."

Charity paused, shock rippling through her. "They didn't."

"Some did." Dustin lifted a shoulder. "Some wanted gossip more than cash. I wasn't interested in answering any of them."

"Well, good?" She offered a sad sigh. "Sorry. That sucks."

"The whole kit and caboodle." Dustin frowned. "Whatever the hell that means."

They both laughed, smiling at each other like the co-conspirators they were.

"Back to the game plan. We just started dating," Charity suggested. "Like a couple of weeks ago. We were keeping it quiet because..."

"Because I have a big, nosy family, and some things are private." Dustin shrugged. "Good enough reason in my books."

"But we were going to say something in another week because the auction organizers, aka Fern's sisters, Tansy and Rose, need to know." Charity considered the possible pitfalls they would need to clear. "By the way, I'm not interested in doing any interviews. That stupid article made me angry because you are not single, and that's that."

"Great stuff." Dustin was typing rapidly on his phone. "...

and I'm not single. Make sure my name is removed from all social media information about the auction."

"And I say we ignore the woman who doxxed you. Because giving her attention would just make her happy." Charity hesitated. But the thought had popped into her head, and if this was brainstorm time, she needed to share it. "We could be there. At the auction, although I can't believe I'm saying this."

His eyes had gone wide. "Aren't you a glutton for punishment?"

"Oh, I'm not saying we have to, but it is one of two choices. If you're not there, maybe people will believe you're unavailable, or they'll think that you're hiding. If we go and put on a show, we can prove you're not single."

Dustin nodded thoughtfully. "Let's think on that one. First, we get my name off the roster."

"Yes." Charity bounced lightly on her toes. "I need a walk. It's been a long day, and after sitting in your truck, I need to get the blood flowing. And your uncle was not wrong about this trailer being small."

"Small enough a person needs to go outside to change their mind." Dustin winked. "I'll take you on a tour of the nearby arenas. We can get some fresh air, and I'll show you where the cookhouse is."

Thank goodness, since they hadn't brought any extra food along. "Sounds like a plan."

It also got them a little farther from the one topic she'd been deliberately avoiding. The double-wide mattress at the end of the trailer that was also going to be noticeably small once she and Dustin climbed into it.

The bed she'd give anything to be sharing with Dustin for real.

Charity bounced herself and her hungry sex thoughts out the door after Dustin.

Patchwork Annie slipped from under the trailer and joined them, walking lightly at Dustin's side. Charity remembered something his uncle had said. "Why did Frank say Annie was his dog?"

Dustin shoved his hands into his pockets as he led her around the edge of a small arena toward a low-roofed building. "She grew up here at Crooked Creek. One of the trips Caleb sent me on a couple of years back, I ended up here during a big storm. One of the hands mentioned that the dog had gone missing. Uncle Frank shrugged and said, 'these things happen.'"

"Damn, that's cold."

Dustin sighed. "That's not the part I can get mad about. He wasn't wrong. Things happen on the ranch that suck. Animals get hurt or go missing. Caleb and Ashton taught me sometimes the kindest thing we can do is to put them out of their misery."

Charity stopped beside him where he'd paused. "So...what happened?"

"I found her by accident. She must have been crossing Crooked Creek and got caught in the high storm surge. Ended up trapped under some branches. I got her out and brought her to the barn."

"She was okay?"

"No." He grimaced. "She was hurt. Badly. I called the vet, but I already knew it would take a miracle."

"Well, you saved her."

He made a soft sound. "The vet did. Back home, I'm pretty sure Caleb would have given her mercy, and I'd have accepted it. When Frank showed up with his shotgun, though, I threw a fucking fit. Mostly because it was him," he confessed. "I was thinking less about the animal's needs than how much I hated to agree with my uncle. I'm pretty ashamed of that part."

"Oh." Charity caught his fingers in hers and squeezed.

Dustin nodded. "The part that makes this an Uncle Frank story is that after the vet saved her and she clearly wanted to be with me, he insisted that since he'd paid the bills, she was staying here." He tugged Charity with him toward the double-wide doors ahead of them. "I said she was my dog now and I'd pay the fucking bills."

Charity waited. "That can't be it."

"No. He sent the bill for the vet to Caleb. Plus a bill for the top price going for a pure-blooded, fully trained border collie, along with a contract saying he got half the pups when I bred her from now to eternity. Or I could pay three times the buyer's fee amount and be done with him."

"Ouch. I have no idea what kind of money we're talking here, but that's cold-blooded."

"Consider the payments on the truck I'm driving the only thing I can currently afford on my salary, even after Annie's first litter." He rolled his eyes. "Billionaire bachelor, my ass."

"That makes me sad. That your uncle wasn't simply content Annie had survived and was happy with you."

"There's been a lot of back and forth between my uncle and me over the years. Nothing much is simple anymore. Except this—" He tugged the doors open and gestured her into a place that smelled heavenly. "Welcome to the best place at Crooked Creek. The chow line."

DUSTIN HADN'T MEANT to complain or tell tales while they were here. In fact, he'd planned to keep his mouth shut as much as possible—not his typical behavior, by any means.

Charity had blown his mind by snarking at his uncle.

She'd also loosened something inside him where he sometimes wondered if he *did* overreact when it came to his uncle. Proof that the man could piss off even-keeled Charity was an affirmation Dustin had badly needed.

Still, it was time to change both the subject and the mood, and the food at Crooked Creek was the best solution to that.

"Dustin."

Food and the *good* people who worked the ranch. He turned at the sound of his name to discover a few of the hands rushing forward. "Amy. Lazing about tonight, I see?"

"Just finished a shift full of hard labour. Unlike someone, who I bet sat on his ass for a few hours coasting down the highway while stuffing his face." The cowgirl threw herself into his arms and squeezed like an anaconda. "Welcome back. We've missed your ugly mug around here."

"We didn't miss you winning all the roping challenges." Coralee held up a hand for him to high five once he'd untangled himself from Amy. Coralee looked past him then and raised a brow. "And who's this?"

Dustin was about to introduce Charity when she slipped into his personal space, hand around his waist.

Right. The girlfriend plan started now. "Ladies. Gents." Dustin lifted his chin at the couple of guys standing beside the table they'd been sharing with the cowgirls. "I'd like you to meet my girlfriend, Charity."

Charity held out a hand and greeted them all in turn as conversation whirled around them.

"See?" Coralee declared. "I told you that article was off the mark."

"Well, the *Silver Stone stud* wasn't seeing anyone the last time he showed up." The young man with a raspberry mark on his cheek smiled far too intently at Charity. He spoke with a thick French Canadian accent. "Bonjour, darling. If you're looking to trade up, the name's Lionel."

"How is a second-rate cowhand a trade up from a billionaire bachelor?" Amy demanded.

"I'm sure he's more than second-rate." Charity winked at Lionel even as she slid her fingers into Dustin's belt loop. "Thanks, but I'm happy with Dustin."

"It must be his conversational skills," the final cowboy of the group, Keith, mumbled.

"He does have a talented tongue." Charity kept a straight face, which sent the group into howls of laughter. It also earned them a sour look from a couple of the old-timers playing cards in the corner.

Dustin lifted a hand to them in apology then pointed to the table. "Let's keep it down. Room for two more?"

Keith hauled a chair over, and Coralee grabbed another.

Amy caught Charity by the arm. "Come with me. We'll nab gabbing supplies. Back in a minute."

Dustin watched the two of them walk away. Charity glanced over her shoulder at him as Amy chattered like a magpie. Charity flashed a quick thumbs-up, and Dustin grinned.

Yeah, she'd handle the crew here just fine. Maybe it would be a good thing, this short stay at the Crooked Creek ranch. Meant he could spend some time with some younger hands. He was pretty much the youngest worker at Silver Stone, and while it wasn't terrible, being around people his age was nice for a change.

He'd take Charity riding. Show her the couple parts of the ranch that were admittedly pretty. Spending time with Charity sounded good.

She feels good at my side.

Keith nudged his arm. "You're staring."

"Am I?" Dustin focused a little harder and discovered his gaze was currently fixed on Charity's ass. "I guess I am."

"I thought for a minute you were kidding around, but you're serious. She's really with you?"

Dustin turned and slapped a hand on Keith's shoulder. "Damn right. She's got some shit to do for Silver Stone. Caleb told me to bring her down and make sure none of you lot tried to steal her away."

Coralee leaned her elbows on the table, gaze fixed on the area where Amy was guiding Charity through the maze of food options still available at this hour. "She's pretty."

"She's hot," Lionel added. "Too hot for you, even if you're a cocky stud."

"Keep opening your mouth, and your feet will mosey right on in," Dustin warned. He offered Coralee a smile. "She is pretty, isn't she?"

"She's not a cowboy, though."

"Nope. Working the office for our foreman. She dances, and knows how to put out fires, although that volunteer job is on hiatus."

"A dancer, hey?" Lionel grinned harder, his brows waggling.

Here they went again. Dustin leaned back in his chair and turned his expression to warning mode. "Watch what you say next, dude. I like a good laugh as much as the next guy, but sometimes your smart-ass comments go too far. Remember what we talked about."

Coralee hit Lionel on the arm. "See? He already knows you're a jerk when it comes to talking about women."

"I *was* a jerk. I'm becoming less jerky." He frowned. "Wait, that sounds wrong. That makes me sound like a preserved beef stick. What's the English way to say it?"

"Less of a jerk," Coralee offered.

Lionel gave her a thumbs-up. "No jerking. Got it."

Charity placed one tray in front of Dustin. Amy lowered

another on the opposite side of the table. Minutes later everyone had a full glass and a plate covered with snacks in front of them.

"I was telling Charity the hours Sam cooks hot meals. But that stuff is available pretty much 24/7." Amy lifted a cookie in the air that was the size of a small plate. "We do not starve."

"Cookhouses on ranches are dangerous places from what I can tell. The one at Silver Stone—Lordy, JP cooks some of the best curries I've ever had." Charity paused as Dustin adjusted his chair so he could stretch his arm along her backrest. She hesitated for a split second then smiled as if remembering the game.

His moment of shock came when she laid a hand on his leg then responded to a question from Keith.

It shouldn't be this distracting. Being next to his good friend, her fingers softly curled around his thigh. The scent of her hair wafted around him, and Dustin was far too aware that Charity was as good as in his arms.

Suddenly, spending time together took on a whole new meaning. His dream rushed back to mind in far too vivid detail.

Only...should they? Be more than friends?

Dustin knew one thing. After the brief moment they'd shared in her apartment—had that seriously been only two nights ago?—he'd love to explore more. Maybe this was the perfect time and place.

Charity leaned into his side to get his attention. "That man looks important. He's staring at you, and he's walking this way."

Dustin followed her head tilt. "Good catch. Crooked Creek's foreman, Adam West."

She stood along with Dustin. "You're kidding me."

The older man overheard their final comments. "Not kidding, unfortunately. My mother always wanted to name a son Adam. Then she married a West, and the rest is history."

Dustin shook Adam's hand. "Good to see you again."

"You always say that, but I think it's more that you like seeing me instead of your uncle." Adam held out his hand to Charity. "You're the young lady helping in the office?"

"Charity Gruzing. I'll try to make it quick and painless."

"It'll take how long it takes. In the meantime," Adam turned his attention on Dustin, "you're my problem."

"I like the sound of that."

Adam grinned. "You'll like it even better when I tell you we're branding this week."

"Hot damn. Good timing, then." Dustin answered the question in Charity's eyes. "Cutting out the calves, roping, all the fun stuff of being a cowboy."

"Sounds like it. I'd love to watch for a while."

Adam nodded with approval. "Your boyfriend's got some skills. I'll make sure someone shows you where the best spots are to safely watch when you're on break."

"Thanks."

"Dustin, early muster. We're leaving at five a.m. I hope no one is late this time." Adam spoke louder to include the cowhands gathered at the table then tipped his chin at Charity. "Night."

"Good night."

At the table, Dustin's friends had begun to clean up. Chairs were put back in place, and food trays and dishes were cleared to the racks in the corner of the room.

"Adam never forgets a thing," Coralee complained. "Five minutes after I was supposed to be there, once, and it's still all *'no one had better be late this time.'*"

"Try being a few minutes early for a change," Keith suggested.

"Are you kidding? Give up sleep?" Coralee looked

outraged. She waved at Charity and Dustin. "See you tomorrow. Dustin at least. Have fun in the tomb, Charity."

"Um, thank you?"

Moments later, the mess hall was empty, and Dustin and Charity were headed back to their trailer.

"They're good people." Charity frowned. "What's the tomb?"

"No idea," Dustin confessed. He caught her fingers in his, and when she startled, he jerked his head toward the group of four walking at a slight angle away from them toward the bunkhouse. "They're watching."

"Oh. Okay." Charity stared skyward. "It's later than I expected. We've lost the light."

"It's cloudy, so no moonlight, either."

They walked in companionable silence until reaching the stairs to the trailer. Charity squeezed his hand before letting go. "You'll be up early."

"Earlier than you think since I need to eat before meeting with Adam. I'll try to be quiet when I leave."

They slipped inside. Dustin kept waiting for things to get awkward between them, but it never happened. They moved easily in two different directions. Charity took a small bag with her into the bathroom. He pulled out a set of clothes for the morning and left them on the kitchen table so he could dress without waking her. Poked in the fridge to see if there was anything there that caught his eye.

Charity popped from the bathroom a few minutes later, face shining, the scent of toothpaste filling the small bedroom. She wore a pretty purple wrap around her head that matched her pyjamas, her curls popping out of the top like a volcanic eruption. "It's all yours. Okay if I take the right side of the bed? I sleep on my side and like to face the wall."

"No problem." Dustin took his kit into the bathroom and

jumped into the shower. Even as the dust of the day washed down the drain, the tension in his body built. Outside the door, Charity was nestled under the sheets. Was her long-limbed body all relaxed, or was she waiting for him to return?

Was this situation affecting her as much as it was him? The wanting to taste. To touch. To take. It was tough to remove his hand from his cock. To not seek release here and now.

Nope. Either they did something together, or he'd abstain. He was not going to stroke one off five feet away from her without her knowledge. That would be creepy. Maybe it was a strange line to draw in the sand, but Dustin drew it.

He cut off the water and brushed his teeth, ignoring his heavy cock as best he could. Tucking the damn thing into a clean pair of boxers was torture.

Even worse, though? Opening the bathroom door to discover Charity stretched out on the right side of the bed, sound asleep.

A soft chuckle escaped as he made his way to the opposite side of the mattress. So be it. Tonight? Sleep.

But tomorrow, once they were in the same place at the same time, he would offer some suggestions for ways they could pleasurably pass their spare time while here at Crooked Creek.

7

———

She wouldn't have believed it if anyone had told her that the first chance she had to get Dustin Stone into her bed, she would sleep through the experience like a baby.

God, she hoped he didn't think she'd been faking it.

Crawling under the covers had sent her into a mental whirlwind—there was that word again, but it was true. She'd considered what seemed to be a million options of how to greet him when he came out of the bathroom.

Sitting up, pretending to read? They could exchange a little more casual conversation with meaningful glances before turning out the lights and spooning together.

Should she strip and stretch out naked, like an old-fashioned dirty postcard? Leave her clothes on and stretch out like a *shy* old-fashioned postcard?

Curl up on his side of the bed? Say nothing now, but snuggle against him in the night?

Gah. See? A ton of great ideas, not one of which was to roll over and instantly fall asleep. Silly woman.

Fern was going to tease the hell out of her for this.

That was Charity's second thought when she woke up after not having seduced Dustin. Her first thought was *maybe this morning,* and then she realized the bedsheets on his side were cold.

Her phone said it was seven thirty, which meant she needed to get her butt in gear if she wasn't going to be late for the deadline she'd been a hard ass about.

Wouldn't that piss off Dustin's uncle? If Charity was late after ordering him to be on time?

A ripple of amusement rushed through her, chased immediately by self-recrimination. Damn it, obviously Dustin's naughty streak when it came to annoying his uncle was contagious.

Charity hurried out of bed and got ready for the day.

She paused to text Fern, though, which she hadn't done the previous day after the girlfriend plan had been hatched.

Charity: *Hey you*
Fern: *Hey. Apartment is fine and de-garbaged. I went in on the way home from the art gallery and made sure that was taken care of. The fridge I'll deal with on the way home today.*
Charity: *You're a wonder*
Fern: *I am amazing, aren't it? I told you all the boring stuff before demanding juicy details.*
Fern: *Hint, hint. Now is time for juicy details.*

Charity started to type then gave up and phoned her friend. "Hey. I'm running late, again, so here's the scoop."

Her friend stayed quiet as Charity updated her on what happened the previous evening. Then Fern snickered. "I don't know if I should be crying or cheering over here. Insults, lies, missed opportunities. Damn, girl. You've been busy."

"Haven't I just?" Charity took a deep breath. Fern had her

back for everything else, so now was time for the deep questions. "Tell me the truth. Do you think I'm terrible for hoping to sleep with Dustin while we're here?"

"Well, technically—"

Charity rolled her eyes toward the ceiling. "Cut to the chase, Fields. The clock is ticking."

Fern laughed. "Sweetie, you and Dustin are two of my favourite people, and I don't say that lightly. I think you'll be dynamite together, in bed and out. The only part I don't get is the part where you're fake dating."

"To throw off the media and make him safe from the bachelor auction. Were you even listening?" Charity stepped out of the trailer door and headed for the cookhouse.

"I was listening. I meant why are you *fake* dating? You two should be dating for real."

"Ha. As if." Charity slowed, paces away from her first dose of coffee. "We don't swim in the same circles. Friends, yes. Anything more than pretend partners isn't in the cards. I need to go, but you don't think it makes me cold to want him, even if it's temporary?"

Fern sighed. "Of course, you want him. You two were meant for each other, which means your swimming pool analogy needs a new filter. But go. We'll talk later. Love ya."

"Love you too."

Charity squared her shoulders, pulled open the door, and marched inside in search of the largest cup of coffee she could find.

The cookhouse smelled as wonderful as the night before. It was also ninety-nine percent empty. The sole occupant waved from his place behind a massive cooktop. "There you are. Hungry?"

"A little. I need caffeine more than food."

"Good thing I can get you both." He winked. "I'm Sam. I assume you're Charity. Adam told me to take care of you."

"Aww, he's so sweet."

Sam laughed. "That would be one of the first times he's been called that. But sure. Let's get you fed."

Five minutes before eight, Charity pushed out the door of the cookhouse with a final wave at Sam. He'd turned out to be a great source of information regarding exactly what the cowboys, including Dustin, would be doing that day. She'd also eaten pancakes so fluffy they melted on her tongue. In her hand, she gripped the largest single serving to-go thermos she'd ever seen.

Pretty much a perfect start to the day—other than screwing up the seduction part.

A piece of yellow paper fluttered in the wind as she approached the door of the office. Charity pulled off the teeny sticky note that read *Gone to town. I put out stuff for you. F.*

Well, good. She didn't need to have the man standing over her watching as she gathered materials, but what if the stuff he put out wasn't the stuff she needed?

Obviously, she'd be making this up as she went along.

Charity opened the door and headed for battle, quickly deciding that the *F* on the note hadn't been shorthand for Frank, but a *fuck you.*

There was no chair in the office.

Charity took her time searching, even checked in the closet, but the room failed to magically spit out anything remotely chair-like.

Also, there were no windows and no air conditioning. With the dark wood paneling on the walls, she now understood Coralee's *tomb* comment.

There were binders on the side table labeled with some of the years she needed to go through. The three sets of vertical files were open to various drawers full of reports. The desk was covered with loose papers, none of which related to her work.

Oh, this was going to be interesting.

Since help wasn't being offered, Charity went for the do-it-yourself solution. She found an empty box in the storage closet, neatly labeled it *office desk* and added the date. It was very satisfying to sweep everything off the desk surface into the box and close it up tightly.

She put the box on the top shelf of the closet, label side out. She wasn't an animal.

After propping open the door in hopes of drawing in some fresh air, she pulled out the list Tucker had sent and began gathering materials to the left side of the desk. Once she had three neat piles, she climbed on the right side of the desk, sat cross-legged, and got to work.

Flexibility in all things was a blessing, she decided.

Two hours later someone knocked on the door. "Charity? You here? Oh, there you are." Coralee frowned. "How are you in that position and still breathing?"

Charity uncurled her arm from around her right leg. She'd adjusted position a few times as she'd worked. "This is about the most pretzel-like I can get without needing a recovery team to detangle me."

The young woman stepped up to the desk, swinging her head from side to side. "In my day, desks were used to write on or sit on, but not both at the same time."

"Ha! You're the same age as me, and yes, I'd prefer the desk to be one or the other, but this is what I've got to work with." She swung her legs over the side and let them dangle. "What's up?"

"Adam sent me to let you know we'll be in the south arena all afternoon. If you plan to take a coffee break, you could watch for a while." Coralee picked up a paper and gave it a glance. Her quick turn around the room increased the size of her frown. "Sometimes I think I should have gone to college like my sister did, and then I see this and think *nope*. Outdoors wins every time."

"It is a little depressive in here," Charity agreed. "But it's short-term. I'd love to come watch if I won't be in the way."

"The cows won't care, and the rest of us like an audience." She winked. "Don't pretzel yourself too hard."

"I'll stand for a while. Just to keep on the straight and narrow."

"Good one." Coralee held out a fist, and Charity gave it a bump.

The other woman slipped out the door. Charity watched after her for a moment, letting the warmth of the sun beat down on her shoulders as she stood in the open doorway.

So far, so good in terms of her work. It was slow going, but she was making headway. Frank Stone might have tried his best to make her day tougher, but he didn't know just how resilient she was. Or how motivating the promise of seeing Dustin in full cowboy mode was.

With the reward laid out ahead of her, Charity put her head down and dove back in.

It didn't matter where Dustin was working, having a horse under him and a rope in his hands felt right.

"You grin any harder and you'll scare the calves." Keith paced forward, settling his horse into position beside Dustin as they guarded the south side of the field and made sure none of the animals tried for a breakaway.

"Your own grin is pretty damn wide," Dustin informed him.

"True." Keith leaned forward and patted his horse's neck. "We'll scare them together, then."

Patchwork Annie pranced daintily nearby, almost under Dustin's borrowed ride, Midnight. Annie's attention darted between the cattle and Dustin, waiting in case he gave her a new order.

It had been such a pretty morning that Dustin's regrets at having to leave Charity had eased away. The sun had barely backlit the sky when they'd rolled out as a group from the barns. An easy half-hour ride took them to the field where the mamas grazed with their babies at heel. After the peaceful quiet of the day's start, the rest of the morning had vanished into a blur of dust, hard riding, and a whole lot of noise from the bawling calves.

Cutting out part of the herd and guiding them back to where Adam wanted them had taken the kind of teamwork Dustin loved. This afternoon promised the kind of personal skill he thrilled to as well.

With three older brothers and far too many older hands on the ranch to count, Dustin had been roping in front of an audience since he was little. Sometimes he'd done well, sometimes poorly. He knew to do the best he could then take the cheers or jeers that followed with good humour.

Cowboys kept a person balanced. Ego? What ego?

"Tell me more about your girlfriend." Keith tipped his hat toward the barn as they waited at the side of the arena for their turn.

Dustin followed his gaze. Charity was climbing up on the railing, a floppy wide-brimmed hat on her head. She looked nothing like a cowgirl, but she didn't look out of place. "Like what?"

"Does she have a sister?"

Dustin laughed. "Yes, but Chelsea's also taken."

"Damn it."

"I thought you were going to make a play for Amy."

Keith sighed. "Lionel."

"Coralee?"

The other cowboy grimaced. "Also Lionel."

Dustin gaped. It wasn't the concept so much as the players. He'd have never imagined Lionel had it in him to keep two ladies happy at one time. He also had never seen any indications that Coralee and Amy were into each other. "They're both seeing him?"

"No, he slept with both of them, separately. When they found out, and after the shouting died down, the two of them decreed there would be no more fun and games with anyone at the ranch."

It was impossible to keep from laughing. "Well, good for them."

"Sucks for us." Keith shrugged. "Truth is it's kind of nice to have sex off the table. We're all getting along much better now without that element constantly on our minds." He grinned at Dustin. "Plus, the ladies make the best wingmen ever when we hit the bar. Who knew?"

"Bonus."

Keith waved back at Adam. "He's ready for us."

Dustin tapped Midnight in the flanks with his heels. "I'm ready for him." He glanced at Keith. "You?"

"Bet I out rope you two to one." Keith's chuckle at Dustin's flashed middle finger was evil. "If I win, you buy when we go to the pub this week."

"We'll work something out." Dustin wasn't sure a trip anywhere he might be spotted was a good idea. Having zero media in his face was a thing he was enjoying immensely.

Then the two of them were back with the group, waiting for Adam's instructions.

The arena was full of people, including the vet and Dustin's uncle. One by one, he and Keith roped the calves and brought them to the ground. While down, they were branded, inoculated, and the males castrated. The entire procedure took only a few moments, but required intense concentration over and over again.

Thankfully, Uncle Frank chose to work the brand on the other side of the yard from where Dustin brought the calves to Adam. The other hands held down the animals, guiding them afterward into a separate holding pen.

Patchwork Annie darted in and out of the two-month-old calves, turning them toward Dustin so that he had a simple shot at dropping the rope over their heads.

One of the older hands opened the gate at the far side of the arena, distracted momentarily by something. A calf made a break for it. Dustin had Midnight turned instantly, rope swinging as they raced after the animal.

Smooth circles overhead—once, twice. On the third, Dustin snapped his arm forward and the rope fell over the beast's head. Dustin was already dismounting as Midnight pulled to a stop.

A quick hold of the calf's flank while lifting the head rope, and the beast was on its side in the dirt. Dustin tied off its legs—front first then the back two—with a half hitch.

He could have sworn the calf sighed sadly as it lay quietly, its chance of escape gone.

Applause sounded from Dustin's right.

He figured the guys were kidding around, but it was Charity, proudly putting her hands together for him. The warm spot in his belly felt damn good.

Coralee rode up and dismounted beside him. "I've got the calf. You need to grab a kiss from your sweetie. She looks thrilled at wonderful you. Show off."

"I'm working." Dustin glanced at Charity though.

Coralee bumped him with her shoulder. "Go on. If you took off for a roll in the hay, people would talk. Now if you don't kiss her, they're going to wonder why." She waved at Charity. "Heck, if she looked at *me* like that, all stars in her eyes, I'd already be over there planting one on her."

Since the last thing he wanted was for people to talk, and the main thing he'd been craving was another kiss...

Dustin undid the rope from his saddle horn, tossed it at Coralee, then mounted up. Midnight obediently trotted over to the railing where Charity sat, shining eyes trained on them both.

"Having fun?" Dustin asked.

"It's fascinating. And you were amazing."

Dustin tipped his hat. "Thank you."

He peeked back at everyone. The hands, Adam, and his uncle were all hard at work. Coralee was staring over her shoulder as she guided the calf back to the lineup.

Dustin crooked a finger at Charity. "I've been told my sweetheart deserves a kiss after being supportive of my cowboy skills."

Charity took a quick inhale, gaze darting toward the arena. He checked again as well, and now there were a few more eyes on them.

Ignoring the audience, Dustin focused on her. "You okay with it?"

Her cheeks flushed. She lifted her chin. "Of course. Just don't pull me off my fence. It took some doing to get up here in the first place."

He laughed. Which meant they were both smiling as he closed the distance between them and connected their mouths.

Her sweetness slammed into him with the impact of a two-by-four. Soft lips on his, innocent even with no tongue and nothing else touching. They could have been skin to skin, naked, for how much he wanted her in that instant.

Far too soon, Dustin pulled back. He took a deep breath through his nose, fighting to keep his smile one of a friend and not the *I plan to ravish you later* thought that rushed through his brain. "Thanks for cheering me on."

"No problem, boyfriend." She offered him two thumbs-up. "This is for the next awesome thing you do, since I have to get back to the office."

"How's it going?"

She shrugged. "Fine. I'll tell you more later. Now you need to get to work before I become the reason you get in trouble with someone, and by someone, I mean your uncle, who is giving us the evil eye."

Dustin pulled off his cowboy hat and scratched his head on the side facing his uncle with his middle finger. "No problem, girlfriend." He snickered. "We need cute nicknames for each other, because that just sounds silly."

"I'll put it on the to-do list for tonight. Brainstorming cutesy code names."

Dustin put his hat back on. He tipped his head then turned back to the job at hand.

It shouldn't have meant so much, their silly plans for the evening. It shouldn't have meant so much in a bad way that Uncle Frank glared at him the entire way back to Adam's team.

Focus on the good stuff, Kelli always told him. *The bullshit will be there whether you think about it or not. Focusing on the good stuff makes your day a whole lot more enjoyable.*

Charity was a good thing to think about.

8

———————

Charity stopped by the mess hall for a drink to take with her and to steal a chair. She'd already had enough desk perching for a lifetime.

Sam hurried to her side when she propped the door open then went to pick up her chosen chair. "You need help with that?"

"No, I've got it. I'll bring it back when I'm done."

He held onto the opposite side as if keeping her in place. "Done with it where?"

"The office. Someone must have borrowed the one in there."

The cook looked outraged on her behalf and then insisted on carrying it all the way for her.

"You have any favourite meals?" he asked en route.

"Spicy dhal. Naan bread. Barbecue anything." Charity smiled as she opened the office door. "But everything you've cooked so far has been delicious."

"Thanks." Sam nodded sharply. "I'll still see what I can do."

It was nearly five when the office door opened, and a dirt-coated Dustin poked his head into the office. "In the middle of something or nearly done?"

"I'm finishing up this chart and that's it for today." Charity eyed him. "Pigpen."

He wrinkled his nose. "Nope, not liking that one as a nickname."

She snickered. "You headed to the shower?"

"Sort of? I don't want to mess up the trailer shower, so I thought I'd hit the bunkhouse shower instead. Only I didn't plan this very well. Can you grab me clean clothes and meet me? One of everything except boots. That will keep where we sleep less ranchy. Or raunchy, you pick the word."

Charity eyed her list then came to the door. "Point me where I'll need to go. It'll be a few minutes."

Dustin lifted his hand and showed her which entrance to use. "No rush. Trust me, it'll take more than a few minutes to get off this grime."

She went back to her chart and entered the last of the missing registration numbers. A final glance around the office proved she'd put everything back that she needed to. Despite the...well, *spite*, Frank Stone had shown, she'd had a successful first day.

The other success, she realized as she gathered Dustin's things, was the quiet. She hoped they'd gotten things calmed down around Silver Stone. At least having Dustin nowhere in sight was a good thing while the rumour mill did its job and informed the masses of Dustin's updated relationship status.

Tucker would deal with the interview nonsense swiftly as well.

She marched across the yard toward the bunkhouse showers, whistling happily.

"Stay away from the working crew."

The rough order pulled her to a stop. Frank Stone stood a few feet away, his favourite expression on his face. Had to be his favourite since the scowl was the only one she'd seen him wearing so far. "Excuse me?"

"I don't need you getting hurt and my nephew blaming me, so stay away from the arena and the horses and anywhere else you might so much as stub your toes." Frank dipped his chin and stomped away without giving her a chance to make a response, smart-ass or otherwise.

Maybe that was a good thing.

Charity stood right where she was for another moment, though. Took a deep breath and let it out slowly as she thought of the things she'd accomplished that day. Of the amazing show Dustin had put on for her—okay, he'd just been doing his job, but it was as if he'd done it specifically for her.

Good mood restored, she continued her way up and through the door he'd pointed to.

"Hey, Charity. Good to see you again." Keith rubbed a towel over his hair while Lionel slipped his feet into boots.

"Looking for Dustin?" Lionel asked before gesturing to the pile in her arms. "Of course. He is a lucky man to have a woman who cares for him as if he's a prince."

"Or a woman who helps when he's forgetful," Charity offered dryly.

"That too." Keith grinned. "He's in there. Go right ahead."

If she hadn't been still slightly distracted by the small scene in the yard, maybe Charity would have clued in before she pushed through the door, and it closed with a solid click behind her.

She wasn't in a locker room, but the actual shower room. Four basic walls with shower heads extended into the room. Steam rose from the one shower that was still running.

Under it stood Dustin in all his naked glory.

Her pulse shot to high.

Head tipped back, his hands scrubbed his hair. Water streamed over his head and chest, joining into thicker rivulets that fell past his hips and legs.

The faintest of tan on his forearms cut off abruptly mid-biceps. Arms flexing, his muscles bulged and lengthened in a hypnotic pattern. She couldn't take her eyes off him. She should—

She absolutely should *not* be staring. Not at his muscular chest or the way his torso curved in toward lean hips. She shouldn't be craving to touch the thick line of the V muscle framing either side of his groin.

He turned to fully face her. Charity clutched the clothes tighter to her chest and gave in fully to this temptation. She drank in the sight of his cock as it thrust forward from dark curls. Not hard, not flaccid, he was long and...

Damn it. Charity should have turned and left the instant she'd realized where she was, but this show only made it that much clearer that she wanted the man desperately.

Fake dating for a good reason should still come with some perks, yes? For both of them? And getting her hands on that ass —the perfect ass that he had turned and presented her direction—was on her absolutely must do list.

Enough. Charity didn't wait for him to accidentally discover her ogling-self in the room. "Dustin."

He straightened and peeked over his shoulder. "Oh. That's some delivery service."

He turned off the water. Paused.

Again, she should have turned her back, but she couldn't. Didn't want to. Didn't want to hide how much she appreciated looking at him. But first things first. "I'm sorry. I should have let you know I was here sooner."

Dustin nodded as he turned, gaze fixed on her face. "Thanks. But it's okay. If you don't mind, I don't mind."

That was clear, because even as he walked toward her, his cock rose like the sun on a spring day. Eager and bold and very invigorating.

Charity hummed happily. "You're gorgeous."

"From the eye contact, I assume you're talking to my cock."

She snapped her gaze back up to his. "All of you."

He dipped his chin. "Thanks."

As he reached for the towel hanging on the wall, the words spilled free. "Can I help?"

Dustin paused with the terry cloth knotted in his fingers. "Tee?"

"To dry you off," Charity clarified, then added, "To touch you. I want to. So much."

His expression grew serious. "And more?"

She nodded so hard and fast her chin vibrated.

They both smiled, and the connection only grew.

Dustin moved closer. The heat of his body enveloped her like a caress. Her skin grew more sensitive, her sex ached for contact.

He cupped her cheek in his hand. Somehow he ignored that he was completely naked and she was fully clothed. His eyes were serious, and yet that part of him that was sheer mischief remained. "There's something between us, isn't there?"

"Friends," Charity insisted. "Always friends, but yes, something more as well."

Dustin smiled softly. "Want to explore that *something* with me?"

So, so very much.

She waited.

He waited.

Oh damn, she knew this one. "You want me to say it."

Dustin stroked his thumb over her lower lip, gaze following it intently. "Consent is sexy."

"Yes," she said instantly. "I want to explore."

She propped his clothes on the small shelf above the towel hook then pulled the towel from his fingers. Moisture and warmth greeted her as she stroked upward over rigid chest muscles. The heavy thump of his heart pulsed under her fingers.

Dustin hummed happily. "Me too. So, let's explore."

It wasn't the best place for this to happen, but considering Lionel and Keith had left the shower room only a few minutes before Charity had come in, Dustin figured he had some willing spotters running interference outside.

Still, he tilted his head to the right. "Hang on."

Crossing the distance to the door, locking it, then returning to her side took only seconds.

He caught her hand in his and replaced it on his chest.

Charity's lips curled upward. "Instant replay?"

"I liked where this was going, so why not?"

Her gaze dropped to her fingers. "This isn't drying you off."

"No. Is it getting you wet?"

Her cheeks flushed. He adored that about her—the change in her skin tone was subtle but oh so clear when they were up close and personal like this.

Charity drifted her fingertips up to stroke along his collar bone, over his shoulder, then down his back as she stepped around him. Dustin focused on not coming before she'd even laid a finger on his cock.

She paused, stroking the small scar on his back. "What's this from?"

"Luke. My fault, though."

Charity leaned in and kissed the spot. "All better."

"You don't know how much I wish I had a million more scars, including a few dozen on my cock."

A sultry laugh escaped her. "I like kissing you. And I have no objections to kissing all of you."

As if providing proof, another one landed between his shoulder blades.

Dustin closed his eyes as she rested her hands on his hips. Caressed up an inch, then down. An inch forward, then back.

"Your ass is a thing of beauty."

"I look forward to repeating the compliment." His voice had gone raspy. Needy.

Charity stepped against him, fully clothed to his naked. "Remember, the universe doesn't require cosmic sexual balancing. Or something like that."

"You have too good a memor—oh God, *yes*." She'd reached around him and wrapped her fingers around his length. Dustin let his head fall back as she stroked with firm, confident glides. "You can do that any time you want."

"Harder? Softer?" She put her teeth lightly to his shoulder, and a shiver rolled over him.

"Perfect right now. *Fuck*." He rocked forward into her grasp.

"Give me a second." Charity released him, stepped around so she faced him, then curled him in tight again. "I want to watch."

"Too short to peer over my shoulder? I'll get you a chair next time."

For some reason that made her laugh. The sound came out a little ragged. "I've never figured out why this turns me on so much. Touching you, watching your breathing kick up as I hold your cock—it makes me ache inside."

"I'll do something about that ache," Dustin promised.

"Fine by me, but you first," Charity insisted. She kept stroking as she eased against him again, lips going to his throat. She nipped, then sucked, and Dustin groaned.

He wrapped a hand over hers and tightened the pressure slightly. "Use your teeth on me. I like it."

She scraped over his jugular, and a hot pulse raced through him. Tingling crawled up his spine, and release beckoned.

Necessity called—

He cupped the back of her neck and moved her into position so he could ravish her mouth. Kisses deep and hot and wet even as their joint hands moved over his cock. Her taste flooded in as she moaned, the sound drifting on the moist air like an erotic soundtrack.

Dustin pushed forward and let his control go. With barely enough mind left, he turned their aim away from her slightly as his semen spurted free. Long hot strands laid over their joint fingers as white spots formed in front of his eyes.

Sweet motherfucking goddamn hell.

What escaped his lips? "Wow."

He stood on shaking legs, trying hard not to lean on her too much as he fought to keep his balance.

She nuzzled his neck. "Have fun?"

"Yup."

Laughter bubbled up. "You're a man of few words once you've come."

The few he still remembered were all curses and the word *more.* "Maybe."

He tilted her chin so he could kiss her smiling lips. Slow and soft and all kinds of *thank you* in the motion.

She patted his butt with her free hand. "You need a bit of a shower repeat, and I need to wash my hand."

"Your turn next," Dustin reminded her.

Charity waved her clean hand in the air. "Cosmic. Fireworks. Eventual. Yada, yada."

He tugged her toward the shower. "It's not going to be a punishment."

"I hope not. And I'm eager—but not eager enough to try anything else right here." She washed under the shower he turned on, reaching into the water stream. "Our trailer seems safer."

"Right." Dustin held the towel out until she took it from him. "The locked door here would only slow down, not stop, the other hands."

He rinsed quickly, shaking his head at the expression on her face as he turned off the water and stepped to her side. "You're going to make my head swell if you keep looking at me like that."

"I can't help it," she complained, holding out their shared towel. "You really are gorgeous."

Dustin laughed. "And...you're talking to my cock again."

Her head snapped up, but her lips were still raised at the corners. "Your cock likes me."

"All of me likes you." Dustin stepped into her personal space and kissed her softly. "I promise."

Charity turned serious for a moment. "Get dressed. I need you to check outside and make sure the coast is clear before I go out there. I don't want any trouble."

He knew a quicker way. "Let me look."

Dustin poked his head out the door. Lionel was gone, but Keith was still there, leaning on the wall and peering at his phone.

"*Psst*. You can leave." Dustin winked. "And thanks."

Keith grinned. "Was just catching up on my reading about one cocky cowboy."

"Fuck off." But Dustin said it with a grin.

His friend winked. "I'll head out. Nothing to see here."

Dustin waited until Keith was gone then opened the door for Charity. "You're safe."

"Thanks." Charity stepped past him and placed his clothes on the nearest bench. "Probably easier for you to dress in here without getting anything soaked."

"Yes." He watched as she made her way to the exterior door. "Want to meet me at the trailer?"

"Now?" The word came out high and squeaky, and she laughed. "Sorry. I'm nervous for some silly reason. I want to be with you, Dustin. I feel funny about marching back to the trailer so we can fool around."

He shrugged. "Then we'll wait until it doesn't feel funny."

Charity paused, hand on the doorknob. "Really?"

"Really." He pulled up his jeans and did up the button and fly. He met her gaze again. "Would you prefer if I picked you up, tossed you over my shoulder, and hauled you back to the trailer to ravish you?"

The way her eyes widened and how hard she swallowed —*holy shit*. Excitement was not the response he'd expected.

Interesting. He strolled forward and captured her chin with his fingers. "I don't mind us playing games once we spell out all the rules. But for now, we'll plan it this way. Food is being served, and I'm starving."

Her stomach rumbled and her lips twitched. "I'm apparently Pavlov's dog. Mention food, and I respond."

"Welcome to ranch life." He kissed her softly, pulling back to make direct eye contact. "It's been a full day. The rest of our sexy cosmic balancing act will follow at the time and place that seems natural. Say yes, and we start. Say no, and we stop."

She nodded. "Same goes for you."

Dustin gestured her out the door. "I'll meet you at the dining hall. Save me a seat."

"Okay." She paused then went up on her toes and connected their lips again for a sweet but intense moment.

She was whistling softly as she slipped out the door and headed to the warmth and fellowship of the chow line.

Dustin dressed quickly then contacted Shim, continuing to ignore the mass of other unanswered messages.

Dustin: *Sorry. Meant to message you last night, and then this morning, but the day slipped away.*
Shim: *At least you do remember how to use your phone.*
Dustin: *I'm mostly pretending it doesn't exist. Sorry I'm not there. Or maybe I'm glad I'm not there. How's the chaos?*
Shim: *Not as bad as the first day, or so Tucker told me. Less media trucks as they've started to get the message through official channels to stay away, but more random strangers.*
Dustin: *Shit.*
Shim: *Caleb's shut the main gate. First time I've ever seen that thing across the road.*

Dustin sighed. He could remember the massive wrought-iron thing being closed once his entire life, and that was for a photo op.

Dustin: *Shit again.*
Shim: *Don't blame yourself. Tucker, Luke, and Caleb have all been repeating to everyone who will listen that this is just one of those things that can happen these days, and we'll ride it out. Ashton is ready to fight on your behalf.*
Dustin: *I know I have their support. I still wish it wasn't happening.*

Shim: *Give it time for the different stories to die down. Now it's about half interested in Silver Stone and her newfound success, and half interested in you.*
Dustin: *And my big, thick...bankroll.*
Shim: *Lol. Right, stud. But now that we're telling everyone you have a girlfriend, that interest should drop soon.*
Dustin: *Hopefully. Means I'll be here for a few more days then.*
Shim: *Yeah. No signs you've been followed?*
Dustin: *So far, so good.*
Shim: *Great. By the way. I'm working on updating the website. Plan to put a "about the family" in there to quell a few of the wilder rumours. I've got a few pictures of you and Charity from past events. Okay with me posting them?"*
Dustin: *Okay by me. Check with Charity first, though.*
Shim: *Will do. Now shut up. I'm in the chow line and it's nearly my turn.*
Dustin: *Food's more important than me?*
Shim: *Hell yes.*
Dustin: *Ass.*
Dustin: *One more thing—*
Shim: *What?*
Dustin: *Kidding. Go eat.*
Shim: *Jerk.*
Dustin: *To you? Always.*

Laughing softly, Dustin shoved his phone in his back pocket and headed to the chow house. Some good food, a chance to finish the day with good friends, and an adventure with Charity. Then back to the trailer for the night with her—

Being banished to Crooked Creek was turning out to be an awesome thing after all.

9

Supper was delicious and the company great. Charity thoroughly enjoyed spending time with the group as they shared stories and teased each other about the small things that had happened as they'd worked with the animals over the course of the day.

Only once dessert was done, Dustin tugged her away from the girls. "Come on. You're late for your riding lesson."

Coralee and Amy both blinked.

Their reactions tickled Charity's funny bone all over again. Maybe she shouldn't have found it so amusing, but it really was a kick. "I should take pictures of people's faces when they find out I don't ride. It would make a great instruction manual for actors practicing *horror* and *dismay*."

"After a couple days you won't be able to announce you don't ride anymore, so that project is short-lived," Dustin assured her. "Ladies, I'll see you in the morning."

"Night, Dustin. Night, Charity." Amy waved them off. "You can have the horses. I'm off to soak in a tub with Epsom salts so I can move tomorrow."

As Dustin led Charity toward the barn, Patchwork Annie came out from the group of dogs nesting together under an old willow tree. She stretched, back arching even as her tail wagged lazily in greeting.

Dustin stooped and petted her. "You should be smart and stay here and get some rest. You worked hard today. Good girl."

Annie's tail turned up the pace at his praise.

When Dustin stood and reached for Charity's hand again, she hesitated. "You sure you want to do this tonight?"

He stopped. "Are you worried or scared? Because we don't have to if it's a problem."

"It's not that," Charity assured him. "I am interested, I just don't want to make you ride for longer when you'll be in the saddle again tomorrow. Annie wasn't the only one who worked hard today."

With a quick nod, Dustin resumed his stroll, pulling her along with him. "Oh, I get it. You're worried about Amy's comment about soaking in the tub. That isn't a problem for me, at least not today. I ride a lot at Silver Stone. Like, I mean a *lot*. I rarely use the ATVs, so I'd guess I'm in the saddle for at least half of each day, probably more. The hands here at Crooked Creek don't ride nearly as much except when there's a task like branding."

"Okay. But make sure you stop the day when you need to so you can get through tomorrow safe and rested."

He squeezed her fingers and flashed her a smile. "You're cute when you're being all protective."

She stuck out her tongue. He only grinned harder.

Charity glanced at their joined hands and decided she didn't want to say anything about not having an audience because she liked holding hands with him.

She had it bad. She'd just outright admit it to herself, if not to anyone else.

"Here we go." Dustin stopped outside a stall with a large pale brown horse inside. Annie turned in a circle and curled up quietly against the barn wall.

Oh boy. This was really happening. "That's not the horse you rode today."

He looked impressed. "Good eye for a non-horse person. No, Midnight *does* need to rest since he did most of the hard work. This is one of the older horses Adam plans to retire. He'll head north with us when we leave to go live with the rest of our retirees. His name is Beach."

"Is that a pun or something?" Charity watched as Dustin stroked the long length of the horse's nose.

"Yup. Short for Son of a Beach. Not sure who named him. Caleb and Ashton would never let us get away with nonsense like that. It does mean when Fern asks what you did tonight, you can tell her you were somewhere on a Beach."

Charity laughed. "Nice."

"Want to say hello?" Dustin stepped to one side. "Put your hand on top of mine to start."

"I'm not that green," Charity complained. "I know he won't melt if I touch him."

"Maybe I just want a reason to have your hands on me."

The way he said it more than the words sent a shiver racing through her. "*Dustin.*"

"It's true. And I like how you quivered, as well."

He moved their connected hands to the spot between Beach's eyes, sliding down slowly. Once. Twice.

Then he switched their position, pressing her palm firmly to the horse's nose. The short hairs scratched her skin, warmth making it clear this was a living, breathing creature and not some inanimate object she was touching.

"On your own, now." Dustin removed his hand. Charity offered another stroke.

Beach lifted his head slightly, and she froze. "Did I do something wrong?"

Dustin laughed, a gentle warm sound. "He's greedy for more of your touch, and I don't blame him one bit. Pet him harder."

"You're making this sound far too sexy considering we're standing next to a horse," Charity complained, the breathiness in her voice impossible to hide. But she petted Beach harder as ordered, and he exhaled heavily, a very contented sound.

Dustin stepped behind her, one hand wrapping around her waist. "You're ready for your Horse 101 introduction class now that you've said hello to the demonstration model."

He guided her hand over Beach as he named parts. Withers, forelegs, saddle, mane. He had her feel the different textures of the horse's skin and mane. Even lifted Beach's hoof and showed her the solid and softer parts, and the sturdy horseshoe.

"Beach doesn't mind all this touching, does he?" she asked.

"Most horses don't. Working horses this old become attached to human companionship. He's probably a little lonely here at Crooked Creek since he's getting too old to ride for some tasks. He likes the attention you're giving him."

"I'm enjoying it, too." One hand rested on Beach's rump. "He's still very big, but not as scary as he was at first."

"I'm glad. But being careful around horses, especially strange ones, is never a bad idea." Dustin nuzzled her neck with his nose. "Ready for your reward for being an A-student during lesson number one?"

She twisted her head and met his lips in a kiss. Sweet, soft. Instinctively, she turned toward him and linked her fingers around his neck. He tucked her body against his even as he deepened the kiss.

Shivers slipped up her spine, an electric sensation of

pleasure and need. He eased his tongue over hers, and she sucked on it lightly, smiling at the hum that escaped him.

Hands settled on her butt, lifting her higher and tighter. His hardening cock pressed against her belly, and it was her turn to hum happily. "You're turned on."

"I'm kissing you. Touching you. Hell, yeah, I'm turned on."

"Good to know." Charity kissed him again, tugging him toward her so she could thoroughly enjoy the connection.

A shot of hot air rushed past her cheek on the left before something prickly bumped her face.

"Son of a Beach," Dustin scolded as he broke off the kiss and pushed the horse's face away from them. "Get your own girl."

She couldn't help it. Charity laughed, trying to keep the sound soft and gentle, the same way Dustin spoke around the horse, but it really was too funny. "Was he jealous?"

"Green with envy." Dustin caught Charity's hand, hooked his free hand into the rope halter, and guided them both from the stall. Annie instantly joined them. "Next lesson, getting up on a horse."

Charity caught herself before checking the time. If she was going to trust him with her body later, she needed to trust him with time keeping now. "Okay."

As if he'd caught some of her thoughts, Dustin squeezed her fingers before stopping beside a railing. He looped the head rope over the center post. "You said it before, horses are big. But they're not a ladder, so it's not like we climb them by stepping anywhere we want."

Keeping as relaxed and calm as possible—she remembered what Kelli had said about horses picking up on feelings— Charity laid her hand on Beach's withers again. "I'm not seeing much to step on to be truthful."

Dustin looped his hands together and stooped over. "Today,

I'm your ladder. Left foot in the stirrup, left hand grabbing Beach's mane. Pull up and stand up, then lift your right leg over. Last thing you'll do is sit up and get comfy."

She stared at his hands for a moment.

Trust, remember?

Right, easy to say, harder to do. Charity dipped her chin, then lifted her foot into his palms.

A moment later she was sitting upright on Beach's back.

"Huh." The fingers of her left hand were still tangled in his mane. Her right hand pressed to his neck, and was Beach mostly standing still under her straddle-wide legs. "I seem to have missed the moment of truth."

"Because you, darling Tee, are a natural." Dustin rested his hand on her thigh. "Mostly, though, you're a dancer. Riding really is a lot like dancing in some ways."

"Kelli said that I needed to let the horse lead."

He laughed out loud, unlooping the rope from the post and draping it over Beach's neck. "I guess my niece isn't the only person I'll get to hear 'Kelli-isms' from." Dustin got up behind her—she had no idea how he did it, but one moment he was on the ground, and the next, he was behind her. "That's enough for the lessons. Now you get to sit back and enjoy."

He wrapped his arms around her, fingers over hers where she held Beach's mane.

Charity leaned back against his chest. "We don't need reins?"

"Nope. And obviously not a saddle, either. Good thing you were wearing jeans, though. Bareback on a horse isn't much fun if you don't have at least a layer of denim for protection."

He took them out the dirt road to the south. The evening sunshine lit up the Waterton range with spectacular brightness. Patchwork Annie ran ahead of them, head up, tail raised, excitement clear in every quivering inch.

An idyllic picture from an advertising brochure.

"It's pretty out here." Charity peered up at the sky. "The mountains are in the wrong place, though."

"For me too," Dustin agreed. "But Crooked Creek is pretty, like you said, in her own way." He paused, his cheek brushing hers, his five o'clock shadow a gentle scratch against her skin. "I might have grown up here if things had gone differently."

"What? I didn't know that."

Dustin tilted their joint hands to the right, leaning that direction with his torso, and the horse eased to the side like magic.

He spoke again, his voice deep and quiet. "After the accident where my parents died. Uncle Frank was married back then. He and Auntie Heather demanded to take me and Ginny since we were still underage."

"Oh, damn. I can't see that idea going over well with your brothers. Especially Caleb."

"No." Dustin took a big breath and let it out slowly. "It's hard. I don't like the man, mostly because Uncle Frank bad-mouths Caleb, and I see red. But when Auntie Heather left Frank a few years back, Ginny and I got to talking. I didn't know this before, but I guess Heather wanted kids but couldn't have them."

Her heart ached. This was turning into a tangled mess. "Oh, no."

"I had never thought about that before. That she wanted us, truly wanted us, so she could have a family."

"But you already had a family with Caleb, your brothers, and Ginny."

"And Dare. So, yes. Heather's heart was in the right place but trying to break us apart was the wrong solution." His body shifted against hers gently as if he'd shrugged. "Things could have been different. They could have supported us and helped a lot in those early years, but it seemed they wanted all or nothing. Which meant they got nothing, and things went downhill from there. At least for me. Caleb is way more forgiving and tolerant than I am."

"He's a good man." Even better than she'd known.

Charity considered her own family and how broken they were because of bad choices—deliberate bad choices. Neither of her parents had been strong and giving like Caleb had been. "I'm glad you've got your people."

"Me too." Dustin leaned back, pulling Charity with him.

Beach stopped walking, resting on the top of the ridge where they could see for miles in every direction. Annie returned to their side, peering up expectantly at Dustin, just in case he needed something.

Charity adjusted her gaze, slowly taking in the scenery. "Okay, I don't have a fair comparison of Heart Falls, but this is epic. I think it's seeing this view from horseback, but it's breathtaking."

"Everything is better on..." Dustin stopped. "Let me rephrase. Because I was about to utter absolute bullshit."

Charity laughed, twisting toward him slightly. "You're telling me those old romance novels I read where they're having sex on a horse overstate the truth?"

"I'm saying I've read those scenes, and while I could maybe coordinate some of the positions, I don't think anyone would be calling out, '*Oh God, Oh God, Oh God,*' except while they were falling off."

"Too funny."

He tucked his fingers under her chin and interrupted her laughter with a soft kiss. "Come on. It's time to go home."

～

He'd wondered if she'd stay quiet on the ride back, preoccupied by what they might do once they reached the trailer.

Obsessing about the unknown, the same way he was.

Nope. She chattered easily about her day. Not the specific details, but that she was finding the information a little at a time. How she'd had a great conversation with Sam, and that watching Dustin rope had been a treat. Charity practiced whistling for Annie, who came when called but kept eyeing Dustin as if asking why someone else was involved in their special relationship.

Just before they reached the barn again, Charity mentioned her sister and sister-in-law and their upcoming get-together.

"We'll probably keep it low-key this year. Since I just started, I don't get much time off. And Chelsea and Suz are saving up for a down payment. I think they might drive to Heart Falls from Edmonton on a Friday. We'll hit Rough Cut on Saturday and hang out the rest of the time."

"I'll join you for dancing," Dustin offered. "If you guys want to come out to Silver Stone and go for a ride, I could arrange it."

"Seriously? They'd love that." Charity paused. "I *think* they'd love that—let me find out for sure. I might take you up on the offer."

Beach happily back in his stall, Charity helped brush him down. They didn't need to do much since they'd only been out for a short while.

Brushed, watered, and given a treat, Beach bumped his head into Charity's hand for a final pat before easing back to rest.

They were barely steps outside the barn when Charity caught Dustin's fingers in hers. "Thanks for the fun lessons."

"You're welcome. You'll need to wear the boots Ivy lent you when we get around to using real saddles."

"What were you two doing?" Stepping out of the darkness like a wraith, Uncle Frank snarled the words like an accusation.

Before Dustin could respond, Charity answered, her tone one hundred percent perky excitement.

Aka, fake as hell.

"Dustin took me for a ride. What a lovely ranch you have. The view with the sun setting on the mountains to the south was spectacular. But tomorrow will be here soon enough, so excuse us. Need to hit the sack. Don't want to keep you. Good night."

With Dustin's fingers in a death grip, Charity marched them to the trailer. Not even four steps past his gaping uncle, she whistled, and Annie zoomed to her side, peering up eagerly.

Well, that was...unexpected.

"Good girl. *Such* a good girl." Charity kept walking, opening up more distance between them and his uncle, but she looked directly at Annie to offer the praise.

Dustin spoke softly. "Somehow you keep kicking my uncle where it hurts without looking like a delinquent."

"It's a talent, I know." She flashed him a smile before pausing and ruffling Annie's ears in a caress. "Such a good girl. That was more than I'd hoped for."

"You been sneaking her treats?"

"When would I have time to do that? She's been with you all day."

Huh. True. "Obviously she's a good judge of character."

"Obviously." Outside the trailer, Charity paused. "Do we need to get her food or water?"

"I put out a bowl of water earlier, and there's food and water in the barn. She'll probably head there in a few minutes."

Charity gave Annie a final goodnight pet. "Sleep tight, pupper. Tomorrow is another big workday for all of us."

Was that a warning Charity planned to hit the sack right away? Dustin opened the trailer door and prepared for anything.

Anything except being caught by the front of his shirt and tugged firmly toward Charity.

"You still awake over there, Stone?" she asked, her smile pure mischief.

"Every damn part of me."

That was all he got out before she kissed him.

Lips to his, firm and demanding. Hands on his shirt, opening his buttons, shoving his top shirt off his shoulders. It fell to the floor somewhere behind him even as she undid the button on his jeans.

Dustin reached over his shoulder, caught a piece of his T-shirt, and ripped it forward over his head. Then he was touching her, separating the shirt she wore from where she'd tucked it into her jeans. Sliding his hands under the material to savour the heat of her torso under his palms.

His zipper was open, her hand pressed over his hardening cock. "You're excited again."

"We've been over this. Touch me and you're guaranteed a reaction. Hell, smile at me the right way, and I'll get hard."

"Easy man to please."

"I'm a man. Easy is in my DNA."

Charity laughed, tugging him farther into the trailer. "I attacked you in the doorway."

"Anytime, anywhere," Dustin returned as he stripped her top over her head to reveal a barely-there bra that ended in line with her nipples. "God damn, Tee. If I'd know you were wearing this, I'd have killed myself on Beach. My cock would have been so hard it would have broken off and I'd have fallen over."

She caught his hands and pressed them to her chest. "Good thing you didn't know until now. I like contact with my breasts. On top of clothes, under, your hands, your mouth."

"Perfect." Dustin cupped her, tracing a slow line along the edge of the fabric with his thumbs and smiling as a shiver rippled over her. "You want anything else, more or less, let me know. But I'm going to do what I like first just so we're not following a list. Okay?"

"Do it," she ordered. She gripped his cock over the cotton of his briefs and jacked him lightly. "I'm on the pill, but we use condoms."

"Yup. In my bathroom kit right here on the table. I also have lube if we need it." He picked her up and spun her around as she laughed. "I want you naked. Except that bra is staying on because it's turning me on so hard I can't see straight, and I fucking love it."

"I can help with getting mostly naked."

As soon as her feet hit the floor, she undid her jeans, shoved them toward the floor, and stepped out. The move gave him a clear shot of her ass in a thong, and any blood he still had in his brain went south faster than geese in a snowstorm.

Control, Stone. Fucking control right now.

He fondled her ass with one hand as he reached past her to the table and pulled out a couple of condoms, tossing them on the table so they were within reach when needed. Then he went to his knees to help strip off her panties.

"Your jeans. Now," Charity ordered.

He ignored her, lifting her onto the small dining room table. "Dessert first."

There were many things he enjoyed when it came to sex, but on the list of his favourites? This—the taste and sensation of her pussy under his tongue and lips was everything he'd been daydreaming about.

"Holy hell—there. That's a..." Charity lifted her feet to the edge of the table and leaned back, supporting herself on her hands as she stared happily between her legs.

He took a quick peek up to make sure she was good, but the sounds and small movements of her thighs told him as much as the flush of passion on her face.

Dustin pressed a kiss to her inner thigh. Another to the crease where leg and torso met. Then he returned to her clit, circling his tongue until she squirmed so hard he hooked an arm around her thigh to keep her in place.

A kiss to the other thigh. Closer...closer. When his mouth covered her this time, he slipped two fingers into her core, and Charity gave a cry that set his spine tingling.

His cock pressed hard to the front of his briefs, the open gap of his jeans the only thing keeping him from losing circulation. The pressure kept building, and he was ready whenever Charity was.

"I want to come with you inside." Charity fisted his hair and jerked hard enough to pull his mouth from her. "Quick. I'm close."

Dustin stood, keeping his fingers lazily moving in and out of her pussy. "Take me out and cover me," he ordered.

Her eyes were glazed with pleasure, but she obeyed. Feet dangling over the table, thighs wide to let him keep touching her. She shoved his jeans and briefs down until his cock was in her fist, stroking with a sure, steady rhythm that threatened his control all over again.

A second later she had a condom unwrapped and was easing it over him, her touch soft on his hot length.

After one final stroke, Charity leaned back, feet back on the tabletop. Gaze on his.

"I want this. I want *you*."

"Reading my mind?"

"I'm a fast learner." She caught his shoulders and tugged his torso closer to hers. "Now fuck me."

"Yes, ma'am."

She laughed. "Oh no, mood killer."

"Sorry." Dustin slipped his fingers from her heat and used the moisture to coat his cock. "How about *take my cock and I'll fuck you until you're screaming*."

"Much better. Okay."

It was such a Charity answer, Dustin was laughing as he slid the head of his cock through her folds. He eased back and forth a few times to make sure she was ready, then pressed down to line up perfectly.

The single slow stroke as he pushed in was enough to make a chill run up his spine.

"Dustin. Oh God, that's good." Charity dug her nails into his shoulders. "Faster."

Dustin withdrew slowly, stroked in. Repeated it again. And again.

"Faster—oh, *yes*."

He circled her clit with his thumb again, enjoying the sensation of her muscles tightening on him. "Faster or good?"

"*Uhhhhh.*"

Her head tipped back, and a long low moan escaped as her pussy convulsed around him. Her climax triggered the end for him as well. Dustin drove in hard once, twice. On the third thrust, pleasure roared through him, spilling out with his shot as he came. "*Tee.*"

Still connected, Charity cupped his face, kissing him as Dustin rocked over and over. Her pussy tightened with an aftershock, and she laughed as he groaned. He scooped her up, shuffling with his jeans around his ankles two feet to the right to collapse into a nearby chair with her in his arms. No longer inside her, things might have gotten a bit messy but remained a whole lot satisfying.

They sat quietly for few minutes before Charity nuzzled his neck. "That was fun."

"Tons of fun." He held her tight and waited for the room to stop spinning before attempting to stand.

Friends. Absolutely. But it looked as if this next, other thing between them was going to be a heck of a good time as well.

Charity laid her head on his shoulder. Her heart pounded under the hand he pressed to her chest between the swoops of her bra. As they cuddled together, all Dustin could think of was how right it felt.

It was more than *okay*.

10

———————

he days that followed fell into a sweet rhythm.

Charity woke each morning after a refreshing sleep to an empty trailer. Breakfast in the cookhouse was usually her and a few of the older hands. Sam cooked up enormous meals for her then sent her to the office with enough coffee and cookies to make digging in musty files tolerable.

Midday she'd join whoever was stopped for lunch. Every afternoon break something of interest was happening in the arena. Crooked Creek might be a smaller operation than Silver Stone, but as far as Charity could tell, people were constantly busy with all the usual tasks of ranching.

Getting to watch Dustin work, though—he was good. Like *really* good. She wondered how much of his skills had been learned specifically under his brothers' tutelage.

At the end of each day in the tomb, she'd put away her completed forms and all pretense of work and enjoy the evening in Dustin's company. Good food, great conversation with the cowhands, and tons of variety in the remaining hours of the day.

Horseback riding lessons. Cards with Amy and Lionel. Sam set up a barbeque dinner on Thursday night with steaks so big Charity thought she needed to share with Dustin.

He laughed as she attempted to put half on his plate. "That's yours. I want my own, so you're stuck with it."

"This is enough protein to feed a body builder for a week," Charity complained.

"Or one meal for a hard-working cowboy."

He winked, though, and silently accepted the piece she slipped onto his plate later with a whispered plea. "I don't want to waste it, and I can't eat another bite."

"Good thing I'm germ-proof these days."

They shared a conspiratorial smile.

She was sleeping so well. Partly the extra outdoor time, but she gave most of the credit to the enthusiastic sex she and Dustin were having every chance they got.

Since the first day when she'd all but jumped him in the kitchen, they'd been enjoying each other's company thoroughly. The second round had happened that first night—immediately after a rinse off in the shower where Dustin had turned her on all over again and proven he knew how to sex her up in a shower as well as on the table.

They hadn't stopped. Charity was damn glad that between them they'd packed enough condoms for an overzealous spring-breaker.

The only dark cloud on the horizon turned out to be Frank Stone's visage. The man couldn't be in Dustin's vicinity for more than two minutes without being rude. Which naturally triggered Dustin's smart-assery, although the smack-backs had become lighter as he was clearly more interested in getting out of Frank's way so he could spend time with her.

Being an unexpected positive influence on Dustin? Too funny.

Friday morning Charity hit a snag in her search. The open paper files had failed to give up the needed information. She was so close to being done, she really hated to stop. Tucker's email response to her question for ideas suggested she might find more information on the Crooked Creek computer.

Lovely. Time to track down Frank Stone and ask for his password. Wasn't that going to be fun?

She started her search at the cookhouse. Sam shook his head. "I know he didn't ride out with the crew. Might be in the barn. I'll keep an eye out."

"Is it okay to go in the barn by myself?"

The cook chuckled. "You didn't grow up on a ranch, did you?"

"Nope."

He patted her shoulder reassuringly. "If anyone questions if you should be there, just tell them you're looking for kittens. There's always kittens in the barn, and it's as good an excuse as any."

Charity laughed. "Now I feel the need to go hunt down some kittens for real. Any suggestions where I'd find them?"

He pointed up. "Loft."

"Got it."

The idea of kittens was intriguing, but Charity stuck to her objective. Find Frank Stone, get the info she needed, and finish her task.

At least until she spotted Beach. Or perhaps more accurately, Beach spotted her, and distraction officially arrived.

The horse poked his head over the low front gate of his stall to nicker at her, lifting his head a few times in a small jerking motion as if telling her to come say hello. After three nights in a row of riding him, each one with more independence on Charity's part, she was comfortable enough to go up and do exactly that.

She held a hand to his muzzle and gave him a scratch. "Hey, beautiful. How are you?"

Beach nuzzled her palm, then her pocket, searching for a piece of apple or carrot.

Charity stepped to the side to pat his neck more easily. "No treats right now. Maybe tonight. I think we'll—"

"What are you doing?" Frank Stone spoke quietly, but anger snapped in his tone. He'd popped up out of nowhere and was suddenly so close that Charity felt overwhelmed.

Beach stepped uneasily in his pen, sensing trouble. Charity retreated instantly to a safe distance from both horse and man. She turned to face Frank. "I was looking for you."

"Well, it's damn obvious that I wasn't in the fucking stall."

Anger rushed in. She'd been innocently petting the horse, not swinging from the rafters or lighting haybales on fire. "There's no need to be vulgar, Mr. Stone."

"There's no need for you to be poking around in the barn, either. I'll ask you again—what are you doing? Snooping for my nephew? Trying to find reasons for Silver Stone to bad-mouth me?"

Whoa, he was going off the rails at high speed. Charity held up a hand. "This conversation is way out of my comfort zone. Sam told me to look in the barn for you. I stopped to pet Beach. That's it. There's nothing nefarious going on."

Frank folded his arms over his chest and glowered. "What do you want, then?"

"Access to the final information Silver Stone needs. Tucker said he'd send you a final email with the details, but I might need to check email or excel spread sheets if you have them."

Frank swore softly, just in general this time, not at her, which was fine. "Computers. Hate the damn things." He lifted his chin. "It's in the office. Second drawer down."

Okay—not the usual spot for technology, but whatever. "You want me to go access the files without you there?"

"I'm not stopping my job to go do yours," Frank snapped.

Such a pleasant man. Charity smiled wider, just to keep her temper in check. "I'll need your password."

He frowned. "What's that?"

They stared at each other for a moment. It would have been funny, only she was more focused on if she'd heard him correctly. "There's no password on your computer?"

"Since I don't know what that is, I'd guess not."

Holy mother. Charity nodded slowly. Her instinct to fix the problem shot to high, even considering the source. First things first, though. "It sounds as if you're good with me going ahead. I'll finish gathering what I need by this afternoon." She lifted her chin. Why not offer? "If you'd like, I could do some organizing in the office for you. Update your computer and add some security."

He lifted a hand immediately, shaking a finger in her face. "Don't you go messing with my damn stuff, adding security or what have you. I won't be able to find a bloody thing."

"Organizing when done right means you'd be able to find things easier, rather than the system you have currently." Damn —she sounded sugary sweet, but even Charity couldn't keep this forced positivity up for much longer. Mischief was sure to sneak out. "That's fine. I'll finish my work for Silver Stone and stay out of Crooked Creek's damn stuff."

"Good riddance." He took a couple steps away and glared back at her. "Don't know how you get anything done with all the time you've wasted watching my nephew. You should stay away from that boy."

"Too late. I've already fallen madly in love with him." She gushed the words intensely.

Damn her tongue. She wiggled her fingers at the stone-cold

man and pivoted sharply, bouncing out of the barn as if she didn't have a care in the world.

Regret arrived too quickly. She needed to control her temper, because smart talking someone older than her, and related to her current bosses, wasn't on any list of smart job moves. What if Frank called to complain about her? She hadn't been *terrible*, terrible, but still...

Maybe a little heads-up warning was a good idea.

With that in mind, she waited until she was back in the privacy of the tomb then called Tucker.

"Hi. How's it going?" Tucker asked.

"How annoying are we allowed to be while we're here?"

He laughed. "Excuse me?"

"Let's just say I was less than five minutes into the job and already decided Frank Stone was an ass." Charity pivoted on the spot and made plans. "Consider how much I want to impress you and everyone at Silver Stone, then let me repeat that—the man is an ass."

"Good to hear from you this afternoon, Charity. Yes, you're right on the mark with that one."

Charity snorted. "You can't talk right now, can you? Someone is there?"

"That's right."

She thought quickly. "Without going into details, he's a hard man to speak politely to during prolonged periods of interaction."

"I've noticed that myself. Don't worry about it."

Thank goodness. "Great news. So, in light of trying to get me and my snappy remarks away from Crooked Creek sooner than later, how are things going over there? Is it safe to bring Dustin home?"

"Wait—what? Hang on a second."

The line went quiet for a minute before Tucker returned.

"I got rid of the hand. Now back up the conversation. When you said that part about speaking politely being tough, I assumed you meant Dustin. Which I totally expected, business as usual. But you meant *you*?"

Oops. "Can we go back to the part where you said not to worry about it?"

He laughed. "It's fine. You're not in trouble, but I am amused."

"At the risk of repeating my point, my grandmother always said I was never one to suffer fools lightly." Charity sighed. "I've got everything you asked for. Well, I will once I fill in this final chart. Dustin's been behaving. Having a good time, I think. How is the media storm?"

"Fading slowly. Caleb and I chatted about it this morning, and if you're done—good job by the way—then you two can head home tomorrow. Tell Dustin to give Adam a head's-up tonight in case there's anything planned he's needed for. I don't want to leave Adam in the lurch since we left your departure date wide open."

"I can pass that on. And if we need to stay until Sunday, that's fine as well. I can keep myself busy." Kitten hunting if nothing else.

"Then it's a plan. Email and let me know what you decide, but in the meantime, try to stay out of trouble." The amusement in his tone stole the sting from the words.

"I will," she promised. "And Tucker? Thanks for being understanding."

"I understand the need for understanding, but you're welcome."

~

CHARITY'S ANNOUNCEMENT pre-dinner to Dustin that they could go home the following day was both welcome and disappointing, especially to Dustin's friends.

"You just got here," Amy complained.

"He has a job at another ranch," Keith pointed out. "He can't do all your work all the time."

Amy took a halfhearted swing at him. "Ass."

"We should do something fun tonight," Coralee said. "Bonfire on the ridge?"

"Brilliant. Let me check with Adam—I have to talk to him anyway. Need to let him know we're leaving and see what timing works best." Dustin brought Charity with him to talk with the foreman.

Adam nodded at the announcement. "Sorry to see you go. You've been a big help as usual. You headed out first thing, or can you still work for a few hours in the morning?"

Dustin had already checked with Charity. "If you need me, we can leave later in the day. We'll load up Beach right before we go if we can borrow a trailer."

"Then I'll see you at nine. We should be done by lunch. You can enjoy one more of Sam's meals before you leave." Adam turned to Charity. "You shouldn't ride by yourself yet, but if you want, Amy and Coralee are off in the morning. I'm sure they'd enjoy a ride with you."

"Thanks, I'll check with them."

In an amazingly short time, Dustin and Charity and their four friends were all mounted up with supplies packed for their evening.

Charity nestled in against Dustin as if she belonged there. "Bonfire on the ridge?"

"Close to where we rode the first night. About thirty minutes from here, so just a gentle, relaxing ride." He tucked the reins into her hands then offered a dramatic sigh. "You drive. I'm having a nap."

A soft snicker escaped her. "I've learned enough in the past few days to know that an old, familiar route, ridden slow and easy, means no one needs to drive. Beach could probably get there with his eyes closed."

"Probably," Dustin agreed. He slipped his hand under Charity's shirt, resting his palm on her bare stomach.

She hummed happy consent. "I like you touching me. In case I haven't said it often enough."

The trail narrowed as the trees closed in on either side of them. Dustin and Charity were last in the line, leaving them in a cozy, private corridor if they spoke quietly.

"You've been nicely vocal about what you like. Makes it more fun for us both."

She leaned back, head twisted slightly until their faces were close. "Sex with you—and I'm not trying to stroke your ego here—it's been good."

Amusement trickled in. "Ego stroked, nevertheless. Thanks, and back at you. Like I said, knowing what's working helps. Much better than wondering if I'm in the right spot or if she's so bored she's thinking about what's on her chore list later in the day."

"Oh God, that's a terrifying thought."

"Hey, I assume I was relatively horrid at sex the first few times I tried. I think we all are. Masturbating lets us figure out what we like. Teamwork to get to the same point takes practice."

Charity's stomach quivered under his hand as she laughed. "That it does. And I like that phrase, teamwork. I think it took a dozen tries before I had my first orgasm during *teamwork sex,* and that wasn't because I wasn't having fun." She paused. "My sister was my source for all things sex related. Chelsea was real, and honest, and blunt. Just the type of person everyone needs in their lives."

Dustin paused. To hell with it—a little embarrassment wouldn't kill him. "I got the talk from Caleb. And Luke. *And* Walker. *And* Ginny. Not at the same time, but during the same time frame. Almost as if they knew I was getting interested and brave enough to experiment."

"Too funny."

"Lots of different perspectives, that's for sure. But while I got the information I needed, and the warnings about how to be careful, plus so many details from Ginny that embarrassed the hell out of me but helped, I have to say two people taught me the most. The first was Tucker. He smacked me down hard a few years ago when it came out that he and Ginny had a sexual past going back for years, and I had a hard time with it."

Her confusion was clear. "But Tucker and Ginny are amazing together."

"They are. But they weren't *together* then. And in my head, I had somehow categorized sex as either a fun thing people did as a one-night-stand, or a thing people in a committed relationship did."

Charity shook her head, her curls brushing his cheek. "Not the strangest of concepts to come up with. I got my uber-embarrassing talk from Chelsea when I couldn't figure out how she and Suz had sex when neither of them has a penis."

It was Dustin's turn to laugh. "Oh boy. That would have been a fun conversation to eavesdrop on."

"I wish more people could overhear stuff like that. Talking about sex—talking *period*—solves so many issues."

"It does. And that's why after Tucker gave me hell, I decided I needed someone to talk to who'd shoot straight with me no matter what."

They were nearly out of the trees, Beach pacing slowly

up the trail. The sun was headed toward the distant mountains to the west, but for now the sky remained bright blue and clear.

Charity rested her hand on his thigh. "Who's your sex guru?"

"Kelli." At Charity's surprised gasp, he laughed again. "I worked with her for years before she and Luke became a couple. She had the best attitude toward talking about sex, and she'd proven many times over she was willing and able to kick my butt if I was being an idiot. I asked her a few questions, and one thing led to another. Luke knows, not because she needed his permission or anything, but so it didn't feel strange. We don't talk as much anymore, and never about specifics between her and Luke, but for a while, it really helped to have a woman I could do a brain dump with. Have her fix my bullshit ideas, and then have my wrong thinking gone instead of hanging over my head forever."

Charity twisted enough to press a kiss to his cheek. "I owe her a beer then."

"I owe her beer from now to eternity. She was the one who really emphasized that consent was key."

Up ahead his friends were guiding their horses to the side of the hill, dismounting and pulling everything from blankets to bags of chips from saddlebags.

Beach walked himself to the edge of the gathering and began to graze lazily. Dustin slipped off then reached up to help Charity down. Sliding her against his body en route to the ground was a nice reward.

"Charity. Sit next to me," Coralee ordered.

"Why would she do that when she could sit with Dustin?" Keith asked.

"Better conversation. If she sits with him, all they'll do is kiss, and that's boring for the rest of us."

Charity squeezed Dustin's hand. "We're being separated. Obviously, we've been kissing far too much."

"No such thing." Dustin proved his point by leaning in and connecting their lips. Short and sweet was the plan.

Charity had a different idea. She wrapped her arms around his neck and kissed him until he was running out of oxygen. Which, fine by him. He'd die happy.

The whistles and laughter were like a warm hug wrapping around them.

Over the next hour the sun slipped below the horizon, turning the sky into strips of gold, red and peach. Conversation flowed and beer was consumed. Coralee had brought a bag of marshmallows, and Keith cut long sticks to roast them over the fire.

Small insects flickered in the fading light, and a colony of bats appeared, swooping in silently to dine overhead.

Charity had returned to Dustin's side by now, leaning back on her hands to stare up at them. "They're not scary at all, are they?"

"Nope." He adjusted position until he helped support her. "My nephew Tyler is fascinated with all things that fly. He calls bats batterflies."

"Oh my God, that's so cute."

"Too cute." Dustin glanced around the circle at the other cowhands, but everyone was busy chatting with their neighbour. It was time for being with friends, but he couldn't resist this one moment. "Hey, want to bore people?"

She took his kiss, lips still softly curved as they connected. Heat rippled through him. Damn going home tomorrow. He didn't want this to end, yet spending every night together once they were back in Heart Falls was out of the question.

Still, that was a problem for tomorrow. Not tonight as the

sky painted the world with sunset hues and the fire crackled in front of them.

Charity shifted position, ending the kiss. But she was still smiling as she curled herself tighter against him and tugged his arms around her.

Amy stood and came back with her guitar, strumming softly as she tuned it. "Time to sing for your supper, Keith."

Keith needed no more encouragement. He wasn't bad, either. Definitely good enough to carry the rest of them as he drifted through a series of country and western they all knew.

Everyone except Charity, who sang along for about half of the songs. But she tapped her fingers on Dustin's leg during the ones she didn't know and joined in on the chorus when they came round the second and third times.

A sweet interlude before returning to the real world, and Dustin reveled in the moment.

11

Her first clue that she'd woken earlier than expected was the darkness. The second was Dustin's arm draped over her waist, cuddling her close to his warm body.

What a wonderful surprise.

He'd been up well before her every day until now, and she wasn't about to let the opportunity slip away. Morning sex wasn't always her favourite, but since this might be the last time in a long time to have Dustin in her bed?

Time to make nookie while the sun shines, or something like that.

She rolled carefully, examining his face. Eyes closed, his breathing smooth. The layer of scruff on his chin and cheeks was just long enough to make her fingers twitch to touch.

Under the covers, Charity slipped a hand onto his shoulder. Stroking gently, she traced the muscles of his biceps, his triceps. Reaching lower to caress the side of his torso.

"I'm having this awesome dream. Could you tell Charity

I'm staying in bed for a while?" His voice was sleep rough and deep.

"Okay with me. You just lie there and snooze if you want. No use wasting a good dream."

"That's what I figured. And if that dream eventually means you and me, naked, there's a few final condoms in the side table."

Charity laughed. "A few? You are an optimist."

"Always and forever."

She tossed off the covers then pressed a hand to his chest, rolling him to his back. Naked except for his briefs—she may as well do something about that issue right away.

Easing the fingers of her right hand under the waistband, she tapped his hip with her left. "Lift."

He arched slightly and she stripped off the fabric, freeing his cock at the same time. She tossed his underwear to the stool beside the bed, then pulled off the T-shirt of his she'd stolen to sleep in. Another move, and her headwrap and scrunchie were gone, messy curls tumbling down to her shoulders.

Both of them naked and ready, especially Dustin, if his erection was any indication.

"You seem to have this obsession with my cock," he offered. "And I'm not saying that it's a bad thing, just that it's a thing."

"You have a pretty cock," Charity insisted.

"Ha. Cocks are functional, not pretty, but I'm glad you like mine." He wrapped a hand around it and stroked. His gaze dipped over her, heat brushing her like a caress. "So. This dream of mine... It's starting out most excellently."

"Glad you approve. I thought we'd go for a documentary this morning."

The slight frown between his brows was adorable. "Umm, sure."

She laughed, covering his fingers with hers and helping stroke a few times. "Today we're learning to ride."

All concern vanished. "Continue. I'm highly motivated to improve my education."

She straddled his thighs, taking control of his hands and pressing them to the bed. "Some people like to use a saddle when they ride, but it's good to know how to give directions with just the smallest of hints from your hands. And mouth. And other body parts."

She leaned down and kissed his six pack. Slipped her tongue along the edges of the rigid muscles and headed south.

Dustin's muscles had gone rock solid, his cock rising skyward. "You're killing me here, Tee."

A small lick to the head of his cock. "Focus. I hear riding is fun. Also, good exercise."

"I'm sold. Holy *shit*—"

She'd taken the head of his cock into her mouth and sucked him deep.

Each long, slow motion over his length brought another gasp or groan, and Charity savoured each one as proof of his pleasure.

"Get up here," Dustin ordered. "My turn."

Charity pulled off with a pop and her own happy sigh. She shook her head, though. "You can't interrupt my lesson like that."

"It will involve riding, I promise," Dustin insisted. "You, riding my face."

He hauled her up, slid down slightly on the bed, and the next thing she knew, he was licking her clit and labia and pussy as if she was an ice cream cone on a hot Sunday afternoon.

One thing was crystal clear after spending time with Dustin. The man didn't just go down on her because he'd been told he should. The grunts and moans of pleasure rising from him were just as loud now as when it had been her mouth on him. He stroked and licked and teased with such enthusiasm that tingling anticipation pulsed in beat with her heart only minutes later.

"So good." Charity stroked her fingers through his hair. Perched over him in such an intimate position, she'd have expected embarrassment on some level.

Nope—nothing but the desire to enjoy and give back as much as she was receiving from him.

Charity leaned to the side and nabbed a condom before wiggling back down Dustin's body. "Got to be sure to ride safely."

She wasn't as quick as he was with the condom, but she got it on him, earning a few extra groans in the process. One slight position change lined her up with his length, and she rocked her sex over him. Teasing them both with pressure on her clit and his glans.

Time to get back to the lesson. She met his gaze. "Then you ease on top and get comfy."

She tilted his cock slightly and slid down. Slowly, an inch at a time, until he was fully buried inside. Everything in her sang with pleasure.

So damn good.

Dustin curled his fingers around her hips, small breaths pulsing out. "You're doing great."

Charity leaned over and kissed him. Teeth nipping, tongues tangling, the entire time she squeezed her sex around the thick length of him inside her, thrilling at each moan she pulled from his lips.

"And then, if you get really good, you can ride without using the reins at all. Just a lot of balance and teamwork."

She sat upright, hands lifted to her breasts. A small hip

raise, then drop. Again and again, adjusting the motion until a beat pulsed between them.

"No reins, but lots of touching." Dustin lifted her hips a little farther and took control. Pulsing upward, he thrust his cock in and out. "Touch yourself, Tee. Play with that pretty little clit for me."

She reached between her legs, pulling moisture from where he slid into her. A half dozen small circles over her clit were more than enough to push her to the peak.

"*Dustin.*"

He eased his fingers over hers, tracing the line where his cock entered her, and Charity let her head fall back as her climax hit. Dustin thrust up one final time and stayed there, buried deep, as his hips convulsed lightly.

His gaze fixed on hers, albeit unfocused with pleasure.

Charity pretty much collapsed on top of him a second later. They lay together, panting hard. Pleasure trickled over her skin like a million small sparks. Stars floated in front of her eyes, her pulse still echoing everywhere including her sex where it surrounded his softening cock.

Dustin pressed a kiss to her temple. "You're a good rider, Charity Gruzing."

"I had a good teacher."

"Really."

She pressed her hands to his chest until she could meet his gaze. Expression straight as possible, she nodded. "Beach is the best."

A burst of laughter escaped and he rolled, trapping her under him. "Terrible woman. My ego is broken."

"Your ego is just fine, Stone. So is your sex game." Charity curled her arms around his neck and kissed him. Happy connection in the move.

They separated reluctantly. "You go ahead and shower first.

I'll lay here for a while and recover from being ravished," Dustin offered.

They tossed the linens and towels they'd used into the bunkhouse washer before heading to the cookhouse. They ended up having breakfast together with the girls before Dustin headed off to help Adam with one final task.

Amy and Coralee excitedly took Charity up on the request for one final ride. It was interesting to have their help and perspective as she saddled Beach mostly on her own.

Charity offered Amy a high five and thanks after copying the other woman's method to get the saddle up onto Beach's back. "Dustin doesn't even think twice about lifting the saddle into place. I'm relatively strong from my dancing and firefighting work, but that swing method you use is a big help."

"You're doing great. And your flexibility is a huge help when it comes to mounting up." Coralee took them on a new route for an hour-long ride, then guided Charity through brushing Beach down and putting everything away when they were done.

Charity was still humming happily as she finished the laundry and packed up her clothes. Final task—gather the work files for Silver Stone.

Stepping into the tomb, she jerked to a stop. Frank Stone stood behind the desk, scowl firmly in place.

Determined to finish better than she started, Charity went for polite. "Good morning. I'll just grab my things and I'll be out of your way."

He glared. "Told you not to organize my shit. Where the hell did my receipts go?"

Such a pleasant man.

"I moved them out of my way nearly a week ago so I could use the desk and not lose them. One minute." She took her file from the corner of the desk and laid it on the chair before rescuing the box from the closet. As tempting as it was to dump the contents on the desk, she restrained herself and instead placed the box in front of him. "Here you go."

His glare increased. "You done, then?"

"Yes. Tucker and Caleb will be pleased to have the information. And you won't have to put up with any more repeat requests, so positive results all around."

"Good riddance." Frank peered into the box then sneered. "They didn't really need that information, you know. They sent you to do busy work so they could have that boy out here to annoy me."

Keep your mouth shut, Gruzing. Shut your mouth and walk away...

Nope. It was no use. It appeared she had no sense of self preservation. "You like to assume the worst about people. You might want to work on that because your assumptions aren't doing you any favours."

His eyes opened wide in shock. "Excuse me?"

"Your family cares about you. They obviously care enough to stay connected, but the entire time I've been here you've done nothing but put down Dustin, me, and everyone connected to Silver Stone."

Frank snorted. "I don't have to explain myself to you, but clearly you haven't seen what I've seen. Disrespect isn't something I need to put up with."

She needed a bigger hammer to make her point. *Fine.* Charity stepped closer and made him look at her.

"The last time I spoke to either of my parents was ten years ago. They've never tried to contact me, as far as I know, and I've got no desire to reach out to them. It makes me sad on one level, but it's for a good reason. The connection between us is broken and can't be repaired." Charity eyed Uncle Frank. "You and the Silver Stone ranch haven't broken yet. The biggest conflict

I've seen between you and the rest of the Stone family is your anger, although it seems as if you've forgotten why you're angry in the first place."

"It's hard to forget when that boy constantly talks back."

Charity laughed. She simply couldn't help herself. "That boy is a man who put in a whole lot of hard days of labour on your land, by your side, without once complaining. In fact, he probably lasted longer than you, and the entire time he was careful to protect your land and animals and have a positive impact on the people he worked beside. Tell me I'm wrong."

The furrow between Frank Stone's brow deepened. It was too much to hope she'd gotten through to him, though.

Sure enough, he ignored all the other points of her argument and returned to the same old tune. "He's polite to everyone else but sasses me. That's not helping your case, young lady."

Good grief. It was worse than talking to distracted eight-year-olds when she taught dance. "Okay, yes, he sasses you. Ever notice *when* that happens? Repeat your conversations in your head sometime, and you'll discover that not once has he ever been rude to you without you being rude first. Or if you're dismissive of someone in his family, especially Caleb."

Frank glared. "Caleb. That—"

"I should warn you," Charity interrupted. "I'm pretty in awe of Caleb myself, all things considered, so if you're about to bad-mouth him to me, *I'll* be the one sassing you, PDQ."

For a moment, Frank went silent. Whether because he'd finally gotten the message or was too shocked to continue, she wasn't sure.

It was past time to leave. Charity grabbed her paperwork. "I've said enough."

"More than enough."

She laughed again, because it was that or hit him over the

head with her file folder. "It's sad, you know. You could be enjoying the respect of some of the best people I know. You have the love of most of them because you're family, despite how you act. The respect, you'd need to earn."

She picked up the chair along with the file folder and headed out the door. If the man wanted something to sit on, he could find his own damn chair.

WITH BEACH LOADED into a borrowed trailer, Dustin said goodbye to Adam then glanced around. Charity was busy offering and receiving farewell hugs from the hands they'd spent time with over the past days. "Know where my uncle is?"

"Office, last I heard." Adam patted Dustin on the shoulder. "I need to tell Tucker to get tired of you more often so you can come help me out. And bring Charity. She's a breath of fresh air."

"She is. Thanks." Dustin tipped his head toward the office. "I'll just let him know I'm leaving."

"Keep it short and to the point." Adam winked.

"I'll try." Dustin always tried.

Patchwork Annie marched happily at his heels as they crossed the short distance to the office. Dustin took a deep breath before pushing open the door. "Uncle Frank? Just wanted to let you know Charity and I are heading out."

Frank was behind the desk. He glanced up, opened his mouth, then paused. It almost looked as if he'd forgotten what he wanted to say because he swallowed hard then stood and thrust out his hand. "Thanks for your help."

Dustin blinked in surprise. Um, no cutting remark or disparaging comment? He hurried forward and accepted the brief, firm handshake. "Thanks for the hospitality. Charity washed the sheets and towels. They're clean and in the trailer. And Adam loaned us an older trailer to take Son of a Beach north. I'll be sure Tucker makes a note to return it during our next exchange."

"Good." Frank dipped his chin and seemed to struggle for words, then just repeated it. "Good. Now get, I've got work to do."

He dropped back into his chair and instantly dove into the papers on the desk, once again ignoring Dustin.

Dustin wandered out of the office, slightly shocked and a lot confused. Mostly, though, happily surprised.

That just happened. Unexpected, but as Charity would say...*okay*.

They were on the road shortly after.

Charity told him all about her morning ride. "And I now know how to saddle Beach without feeling as if I'll break something. Him or me."

"Glad the girls could help with some hints. You're welcome to keep riding Beach once he's settled at Silver Stone. We usually move the retirees out to the farther fields, but not until they're settled." He squeezed her fingers. "I'll talk to Tucker."

"That could be fun. Thanks."

Dozens of topics for conversation bounced in Dustin's brain. They'd always had an easy time chatting. Only he realized he wanted to not just shoot the shit. He wanted to know more about her. As if the sharing during intimacy needed to extend into their daily conversations.

They'd agreed that straight up was the best way to discuss anything, and it was true. So he asked what was on his mind. "I meant to ask earlier. Before we left Silver Stone, you told Caleb it was no use contacting the police over that woman who posted my information."

"Yeah. If you knew her name, you could report a person,

but in general, you can't legally stop social media discussions, no matter how wrong or upsetting they are."

Dustin paused. "I don't know anyone I've dated who'd think posting that info would be a good idea."

"I'd have no idea either if I were in your shoes." She made a face. "The few guys who have my number, I'd hope they wouldn't be terrible enough to post it in public. But we're not in control of what others do."

"No, we're not." Dustin linked their fingers. "What happened in your case? What went viral?"

She paused. "How much do you know about my growing up years?"

He shrugged. "I know you don't get along with your parents. You were living with your grandmother when you graduated school. I've seen your grad pics, and your grandma and your sister are the ones in the photos with you."

Her gaze drifted outside the window. "Figured you and the Stones weren't the type to know this type of drama. My mom was a blogger. Chelsea and I grew up with every part of our family life documented and posted online."

Shock rushed him. "Get out."

"Seriously." Charity sighed. "When I was really little, I didn't know any better. Mommy having her camera out constantly was just how things were. I didn't know she was posting stuff that hundreds and thousands of people looked at on a daily basis."

The idea of that level of invasion of privacy was staggering. He paused, wondering. "My foster sister is a blogger, but she never posts pictures of the kids. And I know she talks about ranch life, even her kids, but only in a tangent-like way. She's the center of the focus."

"Which is just fine. Consent, once again, being the key ingredient." Charity met his gaze briefly then refocused on the road. "I was about twelve when I figured out being talked about wasn't something I enjoyed. I didn't want the attention of people online. I hated when stuff would get brought up at school that someone else's mom had read about my life and shared with her kids.

"Plus, I wanted my mom and dad to really be with me in real time. The breaking point was the day I had a dance recital, but instead of coming to watch, mom took fake photos ahead of time. Casual, real time pictures wouldn't be good enough, you see. I had to pretend—and I'd had enough pretending. I told her I didn't want to be posted about anymore. In fact, I wrote up a cease and desist—like a typical smart-ass twelve-year-old would."

Twelve. Fuck it. "The letter didn't go over well?"

"It started a chain reaction. Turns out the perfect family Mom was posting about online was fraying at the edges. She and dad were fighting all the time about whatever unhappy couples fight about. Chelsea was figuring out her sexuality and lived in fear that area of her life was about to be put on display for the entire world to discuss." Charity lifted her hands in the air. "Mom made the bad choice to pop up something about ungrateful children and she posted my twelve-year-old rant online. Within hours, it was being shared everywhere. By the time it hit mainstream media, people from both sides of the *mommyblogger* debate were reposting my letter with their opinions. It was all about hopping on the drama-train."

At twelve years of age, Dustin had been riding horses, playing with friends, and trusting his older brothers implicitly. "I had no idea."

"Most people in Heart Falls don't, thankfully." She adjusted position in her seat, feet curled under her. "Dad and Mom got a divorce, and he left. Mom had a breakdown and decided she didn't want to be a mom anymore, so Grandma Lily stepped in to take care of me and Chelsea. We took her last name to separate ourselves from the drama as much as possible."

Wow. "Your entire world got shaken up."

"Moving in with Grandma Lily was the start of having a real life, though. She was there when we needed her the most, and I will always be grateful for that." A long drawn out sigh escaped her. "She died of breast cancer about six months after I graduated from high school."

Charity had faced one devastating hard blow after another. "I'm so sorry. Fuck cancer."

"Yeah." She reached her fingers across the space between them. "That's my journey into going viral."

He frowned, a sudden worry striking. "What if you hanging around me makes the old news pop to the surface again?"

Her fingers were warm in his. "I've always figured that at some point the story might come up again, but now I'm older and don't care as much what unknown people say about me, online or otherwise."

Jeez. "I don't want to drag you back through that mess."

"This time it's my choice—and that's what makes all the difference." Charity squeezed his hand. "I mean it. Let it go."

"Fair enough. I'm really grateful you had your grandma. As for the rest of it, social media fame sucks, and may we never experience it again."

A soft chime rang on the dash.

Dustin glanced down in concern, but the trailer brake warning light had turned off as quickly as it had turned on. "That was weird."

Charity met his gaze with a lifted brow. "What?"

He shook his head. "It's nothing. Pick something to listen to and you can tell me what's on your agenda for the summer."

The rest of the trip passed quickly, and soon enough they were pulling to a stop outside Charity's apartment. Dustin hopped out to help her with her things.

She'd already crawled from the truck and was reaching for the back door when he arrived at her side, clicking his tongue as he took over. "I see I need to train you in the fine art of waiting."

"I am capable of opening my own doors."

"Of course, you are. Which is why waiting for me to do it means you're giving me the privilege of taking care of you."

She stopped in the middle of reaching for her gym bag, dropped her arms to her sides, and stared at him. "Really?"

Dustin looped her bag over his shoulder, caught her fingers in his and whistled for Annie, who was sniffing the nearby rose bushes. "Really what?"

"Is that why guys open doors for others?"

He shrugged. "Don't know about everyone else, but that's what Luke told me. I think it's a nice way of showing I care about people." They were in Charity's apartment a minute later. He put her bag on the table then turned to face her. "Need anything else?"

She shook her head. Annie sniffed her way around the room like a bloodhound on a mission.

"I'm going to miss you."

Dustin's heart kicked for a second before falling with a thud—

Damn it. Charity was talking to the dog as she knelt to ruffle Annie's ears.

He kept it cool. "You'll be out at the ranch Monday morning. I'll make sure I stop by when I can so you can see Annie."

"Of course." Charity stood. "Here's hoping things go okay

when you hit Silver Stone. And I'll let you know as soon as I can what Chelsea says about their plans to visit."

"We still need to have a date or two." Dustin tried but failed miserably to keep from fidgeting.

"The bachelor auction as well, but we can play that by ear." She stood opposite him, all awkward with no eye contact. The comfort level built between them seemed to have vanished as soon as they'd walked into the room.

He wanted to kiss her. He wanted to pick her up and take her to the bedroom and strip her down and go back to where they'd been that morning.

Woof.

The bark was both loud and unexpected enough he and Charity's attention snapped to the side. Annie had jumped up on the couch and was now sitting on her butt, front legs braced as she watched them expectantly.

At least her hijinks broke the tension in the room. Charity laughed. "Annie. We're not watching a show. You need to go back to the ranch with Dustin."

Annie put her chin down on her front paws as if she understood but was saying a clear *no*.

Dustin's phone buzzed loudly. "Shit. That's Tucker."

"Oh no." Charity's eyes widened with concern as he checked the message.

Thank goodness, it was nothing. "It's okay. He wants me to pick up an order at the mercantile once I drop you off, and they close soon."

"You should go. Message me, though. Let me know how it is over there. And I'll talk to you on Monday."

To hell with it. Dustin closed the distance between them and caught her cheek in his hand. Then he kissed her. Hot and hard and possessive and damn, it felt so right.

When he finally pulled away, Charity was once again

smiling instead of looking at him all awkward and uncomfortable. He dipped his head and slipped out the door, Annie at his heels.

The dog stared out the window forlornly the entire trip home to Silver Stone. Dustin couldn't help but think that his expression was probably as hangdog as the beast's. Being back in Silver Stone was good, but not being around Charity was bad.

Which meant...

Over the years Dustin had been a front row witness to his siblings finding their perfect partners, so the signs weren't entirely foreign. He and Charity got along like a house on fire in bed. Outside of sex, they liked each other plenty, and they had lots in common.

Which meant it was time to do some thinking about what he really wanted, and whether their short-term pretending should become an attempt at long-term reality.

Maybe the social media storm had been the catalyst Dustin needed to see a good thing right under his nose.

12

One unexpected side effect of having been at Crooked Creek for the past week—Charity was disappointed to discover she had to make her own supper.

Or did she? One quick text was sent to Fern to see when her friend was done with work and if they could get together.

Fern marched in the door an hour later, pizza box in hand. "I want dirt."

"I wanted meat lovers, so we're definitely not sharing."

Fern blew a raspberry. "I know you've been eating like royalty for the past week, so I didn't splurge for wings, but I did nab salad fixings. You need to shop tomorrow. I did a good job cleaning out your fridge."

They threw together the salad, loaded their plates, then settled on the couch.

"Tell me everything, or at least what you want to share," Fern ordered. "But first, I've been watching social media and so far, the storm is settling. Shim was amazing, by the way."

Charity paused with her pizza halfway to her mouth. "I'm terrible. I forgot he'd arrived."

Fern waved a hand. "You were busy using your thinking muscles being mostly polite to Uncle Frank, and the rest of your brain was dissolved by the excellent sex." She lifted a brow. "I assume it was excellent."

Charity smiled. "Most excellent."

Fern sighed happily. "I'm glad one of us is endorphin-ally satisfied."

"Maybe it's time you made a move on your guy." Charity paused. "We did establish it's a guy, yes?"

That got her an eye roll. "Yes. Now back to Shim's excellent work—"

"You are so good at avoidance."

"Thanks for noticing. Shim adjusted the Silver Stone website this week. Look at the *About Us* page.

Fern held her phone up, already cued up to the right spot. She scrolled down slowly so Charity could peek.

There were three brief write-ups, but the pictures caught Charity's attention first.

The black-and-white photo in the upper left corner was an older one. Two families were posed in front of or climbing on the massive wrought-iron gate to the ranch. The Stone parents, the Hayes parents, and all seven children grinned from the screen in *The Beginning* portrait.

Fern scrolled down more, accidentally skipping over a few pictures, but Charity was too busy admiring the shots to complain.

The middle of the page was titled *Today at Silver Stone* and had current day photos of all the grown Stone children with their partners. Kelli and Luke on horseback. Tamara and Caleb perched on a railing by the arena, animals milling in the background. Walker and Ivy seated on a porch swing. Ginny and Tucker on the dock extending into Big Sky lake, sunset glowing around them.

The bottom of the page was titled *The Future* and was a single shot of the next generation of Silver Stone. Hand in hand, the six children had their backs to the camera. In one unified line, from sixteen down to age four, they stood on the ridge overlooking the land, a herd of horses grazing in the near distance.

"*That* is a proper kids' picture. Faces hidden." Something settled inside Charity at seeing the image.

"Shim said he was warned multiple times to keep the kid's images unidentifiable."

"Good. He did a great job. This is amazing." Charity poked at Fern's thumb where she was covering part of the screen. "I can't see the entire page."

"First, I want you to acknowledge that it looks really good, yes?"

"Fantastic. Now move your fingers. Why are you hiding the picture of Dustin? Because I assume that's what is under your big, fat thumb."

"Here." Fern handed the phone over.

Charity scrolled back up. "Oh. *Wow...*"

"You knew he was putting your picture up with Dustin's."

"Yeah. He texted and asked permission. I said it was okay, but wow." It was a little overwhelming to see herself online again, this time next to Dustin and mixed in with the family. And the picture they'd found was...

Wow. Again.

Two Christmases ago Charity had helped organize a Not-So-Nutcracker fundraiser, and Dustin had been a willing victim during the event. He'd ended up dancing with the children she taught, which meant she'd spent time making sure his dance moves coordinated with the kids. Someone had snapped a shot of just the two of them while they were goofing off. She'd never seen it before.

Dustin had his arm around her shoulders, both of their chins lifted in laughter. The wood behind them had been part of the set, but in the picture, it could have been any of the barns at Silver Stone.

Charity wore a pair of fake reindeer antlers on a head band, the fuzzy things poking up through her curls and turning her into an adorable holiday creature. Dustin wore the silver cowboy hat with a princess tiara on the brim that his nieces had made for him.

It was a fun picture, and compared to the others of his siblings, a lot more light-hearted and youthful. They looked good.

They looked good *together*.

"It's great." Charity said the words firmly, as if saying it would make her less aware of how much she didn't belong, no matter what the pictures said. She clicked off the screen and handed the phone back to her friend. "If it makes Dustin's life easier, I'm glad."

Fern accepted her phone silently. But her expression said volumes.

Charity frowned. "What?"

"Nothing. Just wondering what the plan is now."

Good. They needed to move off the topic of the pictures of her and him that made *them* look too connected for her heart's good. "We'll be doing some stuff together with you and Shim over the next while as usual. To make sure the dating story keeps up steam."

"You're really thinking of attending the auction?" Charity nodded, her mouth full of pizza, and Fern looked thoughtful. "It's not a bad idea. I'm helping coordinate, by the way."

Charity swallowed her mouthful then responded. "The bachelor auction?"

"Yeah. Rose and Tansy finished most of the grunt work

already. But my brother-in-law Chance got a last-minute invitation to some swanky art gallery opening in Ireland, and he ended up taking the lot of them with him. Rose, Tansy, his brother Cody. They left yesterday and won't be back until the tenth."

"That's exciting."

Fern grinned. "Rose was over the moon. She's wanted to go to Ireland ever since Chance came to town. But back to the auction, my dad is emceeing, as usual. If you guys are in the crowd, I can make sure Dad knows to do a brief spotlight on you at a time that works for you to get away safely."

Being in the spotlight sounded scary, but at the same time, it might help. "Not a bad idea. I'll ask Dustin, and if he says yes, then your dad is the perfect one to deal with it." Charity laughed. "What's your father going to do this year without Tansy there to annoy him by bidding wildly for every cowboy?"

"There's always some excitement when she's around, isn't there?" Fern shrugged. "You and Dustin will be our excitement this year."

"I hope not." Charity refilled her plate. "Okay, next step. Finish supper, then relax."

"To power relaxing." Fern raised her pizza in the air. "And to friends, whatever that looks like."

Charity's brain chugged like a piston while Fern clicked on a movie for them to watch. Friends, yes. But *friends* didn't look the way she and Dustin did in that picture.

They looked like *more*, and she wasn't sure what to do with that information.

$\sim$

Turning up the approach to Silver Stone ranch was both familiar and foreign. The main gate that had been open forever stretched across the asphalt, blocking his path.

One of the hands popped out from a wooden security building beside the road that hadn't been there before Dustin left.

"Damn." He pulled to a stop and rolled down his window, dipping his head at the familiar face. "Roy. This is new."

"Hey, Dustin. Yeah, Tucker and Caleb decided it was easier to stop the invaders here than to get them to turn around and leave later." Roy stepped to the side and pushed the button to make the massive gate sections roll apart. "You get harassed much when you were down at your uncle's?"

For a second Dustin wondered that Roy would mention the animosity between him and his uncle, then he realized the man was talking about the media bullshit. "No one showed up, thank God. You guys dealt with the bulk of it, I'm sorry to say."

Roy shrugged. "Not a bad thing to get attention on Silver Stone. Your info being handed out—that wasn't right."

"Hopefully it's past us."

The man gestured him forward. "See you on the next shift."

Dustin had barely finished parking the trailer when Shim appeared.

"Finally, the man of the hour returns." Shim smacked him on the back then pulled him in for a firm hug. "Good to see you."

"Good to be back. Sorry I missed your arrival." Dustin paced to the back of the trailer and opened it to release Son of a Beach. "Walk with me? I need to stable him for the night."

"Of course. We need to catch up. And not just about your online status."

"Tucker said it's getting better?" Dustin gestured to the

parking lot area. "No one here who shouldn't be, and I didn't see anyone on the highway."

"Having the gate closed made a huge difference. Everyone's had a blast working a shift up there, by the way. It's a nice, easy change of pace from hard labour to just telling people *no*."

Dustin laughed. "Nice to know there's one good thing from the mess."

Comfortable and relaxed defined the next couple of hours as he and his friend found Beach a stall and rubbed him down.

While they worked, they got caught up. Shim's job at Silver Stone was a brand-new position, and even he didn't know what it would involve. "I've set up a couple of apps remotely for you guys already, like the *Finder* app. Going forward it's all about keeping the tech systems up to date and virus free."

"The new tractors have as much tech as they have old, familiar gears." Dustin grinned at his friend. "I can't wait for the day Luke's poking around for fun and hits something that makes him stall out and get stuck. Hopefully he's in a far-off field and needs to be rescued."

"Terrible, but probable. At least I'll be able to find him quickly."

"We wouldn't want the equipment to be lost for too long."

Shim smirked, then his expression went evil. "You've already caught me up on your family. Good to know everyone's doing well. Now, tell me about Charity."

Dustin put on his most clueless smile. "She's great. We plan to go to Rough Cut this week. Fern's coming along, and so are you."

"Sure. But that wasn't the question, and you know it." Shim closed the stall behind them, and they strolled back to the parking lot so Dustin could grab his stuff.

How much to say? Since he was still figuring it out, probably not a lot. "I like her. Always have."

"Girlfriend, though?"

Dustin paused outside his truck. "Why not? She's a ton of fun, she's kind, and a looker, and her sense of humour is twisted enough to make me laugh without it going off the rails. Us getting involved makes sense."

"It does on one level." Shim raised a brow. "As much as you and I being friends makes sense."

Nope, Dustin was lost. "What does that mean?"

Shim shrugged. "We met because you had a teacher who made you do a writing exchange exercise with someone outside the Heart Falls community to discuss our lifestyles—basically, we were pen pals, which no one does anymore. You're a cowboy; I'm into technology and computers."

"You can ride, at least enough to not fall off. And I can work a computer." Dustin shook his head, grabbed his stuff, and headed for his room. "Also, you're not *that* good a friend."

"Ass." Shim paced beside him, continuing his rambling. "Charity is an office worker, also not a cowboy. She's got a background in dance and she's a community volunteer."

"I both dance and volunteer." Dustin eyed his friend. "This is a weird conversation."

"It is." Shim pushed open Dustin's door and gestured him in. "And I obviously have no issues hanging with you."

"Thanks." Dustin dumped his dirty laundry into the basket beside the bathroom.

"Charity has no issues *being* with you, either, not after what you shared about your week."

Dustin glared at his friend. That was too far. Dustin didn't kiss and tell. "I didn't tell you a damn thing, jerk."

Shim grinned. "Didn't have to."

He pointed at the laundry. Charity's pale pink bra sat on the top of the pile like a cherry on top of a sundae.

"Fuck." Dustin dropped the lid on the basket, hiding the evidence from sight. He pointed at his friend. "Don't you tease her."

Shim looked shocked. "I would never."

"You'd be joking, but I don't want her scared off." Dustin sighed. "I like her, Shim. Seriously like, more than high school girlfriend like nonsense."

His friend only grinned wider. "Well, then it's a good thing you just *happen* to have to pretend to be a pair for the summer. Just to make sure everything's in the clear when it comes to the online drama."

"Great. Remind me that she's only doing this because she has to."

"Dude, Charity is not one to do anything she doesn't really want to do." Shim pointed at the laundry. "She seems to have wanted to do you just fine."

"Shut up."

"Can't. I've been waiting for the mighty Stone to fall, and I'm finding it rather sweet."

Dustin punched Shim in the shoulder lightly, and they wrestled for a minute.

When they stood again, Shim patted Dustin's back, expression gone serious. "I get it. The whole wanting to know if this is right, and living up to expectations, even the unspoken ones."

Because that was hitting the nail on the head. "My family means everything to me. But you and my friends, you're a part of what's important, too."

"And now you're trying to figure out if Charity could be somewhere in both of those camps. Friends *and* family."

Or would she be something even more?

Dustin shook his head. "I've got to think it through, but yeah. This is big. I don't want to rush, but I also don't want to miss out on something good because I've got my eyes closed."

They headed to the cookhouse for dinner, the companionable silence between them something to be grateful for. Especially when Dustin's head was full of tangled thoughts and uncharted territory.

13

———

$\mathcal{C}$harity was still feeling a little unsettled the next morning when she put through a call to Chelsea. Partly because of the image of her and Dustin looking too much like a couple. Partly because her desire kept growing for the pretend story they'd started to inch closer to reality.

A nice catch up with Chelsea would help.

Her sister answered the phone with a yawn and a fuzzy, "*Whatsup?*"

Charity laughed. "I'm sorry. I thought you'd be awake by now."

"Suz had a late shift, and I waited up for her. You home?"

"Got back yesterday. Successful time away, both for my job and mostly riding out the weird gossip about Dustin."

Chelsea hummed. "I watched the story evolve over the past few days—Dustin's not online much, is he?"

"No. He mostly spent a lot of time shaking his head this past week while people told him what was being said."

"Good for him for keeping it separate. Did you look?"

Charity considered. "Only enough to remind me how

much I don't like having things online that are out of my control."

"I hear you, kiddo. But it does seem as if the mess is settling nicely. I saw mention of him having a girlfriend, so that'll help."

Oh no. Charity searched her brain but couldn't remember what she'd told her sister. "Um...about that girlfriend."

"Why do you sound guilty?"

Because big sisters had built in bullshit monitors? "I could have sworn I told you, but I'm the girlfriend. I mean, I'm the *pretend* girlfriend."

"*Tee*." The scolding and the worry in Chelsea's tone was loud and clear.

"I know. It made sense at the time, I swear."

"You're a menace. And I hope to hell you know what you're doing." Chelsea sighed heavily. "Next topic, we've set our holidays. Suz and I have Tuesday night to Friday off, second week of July. Suz's first shift back starts at six on Friday night, so we'll come and hang out for a couple days then drive home Friday, no problem."

"Perfect. I'll arrange with Silver Stone to switch my weekend for those days. Oh, and Dustin says we can borrow horses and he'll take us riding while you're here."

"Oh, really?"

"He's a good guy, Cee. Should I tell him you're interested?"

"Of course, we're interested." Chelsea paused. "You're a grown up, Tee, so I won't ask things that are none of my business, but I will say this; if you need me, I'm there. You need *anything*, I'm there."

"Back atcha, sis. I love you, but everything is okay, really. And I'm looking forward to time with you two in a few weeks."

They said their goodbyes, then Charity got back into the routine of her life. A tidy of her apartment, a trip to the grocery store to restock a few items. Ordinary, everyday things.

She missed having Dustin to talk with.

No—not a place she would allow her mind to go. Instead, she sped up her pace on the walk home from the store, hauling her groceries with her in the rolling basket she used.

A long, low whistle sounded to her left. Charity whipped her head around to discover Dustin beside her, his truck moving at a snail's pace as he grinned out his window. "Hey, Tee. Need a ride?"

"Home is only a couple blocks away," she protested, but he'd already pulled over and was out his door and headed to her side.

"You can be comfy for a couple of blocks, then." He picked up her entire shopping basket and eased it over the side of his truck into the back. He pulled open the passenger door and offered her a hand up. "There you go."

It felt far too good to be in the cab of the truck. "Are you proud of me? I didn't try to open my own door or anything."

"So proud." He leaned over her, smiling face right there in front of her. He lowered his voice to raspy, sex volume. "Can I help with your seatbelt?"

"You just want to grope me."

The words popped out before she thought better of it, but he laughed. "You know me too well."

His hands moved in a quick, gentle caress over her torso. Then he did up the seatbelt, closed her door, and returned to the driver's side.

"You just got me all hot and bothered," Charity complained softly when he put the truck in gear.

"Maybe we should do something about that." Dustin drove slowly, his fingers linked with hers on the bench seat. "If you're free this afternoon."

It was a recipe for disaster, but hell if she had the willpower to say no.

Which was why an hour later she lay panting on her bed, Dustin at her side. They'd both enjoyed a couple of outstanding orgasms.

"My ice cream is melting."

Dustin pushed up on his elbow and grinned. "Is that new slang for what we just did?"

"It's a literal complaint. My groceries were abandoned in the kitchen. God, did we even close the front door?"

He nuzzled her neck, curling against her. "I closed the door, *and* I shoved the ice cream in the freezer. That's all I had time to do before the ravishing began."

"It was impulsive but excellent ravishing." She cupped his face and stared into his dark brown eyes. "Hey."

"Hey."

The slow lean in until their lips met gave her all sorts of time to consider again how terrible of an idea this was. But seriously—between the choice of kissing Dustin or not kissing Dustin?

No choice at all.

The brush of his lips over hers stayed soft. His tongue teased her lips until she opened, and they both made sounds of the *delicious* sort.

When he finally broke them apart, it was to press his lips to her temple and keep snuggling her close. "Any updates to report? I mean about life in general, not the *hashtag social media sucks* topic."

She laughed softly. "I have the dates for my sister and sister-in-law's visit. If that horseback ride offer is still available."

"It is." Dustin trailed his fingers down her arm. "I caught up with Shim. He says hello, and that you owe him a dance when we're out next. Apparently, there was a second picture of the two of us taken during the Nutcracker where you were still wearing the red Rudolph nose. He did *not* use it."

"I bet the picture is cute. But thanks to him for saving me from becoming *hashtag Dustin's Deer*."

"Damn, I need to use that one."

She poked him in the chest. "Behave."

"Why start now?" He winked, though. "Dancing this week?"

She thought over her schedule. "Sooner is better than later. Since the auction is on Saturday, we should get in some public viewing before then."

"Tuesday work? I'm on a late shift tomorrow."

Charity nodded. "Okay."

Making plans to go fake dating while still in bed after real sex. The situation was beyond what she'd expected, but there was no use doing anything right now but go with the flow.

Work on Monday felt far too ordinary. With the security at the front gate, there were no further interruptions in the office.

Tucker showed up with Caleb halfway through the morning, though, and a shot of worry struck. After all, she had been rude to Caleb's uncle. Even if the man had deserved it.

But Tucker and Caleb simply wanted to go over the information she'd gathered the previous week.

After checking through the papers, Caleb sat back in his chair and sighed contentedly. "You're a miracle worker, Charity. Thanks for digging through what I expect was a mess to get this data for us."

"You're welcome." Her grandmother's admonition to always be truthful struck hard. "It wasn't as hard to find as I expected. Your uncle's bookkeeping system is old-fashioned but orderly. Once I figured it out."

She didn't need to mention the chair incident, either.

Tucker and Caleb exchanged amused glances.

"That was nearly a compliment," Tucker noted.

Charity's cheeks heated. "He wasn't *all* bad."

Caleb's chuckle was deep and low. "No, Uncle Frank is not *all* bad, but I agree that he is annoying. Thanks for putting up with him."

She met Tucker's gaze, silently asking what she didn't dare ask in front of Caleb.

Tucker shrugged. "Told you not to worry about it, didn't I?"

"I know he's good at pushing people's buttons." Caleb said, standing as he spoke. He met her gaze straight on. "You didn't swing a pitchfork at him. Which means so far, my *wife* is still troublemaker number one when it comes to family relationships and Uncle Frank."

"Oh my God, really?" Although it didn't surprise Charity. Not really, but she was curious as all get-out what could possibly make even-keeled Tamara react that violently.

"Really." Caleb adjusted his hat then winked. "Like Tucker said, don't worry about it. And thanks again for your help, with the info gathering and the girlfriend thing with Dustin."

"No problem."

Caleb was nearly out the door when she remembered the paperwork she'd prepared for him to sign the previous week, which meant it was nearly thirty minutes later before she had the empty office to herself and a chance to collapse into her chair and breathe out a sigh of relief.

She wasn't in trouble.

First and most importantly, Caleb had acted like the rock-solid big brother Dustin had always said he was.

Second lesson of the day? Tamara was a total badass. Charity couldn't wait to find out the whys and wherefores of the pitchfork incident.

～

OUTSIDE CHARITY'S apartment on Tuesday night, Dustin paused. He passed the flowers he'd bought from hand to hand, wiping his sweaty palms dry on his jeans.

What the hell? He was as skittish as a newborn colt. Ridiculous to be nervous, all things considered. But his brain kept coming back to the idea of making this real, and the best ways to do that, and now he was jumping at shadows.

He took a deep breath and rang the bell.

The door popped open a second later, Charity's smile shining on him. "Right on time."

"Adam would be proud." He held forward the flowers. "For you."

She took the bouquet, and her smile bloomed even brighter. She gestured him in. "Thanks. That's so sweet."

"You always wear flowery things, so I thought you'd like them." He gestured to her outfit. "My proof. Flowers."

She pulled a glass vase out of the cupboard and filled it with water. "I do have a theme, don't I?"

"It works. The bright colours look great on you."

"Thanks again." The vase settled on the kitchen table, Charity stepped back to admire them. "Very pretty. From Rose's shop?"

"As if I could buy from anywhere else in town. Fern was working. Said to tell you she'd be a little late tonight."

"Okay. Just let me put on my shoes and I'll be ready to go."

She paced away. Dustin admired the sway of her hips under the flitty flower-covered skirt that fell to mid-thigh. "You really do look pretty."

"Thanks." Charity twirled, revealing the length of smooth skin that made his fingers twitch with the need to stroke. "Hey. None of that."

He reluctantly lifted his gaze off her legs. "None of what?"

"Undressing me with your eyes. We're going dancing, remember?"

"Horizontal dancing is a thing."

"Really?"

"So I've heard."

She bent to tug a silver shoe strap in place. "Vertical dancing first."

Her ass—*damn*. "You're a strict girlfriend, Tee."

"So I've heard."

They grinned at each other, and his nerves vanished. This thing they were doing, with the time spent together—the dating might be pretend, but the connection between them was real.

Maybe if he kept them doing what they were doing, they could flow from pretend to the next thing, simple and easy.

Outside her apartment, Charity slipped her hand around his elbow. Tucked to his side, they strolled the short distance to the door of Rough Cut pub.

"I assume we'll hear some teasing tonight," Charity warned.

"As long as it doesn't involve stud talk, anything that links us together is a good thing." He squeezed her fingers. "When you want to call it a night, though, let me know."

"Okay." Her lips curled upward. "I owe Shim a dance. And I know Fern will grill you for information. She's attempting to track down your doxxer."

"Won't that be fun?"

Charity snorted.

"On my side, in terms of updates, Luke gave me a heads-up that he and Kelli plan to be there tonight. Offering a bit of family comradery." His turn to grin. "In other words, since Ginny is out of commission until after the baby arrives, us going to the pub was a great chance for Kelli to hold Luke's feet to the fire and get him to take her out."

Getting to be with members of the Stone family in small amounts was easier than the entire group of them. She felt frozen in place when there were more than two gathered. "I like Kelli."

"Me too. Plus, I always enjoy the chance to hang with my brothers outside of a work setting. I helped Tucker move his and Ginny's stuff to the new house today."

"The place is ready?"

"Mostly. The main floor is completely done, including the baby's room. Means they won't have to move after the kid arrives."

They were headed up the boardwalk now. A casual acquaintance from the community grinned at them as the man pulled the door open and gestured them forward. "If it isn't our own homegrown celebrity. How's it feel to be famous?"

"Famous or infamous?" Dustin asked with a wink, tucking Charity closer as he guided her in the entrance.

The place was hopping, but with enough room to move so that it didn't feel like a trap. He waved across the dance floor at Luke and Kelli, who were already twirling to a fast two-step.

"No use trying to find a seat if we're just going to give it up." Charity swirled into Dustin's arms, ending in the perfect position like magic.

He spun her onto the floor. "You move well."

She laughed. "You say that as if you're surprised."

He blinked. *Shit.* "Well, hell, that came out wrong. Of course you move well—ballet and the rest of it. And we've danced before."

"Vertically and horizontally." Her naughty wink sent a shot of fire through him.

"Tee," he scolded. She laughed as he whirled her then dipped her backward.

They did move together well. Both Luke and Tucker had

previously shared with Dustin that they liked dancing because it was a great way to spend time alone with their wives even in the middle of a gathering.

The upbeat song ended and switched to a romantic ballad. Dustin tucked Charity in tight and enjoyed the sensation of her pressed against him. "My brothers are geniuses."

"What's that?" Charity traced her fingers over the back of his neck. Her body swayed against his, and all sorts of naughty plans for later came to mind.

"Remembering some advice they gave me that I appreciate more and more the older I get."

"Nice to have family moments like that. My grandmother told me once to never date a man who drove a fancy truck and didn't offer to wash the dishes."

Dustin frowned at the change of topic. "Good thing I don't have a fancy truck."

She shook her head. "It's the *combination*. If he has a fancy truck but doesn't volunteer to help around the house, she figured he'd be the kind of man more focused on what made him look good than sharing the chores involved in living a life."

Oh, now he got it. "Your grandma sounds awesome."

Charity pressed her cheek to his and sighed contentedly as he guided her around the floor.

She felt so right in his arms. He couldn't wait to take her home, but he was also really liking this time together in public. A chance to show her off—

Yeah, it was to make sure the girlfriend ploy caught on, but Dustin knew it was for more. That made it more...and a moment to truly appreciate.

The song came to an end, and she shifted to upright beside him. Their fingers were still linked as they waited for the next song to start.

Shim shuffled forward, bowing slightly to Charity. "You owe me a dance."

"So I hear." Charity squeezed Dustin's fingers before letting go. "Save me a seat. I'll need a break after this."

"Because we will dance and not simply sway lazily," Shim offered to Dustin before twirling Charity away with an evil laugh.

"You're an ass," Dustin called after them.

Shim didn't break stride in the two-step, but somehow managed to hold up his middle finger so it flashed Dustin every time he and Charity rotated on the floor. Charity laughed out loud.

All was well.

Dustin turned to leave the dance floor. Luke motioned him over to where he and Kelli had settled at a table just to the side.

Dustin sat, gratefully accepting the bottle his brother handed him. "It's a wild one tonight."

"Good turnout, that's for sure." Luke leaned in. "Hate to be the bearer of news—not sure if it's good or bad at this point—but you've been spotted on social media again."

"Fuck."

"No, this time it might be okay. They've bought the girlfriend line." Luke held up his phone. "Has to be someone local."

The social media post was from a generic *@AroundHeartFalls* account.

Look who was spotted out for the night! I think they look adorable. Shipping this hard. #DusTee #SilverStoneStud #CuteCountryCouple

An image of him and Charity all snuggled up as they

walked down the boardwalk earlier that evening accompanied the text.

"Okay, that's slightly creepy." Yeah, it was confirmation that he wasn't eligible to be pursued. But he didn't want this to turn into people stalking him and Charity instead.

Luke eased his legs under the table. "A few more people reposting, and you'll be truly in the clear in terms of the bachelor angle."

"You guys look good together." Kelli poked him in the side. "You being nice to her?"

"Very nice," he assured her. "As nice as she allows."

Luke frowned. "What are you guys talking about? Of course he's being nice. Caleb would have his head otherwise."

Only, Kelli wore the kind of smirk that said she wasn't as oblivious as Luke. She waited for Dustin to say something more, but since there really wasn't anything official to say yet, Dustin kept his mouth shut.

She raised a brow but nodded. Then she turned to Luke and smacked him on the arm. "Your brother is old enough he doesn't need the threat of Caleb hanging over him so he behaves."

"Really? I'm older than him, and you still threaten to tell Caleb when I plan to do shit with Tucker."

Kelli rolled her eyes. "Because you two are hellbent on killing yourself with some of your hare-brained competitions. Only the wrath of Caleb keeps you on the straight and narrow."

Which was both true and hysterical, so Dustin was laughing when a breathless Charity arrived back at the table.

"That was fun. Now hydrate me," she ordered.

Dustin pulled her into his lap so he could whisper in her ear even as Luke handed over an unopened bottle. "Keep a smile on your face, okay?" he warned before presenting her with the phone. "We're in the news again."

She stiffened slightly as she read it, then groaned. "*Hashtag, Dus-tee?* That's what they're going for?"

"I think it's cute," Kelli offered.

"As cute as online notoriety can be," Luke offered dryly.

Charity wrinkled her nose then turned and planted a big kiss on Dustin's cheek.

He blinked. "You realize you're offering more ammunition. Because that picture was taken less than an hour ago. Plus, someone knows your nickname is Tee, and I can't imagine that's common knowledge outside Heart Falls."

She was the one to lean in close this time. "Maybe, but better keeping attention and cameras on us than Kelli, am I right?"

Dustin swore then nodded. He opened her beer and presented it to her with a flourish. "Any time you want to plant one on me, you're good to go."

"I'm shocked and surprised. *Not.*"

Beside them, Kelli laughed. Her pointed glance at Dustin said all over again that she suspected more than Luke. Which was fine by Dustin, since she seemed to approve.

What was it that Keith had said about women making the best wingmen?

Kelli patted the seat next to her. "Charity, I need to talk to you. Since I hear you two are hitting the auction on Saturday, I need your help with some ongoing mischief."

"Okay." Charity kissed his cheek softly then slipped off his lap.

Which meant the girls were soon discussing something earnestly, heads tucked together as Luke and Dustin eased back in their chairs and shot the breeze. Comfortable, easy, right.

Dustin lifted his beer and tipped it toward his brother. "To a well-executed plan."

"To obnoxiously cute online names and the end of clickbait troubles."

They clicked bottles.

The sound rang out crystal clear and sharp like a bell.

A cold sensation rolled over Dustin along with a sense of déjà vu. As if he'd been here before and something was off. He shook the sensation off, but the sense of unease lingered far too long into the evening.

14

———

"I changed my mind. This is a terrible idea."

Charity sat in the passenger seat of Dustin's truck, fingers squeezed tightly. He'd picked her up and brought her to the community hall where the lunch and auction were being held. They'd arrived at the end of lunch to cut down on the total time in public.

It was suddenly all too much.

Dustin twisted in his seat. "Which part?"

It was tempting to say *all of it,* but that was so far from the truth, Charity couldn't say the words without guilt rippling in.

She liked being his fake girlfriend with benefits.

It was the other parts of today's deception that made her hesitate. "We've spent the past three days watching social media play with that silly *hashtag DusTee* label. People who don't even know us have opinions about if we look good together or not. And no, I didn't read all the comments—Fern took my phone away before I found any of the ruder ones."

"Since I also didn't read them, I will tell you that according to Tamara, the only rude comments were from people whose opinions we wouldn't give a damn about in the first place. I'd say we can safely ignore *all* the comments."

True. Still... "Maybe it's enough."

He stroked his knuckle over her cheek. "Okay."

She snickered. "My favourite word, only this time I don't know what you mean."

"*Okay*, we don't have to show up." He shifted back in his seat and gestured to the wheel. "I put her in gear, and we can head to Silver Stone and ride Beach for a bit. He could use some exercise."

She eyed him. "You're serious?"

"Of course." Dustin shrugged. "If you're uncomfortable, then we don't do this. You know the rules."

"This isn't sex."

He grinned. "No, but permission to change your mind is not limited to bedroom activities."

Which somehow made the butterflies in her belly calm down. "Okay."

A blast of laughter escaped him. "Tee. Help me out here. Which *okay* is it? Into the hall or off to the Beach?"

She laid her hand on his thigh. "Into the auction. I did promise to do that thing for the Silver Stone ladies. Which Fern is so excited about, because it seems there's some record for purchasing a bachelor, and Tansy's about to lose her crown or some such nonsense."

"Fern is a great little sister. Knocking older siblings off their perches is in the youngest sibling rule book."

She forced herself to wait until he rounded the truck and opened her door to help her down. When she would have headed straight to the doors, he tugged her against him for a brief, intense kiss. Heat wrapped around them, the urge to lean in closer and just hang on sticking hard.

When he pulled back a few minutes later, Charity was no

longer worried about the auction. She was no longer worried about *anything*. "My brain just short-circuited from a lack of oxygen. *That* was a kiss."

"That was a thanks for saving me." His expression turned more serious, although still happy and content. "I mean it. Thanks, Tee, you're the best. Don't worry about today. No matter what happens, I'll take care of you, I promise."

"I know." The warmth enveloping her was no longer just sexual, but a sweet heat unfurling in her chest. The look in his eyes—

Charity stepped away before she could do something dangerous. She grabbed her purse from the truck before tilting the side mirror to fix her lipstick.

While she worked, Dustin leaned on the door beside her, contentedly watching. When she tucked her lipstick away, he caught her hand in his and escorted her into the hall.

The Stone family had taken over a section to themselves on the far right of the floor. Charity eyed the space, looking for a nice safe place to sit that wouldn't mean being too surrounded.

Ivy wasn't there, and neither was their youngest, but Walker had both Chloe and Carter at the table. Tamara and Caleb's youngest son Tyler sat next to Carter. Their teenage girls were seated with some friends at the opposite end of the table from their parents, Sasha waving her hands excitedly as she spoke. Luke and Kelli filled in the gap on one side of the middle of the table, and a couple of empty chairs remained on the other side next to where a very pregnant Ginny sat beside Tucker.

Dustin guided Charity directly to the open chairs.

So. It was straight into the firepit, then.

Ginny leaned back and put her feet up on the chair Tucker turned for her. "Perfect. I can now continue to be entertained and fed pie."

"You want mine?" Tucker asked, holding out the piece in front of him.

She accepted it happily. "You should go grab another piece."

Tucker winked at Charity. "Of course. What flavour do I want this time?"

Ginny poked at the crust. "Pumpkin again is a safe bet. Maybe apple."

"Two pieces of pie, coming right up." Tucker offered Charity his chair. "And what type of pie do you want?"

"Whatever Dustin picks, apparently. Definitely cherry."

Ginny snickered. "You learn fast."

Dustin just grinned, pacing off at Tucker's side to where the pie table waited.

"They're good, but not up to Tansy's standard." Ginny licked her fork then leaned in close. "How are you holding up?"

Feeling like a fish out of water? Charity shoved down the worries about being surrounded by the Stones and focused on Ginny alone. It was hard to be intimidated by the woman who was glowing like a Madonna.

"I'm okay. Frankly, it's fun to be here without the stress of having to bid. The auction is for a good cause, and I like supporting the community, but the bidding tends to get expensive, really fast."

"Especially when Tansy is around," Ginny pointed out.

"True," Charity agreed with a laugh. "Just my luck that the one year she's not here to drive up the prices, I already have a date."

Ginny joined in laughing, but her expression matched Kelli's across the table. As if they suspected the fake girlfriend thing had gone farther than simply pretend public displays of affection.

Don't go there, Charity. Friends. We're just friends. That's all we can be.

Fern's dad, Malachi Fields, waved to the crowd as he paced to the front of the room. On the stage a group of men had gathered, including Shim. Most in their twenties, although there were a few older gentlemen into their fifties. All were neatly dressed in suits or newer jeans. They all looked nervous, and Charity couldn't blame them.

They weren't Dustin, after all. They weren't the *#SilverStoneStud*.

Ginny caught her sleeve and pulled her close. "You just snorted."

Charity pressed a hand to her nose. "Oh my God, I'm sorry. That's embarrassing."

"Oh, stop that." Ginny waved a hand in the air then leaned so close the swell of her belly pressed against Charity's arm. "You have tells, my darling. And that snort *tells* me that you just had an evil thought, and rules of the Stone women say entertaining evil thoughts must be shared."

Being included in the Stone women was enough to make Charity fight for focus. But she nodded slowly, debating what to say that wouldn't give away things Dustin might not want shared. They never had discussed how much he wanted to tell his family other than knowing he and Charity were "dating."

She went for simple. "All the social media tags from the viral nonsense are whirling in my brain and doing bad things."

Ginny considered then grinned, mischief rolling in hard. "Not enough cocky cowboys on the stage? Or not enough studs?"

Oh my God. "*Ginny.*"

"What?" The other woman winked. "Sorry, I have a bad habit of putting together the clues then blurting out the dirty details."

"You were clearly reading my mind," Charity admitted.

Ginny offered a quick wink. "Can't say I disagree, other than Dustin's friend is cute. Young, but cute."

Charity was saved from having to respond by Malachi Fields, master of ceremonies, turning on his microphone and starting up the event.

"It's time for the annual fund raiser for the Boys and Girls Club and the Hope Foundation. And since we don't want to keep our volunteers waiting too long, let's get started." Malachi waited as a trickle of applause sounded. "The auction will proceed smoother than usual this year—"

"When's Tansy back in town?" some card in the audience shouted.

Malachi snapped up a finger at the man. "My point exactly. Since my daughter isn't here to create chaos, I've decided we have time for a momentary interlude. First, if I could ask Dustin Stone to please join me."

The clapping was much louder this time, along with wolf whistles and hoots. Dustin good-naturedly waved at the audience as he made his way to Malachi's side.

The older man rested a hand on Dustin's shoulder. "Not that you need introducing, but for the visitors to the community, this is Dustin. He's been a solid contributor to many Heart Falls fundraisers over the years, including participating in the auction. But this year, while I know some of you in the audience were hoping to bid on this young man, he's here with his girlfriend, also a well-loved member of the Heart Falls community."

"Go, Charity." The shout went up from the back of the room, and laughter bloomed along with applause.

Ginny laid her hand on Charity's shoulder. Kelli and Luke offered her a thumbs-up. At the head of the table, Caleb glanced over and dipped his chin as if acknowledging her.

Charity's heart skipped a beat. Oh God. It seemed too real. It was too much what she *wanted* to be real.

Malachi smiled out at the crowd. "Since Dustin is not participating in the auction today, I just wanted to say a quick thanks for his past endeavors, and the best of luck as he continues his work with Silver Stone—"

"Hey, Dad." Fern stood and waved her arm in the air. Her prothesis had a Canadian flag sticker with a red flashing maple leaf on the back of her hand. "Forget something?"

Malachi frowned. "Is it a rule that one of my daughters needs to shout at me during every auction?"

"Tansy thinks so." Fern winked as laughter ensued. "But you did forget something."

Her father considered then rolled his eyes. "I have a very good memory, only it's short," he announced to the crowd. "Yes, thank you, Fern. There is one thing, before I let Dustin go. Charity, could you please join us as well?"

She rose to her feet. Ginny gave her arm one final pat of approval. Applause had started again, plus all the firefighters Charity had volunteered with in the past joined in with a foot stomp like they'd do at the fire hall after training sessions.

She waited for her nerves to kick into gear, but they didn't. She'd been a performer in the past with her dancing. She knew all these people, and logically there should be no reason to worry.

All that was true, but mostly, it was because when she glanced up at Dustin's face, he smiled as if she were the only person in the room.

How she felt inside—it was completely wrong. Walking up the steps to his side should not feel so right.

But the truth remained. In spite of it being impossible, by his side was where she wanted to be.

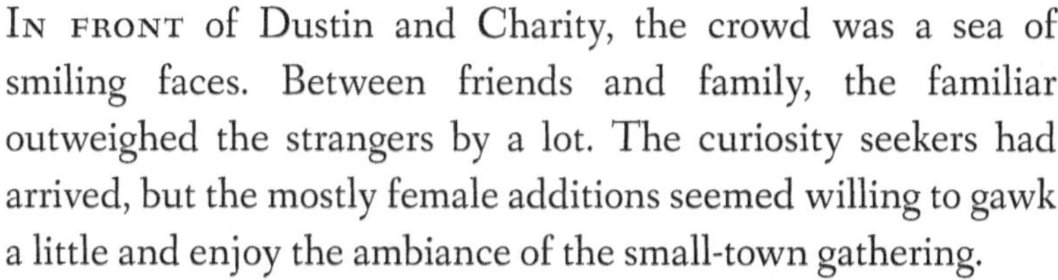

In front of Dustin and Charity, the crowd was a sea of smiling faces. Between friends and family, the familiar outweighed the strangers by a lot. The curiosity seekers had arrived, but the mostly female additions seemed willing to gawk a little and enjoy the ambiance of the small-town gathering.

Malachi finished clapping and gestured for everyone else to quieten down as well. "Charity, welcome to the stage. You're not in dance gear, or I'd invite you to teach us a few ballet steps."

Charity wrapped her fingers loosely around Dustin's arm. "Any time you want lessons, Mr. Fields, I'll happily organize an adult beginner class." She turned to the audience. "Maybe we need another community challenge. Where's Madison Zhao?"

Hands waved, fingers pointed, and the woman who had been the reason Dustin had ended up wearing a tiara while doing pirouettes a few years earlier stood. She was noticeably pregnant, while her toddler son sat in her husband's lap beside her. Their teenage daughter was one of the girls at the Stone table with Sasha and Emma.

Charity motioned to Madison. "Anything else you can dream up that requires my best friend's father to wear a tutu?"

"Oh, that's not—" Malachi attempted, but it was no use. The crowd was already shouting ideas at Madison and approval at Charity.

"Of course," Madison interrupted. "Always happy to put on my thinking cap for a good cause."

"Embarrassing my dad is a great cause," Fern piped up.

Malachi leaned in, still using the microphone so the entire audience could hear him. He shook his head as he spoke and wagged a finger at Charity and Dustin. "I expect these type of..."

"*Shenanigans*," the unknown troublemaker at the back of the room offered.

Dustin wasn't sure why that made Tamara and her sisters lose it, but the laughter in the room was like a living, breathing thing at this point.

Poor Malachi rolled with the punches. He winked where only Dustin and Charity could see before finishing his sentence. "I expect this when Tansy is around, but I see even when she's temporarily left the country, she's firmly placed *shenanigans* into other capable hands."

Dustin had to agree.

Charity gestured to Malachi's microphone. "If I may? In the interest of allowing the actual auction to proceed, I have one announcement, and then Dustin and I will be out of your way."

"It's all yours." Malachi handed over the mic then eyed his youngest daughter. "You. Stay where I can see you."

More laughter as Fern blinked innocently.

Dustin wasn't sure what was going on, but he stayed at Charity's side as she squeezed his fingers tight then lifted the mic to speak.

"This is a fundraiser, and as it appears I've removed one of the participants from circulation—sorry, not sorry—" More hooting and whistling erupted. "I have something to share on behalf of Silver Stone ranch. A few years back the ladies of the ranch started what they call the Silver Heart fund. It's been used to help when needed in the community for several projects, including the school playground upgrades last summer."

"*Go, Silver Heart!*"

Dustin still couldn't figure out who was shouting, but again, he agreed with the sentiment.

Charity nodded. "This year, I've been tasked by the Silver

Heart ladies, Tamara, Ivy, Kelli, and Ginny, to give this donation to the auction since there are no Silver Stone men to offer up as tribute." She slipped her hand from Dustin's so she could pull an envelope from her pocket and present it to Malachi. She turned back to face the crowd. "Bid generously on the rest of the volunteers, and we hope you enjoy your visit to Heart Falls."

She passed the mic back to Malachi then reached for Dustin's hand to lead him off the stage.

"One minute." Malachi had the envelope open and was pulling out the cheque. "Because we want to keep things on the up and up, and because I know you're all as curious as cats in a dairy…"

He paused for dramatic effect.

It worked. The entire audience leaned forward in their seats. Dustin curled his arm around Charity and held her to his side.

"Oh, my." Malachi glanced away from the cheque to Charity, then at the table where the Stone family sat. "I'll keep this short. Thank you, ladies. The Heart Falls fundraiser thanks you." He lifted the cheque in the air and raised his voice triumphantly. "We're starting the auction today with *ten thousand dollars.*"

There was a collective inhale, then the crowd offered up a rush of shouts and clapping loud enough to make the rafters shake. Dustin's sister and sisters-in-law all grinned with delight at the response.

Yeah, it felt good to know that Silver Stone was still helping the community, more than the small contribution he'd arranged on his own that hadn't been revealed yet.

He wasn't sure who started the chant. The refrain began low from somewhere near the back. *Kiss. Kiss. Kiss.* Along with *Dus-Tee, Dus-Tee, Dus-Tee.*

That's when Dustin realized everyone was staring at the stage, attention fixed on him and Charity.

Malachi stepped back, hands raised as if he was leaving the choice up to them. It was a lot of on-the-spot pressure, and Dustin turned to reassure her they could bow out.

Charity caught him by the collar and hauled him in for a kiss, hot and insistent and so fucking right that it took everything in him not to sweep her up into his arms and—

Public place, Stone. Keep it PG.

The voice of reason? Sucked.

She pulled back just far enough to wink at him, her cheeks flushed and her eyes bright, but her smile was real as she whispered intently, "Now, let's get off this stage before someone decides we need to reboot your King of the Pixies barn dance."

"Hell, no. Making a break for it."

They rejoined the rest of the family at the table. Tucker patted him on the back, and Ginny curled her arm around Charity's shoulders. As the official auction began, Dustin sat back and enjoyed the time.

Ignoring the few continuing stares from curiosity seekers was easier now. Also, watching the auction from this side was super entertaining, after being one of the nervous participants for the past five years. Being bid on was just as bad as the fear of *not* being bid on.

Which reminded him of his pre-planned mischief. When Shim stepped forward, Dustin nudged Charity. "Watch."

She raised a brow.

"Back in Heart Falls for his fourth year, Shim Choi is moderately good with computers, can sort of dance..." Malachi raised the note card in his hand and frowned. "...and is somewhat adequate with horses." He frowned at Shim, who had pressed his hands to his temples as if in pain. "You didn't write this."

"No, sir." Shim glared at Dustin. "But go on. Literary endeavors should be encouraged. Even if they're pure fiction."

Malachi sighed as he glanced around the room at the audience. "The actual auction is simply not entertaining enough anymore, I can tell."

"Start the bidding, Dad. I offer twenty-nine dollars," Fern called out. "Hey, Shim." She waved.

He'd barely lifted his hand in acknowledgment when another woman called out, "Thirty-seven."

In rapid succession, the bids of fifty-three, sixty-seven, and seventy-one rang out loudly.

Malachi couldn't keep up, but that was okay because Shim was shaking his head and laughing out loud. "Seriously?"

When Charity leaned against his side, Dustin twisted happily. "Yeah?"

"What's going on?"

Shim heard the question and answered loudly enough it was picked up by Malachi's microphone. "It appears I'm a *prime* example of bachelorhood. Because all the bids so far are prime numbers."

Dustin's game ended soon enough when someone not in the know bid high enough to knock his prearranged partners out of the running.

As soon as the final bachelor was bid on, the room erupted into the cleanup stage. Chairs were stacked, tables broken down, while people milled about enjoying final conversations.

The Stone family gathered themselves up. Kelli paused beside where Dustin and Charity were saying goodbye to Ginny and Tucker.

"Good turnout. Hey, Tee, just wanted to let you know

we've set the girls'-night-out gathering to Ginny's house on Tuesday. Prepare to get crafty."

Charity blinked. "Oh. Okay. Thanks for the invite."

Luke shrugged as he gave Charity a kiss on the cheek then patted Dustin's back. "Don't look so surprised. All the Stone gals will be there. Dustin, see you tomorrow on early shift."

They were gone, leaving Dustin with a very subdued Charity as they said their goodbyes and he guided her to his truck.

He waited to hear her thoughts about the event, but she stayed quiet. They were at the end of the first block when he offered a bit of a prod, just in case. "You dealing with over-stimulated fallout?"

She glanced his way. Nodded slowly. "Maybe a bit. That was bigger than I expected with all the people who showed up. But it's more—" She took a deep breath and shook her head. "No, just a little overwhelmed. I'm glad I don't have to work tomorrow."

It wasn't what she'd been about to say, but Dustin let it go for now. He'd get her safely behind her apartment door and then find a way to loosen her up enough to spill the goods.

He pulled to a stop in front of her apartment, coming around to help her down. "A good night's sleep and a day off will make Monday feel like a breeze."

"You're right."

"This time at least."

She unlocked her door, paused again, then twisted toward him, chin rising determinedly. "I know you're working tomorrow, but would you like—" Her bright gaze drifted into her apartment and a gasp escaped. "Oh my God."

The door swung open to reveal a disaster zone.

"What the hell?" Dustin pushed past her, gaze darting around the room. The place was in shambles. Kitchen chairs had been tipped over, and broken dishes lay in pieces on the counter and floor.

The flowers he'd given her earlier in the week had been ripped apart, the petals strewn on the floor, scattered over the broken stems and shattered vase.

15

———————

Only seconds earlier, Charity had been fighting for the courage to speak her mind to Dustin. Being casually called one of the *Stone gals* had hit hard, an open present she wanted to peek into so badly. No matter that the group of them as a whole still intimidated her, the open door had tempted.

All her concerns about fake dating and who belonged where were wiped away by the devastation that was her apartment.

"Oh my God," she repeated, taking one step into the room.

Nothing was where it should be. From the pictures that should be on the walls, to the items on her bookcase, to the tipped over couch and torn up pillows. It all looked as if a tornado had landed in the middle of the room and blasted everything.

When she would have stormed forward, Dustin stopped her with a hand to the shoulder, fixing her in place with a firm look. "Stay put," he ordered. "I need to make sure no one is still here."

She drew in a sudden breath. She hadn't even thought of

that, considering the door had been locked. "*Dustin*, be careful."

Her stomach muscles clenched with fear as he quickly shoved open the bedroom and the bathroom doors, gaze darting into each space. A low curse escaped him.

Antsy enough to jump out of her skin, Charity fisted her hands. "What?"

He shook his head as he turned to face her. "There's no one here, but both rooms are a mess."

Shockingly, a swoop of relief arrived, making her head spin harder. An audible quiver rocked the words as she asked, "Who could have done this?"

He was back at her side, pulling her against him. "I don't know, but I'll take care of you. I promise."

Which was a good thing, because as much as she liked to credit herself with being able to roll with the punches, knowing someone had been in her place and torn it apart—

She curled against him, body shaking. Adrenaline hit hard. It was nice to have his arms cradling her close, the heat of him knocking against the icy sensation encircling her.

But as good as it felt to have him there, she had to concentrate. "We need to call the police."

"On it. You want Fern too?"

Why...? Her brain offered up the reason far too slowly. As support. It was a good idea, she supposed, but denial came easily. "No, she's helping her parents clean up the hall."

Dustin had his phone out but paused to tilt his head and offer her a look. "*Tee*. You really think the Fields will expect her to stay if you need her?"

No, but another person in her invaded, messed-up space, even her best friend, wasn't what she needed. "Will you stay?"

"Of course." He looked shocked that she would ask. He lifted a finger. "RCMP? I need to report a break-in."

By the time he got off the phone, Charity had got her head on straight enough to check for details. Nothing was stolen—her electronics remained on the wall and on the bookshelf.

Broken items were limited to the kitchen area where her cupboards were now bare. The mess in her bathroom involved upended open bottles of expensive shampoo and body wash—dammit, her only luxury literally down the drain.

Her bedroom—there was no other descriptor than gross. Everything in her drawers and closet had been tossed on the floor. Then the contents of her fridge had been dumped on her clothes and bed, and while at first glance, everything looked soaked with blood, it was mostly ketchup and salsa.

The place was a mess, but that seemed to be the extent of it. When the RCMP arrived, she told them that. "Nothing's missing as far as I can see."

"Lock wasn't forced, so it had to be someone with a key. There're no security cameras in the building." The officer in charge shook his head "We'll do what we can, but for now I suggest a change of locks. Plus, start a list of anyone from your past who might have access."

Which was a very short list of absolutely trustworthy people. Charity didn't bother to point that out before the RCMP left.

She glanced around at the mess and debated the best way to start cleaning up. Maybe a garbage bag? Maybe her laundry basket? She couldn't concentrate. Her gaze kept flitting from one item on the floor to the next.

The next minute, Dustin placed her travel bag on the table in front of her. "Pack what you need for a few days."

That didn't make sense. How would that clean up anything? "What?"

Dustin shook his head then curled his arms around her and tucked her against his chest again. "Tee. Trust me?"

"Yes." Instant and pure. God, it felt good to be in his arms. Being there was the only thing that made sense. She rested her cheek against his chest, the warmth soaking away some of her fear and edging away the ice on her limbs. "Why?"

"You're in shock, baby. Come on. Let's pack a bag and then we're getting out of here."

"But I need to clean up." Didn't she?

He tugged her toward the bedroom, "Clothes. What you need for work on Monday. Something to ride in. Sleep stuff. Can you do that?"

"Sure." She eyed the stuff on the floor. The open empty drawers. The spray of ketchup across her bed. "Maybe."

Dustin swore, wrapping his fingers around hers and tugging her from the room. "Change of plans. Come with me."

The next minute she was back in his truck, and he was headed down the road, chatting quietly with someone. All she saw was her things—ruined and messed up for no reason.

She leaned back on the headrest and closed her eyes. "I trust you."

It seemed like a good thing to reaffirm.

Fingers linked with hers. "I know, Tee. It'll be okay."

A small moment of curiosity managed to break through the haze in her brain. "Where are we going?"

"I'm taking you to Silver Stone."

Oh. That was a good idea, she supposed. There should be places to sleep that weren't covered in fridge contents. Maybe Tamara and Caleb had a spare room. Caleb might intimidate her on one level, but he also made her feel safe.

So does Dustin...in an entirely different way.

"Okay."

Dustin chuckled, and it was such a nice normal sound that she opened her eyes and looked him over.

The crease between his brows wasn't something she'd seen

often. Concern—for her, she realized in her fuzzy state. He looked older, as well. Spine straight, shoulders back, and determined.

"It's going to be okay," she offered, tightening the fingers tangled with his.

Another soft laugh. "You're unbelievable. Yes, everything will be okay. Now hold on. I need to make another call."

Charity leaned her head against the cool glass of the window and watched as the streets of Heart Falls changed to the rolling fields of the countryside. Cattle grazed on one on the hillsides. Men on horseback crested a trail, ranch dogs darting at the horses' heels.

The entire way down the long drive to the Silver Stone ranch gates, Charity kept thinking how normal everything seemed. Except for her.

She felt—lost.

Beside her, Dustin finished speaking quietly into his phone, his serious expression settling into rock-solid resolve. The gate slid open, and he took them through and parked outside the main ranch house. Fingers still connected with hers, Dustin tugged her to face him.

"Fern's bringing you a bag of stuff."

"From my apartment?" Charity shook her head. "She's not a miracle worker."

"Don't worry about the details." Dustin pressed a hand to her cheek. "We'll check in with my brother, then I'll get you settled."

She caught herself staring out the window, zero thoughts in her brain, as he paced the exterior of the truck to come around and open her door. A flutter of amusement somehow stole in as she took his hand and let him help her from the cab.

He raised a brow. "Laughing, Tee?"

"Just thinking that shock is one way to train me to stay on my ass."

A soft snort escaped him, then he had a hand pressed to her lower back and was guiding her to the door. "I'd recommend other, more pleasurable training methods."

He knocked once then pushed the door open.

In the kitchen, Tamara glanced up from the stove. Caleb sat at the island across from her, peeling potatoes. They both stopped what they were doing to face her and Dustin.

"Hey, guys. Did I know you were coming over for supper?" Tamara asked. "Not a problem, but—"

"What's wrong?" Caleb was on his feet, gaze darting between her and Dustin. "More social media bullshit?"

"Someone broke into Charity's apartment during the auction. Trashed the place." Dustin tucked her harder against his side. "She's staying here at Silver Stone until we figure out who did it."

"Of course she is." Tamara wiped her hands on a towel and moved forward. The concern in her eyes clear behind silver-rimmed glasses. "I'm so sorry, honey. Come here."

Her open arms were a welcome haven, and Charity closed her eyes and leaned into the embrace. "Thanks."

"You deal with the police already?" Caleb asked.

"Yeah, but not much they can do." Dustin shared the rest of his news, speaking softly to his oldest brother.

Meanwhile, Tamara patted Charity on the shoulder then tilted her head toward the living room. "Want to sit?"

"God, no." Charity shook her head. "Too twitchy. Put me to work."

She snagged the pot of potatoes and prepared to take over Caleb's task.

Tamara examined her, as if checking her hand-eye

coordination, but eventually nodded. "I get it. Knock yourself out. We'll talk beds later."

Charity was only halfway through the second potato when Dustin's arms surrounded her from the back. His stubble-roughened cheek brushed hers as he spoke quietly. "I'm going to get your place ready. Back in a bit. You okay sticking with Tamara?"

"Of course."

The question on Tamara's face was clear, but Charity was too numb to ponder the whys of it. She reached into the pot for the next potato.

Dustin had asked if she trusted him. She did.

Maybe more than she should.

But right now she knew enough to recognize she wasn't firing on all cylinders. Which meant, as her grandmother had always said, it was time to lean on the people she could trust.

That was Dustin. He'd take care of her.

Numbness slipped in as Charity fell into the mindless task.

Both Tamara and Caleb had been giving him the eye since he'd walked into the house. Since he wasn't about to make his announcement where Charity could hear, Dustin tipped his head toward the door. "Caleb, give me a hand?"

His oldest brother exchanged a wordless conversation with his wife before his gaze landed on Charity. Everything in his expression tightened, which Dustin got on a core-deep level.

"Back in a bit. Message if you need us," Caleb said quietly.

"I've got her." Tamara's voice held more than a hint of fire.

The instant the door closed, Caleb laid a hand on Dustin's shoulder. "Tamara's trained. She can deal with Charity if she goes into shock after the break-in. How are you doing?"

"Pissed off to high heaven and ready to knock heads, but there's no clear signs of who did it. So I'm going to focus on what I can do, which is ensure Charity is safe."

"Good plan." Caleb stepped back, one brow raised. "Why are we out here and not getting the guest room set up?"

"I'm moving her into the cottage."

His brother frowned. "You think being alone in a new place is what she needs right now?"

"She won't be alone." Dustin turned and marched toward the cottage, confident Caleb wouldn't leave the conversation at that.

Sure enough, his brother was at his side as they crossed the space to where the other homesteading family of Silver Stone had lived. Since the Hayeses had died, the small, two-bedroom building had become home to a changing list of occupants. First, and for the longest time, it had been Dare's private space, then Dustin's for a brief period before he'd given it up for Ginny, then Ginny and Tucker. Now it would be a safe spot for Charity.

With him.

Of course, that final addition, and why it was exactly what was needed, would require a little extra explaining before things settled properly.

As expected, Caleb took the bait. "Fern coming to stay with her?"

Two quick steps put Dustin at the top of the porch. He took a deep breath as he turned to face his brother. "I'm staying with her."

Caleb folded his arms over his chest. "She's your *fake* girlfriend, Dustin."

"Nothing fake about it. Not to me." Dustin shook his head, a chuckle escaping in spite of it all. "Damn, your face right now is hysterical."

"I'm trying to keep up, but you're going a little fast for me." Caleb raised a brow. "Don't you think you're going a little fast, period?"

Not that he wanted to tell tales, but Caleb being solidly on his side was important. Dustin stood a little straighter. "We got close while we were at Crooked Creek. I want more."

His brother had his poker face on. Stone-like, blank. No sign whether approval or a reprimand was about to arrive. "You're talking sex. I'm talking—"

Dustin held up a hand. "Sex is part of it, yeah. But since Charity and I are both adults, consenting and able to make decisions about who we want to be with, that's not the part I'm talking about." He pressed a hand to his gut. "Talking with her, spending time with her—it hits me here. Makes me want to rip apart the ass who scared her by messing with her stuff. Makes me want to curl myself around her and protect her from anyone who'd fuck with her on any level. So, yeah, I want more sex, but I want more of *her*. In my life, and in our family.

"And if it seems fast, it's not, though I still don't know how the hell *she* feels. But right now, I need to do what I can to protect her. No matter how fast it seems. *Period.*"

He met Caleb's gaze straight on. Held it.

His brother nodded slowly. Then he caught Dustin by the shoulders and dragged him in for a back-pounding, rib-creaking hug.

"You always did have a heart bigger than you knew what to do with." Caleb backed off slightly, his expression still thoughtful. "Let's take this slowly, or at least as slowly as you can. If Charity agrees, I'll back your play. Tamara is probably already planning how to redo the guest room. I'll run interference with her."

"Appreciate it."

The next fifteen minutes were spent doing the most boring domestic tasks Dustin could imagine. He and Caleb made up the bed, pulled out towels and put them in the bathroom, checked the heat and lights, and basically prepped the cabin so Charity and he could walk in after dinner and have no unwelcome surprises.

But even the mundane tasks were somehow special with Caleb's clear support.

They were headed back to the main house, Patchwork Annie bouncing at Dustin's heels, when Caleb cleared his throat. "Not that I want to go there..."

Hell, no. "Your tone of voice says you're about to try to deliver a sex talk. If so, I don't need it, don't want it, move along."

Caleb outright laughed. "Yeah, no. If you're not clear on that topic yet, I'm not saying a thing unless you straight up ask. I was thinking about your time down at Crooked Creek. I guess the fact I haven't heard from Uncle Frank, complaining about your attitude, means I can thank Charity for keeping you on the straight and narrow." He offered Dustin a wink. "Or for distracting you enough you behaved."

God. That was both funny and slightly skin-crawling. "I don't want a lecture, but I don't know that I'm ready for you to tease me about sex, either." Dustin grimaced as a shiver rolled over his head and shoulders.

As they closed the final distance to the house. Caleb leaned in close and murmured, "Bad move. Never let a person know what makes you nervous."

"Ass."

But the teasing felt good. As if a new page had opened between them in spite of the age difference. Less with Caleb as a father figure, more as simply brothers.

After one final pat to his shoulder, Caleb paused with his

hand on the back door. "I do like her. She seems like a good person."

"Charity's the best sort of good," Dustin responded. "She's kind, but not nice. Can kick some ass when needed—including mine. Right now, I want to be her safe place."

His brother dipped his chin slowly before meeting Dustin's gaze. "Then the Stones will be there to make that happen. Whatever she needs."

The pulse inside his chest made Dustin stand up straighter. "Appreciate it."

Childish laughter rang out when the door swung open. Four-year-old Tyler rushed forward and caught Caleb around the knees. "Dapa!

Caleb chuckled as he swung his son in the air. "Kiddo, you gotta pick one name. Daddy or Papa. Either works."

In the mud room beside them, Emma's white-blonde curls bounced as she turned from hanging up a coat. She tousled Tyler's hair as she passed. "Face it, Papa. You've got three kids and three names."

"Heck, he's got more than that. Four, maybe five or six if I remember correctly," Dustin told her before meeting Caleb's confused gaze. "You said something about never letting on where to hit you..."

"*Dustin...*" Caleb warned.

Emma all but bounced with glee. She could have been three instead of thirteen as she leaned into Dustin and loudly whispered, "Spill. What other names?"

He opened his mouth as if to answer, then winked at Caleb. "Maybe some other time."

A heavy sigh escaped Emma, and she mock pouted, her lower lip sticking out slightly. "Meanie."

Dustin hugged his niece and changed the subject. "Where's Charity?"

Emma slipped her arm around his waist and inched him toward the living room. She spoke quietly as he matched her extremely slow pace. "I'm sorry her place got messed with."

"Me, too."

Emma turned her big blue eyes on him. "It's kind of scary."

He wasn't going to downplay that part, especially to a woman, no matter that she was young. "Nothing *kind of* to it. Scary as hell, I agree." He leaned down and kissed Emma's temple. "That's why Charity will stay with us at Silver Stone until we know who did it. She'll be safe."

"Good." The depth of conviction in Emma's tone made him smile.

She was a fierce thing these days. Might still look like a cherub with the bouncy blonde curls, but she had a hot temper when it came to anyone being mean to others.

Made sense, all things considered. She'd had a ton of bullshit handed her way when she was just a kid. Horrid stuff that he'd been totally oblivious to. And damn if that didn't make him want to hug her all over again.

So he did. Just pulled her in tight and squeezed her, continuing repayment for all the times he hadn't been there for her when she was little.

She squeezed him back with easy affection that made his heart happy. "Thanks, Dust-man."

He chuckled. Yeah, Caleb wasn't the only one with more nicknames than he could count. "No problem, *monkey*."

She stuck out her tongue as she left him beside Charity.

His girl was curled up on the couch, the children's books scattered nearby a clear clue to what she'd been doing before being abandoned by Tyler.

Dustin settled next to her and picked up her hand. "Hey."

Her fingers were cold. She smiled, though, as he rubbed her hand between his. "I thought I was being entertaining, but obviously not even my funny voices can top Caleb coming in the door." She leaned her head on Dustin's shoulder. "As it should be."

"Agreed." He pushed back her hair and pressed a kiss to her temple. "Hanging in there?"

"Yeah. Part of me wants to wallow, so being surrounded by your family is a good distraction." She tilted her head and sighed up at him. "Thanks for being my brains right now when I don't have any."

"No prob, babe."

It didn't sound right. Babe, as a nickname. It worked on one level—the word had a kind of intimacy that he didn't use with anyone else. But it wasn't enough to make it clear that she was *his*.

Getting ahead of yourself, Stone. How about getting past the fucked-up current chaos before declaring yourself?

Damn his conscience, being all logical and shit.

"Come to the table," Tamara called. She met Dustin's gaze. "At least try to eat."

"I'm good," Charity insisted, rising to her feet and approaching the kitchen. "Sorry. I was sitting on my butt instead of—"

Tamara caught her by the shoulders and leaned in until they were face to face. "Honey, you helped earlier. Now it's our turn, remember? No apologies. Not with us."

Charity blinked hard. "Right. Okay."

Dustin curled his arm around her. "Just a quick bite, then I'll take you to the cabin so we can relax."

If he'd expected supper to be a subdued event, he'd have been wrong. It wasn't full of laughter and hijinks, but conversation flowed around them easily. Between Tyler's prattling about everything he'd seen that morning at the petting zoo, to Sasha explaining some of the competition events she was training Secret Path to complete, the meal passed quickly.

Charity didn't eat a lot, but enough that when it was time to gather up plates, Tamara nodded her approval before pointing to a basket on the island. "Dessert for you guys for later. Plus some stuff for the fridge so you can have breakfast in the morning when you want without having to pop over here. But feel free to pop over if you feel like it." She pulled an empty plate from Charity's fingers. "Go. Put your feet up, or have a hot shower, or whatever you need to do."

"But I should—" Charity stopped, sighed. "Right. *Next* time I'm on cleanup duty, though. I want to do my share."

"Sharing is caring," Tyler piped up.

Dustin laughed. He scooped up his nephew and bopped him on the nose. "Exactly, Tyler-bug."

Tyler squirmed to be let down, so Dustin went to make sure Charity had what she needed.

She pulled on her light jacket, a wry smile aimed at Tamara and Caleb. "Thanks for dinner and for the place to crash."

"Not a problem," Caleb insisted. "You're welcome for as long as necessary."

"Share." Tyler raced up and held aloft a couple of his favourite books. "You want books, Char-tee?"

She squatted to accept them gratefully. "So kind of you, Mr. Tyler. I will enjoy these very much."

Tyler pressed his hands to her cheeks and planted a kiss on her. Then he patted her gently and raced away.

Charity stood, amusement in her eyes. "He's not shy."

"Kissing pretty girls is a skill that's well worth learning at a young age." Dustin picked up the dessert basket with one hand then opened the door with the other. "Come on. Let's get you settled."

16

Charity had been in the small cottage a couple of times over the past years, dropping off items or picking them up for Ginny. But never more than a surface glance from the front entrance.

"Explore," Dustin ordered, resting Tamara's food basket on the kitchen table. "I'll put this stuff away."

"Not as if I have a big bag to unpack," Charity grumbled.

"Not as if you have a big house to explore," Dustin countered. He tipped his head down and gave her a stern look. "Go."

"I'm going. Hashtag bossy bastard."

His soft chuckle followed her down the hallway.

The cottage *was* small. The hall led to the bathroom on one side and what she supposed was the master bedroom on the other. She'd seen the second bedroom door off the living room. Ginny had used it for crafting.

Charity hung in the doorway of the bathroom. The shower was enticing. It had been a full day, and her aching head and heart had turned into full body exhaustion.

Considering she had nothing to change into after a shower, though...

A wall of heat pressed to her back. Dustin's firm arms surrounded her and kept her upright. "Wait two minutes, then you can hop in."

She turned in his arms and shamelessly leaned closer. "Water pressure issues?"

A knock sounded on the front door. Dustin tucked his fingers under her chin and lifted her face to his. "Technical details. Come with me."

She followed as he glided ahead of her. "I feel as if we should have a rope I can just hold onto and let you lead me around. That's all you've done all afternoon."

"Skip the rope and grab whatever you'd like to stay close," he suggested. He slipped her fingers into one of his belt loops. "I like this one. Works for me."

Charity was still blinking when he tugged the door open, and Fern and Shim appeared on the doorstep.

"Talk about coming down off a high." Fern wrapped her arms around Charity and squeezed tight. "There you two were, rocking the auction. And now this. By the way, my mom and dad say *what the fuck* and anything you need, you've got it."

Her friend guided her to one of the upright chairs by the small kitchen table. "Your dad did not say what the *fuck*," Charity protested.

Fern snickered. "No. Grandma Sonora did, though. Along with a few other choice words. I think her cursing scared a couple of the bachelors still hanging around the hall."

"Your grandma is feisty," Charity agreed as a hard pulse of sadness struck. "My grandma wouldn't have cursed, but she would have had something to say about inconsiderate, selfish hooligans."

"So basically, *what the fuck.*"

Charity had to nod. "Yeah, I guess."

Fern caught her fingers and squeezed tight. "We'll keep this short and sweet. Shim and I are delivery boys. I brought you clothes—some stuff you left at my place. It's not a lot, but I tossed in a few other things I know you'll need, so you're good until we can finish washing the mess at your apartment."

A bag covered in bright Hawaiian flowers landed at Charity's feet. A second later, Shim was there as well, resting lightly on his heels as he smiled at her. "Hey, you. Sorry to hear about the vandal. Fern let me into your place, and I grabbed your electronics. Everything you need, including charging cables, are on the coffee table."

"Thanks."

He touched her cheek gently then winked. "I also stopped at Dustin's and packed him some clothes. You two are set for tonight."

The two of them? "We are?"

Fern popped upright and caught Shim by the arm, dragging him to his feet. "You are. Call me tomorrow morning, and since I plan to sleep in, make it after ten. I'll explain the rest then. But for now, if you're good, we're heading out."

Charity accepted their hugs then waited as Shim did that back-pounding thing to Dustin that always made it look as if the guys were trying to knock each other over.

"Tomorrow, Tee," Fern called in reminder before the door swung shut behind them.

Whirlwind, again.

"That was...odd," Charity decided.

"A bit, but they're our odd." Dustin turned her to face him. "Unless you absolutely need to call someone else, time to hit the shower."

Calling Chelsea was out. It would only worry her sister needlessly to catch her up tonight. "The morning is soon enough." Confusion remained high, though. "I'm very glad Fern had some of my stuff to bring over, but why did Shim bring you clothes?"

"Because unless you hate the idea, I'm staying with you." Dustin marched her down the hall toward the bedroom, dropping her borrowed bag on the mattress. "Scratch that. If you hate the idea, I'm still staying. I just won't sleep with you. I'll use the couch instead."

His arms around her, all night long? Sounded like the perfect way to get some needed rest.

"Screw the couch. I want you in my bed." It came out with enough conviction and power she almost sounded like herself.

Dustin kissed her cheek. "That's my girl. Now hop in the shower. Use all the bubbles and soap you need."

She slipped open the bag Fern had left. Thank goodness her friend had thrown in a sturdy shower cap along with a couple of head scarves and scrunchies. Dealing with her curly hair without them would have been a nightmare.

Dustin disappeared, and Charity stripped, abandoning her clothes on the floor where they fell. As if leaving the lingering contamination from the day behind, she walked naked across the hall and into the small bath.

With the water as hot as she could stand it, Charity soaked under the high pressure spray. Hard needles of hot water bounced off her neck and back, and tension slowly eased away as she breathed out the grossness of their afternoon discovery.

There had been good parts to the day she could celebrate. Things that had gone very right. Like the auction. The money raised for local charities, the gathering of people all building up Heart Falls.

While someone was tearing my place apart.

She shook her head and put her face directly under the

water. She knew better than to allow other people to dictate her attitude and choices.

She stood a little straighter. The vandal was wrong. Charity was not.

Didn't matter if it was the truth, though, she was tired to her core. Drying off, she avoided looking at herself in the fogged up mirror for too long. A ghost reflected back during each brief glimpse. A ghost with sadness in her eyes.

She hung up the shower cap, wrapped herself in a towel, and cracked the bathroom door open. About to call out Dustin's name, she was greeted by the flickering warmth of amber lights.

Candlelight?

Quietly, she slipped down the hall on bare feet, the overlapping layers of the towel tucked firmly into position just above her breasts. The soft yellow glow increased in strength until she stepped in line with the kitchen area and got a full view of the open living space.

Candles were everywhere.

Okay, at second glance, there weren't as many as she'd imagined. But the dozen or so that were lit had been strategically placed in front of reflective surfaces, doubling the impact. It turned the mood of the simple cottage from rustic chic to romantic escape.

Not that she was looking for romance right then, but the thought was sweet.

Dustin glanced up from his spot on the couch. He laid his phone face down on the coffee table. "Hey. All warmed up?"

"Yeah. Almost tempted to crawl into bed, but after checking the time, I don't think hitting the sack at six thirty is a good idea." She flicked a finger at the phone. "Anything new?"

Dustin patted the spot next to him. "Couple of shots of us at the auction. We look *hashtag cute country couple*, again. No mention of my cock."

He said it so dryly a snicker escaped as she sat, leaning against his side. Far, far too comfortable there. "Well, I hope your cock's ego isn't hurt."

"He's big enough to handle it."

Charity snorted, tilting her head back to grin at Dustin. "Bonus points for saying that with a straight face."

"It was hard," he deadpanned. "Long and hard, and—"

She tapped his chest, laughter welling up faster than she'd thought possible. "Stop it."

He laid his hand over hers, trapping her fingers against his soft blue T-shirt. "There's only one way to shut me up."

Charity pressed her lips to his. A soft kiss that grew more heated as time passed. Dustin curled his fingers around the back of her neck and tugged her closer, tilting her head so he could take control.

She liked that. A lot. Maybe today more than ever as she left behind the worries of what and when and who and simply felt.

The caress of his tongue over hers. The brush of his thumb stroking the side of her neck. The scratch of his five o'clock shadow over her neck as he kissed a path across her jaw and lower.

The towel loosened, slipping to pool around her waist. His lips meandered in loops over the top of her breast curves to her nipples, then under and over again.

Charity closed her eyes partway, far enough her vision blurred, but wide enough that the happy, contented glow of teeny candle flames danced against her retinas.

Dustin groaned against her belly. "I made a tactical error not setting this up in the bedroom."

She stroked her fingers through his hair, over and over, the coarse texture teasing her senses. "I'm not complaining about anything so far," she pointed out.

A soft chuckle brushed the curls over her mons. "Good to know."

She'd been all sorts of wrong earlier when she'd dismissed the candlelight as a lost cause with her messed-up brain. Turned out having Dustin slowly but earnestly eat her up was exactly what she needed.

He slipped his fingers through her curls, opening her to his searching tongue. Charity eased her legs wider and lay back more fully on the couch.

"I trust you," she whispered.

"Let go. I got you."

The next second, his tongue was on her, small intimate licks over her labia and clit. Teasing touches with his fingers dipping into her sex then retreating. His mouth closed around her clit, and he sucked lightly as one finger slipped in deep. Then two, a steady stroke in and out that sent tingles along her spine. Charity raised her hands to her breasts and cupped them, pinching her nipples with thumbs and forefingers.

The stroking continued, but Dustin's licking stalled out. "Goddamn, Tee. You're killing me."

"Feels good."

Another set of easy but precise licks followed before he spoke again. "Squeeze your breasts again. That's it. I love watching you. Your skin glows, your nipples so tight."

He groaned as he pumped his fingers, curling the tips against the sweet spot inside her, and Charity gasped.

"Someday I'm going to fuck you in a chair. Reverse cowgirl. Maybe find a mirror so you watch my hands on your breasts, my cock shuttling in and out of your pussy. Me, all around you, taking you up and over."

"God, this feels good. Lick my clit, again, Dustin. I'm so close."

"Do it. Let go," he ordered, his lips on her again.

A solid pulse of pressure, and she was breaking. Hips rising toward his mouth, fingers fisted in his hair to keep him right where he was. Giving to her, loving her with his mouth and hands and eyes. The dirty words and the candlelight and all of it, for her.

The aftershocks of her orgasm pulsed as hard as the initial blast, and Charity welcomed each one, the cares and worries of the day erased for now in the best way possible.

She closed her eyes and sighed happily.

His girl all lazy and satisfied was the biggest turn-on ever.

A soft laugh escaped her lips when he scooped her up and carried her to the bedroom. "I'd offer to walk, but I've forgotten how." She turned her head and rested her cheek on his chest, stroking one hand along his jaw, heavy-lidded eyes staring at him intently. "You're so damn sexy."

"You're fuck drunk," he said with a smile.

"Not possible." She pressed her finger to his lips. "You didn't fuck me."

"Yet." He laid her on the bed, her naked skin a soft brown in the faint sunlight coming in the window. "Stay here."

Charity lifted a hand and waved it randomly. "No running a marathon until you get back. Got it."

Man, if he wasn't worried about burning the place down, he'd have said screw it to the candles and stripped down and stayed by her side.

Most importantly, though, his plan to fill her head with something other than the disasters of the day seemed to have worked. That was what mattered, not the fact he was so fucking hard he wondered if he might break something rushing to and from the bedroom.

Candles extinguished, he tore his shirt over his head as he entered the room, not sure what he was going to find. Heck, she could have fallen asleep—which would be good for her.

Nope. She sat upright on the bed, perfect breasts right there on display. Curves and soft skin and a smirk on her lips.

A pair of his boxers dangled from her fingers. "These are interesting."

"Tee?"

She eased back into the pillows propped against the headboard and gave the shorts a swing that sent them twirling in a circle. "I dipped into the bag Shim packed you. I *was* looking for a T-shirt to wear because that's kind of a comfort thing. I found these."

Dustin was going to kill his best friend. "I don't suppose you could just forget you ever saw anything?"

She tilted her head to the side as if considering. "Well, maybe *these* with the *Where's Waldo* theme can slip my memory. But these other ones?" She pulled a second pair from under her pillow and held them up. "These are kind of burned onto my retinas. You may as well put them on."

The butt and sides of this pair were white and black Holstein spots. The entire triangle of the groin was an enormous cow's face.

Dustin caught them as she tossed them his direction. "And here I thought for sure he'd have packed the ones that say *Stop staring at my dinosaur.*"

Her grin was huge as she wiggled up on her knees, briefs abandoned to the side. "Tell me there's a T. rex on the center panel." She made a scary dinosaur face but held her arms tucked into her body and wiggled her fingers as if she had teeny-tiny arms.

Dustin laughed as he jumped on the bed, rolled her under him, and smiled down at her. "Sadly, it's a brontosaurus."

"Ah. Long and thin, not thick and meaty."

He dropped to his elbows and pinned her even tighter. "You've got a dirty mind, Tee. I love it."

She took a deep breath, pressing her torso to him, easing her legs open and sighing as his hips settled between her thighs. "You're distracting me."

"I am," he confessed. "Nothing else we can do tonight, except hopefully get a good sleep."

"I'm on board for that." She nuzzled her lips to his neck. "Now, I felt the cosmos tip to the right, again. Maybe you should get your cow face over here and do some universe balancing."

"Maybe I should."

She was already naked, and he only had a couple of things to remove, which vanished surprisingly quickly with Charity's help.

Her hands stroked and caressed, lips touching his abs and hips. When she curled her fingers around his cock, though, he caught her wrist. "I'm too close. I want to be inside you."

"I can work with that." Charity eased back on her knees, sliding a hand under the pillow and coming back with a condom.

"I'm afraid to ask what else you have hidden under there," Dustin teased before groaning as he fought for control. "Your hands on me are going to make me fucking lose it."

She finished rolling the condom down, then tugged him over her. "I won't touch anymore. Much."

Her hand guided him to her sex.

Dustin rocked over her, feeling his way. Checking she was ready, that every step of the way was what she needed, too.

"Inside me," Charity whispered. "Oh, *yessssss*."

His arms shook as he stroked into her again, slow and steady. Small pulses that brought them together intimately, every inch of their bodies connected. Skin to skin, mouth to mouth. Moving inside her, over her—Dustin could stay here forever.

Except that he was about to lose his goddamn control in seconds flat, it felt so fucking good.

Charity pulled up her knees and he sank deeper.

They both moaned. Gazes met, and amusement rose.

"Teamwork sex. I like it," she offered.

"I like *you*," Dustin returned quietly. "Now kiss me."

Her eyes had widened for a split second at his words, then she cupped his face and kissed him with a passion that sent slow out the window. Deeper now, harder. Pulsing on the bed, her fingernails dug into his shoulders as she urged him on.

Dustin slipped a hand between them and stroked her clit, leaning to the side to give her that extra touch.

"*Dustin.*" She scratched his back hard, hips pressing to his as she arched against him.

He let go. Let the power of pleasure roll through him like an express train. Her under him, soft and drowsy and holding him close.

Perfect.

Tangled together after, Dustin rolled only enough to not crush her. Lingered there to catch his breath until he couldn't wait any longer. "Back in a second."

"Mmm-hmm." Charity sprawled as he left.

He dealt with the condom and was back in seconds, pulling her over him on the mattress. "So, what do you want to do for the rest of the night? Good to just Netflix and chill?"

She chuckled softly, tracing a finger down his jaw. "Didn't we already do that?"

"Funny girl." Dustin cupped her face in his hands so she couldn't get away while he blew a raspberry against her cheek.

They wrestled for a bit before Dustin miscalculated and his butt slipped off the bed. He hit the floor with a thud.

Charity hung over the side, eyes wide, smile wider. "Since you're up, grab dessert. I'll find something for us to watch."

"Sounds good." He stood and nabbed the cow print briefs off the mattress. Her laughter followed him as he pulled them on then slipped from the room.

By the time he had thick slices of apple pie slathered with whipped cream on the coffee table, she had a nest of blankets waiting for him to join her on the couch.

"Sad to see you found my T-shirts." Dustin pulled her closer, nuzzling her neck. She'd put her hair up for the night like usual, a pouf of curls escaping the top of her silky headscarf. "God, whatever you put on your hair is like crack."

"Glad you like it." She giggled as his nose slid lower. "Dustin, feed me."

He offered a mighty sigh but obediently settled down. Arm tucked around her, balancing his snack so he could keep her close.

The show she turned on seemed to involve people baking cakes that didn't *look* like cakes. Whatever.

When it was finally late enough to hit the sack, they moved companionably back to the bedroom. She took her side of the bed. He took his. She sighed softly and snuggled into her pillow, her butt tucked to his groin as if that's where she always slept.

As if that's where she belonged.

Dustin spoke softly, tracing circles on her belly. "I have an early shift. Want me to call to wake you?"

"No. I'll be up before anyone misses me."

She was breathing smoothly, asleep long before Dustin felt himself about to go. Which meant it was safe to say it. "*I'll* miss you. I like having you around, Tee. I think we're good together."

No response other than a soft hum.

Untangling himself from her and crawling out of bed just before five a.m. was hellish. He had one more thing to attempt before starting his day.

Patchwork Annie met him outside the cottage door. Dustin stopped to talk to her, petting her first as he hoped like hell his idea worked. "Hey, girl. I have a big job for you today. I need you to guard."

He put Charity's boots on the porch and pointed at them.

Annie sat obediently, but her expression said she wasn't sure she liked what was going on.

"You need to stay with Tee. *Guard*," he repeated as he rose to his feet.

He checked once when he was halfway to the barn. Annie remained where he'd told her, although her head hung a little lower than usual. Probably wondering why he'd left her behind.

Couldn't be helped. She was where she had to be.

Inside the barn, Luke was saddling up Thunderbolt. He lifted his chin as Dustin walked past to his own horse.

"Sorry I'm late," Dustin offered even though it was only by a few minutes.

"Don't worry about it. I just got here myself. How's Charity? Did she get any sleep?"

"She's okay. I got her to relax pretty quickly last night, and she's still asleep now." Dustin turned back with a saddle blanket in his hands to see Luke eyeing him closely. "What?"

His brother grinned. "Kelli spotted you going into the cottage last night. Also, I saw you come out the door this morning."

For fuck's sake. Which meant Luke was going to tease the hell out of him, not knowing the whole story. "Yeah?"

Luke shrugged and went back to tightening the clinch on his saddle. "So the last eligible Stone has fallen. Next thing we know you'll be sending out *save the date* cards and booking the church."

"When it's right, it's right." Dustin reached for his own saddle and discovered his brother in his way, eyes wide, jaw hanging open. "*What?*"

"I was kidding around. You and Charity, for real?" Luke held up a hand. "Not that I don't like her, but damn, Dustin, you're just a kid. You're really ready to settle down?"

Dustin laughed. "You make it sound as if finding someone to be with means getting boring and one step from the grave. I haven't noticed you and Kelli being— Wait, let me start again. *Kelli's* not a stick-in-the-mud. Can't say that about you since you guys got hitched, old man."

"Fuck off," Luke offered.

"Don't be an ass," Dustin countered.

"Don't..." Luke made a face. "Don't be so fucking right. Yeah, you just surprised me, that's all. I thought this shit between you two was a pretend thing."

"It was. It's not anymore—at least not to me." Dustin shoved his brother out the way and returned to saddling Molasses. "I still need to work on Tee, so please don't screw things up by implying we're a done deal or some bullshit that scares her off."

"Of course not." Luke grinned evilly.

Dustin threw a brush at him. "Jerk."

Luke only grinned harder. "Oh, this promises to be fun."

By that point, the wrestling match that followed was a forgone conclusion. They were smart enough to wait until they cleared the stalls before Luke wrapped an arm around Dustin's neck and tried to overpower him. Dustin countered by flipping Luke over his hip and dropping to his knees.

They were into the grunting and laughing stage when someone cleared their throat behind them.

Luke released his grip, Dustin did the same, and then they were sprawled on the ground and looking up at Ashton Stewart, disapproval painted on his face. "Thought I trained the stupid out of you boys years ago."

"Momentary relapse," Luke offered. He popped to his feet and held a hand down to Dustin. His brother hauled him upright, and the two of them turned to face their semi-retired foreman.

Dustin knew his expression had to be sheepish, but at the same time, the situation felt right. Another layer in the growing up and growing together of brothers in a tight-knit family.

Ashton raised a brow, but he nodded. "See that the moment passes quickly." He shifted his gaze to focus on Dustin alone. "Caleb told Tucker you'll need extra time off over the next while. So you can be available to help Charity," he added. "Until the vandal is caught, she'll need someone with her when she has places to go. And you're top on the list of people to accompany her."

Which was a step beyond what Dustin had hoped for when he'd asked Caleb for help. "Appreciate it."

"It makes sense. Tucker's already working the schedule." Ashton's serious expression softened. "You'll enjoy this—I'm your last-minute replacement."

Again, more than he'd expected. "I won't take advantage of it."

Ashton lifted a finger and stuck it in Dustin's face. "You'll do whatever it takes to keep that girl safe and happy. If I have to pull a few shifts to make that happen, so be it. Sonora agrees."

Dustin held out his hand. Ashton took it solemnly and shook it.

The moment felt huge, especially when after shaking his hand, Ashton patted him on the shoulder then shoved him not too gently toward his horse. "Now get your asses in gear, you two."

Moments later they were out the door and in the saddle. Luke stayed quiet for the first part of the ride. The morning promised a gentle warmth instead of killer hot. Dustin rocked easily in his seat, thoughts of Charity filling his head.

How to keep her safe. How to make her know they needed more of each other.

"You're growing up all right."

Dustin shifted his attention to the side. "Come again?"

Luke shrugged. "I should say, you've *grown up* all right. You're a good man, Dustin."

Warmth swelled in Dustin's gut. He dipped his chin at his brother, then did the only thing possible under the circumstances.

He put his heels to Molasses's sides and took off like a streak before Luke could grab his reins. They raced over the trail toward the far fields, running the horses with a carefree delight that was only possible with family. Knowing they were there for each other.

For him. For Charity.

They pulled their horses to a walk just before cresting the final hill, companionably side by side as they reached the top. It was one of Dustin's favourite routes to ride. He often added the loop to his chores even when it wasn't assigned. The sky had brightened now, sun above the horizon. Colours of gold and yellow and darker shadows from the trees spread fingers across the wide fields. It was such a beautiful spot.

Luke pointed to the west, shaking his head. "Trespassers."

No one was there now, but ATV tracks were clear in the new grass. Dustin and his brother made their way to the small shelter built near one of the northernmost Silver Stone fence lines.

The open side of the lean-to faced east. Inside the shelter, it was shadowy enough Luke opened his phone and hit the flashlight on. With the bright light, it was clear to see someone had arranged a few log stumps into a semi-circle. Pop cans and beer bottles were thrown in the far shadowy corner, and a mess of cigarette butts littered the ground, stretching toward the still-dry grass of the field.

"I was worried it was media hounds hiding out, but this looks more like kids," Luke guessed.

"Good thing they didn't start a fire." The pile of cigarette butts was more than annoying. "I don't know. I can put out a few feelers. Check if there's any new teenagers in town searching for places to hang out, but I somehow doubt they'd go to the trouble of coming all the way out here."

"Check it out, anyway," Luke returned. "I'll mention the issue to Tucker. He can put the shelter on the rotation for us to check more often."

"I'm out here at least once a week," Dustin shared. "I can up that for a while, just to discourage repeat visitors."

"Good idea."

They cleaned up the mess then tucked the garbage bag to the side to be picked up the next time one of the hands was out on an ATV.

Dustin checked his watch. Nearly nine a.m. Hopefully Charity was still asleep, but she'd soon be awake to discover that she wasn't truly alone. Not last night, not today.

He mounted up and rejoined Luke as they headed to the next job.

17

———————

*A*dmiring the breakfast set out in front of her took a moment. Charity peeked in the fridge to discover muffins, a pre-cut fruit salad, bacon wrapped cheesy-egg things, and a note that read, *Hit ON. The coffee is set to go.*

A touch of decadence in the middle of chaos. Charity offered up thanks to Tamara, Dustin, and the gods of breakfast, popped the egg thingies in the microwave, then called Fern.

"Video chat me," she ordered, leaning her phone on the vase in front of her that held silver and blue dried flowers—some of Ginny's creative work, she assumed.

Fern popped up a moment later and eyed her closely. "You look better."

"I feel better. I had a good sleep, and now instead of being panicked and upset, I'm pissed off and upset."

"Good progress. Sex will do that to you, I hear."

Charity raised a brow. "You should try it."

"Someday," Fern offered perkily. "In the meantime, here's the update. Your apartment is being straightened up as we speak."

"What?" Charity leaned forward. "*Who?*"

Her friend offered a cheeky grin. "A wild variety of volunteers who know and love you, and who aren't otherwise ineligible to be here. Which means not Ginny, since she's an easter egg about to pop, and not my sisters, who are MIA in Ireland. But that leaves a lot of us. One second."

She walked a few steps then opened a door, stepping into a bright room. She lifted the phone and twisted in a slow circle. She stood in the middle of Charity's apartment, and one by one, friends from Heart Falls appeared. Tamara was there, plus two of her sisters, Julia and Lisa. Hannah Ford, the fire chief's wife, was working in the kitchen area with Yvette, one of the local veterinarians.

Even Madison Zhao was there.

When she spotted Fern and the phone, she hurried forward, clipboard in hand.

"Hey, Tee. Don't worry, since I can already hear you complaining that the preggo is working and you're not—I'm coordination, not grunt labour." She winked then whispered conspiratorially, "Helping here is letting the family set up the new baby's room with the surprise stuff they bought that they think I don't know about." When Charity smiled, Madison flipped her a thumbs-up. "We've got this under control. Everything clothing-like that needs washing is getting taken care of then will be brought to Silver Stone. Household stuff will be cleaned and kept here."

It was too much. "But..."

The phone flipped in an instant to where the ladies were now gathered in one group, all waving at Charity.

"We love you. Don't worry about a thing," Tamara's youngest sister, Julia, called.

"And you get to say thank you at the family girls' night out on Tuesday. That's your job," Tamara shook a finger at the screen, "to say *thank you*. Nothing else. Let us be here for you. Got it?"

Charity was on the edge of tears again for an entirely different reason. "Got it."

Fern flipped the phone again. The spinning screen sent Charity's brain whirling.

"We love you," Fern declared.

"I love you too, but flip me again like that, and I will find a way to get revenge." Charity shook her head, lowering her voice. "It's too much, Fern."

Her friend also lowered her voice. "It's not too much, because we do love you. Plus, dealing with this is something we can do easier than you can because there's a layer of separation. We're mad and upset on your behalf, but it doesn't hit the same way it would if you were here dealing with it. Let us take care of you, please?"

"When you put it that way, there's not much I can do," Charity complained.

Fern perked right up. "Nope."

Charity considered, then another worry slithered in. "Okay, let's pretend I'm able to accept this enormous gift without getting teary. Why are they bringing my clean clothes to Silver Stone? Just put them back in my apartment."

Her friend's stern face was back in an instant. "Not until we catch who did this. Nope, Dustin is right. Your safety comes first. You'll be staying at Silver Stone until we know the vandal is not going to be an issue." Fern shook her head when Charity would have protested. "You weren't here, so we're dealing with a mess. That's an inconvenience, nothing else. What if you had been home? What if things had escalated?"

"I hadn't thought about that." Charity sucked for air. "Okay, my peaceful Zen just took a hit."

"Don't panic too hard, because you *weren't* here, and you

won't be here until it is safe. Dustin said it needed to happen, Caleb agreed, and Tamara is fully onboard."

"Go, Stones." The response was instantaneous and real.

Fern walked somewhere new, the background changing to dark and then daylight bright. When she spoke, it was gentler and pure Fern. "They care about you."

"I know. They've been so giving. I feel like a burden."

"Tee, you do realize the only reason we're cleaning up a mess is because you stepped in to help Dustin. Yes? The vandalism is a direct result of you being associated with him." Fern crooked her finger as if trying to make Charity move in closer. "You did the girlfriend thing to be there for him because you care about him. Admit it."

One deep breath later, Charity nodded. "Yes."

"Yes. So the fact they care— Wait, *reboot*. The fact that *Dustin* cares about you shouldn't seem like such a strange impossibility."

"He doesn't..." Charity stalled out, suddenly aware she was about to utter a lie. "He told me he liked me."

Fern made a face. "Gee, *really?*"

"Get lost," Charity mumbled.

"Can't. I know Heart Falls like the back of my hand." She held up her left arm—the one with the prosthesis—then frowned. She wore a hook attachment instead of a hand. "You know what I mean."

Charity snickered. "I love you."

"Of course you do. And we love you because you're very lovable."

Which was a warm affirmation until the reason they were chatting right then kicked back into focus. "Someone doesn't love me. Aka, *hashtag home trasher*."

Fern's expression tightened. "Yeah. Which is why you'll

stay at Silver Stone where you'll be safe. If you need to come to town, one of us will come with you."

Charity wanted to complain. Wanted to protest that being on lockdown wasn't on the table and being even more of a burden to the Stones and her friends was the last thing she wanted.

Then she remembered the look on Dustin's face. Serious and determined. So caring.

"Okay."

Her friend raised a brow. "I figured it would take wrestling and duct tape to get you to agree."

Charity shrugged. "I was willing to put myself out there to keep Kelli and the kids and the rest of them out of the spotlight. If I'm safe, and the light's still on me, I can take it."

She wouldn't like it, but that was a separate matter.

"I don't know what time we'll be done, but this is no longer your worry," Fern informed her. "It's your day off. Kelli will be over this morning to take you riding and on a picnic lunch. This afternoon, you are being taken kitten hunting by Tyler with Sasha Stone supervising. For supper, I'm bringing over taco fixings, and Shim is bringing some board game that he insists we'll all love. That's dinner and your evening's entertainment all arranged."

"So glad it's *my* day off," Charity teased.

"Right? You have excellent taste in activities." Fern blew a kiss. "Gotta run. Try to relax a little. We got this."

Charity blew her a kiss back then disconnected the line.

Another whirlwind. This time of an entirely different sort. A warm wind wrapping around her made of friends and caring people. Charity stood in place, closed her eyes, and took a minute to silently appreciate the gift she'd been given.

When she opened them again, the bright sunshine pouring in the living room window beckoned. Charity grabbed her warm breakfast treats from the microwave, topped up her coffee, and headed out the front door to the small table and comfy chairs she'd seen the night before.

She'd taken one step onto the porch when Patchwork Annie scared the hell out of her with a welcoming *woof*.

Charity snapped her head to the right to discover the dog resting belly down on the edge of the porch, tail wagging madly. "Hey, girl. Where's your boss?"

A moment's glance around the area revealed no sign of Dustin, which was beyond strange. A closer check revealed the dog lay stretched out with one paw on either side of Charity's borrowed cowboy boots.

"What the heck are you up to, Dustin Stone?" she wondered, standing over his dog.

Her tummy rumbled at that moment, though, so she sat down to her breakfast to try to puzzle it out. As she ate, she attempted to get Annie to join her. But no matter what enticements she offered, Charity couldn't get the dog to budge. Not even for a piece of bacon, although the pup's nose did twitch frantically.

Charity rose and crossed the distance between them and gave Annie the treat before ruffling her furry head. "I don't know what Dustin said to you, but damn, you're a good girl. Thanks for keeping me company."

Fortified in the belly, Charity pulled out her phone and prepared for the not so pleasant task of informing her sister of current events.

Charity: *Got something to tell you that would be easier over the phone. (I know—ugh) Call me when you're free. Don't worry, everything's fine.*

It wasn't a complete lie. Things were fine...ish. At the moment.

Her phone rang almost immediately. "Baby sis. How's it going this fine and sunny day?"

Chelsea's cheery greeting was echoed in the background by Suz's happy call of, "And how's your fake boyfriend?"

"Today, things are going great. Wonderfully, even, but I need you to put me on speaker so you and Suz can listen for a minute."

She got through the description of the auction and the follow up discovery of her apartment without too many interruptions. When she paused, finally, it was to silence at the other end of the line.

"Cee? Suz?"

"We're here," Suz assured her. "I'm sitting on your sister to make sure she doesn't grab the car keys to come sniff out your vandal like a bloodhound."

"If she could, I'd have her here in a second. But I didn't call until now because there was nothing more that could be done last night. And today my friends have taken over, so there's nothing to be done now, either."

Chelsea sighed so loud the sound echoed over the line. "I could give you a hug."

"I think Dustin's got that part covered," Suz teased.

"Dustin's been amazing," Charity offered quickly, ignoring the innuendo. "He left his dog to guard me, and I don't know how he did that because she's usually his shadow."

"That's sweet," Suz said. "Cee, you going to be okay, darling?"

"I'm just worried about Tee. That's all." Her sister's voice was soft and gentle. "Do you want us to come out?"

"Yes, but later, when you already planned to." Charity shoved down her flash of concern about overextending her reach by inviting her family onto Silver Stone land. It was the right thing to do, she just knew it in her gut. "There's more than enough room for you two here in the cottage. I'll double-check that it's okay with Dustin. We can horseback ride and all the rest. It'll be safe and exactly the type of fun we need to forget about the ignorant hooligans in the world."

Her sister laughed softly. "That's exactly what Grandma would have said."

"I know. I keep thinking about her and what she'd have done in this kind of situation. If she'd been in my shoes, she would be gracious, and accept the help. If she'd been on the other side, she'd have offered exactly the kind of help I've been given by the Stones and Fern. So really, she's here. And I need to trust that this is where I need to be, too."

Chelsea spoke quietly. "If you're sure. You check with who you need to, and if it's okay, we'll be there in just over a week as planned. Send me details."

"And if anything changes, you call us," Suz interrupted. "Anytime. You're not ever a bother. You're *ours*. Remember that."

Charity blinked hard, moisture blurring the image of Kelli Stone leading Beach and another horse across the yard toward the cottage. Both horses were saddled and ready to roll. "My morning ride is on the way. I love you guys. I'll message you soon."

"Bye, Tee. Love you too," echoed in stereo from the phone.

Charity stood, wiping the tears from her eyes as Kelli pulled to a stop and dropped the reins over the nearby hitching post.

The pixie of a woman examined her for a moment. "You good?"

"Really good," Charity insisted.

Kelli dipped her chin. She glanced at Annie and whistled. "Well, damn. That boy is a miracle worker."

"That *man*," Charity corrected her gently.

The other woman grinned. "Got it. So, did you want to head out on a ride? I know someone—*cough, Fern, cough*—has organized your life for you today, but it really is up to you."

"I'd love to go," Charity said honestly. "Let me put my plate inside and get dressed."

DUSTIN DIDN'T OFTEN GET to have uninterrupted hours with any of his brothers these days. The morning spent with Luke was all the more special because of that.

They had just returned to the barn, and it felt necessary to say something. Dustin didn't want this to just be a sometime thing.

"Maybe once things settled down around Silver Stone, we could get Tucker to do some finagling of the schedule." Dustin met Luke's questioning gaze as they slowly led their horses to their stalls. "You, Caleb, and Walker are all so busy with your wives and families. And yeah, I hope to get more involved with Charity. We have joint family gatherings, but I miss this. Time working one-on-one where we can shoot the breeze easier."

Luke nodded slowly. "I know what you mean. We work together all the time, but there's not a lot of conversation happening when one of us is up the back of a horse getting our teeth rattled loose."

"I think Ashton called those conversations *trash talk*."

"We're not that bad," Luke complained.

"We can't be. Never know when one of the kids will show up."

His brother laughed. "True. I'd hate to face Tamara or Ivy after cursing you out in earshot of any of their babies."

Amusing as hell, but Dustin raised a brow. "You obviously have not yet heard Sasha let loose when things don't go well in the arena."

"Sasha?" Luke's jaw hung open.

Dustin dipped his head. "Knows everyone of Caleb's pet phrases, and a bunch I'm sure she learned from Tamara, and can toss them off like a sailor on shore leave."

"I'll be damned." Luke grew a little serious. "Everyone is growing up, aren't they? The girls are both well into their teens. Tyler's not a baby anymore. Walker and Ivy have a full-blown family. Tucker and Ginny's baby will arrive soon."

"Kelli's and your kid later this year..."

Luke nearly tripped over his own feet in the middle of guiding Thunderbolt into his stall. "What?" He glanced around then glared at Dustin. "Who told you?"

"You. Right now. Congrats." His cheeks were going to be sore tomorrow from smiling so hard.

"Goddammit, Dustin." Luke rolled his eyes to the ceiling.

Dustin grinned harder. "Didn't know a thing until you opened your big mouth, bro, but hey, I'm happy for you."

"You're an ass." Luke slid the clinches loose.

"I won't tell a soul," Dustin promised as he got to work on his own horse. "So...tell me more." Because it was clear his brother wanted to share, now that the beans had been spilled.

Luke took a quick peek around, then spoke softly. "She just found out. We were going to wait a bit before announcing anything. Don't want to steal Tucker's thunder right now."

God, it was too funny. The whole competition thing between Tucker and Luke was never going to go away. "He beat you on that one, didn't he?"

"Yeah, well, Ginny is older than Kelli, so we weren't in as

much of a rush. Besides, in this family, it looks as if we'll have babies showing up on a steady basis for a few years if things work out with you and Charity." Luke paused. "God. That's a thought."

"What?"

"You as a dad. Not that you won't make a great one," Luke hurried to add. "You're awesome with kids, and always have been. Right from the get-go with Caleb's girls."

"I was more brother than uncle to them a lot of the time," Dustin pointed out. "But yeah, I like kids. I know Charity does too, but that's absolutely not a conversation we'll be having for a while."

"Of course not." Only Luke flashed that evil smile again. "I might casually ask what her thoughts are on big families."

Dustin stared him down. "You tell Kelli yet about your plan to have five kids?"

"She knows I want more than a couple," Luke returned. "If she doesn't kill me after delivering the first one, bartering will begin at that point."

"Smart plan." Dustin resisted the urge to comment that he was certain the 'more than a couple' actually meant one more than Tucker.

They chatted for a few more minutes, getting ready to head back out to finish their list when a sudden ruckus rose from farther in the barn. Loud voices back and forth, shouting and calls of, "*Wait.*"

Dustin braced himself. More social media bullshit?

"I know where the hell I'm going. Now get out of my way." The voice was familiar, but completely unexpected at Silver Stone.

Dustin blinked. His gaze snapped to Luke's. "Uncle Frank's here?"

Luke shrugged. "I guess."

The older man was still muttering as he rounded the corner and spotted them. He marched right up to Dustin. "There you are. I came to drop off some animals and heard there's been trouble. Why the hell didn't you call me?"

Shocked speechless, Dustin had no time to do much more than open his mouth before his uncle was moving again, gaze snapping around the barn.

"Where is she?" Uncle Frank's eyes were on the wild side, his hair a mess as he lifted his hat and ran his hand through it for what must have been the twentieth time, it was such a tangled mess. "Tamara said to look in the barn, but she's not in the damn office."

"Uncle Frank," Luke stepped forward "who are you talking about?"

"His girlfriend." He jerked a thumb at Dustin then whirled on him. "What the hell is going on? I heard her place was trashed. Is she okay? Who did it? What's being done to catch them?"

Jesus. Dustin couldn't in a million years have dreamed up this scenario. First things first, though. His uncle was one step shy of a panic attack, and while he'd shouted, his tone and expression said he wasn't being an asshole.

If he had to guess, Dustin would say Frank was scared.

"She's fine. She's safe here at Silver Stone. We're doing what we can to figure out the rest, but she's okay." Dustin laid a hand on his uncle's shoulder, easing him down. "We're taking care of her."

The frown on Frank's face was fierce, but he nodded as Dustin's words slowly sank in. "She wasn't hurt?"

"She wasn't there," Dustin affirmed. "She's okay."

Frank straightened, took a deep breath, then let it out in a sudden puff. "Good. Good."

Luke was checking his phone and now held up a hand.

"Kelli agrees that Charity should be here in the barn. We'll find her." He raised his voice and shouted, "Hey, Charity, you around?"

"Up here. One minute."

Footsteps rang out on the stairs from the hayloft, the distinctive sound of creaking boards mixing with childish conversation. The next second, Charity came into view with Tyler in her arms and Sasha following behind.

Patchwork Annie followed Charity close enough it was amazing she wasn't tripping over the dog.

Charity stopped when she reached them, blinking hard. "Oh. Hello, Mr. Stone."

"Thank God, you're safe." Frank moved in an instant, and the next second he had Charity and Tyler wrapped up in a hug.

Dustin could see Charity's face, and while shock was first and foremost, she wore a bit of a smile as well. She met his gaze and lifted her brows as if in shrug.

Tyler took it all in stride and patted Uncle Frank on the back. "Super Frank. Come see the kitties?"

A moment later Frank had pulled back and held out his arms for his great-nephew. The kid nestled in as if he were held by the older man on a regular basis. "Were you showing Charity the kittens?"

"Yup." Tyler nodded seriously then held up a pudgy hand, fingers spread wide. "Five kitties. Come see," he ordered, tugging Frank's collar toward the stairs.

"He's obviously very shy and retiring," Sasha offered dryly. "Hi, Great-Uncle Frank. Let me take the kiddo for a minute so you can talk. We'll wait on the stairs," she told her brother, who had latched onto Frank like an octopus and begun to wail in protest. "Better yet, let's go make sure the kittens are still hiding in the same spot. So when he comes upstairs, you can show him."

Tyler considered this seriously before all but throwing himself at his older sister. She caught him without even blinking, spinning him in a circle as she made airplane sounds and rushed him up the stairs.

Meanwhile, Charity had made her way to Dustin's side. She slipped an arm around his waist and leaned into him, speaking softly. "Hey. I thought you were cowboying all day."

"I am. Still cowboying, that is." He pressed a kiss to her temple. "You good?"

"Had a great morning with Kelli, my friends are being my angels, and I have a good dog by my side. I'm very good." They both glanced at Annie, who was all but vibrating, her tail wagging hard as she stood between their booted feet.

"So it worked. Damn." Dustin leaned over and rubbed her head. "Good girl."

Annie plopped her butt down, opened her mouth, and gave a happy yip.

When he stood, leaning in to give Tee a kiss seemed the most natural thing. He slipped their fingers together as he explained. "I ordered her to guard the boots."

"I figured as much. She thought really hard for a minute when I slipped them on, but as long as she can see them, she's happy."

He'd pretty much forgotten about Uncle Frank, as shocking as that was. Charity however turned to face the man. "I'm sorry you were worried. Dustin and the rest of the family are taking good care of me. It's just an inconvenience, really."

"Home invasion is not just an inconvenience." Frank folded his arms over his chest and glared.

She raised a brow.

He downgraded the glare to a frown.

Damn, watching the two of them was like being at a performance. "Are you staying for supper, Uncle Frank?" Dustin asked. "Would you like to join us?"

His uncle appeared as shocked to hear the words as Dustin was to have uttered them.

Then he shook his head. "No, thank you, though." He eyed Charity and the grip she had on Dustin's beltloop. "I wanted to invite you to come to Crooked Creek if you want. Both of you. If that would help."

Charity stepped forward. "That is a generous offer, and I'm grateful you made it. But for now, I'll stay here at Silver Stone. Once things settle down, I'd love to come visit again. If that would work."

It was one miracle after another as the older man nodded then tilted his chin toward Dustin. "Come when you can. Adam enjoys having you around." He swallowed hard as if trying to fit the words together. "I appreciate you being there, too."

He held out his hand to Dustin, who took it in spite of the shock to his system. A compliment from his uncle? An offer of a place of refuge? "Always willing to help family."

"Yeah, I'm finally figuring that out," Frank muttered.

Dustin ignored that part because this was more important. "Thanks for offering Tee a safe spot to land. That's really good of you."

"Well, it looks as if you're being taken care of." Frank eyed them both again then tipped his head at Luke. "Give my regards to Caleb. I'll be in touch."

Charity moved in his path before he could leave. "Thank you."

He chuckled, a low rusty sound, as if he wasn't used to using it. "Young lady, thank you. And you." He stabbed a finger at Dustin, suddenly sounding like his bossy old self. "Get your ass in gear before someone else snaps her up."

"Uncle Frank?"

His uncle caught Charity's wrist and lifted it up to show her bare hand. "If you know what's good for you, you'll put your ring on here sooner than later. Excuse me, I have some kittens to track down."

Then he was gone, headed to the loft. His boots clattered on the wooden floorboards of the stairs, leaving a stunned group of three behind.

Luke stared up the stairwell for a moment. "Well, wasn't that the most peculiar thing I've ever seen." He turned on Dustin and Charity. "Either of you know what's gotten into him? I vote for possession by little green aliens."

"I have no idea. The last time I spoke to him, I gave him hell for being a fool." Charity wrinkled her nose in an adoring manner. "Let's not share that too widely with the rest of your family."

Now that was an interesting tidbit. "Well, the last time I talked to him, which was after you did, he was not as possessed as today, but he was polite for the first time...*ever*." Dustin met Luke's gaze then tilted his head toward her. "It appears we've discovered patient zero in infecting Uncle Frank with a heart."

Luke grabbed Charity's hand and shook it vigorously. "Miracle worker."

She laughed, pulling her hand free. "Whatever. Maybe he needed a plain speaking-to. Anyway, that was a very kind offer from him."

"It was. And when we can, we'll go visit Crooked Creek and our friends," Dustin promised.

Uncle Frank's odd behavior aside, work beckoned followed by the promise of a fun evening with Charity and his friends. Dustin kissed her cheek quickly before hurrying off after Luke.

18

———

*M*onday morning, Charity marched herself across the yard from the cottage to the Silver Stone office, determined to get back into productive mode. Patchwork Annie paced at her side, once again having been told by Dustin to guard. This time he'd used her runners, but Charity thought maybe Annie was getting the idea it was the feet inside the shoes she was supposed to keep an eye on.

The previous day had been all kinds of unexpectedly wonderful. Between her friends caring for her, the ride with Kelli, kitten time with Tyler and Sasha, and the evening spent with Dustin, Fern, and Shim, Charity had pretty much been surrounded by a supportive community.

Dustin's arms around her all night long had been the cherry on top of a good day.

But now she needed to focus. Time to do her job and maybe find a little emotional distance between what was real and what wasn't.

That people cared for her—real.

That she was truly a part of Silver Stone—fake.

And that was okay. Really.

Maybe.

No, it sucked.

She batted down the tight knot in her belly. Today was about taking new steps forward. Go forth and do the right thing, tallyho, and full speed ahead.

Chin lifted, a bounce in her step, she pushed open the door to the office and jerked to a stop. "Shit."

A goat stood on her desk.

The grey and white beast had a very debonair look to him, with a neat little beard and a black bow tie. But he was a *goat*, and on her desk.

Charity folded her arms over her chest. "You know, two weeks ago I might have run screaming from the room. But now? You're just one more box to check off on a long list of 'didn't see that one coming.'" She snapped her fingers and pointed at the floor. "Get down."

Patchwork Annie looked up at her in confusion, uncertain if her butt should be up or down.

"Not you, sweet thing, the goat." Charity eyed the beast. She could walk to the side with the door open and get Annie to chase the goat from the room. But that would leave the creature running loose in the barn—probably not a good idea.

Instead, Charity backed up and closed the door, locking the goat in before sending up a shout. "Hello? Anyone around? Tucker? Any of the hands?"

She peeked down both of the main hallways off the office, but nothing.

"Hello? I need some animal help."

"Hey."

A feminine voice rang from behind her, and Charity whirled. "Oh, Emma. Hi."

"Hi." The teenager stepped forward, her motion such a

combination of Caleb's saunter and Tamara's get-it-done strut that Charity had to smile. "What's up?"

"Oh, I have a small infestation in the office I need a hand with."

Emma wrinkled her nose. "Mice?"

"A teeny bit bigger. Try goat."

The teenager snorted. "Oh, drat. *Them.*"

"Maybe infestation is too dramatic a word since it's only one goat," Charity admitted.

"Oh, you're not being dramatic at all," Emma assured her as she pointed back down the hall to the office and started the return trip. "Eeny is an entire troop of trouble, all by himself."

"Oh good, you know his name."

"Chances are high. Was the door open?"

"Closed."

Emma nodded, hand on the doorknob. "Definitely Eeny. He's our escape artist. Trouble is, once he knows how to get in or out, the next thing you know..."

She pushed open the door, and suddenly a chorus of *bahhhhs* greeted them.

Three pairs of bright eyes set in bearded grey faces turned toward the door. One goat on the desk, number two was perched on the top of the filing cabinet. The final one balanced on the seat of Charity's chair.

That was going too far. She folded her arms again. "I doubt you guys are planning on doing my paperwork, so I'd like my office back, please."

Emma grinned, even as she gestured Charity forward then carefully closed the door behind them. She eyed Patchwork Annie, but as usual, the dog seemed content to remain at Charity's heels.

"Don't want them escaping in a direction I can't control," Emma explained when Charity lifted a brow. The teenager paused. "Are you comfortable holding a rope if I give it to you? They won't bite or kick once I've gotten them on leads."

"I think I'll be okay. They're not nearly as big as the horses."

"They make up in annoyance factor what they lack in stature," Emma joked.

It was like watching a dance. Emma lifted ropes and leads off the wall, stepped forward, and immediately caught the desk percher. She tugged lightly, and he jumped down with a grumbled *mahhh*.

"That was simple." Emma handed Charity the lead. She twisted, caught the ear of the chair goat, slipped the rope over his head, then rolled the chair, goat and all, toward the filing cabinet.

Goat three jumped to the side, directly where Emma stood. A moment later, he too was on a leash.

Emma grinned across the room at Charity. "And now we walk them back to the pen and try to block the holes so they don't get out for at least a day."

"You were amazing." Charity concentrated on keeping her fingers tightly wrapped around the rope she'd been given. No way did she want to let the creature slip away at this point.

"I've been well-trained," Emma said back as they crossed out of the barn toward the wire enclosure Charity had seen before without knowing what it was. "We've had the beasties for a while now. There's not a lot of mischief that we haven't dealt with over the years."

"Well, you did great. Thank you."

Emma eyed her a little harder as she pushed open the gate. She chewed on her lower lip, obviously thinking about something.

Once the goats were safely let loose and the pen completely sealed up again, Charity stepped to the side and leaned on the railing. She admired the enclosure and smiled as the three goats immediately sought high spots to glare down disapprovingly at their jailers.

"Charity..." Emma stalled out.

Charity had dealt with children too many times during dance classes to not read the signs. "Did you have a question?"

The young girl considered again then nodded. "It's just, you and Dustin."

Hmmm. Time to tread carefully. "Yes?"

Emma lifted her chin. "He's special. I know he's our uncle, but he's always kind of been like a big brother, and I just..."

"Just want to know that he's okay?" Charity guessed.

The girl laughed. "He's more than okay. He's happier than I've seen him in ages. I just wanted to tell you that I'm grateful you did so much to make things easier for him when the media stuff hit. And that I'm really sorry your apartment was broken into."

Charity stepped closer, delighted by the conversation. "Thank you for that. It was not pleasant, but a lot of people, including your mom, helped me. And here's a secret." She lowered her voice. "Your big brother-slash uncle—bruncle?— there we go. Your *bruncle* is easy to be nice to."

"Oh my God, that's perfect. Bruncle Dusty." Emma grinned, and her beautiful blue eyes flashed bright with mischief. "He was teasing Papa the other day about how people have many names. That's going to be his from now on."

Charity made a little curtsey. "Thank you for your help with the goats. Now I should get back to work."

Emma nodded then wiggled on the spot. "Can I give you a hug?"

God. "Of course, sweetie." Charity opened her arms and accepted the warm embrace.

It had been four years since she'd met the girl for the first time, and the difference couldn't be more stark. Young Emma had fought for words, hidden from the spotlight, and been happy to stand back and let her sister be the one to speak to their dance instructor.

To see how much she'd bloomed was a treasure.

Charity squeezed her one final time. "Now, I need to work, or they'll put me in the pen with Meany."

"Bruncle Dusty would break you out," Emma teased, waving her fingers as she sauntered away with a bold whistle.

Dustin got a kick out of the story that night as they shared dinner. "They're good kids, Sasha and Emma. I'm glad Tamara came along when she did, but Caleb did his best. And Ginny and Dare helped a ton after their mom left."

"I heard Dare arrived today. Fun name."

"Short for Darilyn, if you hadn't heard that yet. You'll get to meet her tomorrow night, if not earlier."

At the girls' night out at Ginny's place. "I can't believe Ginny is hosting a gathering on the day she's due."

"Distraction is a good thing right now. So I hear."

She eyed him. "Are you planning on distracting Tucker?"

Dustin's grin widened. "Hell, yeah. Might try to lighten his pocketbook a little as well."

Charity put her fingers to her mouth as if shocked at what she was hearing. "You dastardly wicked villain. Planning to fleece your poor, preoccupied brother-in-law."

"Ain't it great?" Dustin threw back his head and cackled maniacally.

His outburst set her off, and they spent the rest of the evening sending each other into fits of laughter.

A day later, Charity knocked her fingers against Dustin's knee. He sat on one of the porch chairs, pulling his boots on. "You guys aren't meeting at Luke's for another half hour. You don't need to walk me to your sister's house now."

"I know." He rose to his feet and offered his hand. "I don't have to, but I want to."

Not much she could say about that. "Well, okay."

He grinned.

They strolled slowly, hand in hand, across the meadow between the cottage and the two houses above Big Sky Lake. Almost all of Silver Stone's living quarters were built to the south of the lake, starting to the west with the main house that Tamara and Caleb lived in. Her borrowed cottage was just to the east of them. The barns and arenas and the bunkhouse lay in the middle more to the south. To the far east were the two homes that sheltered Kelli and Luke, and Ginny and Tucker.

The only building to the north of the lake was a smaller cabin nearing completion that was the future home of Ashton Stewart and his wife Sonora.

The entire collection of homes looked as if they'd grown up from the land. Natural and a part of the terrain instead of unsightly outcroppings.

Charity raised a hand to fend off the sun glaring up from the still water of the lake as Patchwork Annie bounced past them.

"That has got to be the happiest creature in the world right now." Charity gestured to the dog who was prancing between her, Dustin, and the nearest interesting thing to sniff with the abandon of a pup.

"She's done an amazing job of guarding you, but yeah. She loves me best." Dustin winked. "It's my charming ways."

"It's the fact you're super clumsy when you eat," Charity countered. "I swear you had a small fit yesterday. The size of burger that *accidentally* flew her way was embarrassing."

"Spoiling her is a bad habit." Dustin stopped on the back stoop and pointed Annie to the side. She happily joined Luke's and Tucker's dogs in the warm shelter off the path.

Charity braced herself before opening the door. All the Stone ladies in one place at one time, and she was about to be a part of it.

They are nice people, she reminded herself as the door swung open. *It will be fine.*

It was like opening onto a loaded stage with all the performers waiting for their cues. Not only the ladies were there, but their husbands, as well.

Plus, a lone single female. Charity had been introduced to Darilyn Coleman earlier that afternoon. They'd fallen into a frank discussion regarding blogging and children's right to privacy that had reassured Charity that Dustin was right about his foster sister Dare not being a *mommyblogger* of the dangerous sort.

Which meant Charity had all the names to put with the faces.

But, oh my God. So. Many. Faces.

Tamara caught Charity by the arm and pulled her farther into the room. "You're just in time. World war three is about to break out."

"It's not a war," Tucker insisted from where he stood hovering over Ginny. "I decided to have a casual game of pool with my best friend and my brothers-in-law. That's all."

"On the same night I'm having girls' night out?" Ginny demanded.

"Coincidence," Tucker claimed.

"Bullshit." Ginny glared up at him. "Fine. Go play at Luke's house. That's only fifty meters to the south."

"If you think I'm going farther than shouting distance from you right now, you're fucking delusional," Tucker growled.

Ginny caught him by the collar and pulled him toward her, not the least stymied by the enormous swell of her belly. It took a little creative bending on Tucker's part, but an instant later he was accepting her kiss, while around them loud cheers rang out.

When they came up for air, Tucker's cheeks were flushed.

"Okay, small adjustment," Ginny announced, hand resting on her belly. "Ladies—head to the kitchen. Guys, downstairs. Stay in your corners for the evening, and we'll pretend the other sex doesn't exist for the night. Except Dustin—you're our gopher between the sexes."

"Why him?" Tucker complained.

Ginny glared at her husband. "Because I trust him not to hover over me every three seconds reminding me to get off my feet. Now *get*."

Like the parting of the Red Sea, the groups divided in two directions.

Only there was a lot more kissing that took place before the guys vanished down the stairs. Ivy had tucked herself into the corner of the room, and Walker paused, kneeling as he lifted her chin with a finger then gently pressed their lips together.

Caleb straight forward scooped Tamara into his arms and kissed her possessively. Luke whirled and then dipped Kelli, a long, hot kiss that made Charity's cheeks flush.

Dare wore a long suffering smirk. Dustin's foster sister folded her arms over her chest then shook her head as she looked around the room. "There are far too many PDAs happening right now. Very inconsiderate of you, considering I left my *kissee* up north."

A rather breathless Tamara adjusted her neon-green glasses then linked fingers with Caleb and raised a brow at Dare. "I imagine Jesse would be here in record time if you called him."

Whatever Dare responded back was lost as Dustin stepped into Charity's line of sight, a heated expression on his face. "Stop watching everyone else pucker up and get your lips ready for me."

Charity caught her lips in her fingers and tugged them—right, left, up, down. "Like this?"

He snickered then cupped her neck, sliding in close, brushing his nose along hers. "Perfect."

Their lips made contact, and it *was* perfect. Sweet yet hot, new and yet already so familiar. She could have stood there all night with his mouth on hers. The soft caress of his thumb on her neck a contrast with the panic-inducing yet sweet thrill of being included in the whole family.

The desire for this to be real grew with every breath she took.

IT WAS the best and strangest of evenings.

Being designated the go-between, Dustin got in time playing pool, then was sent off to grab another round of beers from the kitchen fridge, next to where the women were gathered.

Every time he was upstairs, his sisters-in-law and sisters ordered him around with great enthusiasm as they got him to fetch things from top shelves, open jars of uber-sweet treats, and otherwise handle physical labour.

He didn't care. In some ways it was like getting permission to briefly enter a world he'd always been forbidden to be a part of. Also, the ladies did not fuck around when it came to having a good time.

They had him move an oversized comfy chair closer to the main table so Ginny could have her feet up and still be in the middle of the action. Multiple trays of cheese-filled, gooey snacks magically appeared and were shared. Bubbles in tall glasses made it look as if all of them were having fancy drinks when he knew damn well most of it was nonalcoholic.

"The pizza for you guys will be ready in five," Dare announced. His foster sister eyed him, gaze dancing to where Charity was helping Tamara assembly-line some craft involving cute snowman candles.

"I hope you made enough. Your husband isn't here, but I promised to eat a few slices in his honour."

"Jesse is probably eating pizza right now and feeding it to my babies as well." She smiled. "Some things never change. He still cooks like a cowboy."

"Straight from the box to the table?"

"If it can't be microwaved, toasted, or grilled, it can't be good." She slid in closer. "So... Charity."

"So?"

Dare grinned harder. "She's adorable and gorgeous."

"Yeah. Plus, she's got enough backbone to give you a run for your money." He leaned in close. "Thanks for not accepting my proposal all those years ago."

She laughed out loud. "You're very welcome."

Charity glanced over, brow raised in question. Dustin winked, then loaded up with the pizza and headed back downstairs.

Tucker was waiting for him, leaning on the wall at the base of the stairs. "Everything okay?"

Dustin snickered, walking past Tucker to the makeshift table to deposit his armload. "Ginny is still pregnant. Sitting down, having fun."

His brother-in-law glared at him. "You shouldn't find this so amusing."

"And yet I do."

"Ass."

Dustin scooped an enormous slice of pizza onto a plate and shoved it at Tucker. "Eat. You'll need your strength soon enough. You'll have to keep smiling as everyone says what a beautiful baby you have, when we all know newborn humans look like crumpled old men."

"God." Tucker stomped off to rejoin the others.

Snippets of conversation mixed between the masculine voices of the basement and the higher lilt drifting from upstairs, and Dustin found he wore a grin most of the time. Getting to see Charity with the rest of them was sweet.

Getting to hang with all his brothers—also sweet.

He dropped the final ball in the pocket and let loose an evil laugh. "We win again."

He raised a hand to Walker, and they high-fived each other.

"You're cheating." Caleb eyed them, gaze narrowing. "I don't know how, but you're cheating."

"It's our far younger eyes and steadier hand-eye coordination. Just hard cold facts," Walker drawled.

Caleb let out a snort. "Again. This time, Tucker and Walker, me and Luke."

"Perfect. That leaves Dustin free to make a beer run." Luke slapped Dustin on the back. "This century, bro. You were gone so long last time I wondered if you'd snuck out for a quickie with Charity."

"Damn, good idea." Dustin ducked under his brother's swing and took the steps two at a time.

As he reached the top, the already lively room exploded with howls of laughter. All around the table, the women held their stomachs or had hands raised to their lips, delight spilling into the room like sunshine.

"What's up?" he asked Charity as he crouched beside her chair.

She pointed at the table, unable to speak through her amusement.

The snowman candles he'd glimpsed before were now wilted forms of their former glory. With misaligned eyes and tree limb arms sticking out in awkward directions, they were nothing that could grace an elegant table.

"Cool. Zombie snowmen," Dustin offered.

Ginny howled even louder, one hand cupping her belly, the other pointing at him. "Yes," she got out between gasps. "Oh my God, we've got a new winner. Zombie snowmen for your perfect holiday décor."

The laughter turned out to be the final straw.

Suddenly, the basement emptied, and the guys were all upstairs, unable to stay away a moment longer. Together they appreciated the disaster of the craft, sliding more chairs together so conversations could continue and expand.

Charity pulled Dustin with her to the kitchen counter. "More food, stat. I saw nacho chips. Let's make a couple of trays."

He nodded even as he stole a kiss. "Nachos will always make me think of germ-sharing." He leaned in close and spoke softly as he brushed a finger over the dip at the base of her neck. "And the flush you get right here when you come."

"Dustin," Charity warned, but her eyes danced.

The evening ended before eleven. Ginny got Tucker to help peel her out of her chair. "You guys can stay, but I'm going to bed. My watermelon is tired."

"We all should call it a night," Luke suggested, trying not to look at Kelli, but failing spectacularly. Or at least to Dustin, who knew his brother was already obsessing about the coming baby and how to make Kelli slow down.

"It's been fun, though. *Adults only* time needs to be a regular event in the family future," Tamara suggested, stretching out and yawning. "Come on, Señor Stone. Take me home to bed."

"What is it with everyone hinting that I'm old?" Caleb grumbled. "I'm not old."

"Señor, as in español," Tamara assured him. "Which reminds me. I need to schedule you a hearing test."

Walker and Dustin snickered so hard the entire family got triggered to join in, including Caleb.

Charity was still smiling as she got ready for bed. Hands moving smoothly as she put up her hair, wrapping silky fabric around her curls. "Your family is wonderful. Thanks for the lovely evening."

"You made it special, too," he told her.

He wanted to say more. Point out how she'd fit in, but instead he curled himself around her and bided his time. This thing between them needed to be talked about, but right now wasn't the moment.

It was *leading* to the moment, he was sure of that, but now was special all on its own.

They'd been in bed for a couple hours when Dustin's phone buzzed. Since it was on Do Not Disturb, had to be Tucker or Caleb.

He slipped it off the side table and took a peek.

Tucker: *Ginny's in labour. Headed to the hospital.*
Tucker: *Can't reach Luke. Let the family know?*
Dustin: *Of course. You guys got this. We'll all be there as soon as we can.*
Tucker: *Hey brat, this is Ginny. Tucker's driving. I'm being squeezed through the portals of hell, but hey, having a baby is great! Fucking Christ on a cracker.*
Dustin: *Your kid is going to be the most awesome swearer in the family. You okay if we invade the hospital while you're cursing out Tucker for getting you into this predicament?*
Tucker: *Still Ginny. Yeah, I don't know how long this is going to take—sweet mercy I hope it's over in like five minutes because FUCK. But hey, yeah. Gather the troops. Dare is with us already.*

See you soon. Well, I won't see you because I'll be busy, FUCK this SUCKS, but hey, you know what I mean.
Dustin: *Love you, big sis. You can do this, you stubborn, rock-solid Stone.*
Tucker: *Love you too. FUCK.*

Maybe it wasn't in the plan, but dammit, he wanted to be there. This was part of why they'd done what they had to do to deal with the media BS. To make it so that they could roll with life and do what was important.

Excitement spiraling through him, he lifted up on an elbow and kissed Charity's cheek. "Tee. Wake up."

She rolled slightly, eyes blinking gently. "What's up? You okay?"

"Fine. Ginny's in labour, though, so we're going to the hospital. Come on. Get dressed while I call the rest of the family."

Which is why only hours after they'd been together, they gathered again.

The sterile setting of the hospital waiting room was a night and day contrast with the warmth of the home Ginny and Tucker shared. Instead of warm candlelight and creamy yellow walls, generic grey paint surrounded them and nondescript beige flooring was scuffed underfoot. No comfy overstuffed chairs, just sturdy individual seats lined up in rows along the walls.

Didn't matter. The heart of the room was the people, and his family were all there. Everyone except Ivy and Emma, who'd stayed home to watch the children.

They'd arrived just before three a.m. For a couple of hours they talked quietly, switching chairs to visit with someone new every now and then. Sasha and Charity went and grabbed coffee for everyone. Dare came out with updates when she could.

Closing in on five a.m., Dare rushed into the hallway. "Close now. Ginny is no longer offering us threats and has moved onto the bartering stage, which means the baby is nearly here."

Dustin was sitting beside Charity at this point, his fingers linked with hers. She quivered on the spot, and he leaned his cheek against hers. "She'll be okay. They both will."

"I want it so much for them, and for Tucker." She buried her face in his neck and breathed deep. "I can't believe I'm here, getting to share this precious moment."

He squeezed her fingers, tongue tangling around the words to say that wouldn't freak her out too much. "You need to be here. It's...right."

She pulled back slightly, eyes shining. "Thanks."

The next time Dare stepped into the atrium, her cheeks were flushed but she wore an enormous grin. "Ginny and Tucker are delighted to let you know, and I quote, 'their daughter is ready to receive her due homage from her adoring family.'"

"Oh my God, a girl." Sasha gave a fist pump. "*Yes.*"

Laughter spilled even as Caleb and Tamara rose to their feet to head in to see the baby.

"They want to share her name," Dare said quietly.

It was nearly twenty minutes later when he and Charity finally made it into the room. Ginny looked tired, but she was glowing with happiness, and that outweighed everything else.

Tucker held a teeny bundle in his arms, staring in astonishment at his little girl. The grin he flashed Dustin was blinding. "God, you need one of these, stat."

Dustin was getting steamrolled by his entire family. He ignored the comment—a baby-drunk brother-in-law couldn't help himself, he supposed—and focused on Ginny. "You look amazing, and I'm glad she's here safely. Congrats."

She accepted his kiss then held her hands out to Charity. "Please don't be scared by the family. They're all high on baby fumes right now."

"I'm floating about five feet off the ground myself, so I get it. Congratulations."

"What's her name?" Dustin asked quietly, slipping in behind Charity and squeezing her shoulders.

Tucker stood then gestured to the chair with his head. "Nope. You gotta hold her to hear her name."

What Dustin wanted was to pull Charity into his lap and have them hold the kiddo together. What he did was settle her in the chair and pass the baby from Tucker to her arms. Then he knelt, curled his hands around Charity's shoulders, and looked into the baby's eyes.

"We'd like you to meet Demetria Joy," Ginny announced. "Demi for short."

The baby twitched, nose wrinkling as she squirmed briefly then settled back into the curve of Charity's hold. Eyes only partially open, she looked as wrinkly and puckered as all newborns.

"She's so beautiful," Charity said reverently. "Hello, Demi. So nice to meet you."

Dustin exchanged a grin with Tucker then focused back on the baby. "Hey, Demetria Joy. Welcome to the family."

19

By Tuesday afternoon, Dustin was ready for a little time off.

Hurrying to make it back to the ranch on time after checking fence lines, both he and Shim were covered with a fine layer of dust from riding hard.

Dustin steered his horse close enough he could land a solid pat on Shim's shoulder. "You rode well today."

"For a moderately talented rider?" his friend teased.

They grinned at each other then turned their horses back toward the barn, walking them slowly to cool down.

"I feel bad we haven't had more time together so far this summer," Dustin confessed. When Shim gave him an odd look, Dustin continued. "You got here, and I was gone. Since then, I've mostly been doing stuff with Charity or with my family. I suck as a friend."

Shim waved a hand at the comment. "Don't be such a princess. We already talked about why you weren't here at the start. Spending time with Charity makes sense for many reasons. And your family is just this huge juggernaut you couldn't avoid if you tried, and there's no *need* for you to try." He turned his horse toward the arena, shoulders lifting in a soft shrug. "I'm here at Silver Stone for good—or at least until the end of this contract. We've still spent time together every day, even if it's only been saying hello at lunch. I'm good, so fuck off with the guilt trip. It's annoying to listen to."

Dustin snorted. "Yes, sir."

Shim winked. "I am putting in my request for your presence at a guys'-only event, though. I won a river rafting fishing trip for four during August. It's on the Bull River, near Crowsnest Pass. Interested?"

"Hell, yes." Dustin's brain went into overdrive. "You got ideas for the other two guys?"

"Open to suggestions."

"We'll talk later." Because Lionel and Keith from Crooked Creek would eat up the activity and be good company. "But first put my name down in stone."

Shim nodded then checked his watch. "Hell, give me your horse. You need to go get ready."

"I can—" Dustin protested.

"Go," Shim insisted, taking the reins as his expression lightened. "You're meeting Charity's family in under an hour. You need to smell a hell of a lot better than you do right now if you want to make a good impression."

"Ass."

"Exactly what you smell like," Shim muttered, tugging the horses with him as he waved Dustin off. "Only the truth, my friend. Only the truth."

Dustin took a deep whiff and grimaced. Shim probably wasn't wrong.

Sending up thanks to his family and friend, Dustin sauntered out of the shower thirty minutes later, ready to enjoy the next three days with Charity and her sister.

As he pulled on clothes, he considered how to make the most of the time. Not just with Charity, but in moving toward the next stage.

God, had it only been a week since Demi's arrival?

In the work world, things had settled back to normal. There were still a few new social media buzzes every now and then, and the requests for interviews had slowed, not stopped, but for the most part, Silver Stone was back to business as usual.

No word yet on who had gotten into Charity's place, though. Which was both good and bad. He wanted to know whose ass to kick.

But he liked having Charity right where she was. And the past week had been extraordinary in terms of time spent together. As if they were already savouring every moment.

Did he even need to say that they should take their relationship in a new, solid direction? Because it felt as if they were already mostly there.

No. He scrubbed a hand over his hair to tidy it. That was the coward's way out. He had to straight up tell her how he felt, and sometime soon. He was meeting her family. She'd already dove in headfirst with his.

Wasn't that supposed to be one of the biggest steps in a relationship?

He found Charity pacing on the front porch, gaze fixed on the driveway as she twisted on the spot and fidgeted impatiently.

She lifted her gaze to his. "I think this is the most excited I've been since going to the Calgary Stampede for the first time and riding the Zipper."

"You're vibrating." He couldn't keep the amusement from his voice if he tried.

"They're late," Charity complained, but she was smiling as she moved closer. "You're going to love my sister. And her wife is the most darling person in the entire world. So smart. And really kind. Suz is like this big ball of happiness in human form."

He pulled her into his lap. "You've told me so much, I feel as if I've already met them. You, though, are going to fall over if you don't stop bouncing."

"I just miss them. And you need to meet them," she repeated.

"I know. Now, you have something right here..." He touched the corner of her mouth for a moment. Charity stilled, and he leaned in. "Don't worry. I got it."

His lips covered hers, and the sweetness of the kiss bloomed from tender to something hotter, and damn, he wondered if he had time to pick her up and take her to the bedroom for a little ravishing.

She held onto his shoulders tightly, lips curving into a smile. "You have an amazingly good distraction game."

"I aim to please." He spoke against her lips, keeping her in contact even as she swung her leg over his thighs and nestled in more comfortably. "Thanks for inviting your family over so I could have a holiday."

"Thank you for taking us not just riding, but camping." She sat back a little and traced her fingers along his jawline. "I really think it would be fine for us to go back to my apartment. Whoever broke into my place must be long gone by now. The other nonsense has slowed to a trickle."

"We're not arguing about this again," Dustin warned. "Focus on what *will* be happening, which is making sure your sister and sister-in-law enjoy their holiday."

She wrinkled her nose. "Okay."

God, she was adorable. And spunky and bright and everything that made him want to be a better man.

Dustin leaned his forehead on hers. "By the way..."

She lifted a brow.

"Who do I need to talk to about checking into this dude ranch?" a cheery voice rang out. Charity straightened in shock.

"...your sister is here," Dustin finished.

Charity shook her head at him. "You are trouble." Then she bounced off his lap, down the stairs, and into her sister's arms.

Dustin waited on the porch as a slightly older version of Charity finished squeezing her tight then turned her gaze on him. Chelsea also wore her tight curls loose and natural, only hers were cut a lot shorter, turning her hair into a dark, shining halo.

He stepped down and held out a hand. "Welcome to Silver Stone."

Chelsea eyed his hand and raised a brow. "Really? A handshake?"

Dustin opened his arms. "We have options."

An instant later Chelsea had enveloped him in a hug tight enough to give his brothers' rib-creaking squeezes a run for their money. That was followed by one from Suz, who turned out to be a tall, extremely thin woman with darker skin than both the sisters and a mass of blonde dreadlocks.

Charity linked her arms through theirs. "What do you want to see first? The kittens? The horses? The goats? God, I'm even excited for you to see the *goats*." She met Dustin's gaze. "I'm obviously feverish."

"You're obviously not fresh from a four-hour car ride," Suz inserted. "Bathroom first, please. Then the kittens, the goats, and the horses, in that order."

"Deal."

Dustin carried their bags from the car to the second bedroom as conversation swelled between the ladies, flowed into the house, out of the house, then headed toward the barn.

When he would have hung back and given them time to

themselves, though, Charity slipped her hand into his and brought him into the group. The entire time she showed off the office where she worked, and where the newest batch of kittens were, Suz's and Chelsea's gazes burned on him like a laser.

They were just at the bottom of the loft stairs when Caleb and Tamara unexpectedly stepped into view. Dustin prepared to introduce them when Charity beat him to it. She slipped in front of Caleb with a happy bounce then lightly rested a hand on Tamara's arm.

"Caleb and Tamara, I'd like you to meet my sister, Chelsea, and her wife, Suzanne. Cee and Suz, this is Dustin's oldest brother, Caleb, and his wife, Tamara."

"Nice to meet you both." Caleb held out a hand and they went through the dance of leaning and reaching until everyone had said hello. "Glad we caught you."

Tamara patted Charity's fingers then slipped her arm around Caleb's waist. "We wanted to invite all of you to join us for dinner on Thursday night if it works with your plans."

"We'll be back from camping sometime that afternoon," Dustin pointed out.

Chelsea exchanged a quick glance with her wife, then smiled and nodded. "We'd enjoy that very much."

The next hour vanished in a rush of visiting the goats and the horses they'd be riding the following day.

"It's been a while since I was up on a horse," Suz admitted when they were at the dinner table in the small cottage. "But I'm looking forward to it."

"I've only ridden once before," Chelsea shared.

"Dustin will take it easy on you." Charity passed the potatoes to Dustin. "We'll go slow. I'm still learning, but riding is fun."

"Glad it's moved up from 'it's weird in a good way,'" Dustin teased before reassuring the others. "You'll both do fine. Plus, we won't be riding for too long. The campsite is close enough we could walk out if necessary."

Dinner was still being cleared away when Chelsea hauled out an *Exploding Kittens* game and shook it in the air. "You are losing tonight," she warned.

"Bring it." Charity waggled her brows at her sister. "Losers wash dishes tomorrow morning."

A simple evening of games was followed by time on the porch. Dustin sat beside Charity and listened as the ladies continued to catch up.

Suz eyed him at one point. "You're very willing to open your ears and keep your mouth shut."

"Youngest child," Dustin explained. "Five older siblings. Someone else was always talking." He winked then said good night, leaving them to chat until darkness had fallen.

Charity joined him in bed with a happy sigh.

"Good evening?" he asked.

"Nice and relaxing, thanks." She rolled over him and kissed him firmly before whispering an order. "Now, no nookie—I can't with my sister within hearing distance."

"You're the one who rolled of top of me," he protested, tracing his fingertips along her ribs until she giggled then outright laughed.

"Hey. No fooling around where I can hear you," Chelsea shouted from the other side of the wall. "Lordy, girl. Behave."

"Sorry." Charity grinned at him then kissed his nose and rolled to the side, cuddling in tight.

With a short way to go and very novice riders, Dustin was in no hurry the next morning. Which meant lazing in bed with Charity was followed by a leisurely breakfast with more bacon than he should have consumed.

They were saddled up and on the trail by ten a.m. After helping them load up, Shim waved them off. Kelli and Luke both stopped what they were doing in the nearest arena to offer cheers and encouragement.

"Make Dustin do all the chores, okay?" Luke shouted after them.

Charity lifted a thumbs-up. Everyone laughed as Dustin raised a hand as well, his middle finger on display instead of his thumb.

He guided them slowly but surely away from the ranch along the well-worn path toward the waterfall before switching to a smaller, more secretive route.

Charity was riding well. Suz sat bolt upright but safely on her horse.

Chelsea seemed a little more nervous, so he casually slipped beside her. Rocking gently in the saddle, he eased back and sighed happily. "Gorgeous day for a ride.

"It is." She glanced at him. "I'm doing okay."

"You're doing great. Samson is a very reliable horse. He's also fat and lazy. If you want him to go faster than we are now, you'll have to work your ass off to make him pick up the pace."

She visibly relaxed. "I'm now more okay than I was."

He laughed. "Good. You really are doing great, Cee. Suz as well."

A moment passed, then she spoke. Statement, not question. "Your brother didn't blink yesterday when Suz was introduced as my wife."

Dustin paused. "Um, no. We knew you were married. Charity talks about you guys all the time."

"I'm glad." Chelsea's grin widened. "Let's talk about my sister. You should tell me all about how wonderful you think she is."

The razzing was as familiar as if Luke were there. "You want that list in alphabetical order?"

Chelsea laughed. "That would be a neat trick." She eyed Dustin then nodded. "I like how you look at her."

"She's become important to me," Dustin admitted. He didn't want to go further, though. Figured Charity should be the one he admitted his feelings to for the first time. When it was appropriate and she wasn't about to run away screaming.

Chelsea nodded slowly, as if hearing what he wasn't saying. "You've got to understand that when Charity stands with you, she's all in."

"I'm realizing that. She's been amazing. Throughout the entire social media circus, she just took it all in stride, which is even more amazing considering your upbringing. Even the home invasion—I mean, she was upset, but after the shock wore off, she's just kept going."

"That she does. We have our grandma to thank for that. Lily Dachice stepped up and became the supportive, rock-solid person we needed. She made up for a lot of the things we didn't get from our parents when things fell apart."

"Charity told me about the whole disaster. It sucks that you guys had to deal with all of that. The childhood in the spotlight and losing your family after."

Chelsea considered him. "Sucks that you lost your parents when you were so young."

He shook his head. "Yeah, thanks. But one thing I've been taught over the years by *my* family is that life is not a comparison game. You don't have to turn us talking about your bad shit into talking about what I dealt with. I'm not thinking about me right now, I'm thinking about you guys. I'm glad you had each other and your Grandma Lily. I wish I could have met her."

Those so very watchful eyes were on him again. "I think she would have liked you."

"A high compliment. Thanks." The offered acceptance

started a warm glow in his gut. He turned the conversation in a new direction, pointing to the north. The small clearing tucked beside the creek that flowed out of the lake at the base of the Heart Falls cascade was just visible ahead of them. "There's our campsite."

20

Dustin had taken them in a big circle. Heart Falls cascade and the lake at its base were a landmark in the area, and Charity had been to the overlook dozens of times over the years. Which meant she knew the lake was *here* and the Silver Stone homestead buildings were only just over *there*, no more than a fifteen minute walk away.

But staring at the water from the back of horse, carrying all their camping gear and with plans to stay out for the night, they could have been alone in the wilderness, miles from civilization.

Turning the ordinary moment into something magical.

He led them to the edge of the lake farthest from the mountainside. The water fell from the land above them, bouncing down the rock face in a spray that carried teeny water droplets to mist against her skin. The lake itself was steady, its mirror-like surface reflecting the robin-egg-blue sky overhead.

"That is so pretty." Suz lifted a hand and traced the shoreline with a finger. "The heart-shape really is visible."

"It's amazing." Chelsea shifted in the saddle. "Not to ruin

the moment, but my butt is ready for me to be a walker instead of a rider, ASAP."

They had tents to pitch, a cook station to set up, and horses to be settled. All of which happened in a sweet, lazy rhythm as Dustin directed them from task to task.

"No rush," he insisted. He eyed the food stash. "Well, a little rush, since I'd like lunch sooner than later."

"You and me both." Suz jumped to attention and offered him a salute. "Show me where to set up, and I'll get the food ready."

While Suz focused on lunch, Charity and her sister raised the two tents. Dustin took care of the horses in the small shelter just to the north of their campsite.

He also arranged a bathroom area out of sight from the tents.

When he wandered back from the horse shelter with four folding lawn chairs in his hands, Charity laughed. "You're not making us rough it."

"Wait until you see what's for dinner before you make that type of claim."

She hurried forward to help him arrange the chairs around their firepit. It wasn't luxurious, but it was a lot more comfortable than she thought a typical campout might be. "Did you hide those earlier today?"

He nodded. "Shim and I brought out a few things ahead of time. No use in making this too prickly for you greenhorns. It's supposed to be a holiday."

Charity slipped in close and stole a kiss. "Thank you. And my butt thanks you."

He patted her hip affectionately before she could pull away. "Your butt is very welcome. Although now I'm sad I can't offer to rub any sore spots"

She eyed the distance between the two tents and

considered how quiet she could be while being playful with Dustin. "Maybe there can be some rubbing later tonight. Strictly therapeutic, of course."

"Of course." He kissed her again then murmured, "Just to remind you you're very loud when you come."

"That's not increasing your chances of rubbing," she warned, dancing out of reach while she planned her next bit of mischief.

She glanced over to discover Chelsea with a handful of LED lights and a solar panel shaped like a small free-standing lantern. "You remembered."

"As if I'd forget." Chelsea eyed the campsite. From where they were, the lake was out of sight, and the steady hum of the waterfall distant white noise. She pointed to the small gathering of trees at the edge of the nearby creek. "There?"

Charity finished rummaging through her day bag and pulled out her own set of solar-powered lights. "Sure. You do the trees, I'll do the path."

Chelsea paced forward to get started.

"What's happening?" Dustin asked Suz as he carried up one final item—a small folding table that he put down beside the woman.

She was relaxing beside the firepit, watching the action. An enormous stack of sandwiches, cookies and fruit were laid out on the flat surface of a nearby rock.

Suz patted the chair next to her. "Come sit, my fine young man. And I'll tell you the tale of the never-ending lights."

"Tell her to use the fun voices," Charity called as she joined her sister.

"Hush, child. Storyteller mode engaged," Suz scolded.

Dustin nabbed a sandwich and sat. Chelsea and Charity both moved quietly so they could listen while setting up a small oasis on the bank of the creek.

"A young woman woke one morning feeling sad and alone. 'Feelings are feelings, but I don't want to stay sad. How can I make myself happy on this cold, dark day?' she asked herself. She decided that a touch of brightness was the answer. Something she might not see during the daylight but that could be a guiding light at night and in future dark moments." Suz took a sip from her water bottle. "Your turn, Cee."

Chelsea twisted a cord of LED lights into the branches of a rosebush as she told the next part of the story. "The first night when she looked outside, the small light was barely visible against the darkness. But day after day, the girl did what she could to add brightness to her world."

"Days passed. Weeks. Years. Until the young girl became an old woman," Suz said, speaking slower, her voice changing to that of someone who'd lived a long life. "And when she looked out of her house at night, the small, insignificant touches of brightness were now so many, that an entire universe of stars shone back through the darkness."

The story was such a part of her past that Charity felt it bubbling inside. She pushed her final solar charger into the earth and crossed to Dustin's side.

He tugged her into his lap, and she laughed, settling comfortably.

"It's a beautiful story," Dustin said, his gaze drifting over Charity's sister and her wife as they tucked their heads together and kissed softly.

"Small touches of brightness add up. Our grandmother taught that story, and she demonstrated how to live the lesson daily." Charity laid her head on his chest to listen to his heartbeat. She wanted to say something else. Something profound. Something sweet—

Something more than silence, but that's what came out.

She didn't want to break the unspoken connection between them.

His stomach rumbled a moment later, loud enough everyone heard, and amusement carried on the air.

"Don't worry, Dustin, we'll save you." Suz pulled Charity from his lap. "Get your own seat, Tee. Time for lunch."

Chelsea passed Dustin a filled plate with a firm order. "Eat. We have an entire afternoon and evening of adventuring to enjoy, and we can't have you fading away from hunger."

Another short ride after lunch was followed by a walk around the lake. Charity held Dustin's hand as they strolled, the temperature heating up to scalding summer conditions.

When they gathered around the fire to cook hotdogs to go with premade salads and an assortment of chips, Suz shocked her wife by joining Dustin in singing some off-colour songs involving buckle-bunnies and rodeo stars.

Chelsea stared at Suz. "You never told me you knew cheesy country and western—"

"Cheesy, *dirty*, country and western," Dustin inserted, shoving his roaster stick farther into the flames. "You're my fave, Suz."

"Of course, I am." She held up a hand and he high-fived her.

It was late before the sun dropped behind the mountains, and even later when the sky changed from crimson and gold to twilight pinks. On the opposite side, the moon was already up, its surface glowing brighter and brighter in the eastern sky.

Suz and Chelsea sat side by side, staring into the fire and talking quietly, hands linked and heads close together.

Dustin caught Charity by the fingers and tugged her toward the darkness. "Come on." Patchwork Annie made as if to rise and join them, but Dustin waved her back. "Stay."

The pup resettled with an enormous sigh, sad eyes watching them leave.

"Poor pupper," Charity whispered.

"Poor pup, my ass. Your sister-in-law fed Annie three hotdogs on the sly at suppertime. The dog can stay by the fire and enjoy her full belly."

Charity chuckled as he led her away from camp. The glow from the fire and the lights she and her sister had set up faded behind them quickly. The moonlight overhead and the rising sound of the waterfall was her only clue of what direction they were headed. "Are we going to the lake?"

"You'll see in a second. Around the corner, and..." The trees vanished to their right, and a shimmering oasis greeted her.

He'd set up his own set of lights.

They reflected off the water like dozens of twinkling stars. A small semi-circle tucked to the edge of the lake away from the falls.

Dustin guided her over the rocks, slowing his step. "Careful here. That's it. And...we're here."

The rock nearest to the water was flat and smooth, and another of his pre-planned setups appeared. "Is that a picnic blanket?" she asked.

Dustin scooped her off her feet, ignoring her inhale of surprise. "It's a blanket, but I failed to pack a picnic."

"Oh," she said, nodding sagely. "It's a sleeping blanket."

"*Buzz.* Second wrong answer."

He lowered her feet to the ground and pulled their bodies together, his solid muscles pressed to her softness—the hardness of his cock clear and rising.

Charity hummed happily. "Oh, I get it. It's a *naughty* blanket."

He eyed her, amusement tinged with suspicion. "I'm not sure if I should say yes to that or not."

"It's where naughty people get sent for time out when they've been bad." Charity squealed as he spun her in a circle. "But you're never bad. You're very, very good. Does that mean *you* don't get to be on the blanket?"

Dustin tugged her shirt free from her shorts. "You said we can't have sex where your sister can hear." He lifted his brows. "Problem solved."

"Okay." She ripped off her T-shirt then reached for his clothes. "In case that wasn't clear, sex on the naughty blanket is a go."

The warm night air caressed over the faint sheen of sweat on her skin as he stripped her naked. There was something deliciously...well, *naughty*... about being nude outdoors. Tucked into the little alcove, no one could spot them, yet with the stars and moon overhead, they were clearly right there in the open. The perfect balance between risk and safety.

The small lights Dustin had strung along the water's edge glowed candlelight yellow over flexing muscles as his strong body was revealed. Fingers drifting over his skin, she paced around him in a circle, amazed that she got to do this. To touch, kiss, taste.

Lips pressed to his, skin to skin. Breasts to his chest, his cock against her belly, they tangled around each other with reckless abandon. His hands on her ass squeezed tight before he cupped her breast, dipped his head, and sucked her nipple into his mouth.

She scratched her nails over his shoulders, digging in when he nipped. "God, yes."

Dustin took her to the blanket and covered her. Kisses to her skin, over her breasts. Teasing and tasting and taking in her gasps of pleasure with obvious delight as he moved down her body.

He pushed her knees up and stared down, head shaking slightly. "Such a pretty pussy. I've missed you."

Charity laughed, the sound morphing into a moan as he covered her with his mouth. Tongue sliding into her sex, licking her clit and over her labia. Quick motions that rapidly sent her tumbling toward an orgasm. "Tell me you remembered to bring a condom."

He licked slower, edging her need higher before he paused to grin at her. "I brought a blanket and lights. Hell, yes, I remembered the condoms."

Dustin patted the blanket to one side, running his fingers over the surface until he found a pocket she hadn't even noticed. He slid out a condom, and she curled upright to open it.

They worked together to put it on him, laughing between kisses, curling around each other. Skin contact seemed vital, and when she finally crawled into his lap and eased over his length, they both sighed happily.

His arms tight around her, torsos gliding skin on skin through each lift and lower. The thick length of his cock inside her rubbed perfectly on each stroke.

She relaxed her head until her curls brushed her back. The position arched her torso toward him, and Dustin teased a nipple with one hand. The other hand pressed firmly to her lower back to keep them connected, rubbing together, sliding sweat-slicked skin over and over as he pulsed upward.

Her orgasm broke sharply, bright and beautiful and perfect. A shimmering moment of pleasure echoed a second later in his face as Dustin let go and joined her. His body rocked, fingertips indenting her skin where he grasped her. Bodies shaking with their releases.

Moments after, she rested her forehead against his shoulder. Their breathing was still ragged, bodies quivering with pleasure. She lifted her gaze to his and the corners of his eyes crinkled as he smiled back. It felt real. *They* felt real.

A sudden light flared overhead as a shooting star raced across the sky above them, and Charity made a silent wish.

Please let it be real.

21

_L_ess than twenty-four hours later, they were gathered by another fire, contentment soaked into Charity's bones.

They'd had an amazing camping trip. Suz and Chelsea had been over the moon about everything Dustin had done to make the time special. They'd all slept in, and the lazy morning that followed, with a swim in the lake before the short ride back to the barn, had been picture perfect and full of memory-making moments.

They'd showered, relaxed some more, then made their way over to the main ranch house in time for dinner.

Tamara handed them each something to carry then pointed outside. "The kids voted for a picnic dinner, since you obviously didn't get enough outdoor time the past two days."

"Picnic by the fire sounds wonderful. It's not something we get back home," Chelsea assured her.

"We have squishmallows," little Tyler announced, catching Suz by the hand and tugging her toward the door. "You sit with me."

"I would be delighted," Suz informed him, winking at Tamara. "I'll need help with the squishmallows, but after we eat our suppers."

"'kay," he agreed somewhat reluctantly.

Tamara chuckled as she walked beside Chelsea and Charity to the firepit area. "Your wife knows the secrets of dealing with children."

"She works in pediatrics," Chelsea offered.

"Interesting. I used to be a nurse. We'll have to exchange war stories."

Dustin helped Caleb with the barbeque while the rest of them found seats around the fire. Emma and Sasha instantly latched onto Chelsea, asking questions about her job as a recreation director at a large fitness facility.

Charity settled beside Tamara, content to watch and listen.

The older woman beside her examined her family, a satisfied smile on her lips before turning her attention on Charity. "You have a good time camping?" Tamara asked quietly.

"We really did. Thanks for letting Dustin have the time off."

Tamara shrugged. "He's never been one to ask for vacations. Silver Stone probably owes him a ton of holiday hours."

"He's not complaining about his workload," Charity assured her. "He adores the ranch and the time he spends on horseback. He likes the chores and the time with his brothers. And your girls and the chores with them." She snickered. "He likes chores a little too much, it seems."

"You guys have had a lot of time to talk over the past weeks, haven't you?" Tamara's gaze was still accepting, but there was something else there as well. A question that Charity wasn't sure how to answer.

She went with the bare minimum truth. "We did. I mean, we've always been friendly, but now I think we're really friends."

"Burgers are ready," Caleb called. "Build your plate at the table here. Dustin will bring you your drink."

Everyone stood to put together their meals, and the moment was pushed aside, which was good because Charity wasn't sure how to deal with the emotions welling up inside.

Friends, yes. But what did she do with the part that said they were more?

They'd barely settled back in place, full plates balanced on laps, when a call rang out from the direction of the house. "Hey, Stone family."

Fern came rushing up the path, aimed straight at Charity and Dustin. At the last second, though, she twisted and stopped short, gaze jumping between the two of them and Caleb and Tamara.

"Sorry for crashing your party, but I couldn't wait."

Tamara gestured for her to continue. "It's not a problem. Are you okay?

"Yes. I mean, I don't have a problem; I solved one." Fern shook her head. "I'm befuddled. Hi Chelsea, hi Suz. I'm Charity's friend, Fern. The point is, I figured it out. I know who doxxed Dustin."

Stunned silence greeted her announcement. Charity had to switch her brain from the family gathering mode to social media circus.

Chelsea caught up the quickest. "You did? How? All her posts were screenshots with her name scratched out. There was no way to follow those back to the source."

"That's what we figured." Fern's gaze sharpened to daggers. "But if it was an *accidental* screenshot share, it should have been limited to one or two at the most. The fact that so many shared and it went viral means someone deliberately set it up. They posted a comment, took a screenshot, and deleted the original before anyone noticed. Over and over. There were time stamps of four a.m. on a couple of them."

"Deliberate, then." Tamara nodded. "Makes sense if she was trying to keep her information offline."

"Yes. But once she'd scrubbed out her info, she still needed people to share without her name involved. A few people looped in automatically because she linked to the article when it was getting a lot of eyes on it. Used their *#silverstonestud*. But all the initial sharing was done by one woman who set up new accounts the day everything went out."

Caleb shook his head. "I'm not up on all the social media business, but if you say it can be done, it can. The main question is, *who?*"

Thank goodness Fern got straight to the point this time. "Patricia Hawkins."

Beside Charity, Dustin cursed softly enough that Tyler wouldn't hear it. "No. Way."

"That was going to be my next question." Charity frowned at him. "Do you know this woman?"

Tamara answered for him as Dustin had shot to his feet and stomped away from the gathering, glaring up at the sky. "She used to live in Heart Falls. She bought Dustin during his first year in the bachelor auction."

Sasha's jaw dropped. "Her? She was the one who went stalkerish on him, right?"

Tamara's expression hardened. "Sent him flowers every day for a week before Caleb tracked her down at work and told her that was enough."

It was Caleb's turn to mutter a curse. He turned to face Charity. "I guess that answers another question. Back then she was the supervisor at the complex your apartment is in."

God. "She must have still had a set of master keys, so she didn't need to break in."

Tamara nodded slowly, taking in all the twists and turns before asking Fern, "Did you figure this out by yourself?"

"Most of it." Fern grinned widely. "Shim helped. And when we ran out of technological ability, we called in a secret weapon."

Tamara raised a brow.

Fern pointed at her. "Your sister Julia has a major geek in her husband's family. Petra Sorensen can make computers spill all their secrets."

"A good person to have on our side, then. Thanks." Tamara narrowed her gaze. "Now we'll be able to put an end to this nonsense."

Charity held up a hand. "We can't change what she's done."

"No," Caleb agreed, "but legally we can convince her to stay offline in the future, away from you, and away from Stone property."

Dustin returned then, settling into his chair beside her with a heartfelt sigh. "I feel terrible about all of this. I'm so sorry, Tee. It's all my fault. You shouldn't have had to deal with any of this crap."

"Oh, that's enough of that nonsense." Again, Chelsea beat everyone to the punch. She folded her arms over her chest and glared at him. "Speaking from experience, if you didn't choose for it to be posted online, it's not your fault. Someone else's bad choices are *not* your responsibility. How you reacted to the nonsense was your choice, and you did everything you could. So skip the guilt, and thanks for taking care of my sister."

Dustin was speechless for a second before nodding, the tension easing from his strong body. "You're welcome."

"'Tee, this means you'll be able to go home." Suz breathed a sigh of relief before turning toward Caleb and Tamara. "Like Cee said, we're so grateful you gave her a safe place to stay."

"We were happy to do it," Tamara said before her gaze returned to Charity. "But you're not going anywhere until we confirm Patty has been dealt with. She doesn't even live in Heart Falls anymore as far as I know, so this might take a while to untangle. For now, you'll stay put, understood?"

"Thank you. Again."

Except the warmth inside had vanished. Not even Dustin's arm around her waist could help.

Charity glanced around the firepit, something uncomfortable twisting inside her. The social media circus had died down. The fake girlfriend idea had no reason to continue past the day of the auction in the first place. Her time at Silver Stone for safety reasons was nearing an end.

This wasn't what she wanted. To be done with Dustin and his family. The thought made her ache inside.

Which meant somehow, sometime soon, she needed to be brave enough to do the right thing. To share how she felt and pray that Dustin felt even the slightest bit the way she did.

It's not always easy to do what's right, but we do it anyway.

Charity had always related her grandmother's words to actions. Breaking from the toxic situation of her childhood. Stepping up to be there for someone who needed her. Now she saw a glimmer of the truth that the message was broader.

Just like the lights in her grandmother's story were a physical representation of the very abstract concept of *acts of kindness*. Doing what's right meant being brave enough to not just stand with Dustin when he needed her, but to share that now, she needed him.

Physically, yes. But more importantly, on an emotional level. As more than a friend.

I'm falling in love with him.

Even saying the words in her head came reluctantly. Which meant she was going to have to be extra brave and pony up an extra serving of courage.

If she could give a virtual stranger hell for not appreciating his family, she could tell one generous, kind, gorgeous young man that he'd stolen her heart.

She'd just have to pray that he wouldn't break it by giving it back.

22

———

ustin's first shift back started so early on Friday that he said goodbye to Chelsea and Suz before hitting the sack. Kissing Charity and leaving her all warm and cozy in bed at five the next morning sucked.

"I'll message you when I'm on break," he whispered.

"'kay," she whispered sleepily. "'nub ya."

His feet were glued to the floor as he tried to figure out the whispered gibberish. "Tee?"

But she was asleep again, fingers curled around his pillow as she cuddled it to her body.

He'd never been more jealous of an inanimate object before in his life.

He went through the motions that morning, most of his brain still pondering her words. Another part was rehashing the revelation that all the social media bullshit and his phone number getting out were from a past bachelor auction date.

A sharp jab in his arm made him jerk upright. "Ouch."

He glared at Shim, who still held the shovel he'd tagged Dustin with in his hands.

"You were sleepwalking. I hear it's dangerous to wake people like that." His friend nodded toward his pocket. "You're buzzing."

Shit. Dustin pulled out his phone to find a message from his brother.

Walker: *You and Charity still on for supper tonight?*
Dustin: *Umm, maybe? Did I know about this?*
Walker: *Ivy said you did. Does it work?*
Dustin: *Good by me. I'll double-check with Charity and get back to you.*
Walker: *Perfect. The kids are over the moon at the idea of seeing you two, but we can always rebook if she's busy.*

Dustin checked his watch, considering if it was too early to message Tee. She'd be spending her last bit of time with her family before they left. Still, she could answer when it worked.

He sent off a quick note then put his back into the job at hand, helping Shim dig a new trench to install power to an outbuilding.

"Everything okay?" Shim asked.

"Just Walker checking in." Dustin shook his head. "Sorry. I've had my head up my ass all morning. Thanks for your help in figuring out who posted my info."

"No problem. I liked the challenge, although it sucks who it turned out to be." Shim cleared his throat. "Not that you have to share, but since I'm now imagining all the terrible things that might happen after my bachelor auction date..."

"Oh God, no. You should be fine." Dustin paused. "And I'm not saying that to be reassuring. Looking back on it, Patty was off from the get-go. I was eighteen, and she was in her late twenties. I took her for lunch at Buns and Roses for our date, and all she wanted to talk about was how she knew she was destined to be a rodeo princess."

"Good rider?"

Dustin shook his head. "Nope. She figured marrying the right rancher meant she'd have all the horses and land and adoration she deserved without needing the skills."

Shim made a face. "I'm sure eighteen-year-old you was thrilled at the discussion of marriage."

"She talked in circles. I have to admit I wasn't smart enough to figure out what she was hinting at until years later. The flowers she sent me daily for a week after the date were strange enough to make me gun-shy."

His friend stomped on the head of his shovel then tossed another load of dirt to the side. "I'm glad she won't be an issue in the future."

"Caleb said he talked to the RCMP again this morning to make sure his complaint from last night is being dealt with. That should be the end of it." Thank God.

The rest of the shift was ordinary. Charity confirmed their dinner plans. Dustin enjoyed working with Shim, who admitted he really should be in the office but had switched stuff up.

"I asked Tucker to make sure I'm on the regular chore list as well as tech support. Even if I'm busy with computer stuff, I need time like this."

"Agreed." Dustin tossed a dirt ball at his friend and laughed as he avoided the return volley.

By four thirty he was washed up and ready to roll. Charity blasted through the doors of the cottage, rushing to the shower. "I need fifteen minutes," she shouted. "There were goats. Again."

He caught her by the arm and halted her forward

momentum. "You can have thirty, but there's a toll to pay before you go any farther."

She raised a brow.

Dustin puckered up.

Charity smirked, reached into her pocket, and pulled out a lip balm. "Here you go."

When she would have smeared his lips using the tube, he scooped her up and kissed her soundly. Dropping her to her feet, he patted her on the butt toward the shower. "Nice try."

Patchwork Annie was curled up on the porch when they left half an hour later. She wagged her tail but happily stayed in place.

"Lazy beast." Dustin opened the truck door for Charity. "I guess that means she feels the cottage is home."

"She was a good girl, staying with me all day." Charity hummed thoughtfully. "I guess we don't need to worry about her doing that anymore."

Dustin was already closing the truck door, but the comment gave him a bit of a jolt. He pondered the idea the entire walk to the driver's seat. Charity didn't need protection anymore. She didn't need to stay at Silver Stone once Caleb confirmed Patty had been dealt with.

Except, she had to stay.

Screw it. What he wanted, and his new plans for the future, *had* to be discussed as soon as dinner with his family was over.

Charity was quiet as well, staring out the window as if deep in thought.

"Missing your family already?" he asked, closing the distance between them to take her hand.

"Hm, what's that?" Charity blinked then pulled on a sort of smile. "Oh, yeah. It was great to see them."

He wanted to offer for the ladies to come visit anytime, but that discussion needed to come after dinner as well.

Nine-year-old Carter opened the front door for them and all but shouted a welcome. "Hey. Dad is burning something. Mom went outside to help."

"It's always nice to have help burning things," Dustin replied, hand on Charity's back guiding her inside.

Charity stepped into the house and was mobbed by Carter's sisters. Harper and Chloe immediately demanded she watch their dance steps.

Carter took Dustin by the hand and pulled him into the family room. Little boy super-serious expression on his face, he folded his arms over his chest. "I can dance, too."

"Really?"

Carter lifted his chin as if daring him to say something rude.

Not happening. Dustin just nodded. "Good for you. Charity taught me to dance a few years ago. I'm out of practice, but do you want to see *my* routine?"

Carter's jaw dropped, then he nodded eagerly.

Which meant when Charity walked into the room with the girls, Dustin was in mid-pirouette. By the time Ivy and Walker entered the house, Dustin had all three children copying his pliés while Charity applauded furiously.

"Well done for an impromptu performance," Ivy said. She pointed to the hallway. "Wash your hands and come to the table."

Conversation was never dull when there were children involved. Dustin and Charity chatted with his brother and sister-in-law while answering endless questions about the horses, the trucks, how much water fell into the lake every day, why blue was better than green, and how much dirt weighed.

By the time dinner was over, Dustin's ears were ringing in a good way.

Ivy shooed all of them to the backyard. "Walker cooked, so I'll clean up."

Walker kissed her temple. "You'll have a quiet house for an hour," he promised.

"Thank you," she whispered before winking at Charity. "You too, outside. Washing up alone, in the quiet, is one of my coping strategies."

"I'm all for a good coping strategy," Charity said, scooping up Harper and heading for the backyard. "Say 'have fun with the bubbles, Mama.'"

"Have fun bubbles, Mama," five-year-old Harper repeated, hanging off Charity to offer Ivy a smacking kiss.

A few years back, Walker had gotten his brothers' help to build a playhouse in the backyard with swings and monkey bars and a small house section with a porch. Plastic flowers grew in the window box, and the entire thing had been painted in bright, rainbow colours.

The kids ran wild, laughing and shouting. A near constant chorus of, "Look at me, Uncle Dustin. Push me, Auntie Tee," rang out as well.

Walker nudged Dustin's arm. "You plan to do something about that?"

Dustin paused. "Which part?"

"The kids are calling her auntie." Walker shrugged. "I don't mind, but you should make sure she's onboard with it."

Tongue-tied, Dustin watched Charity dance with Chloe around the sandbox. "Soon."

Walker stared out at his children, grin growing wider. Then he made a clucking noise.

For fuck's sake. Dustin glared at him. "I'm not chicken, I've been waiting until—"

He stalled out. Waiting until...what?

The truth up and smacked him with a two-by-four. There was no reason to wait. He'd liked Charity and planned to tell her that they should date for real. Then the vandalism had happened. Since then the connection between them had simply kept growing, even without him saying a word.

What the hell had he been thinking?

A hand waved in front of his face. "Earth to Dustin."

Shit. He snapped his attention to his brother. "I'm an idiot."

Walker shrugged. "It seems we all are at some point when it comes to our women." He pointed to the graveyard beside the house. "Maybe it's time to talk more and idiot less."

Dustin wasn't sure why she was there, walking through the cemetery. The children were all happily making a massive sandcastle, so he left his brother with them and hurried after Charity.

A graveyard. Seemed as good a place as any to straighten out the mess he'd made of things.

He approached slowly, partly because it was a place to be quiet, and partly because Charity was kneeling beside the fence, working intently on something.

Stopping far enough away he wouldn't frighten her, he spoke. "Hey, whatcha doing?"

23

———————

Caught red-handed with a small solar light in her hand, Charity decided to tell the truth. "Changing some batteries."

A line creased between his brows then cleared as Dustin put two and two together. "You're the one who's been putting the lights up. For the past four years, no one could figure out who's been doing it. It was you all along."

Charity finished her task then stood, fingers tangled together. "I know Grandma's story was about acts of kindness, but putting out actual lights made me feel closer to her. And once I started, I didn't want to stop."

Deep-felt emotion welled up, and everything she'd been holding back for so long rushed out of her. No longer could she hold this inside. No more waiting and wondering.

It was time.

She snatched up his hands. "I don't want to stop this either."

Confusion returned to his face. "Tee?"

She swallowed hard then hurried ahead. "Being your

girlfriend. I like it. I don't want to go back to just friends. And I'm not only talking about the sex."

She squeezed her eyes tight. She couldn't bear to see him try to find a kind way to turn her down.

Concern laced his voice as he stroked his palms up her arms. "What's wrong? Why are you looking like that?"

She opened one eye a sliver, fighting for courage. "I don't want to hear you tell me that it's been fun but it's over."

The noise that escaped him was part cry and part laugh. He snatched her up and held her so tightly his heartbeat pulsed against her torso. "We're not just friends," he told her firmly. "Fuck that noise."

Relief swamped her, and she buried her face in his neck. Fighting back tears of fear and hope.

Dustin stroked her back and made reassuring sounds "I'm sorry you were worried. I should have said something sooner." He shook his head. "Somewhere between us germ proofing each other and now, I lost the ability to be straight up and say what I think. So fucking stupid."

She snorted. "Not really. It's hard. I mean, I feel as if people might know what they want to say but actually saying it has got to one of the toughest things in the world."

Determined expression back in place, Dustin led her to the bench under the tower maple in the center of the yard. They sat, and he held her hands, staring at their linked fingers. "Last night, when Suz said how you could go home now, my gut said you already *were* home."

Which was how she felt inside. Panic began to fade.

"It's like in your Grandma Lily's story." Dustin curled his arm tighter around her as if trying to mesh them together.

"The lights?" She glanced at the solar lights all around the cemetery. There really were a lot of them after all these years.

"No, although it is nice to finally have solved the mystery of who put them up. Everyone in Heart Falls has been wondering."

"It's been fun to keep it a secret." Guilt struck for a moment. "Although, I'm not really doing it for others—if that doesn't sound really selfish."

"I get it," Dustin insisted. "Consider it a side benefit. They're very pretty, and people appreciate the cheeriness." He cupped her face, turning her toward him. "I was thinking about how in your grandma's story, each small moment seemed insignificant by itself. But they added up, over and over, until they were as bright as a starry night."

She waited.

"That's like you and me. We've been friends for a while, but these past weeks have been full of bright moments. It feels as if *here* is simply where we were meant to be. We never had to take a ninety degree turn in the road, we never had to up and announce *hey, we should date.*"

"But we are saying that. Yes? We should date?"

He laughed. "Yes. Definitely, yes."

"I want to be with you." She said it as plain and simply as possible.

The brightness in his eyes was nearly blinding. "I think I'm in love with you."

Her heart skipped a beat. "Oh, wow."

Before she could say anything else, he leaned in and kissed her. Sweet and soft and heartachingly tender. Her heart pounded and everything inside was singing with hope.

They pulled apart far enough Dustin cupped her face in his palm. "That's for you, because you were brave enough to tell me the truth even when you weren't sure what I'd say. Because you were brave enough to make this stubborn cowboy want to do better."

She met his gaze straight on. "I'm pretty sure I'm in love with you, as well."

His grin flashed this time. "Convenient. Practical."

Charity snickered. "Magical."

"That too."

He lifted her into his lap and held her close, chin resting on her curls. A moment of peace in the middle of the storm.

The sound of his nieces and nephew playing drifted from the yard beside them. Happiness clear in their laughter.

He stiffened slightly then spoke softly. "Not that I want to scare you away right when we're finally getting our shit together, but are you okay with my family? The whole big, overbearing, in-your-face lot of them?"

Charity took a deep breath before answering. "They did kind of scare me at first, especially Caleb. Your family can be intense, but it's kind of like horseback riding."

"It feels weirdly good?" he teased.

She pressed her fingers to his mouth, her own lips curling into a smile. "It felt like a sport that looked interesting, but I could never join in. But that was my lack of experience. Once I put my foot in the stirrup and went along for the ride, your family feels right. Comfortable yet exciting, and something I can enjoy."

The relief on his face was crystal clear. "Your family is wonderful, too."

"Chelsea likes you. Suz is crazy about you," Charity teased.

He turned her in his arms, nestling her in tighter. "I'm a one-woman man, and you're it, Tee. Let's figure out how to make this work for real. No more pretend, nothing because we have to."

"But we're still a *hashtag cute country couple.*"

He laughed. "Yes, we are. And chances are we'll be a few more hashtags in the future since that sort of nonsense never really goes away. But I'll do my best to make sure anything I say that ends up online will be with your consent."

"Easy promise since you're never online," Charity said.

Dustin paused. "I'm thinking about all the interview requests. Maybe Silver Stone should do one. And of all the family members, I'm the most logical to deal with the media right now."

She hadn't considered that a possibility, but even as they sat there, tangled together, the idea made sense. "I'm not jumping up and down excited, but it might be a good plan."

"Just starting to consider it." Dustin tucked her hair behind her ear. "That's a question for down the road. Now I have other more important things for you to consider."

"While sitting in a graveyard?"

His brown eyes flashed with amusement. "No one here with buttinski habits. It's just you and me. And a hundred solar lights."

She laughed then sobered. "You're right. This is a good place to make decisions."

Dustin tucked his knuckles under her chin, gaze caressing her gently. "Will you move in with me for real? Be my girlfriend and learn new things with me? Will you give us a chance to see if maybe this in-love thing is as sweet as I think it is?"

Her heart up and overflowed. "Okay."

Laughter burst from him in one huge explosion of happiness. "Okay from me too."

Charity found herself swept up in his arms. Twirling in a circle, her feet so far off the ground she could be flying, she held on for dear life until Dustin slowed and lowered her, still tucked against his body.

She pressed her hands to his face. "You make me happy."

"Ditto." He leaned in and kissed her again. This time with enough heat to make her toes curl.

A long sharp whistle rang from her left. Charity snapped her attention to the side to discover Carter stood on the fence railing, his faced screwed up in confusion. "Dad says you need to stop kissing before someone complains." Carter frowned harder, looking all around the cemetery in confusion. "Who's going to complain? Dead people don't talk."

Dustin chuckled. He caught Charity's hand in his and led her toward the fence. "You're right. No one in here minds kissing one bit. But your Dad is right too. We should come back to your house."

"Mom is still having quiet time," Carter warned. He bounced his way to Charity's other side, and suddenly she was holding hands with two Stone men, albeit one only nine years old. "Can you show us some other dance stuff, Auntie Tee?"

"Of course." Charity glanced at Dustin who was grinning at her. "Uncle Dustin will help."

"*Wheeeeee*." Carter took off like a shot, racing across the yard ahead of them to share the news with his dad and sisters. The three of them were now blowing bubbles, and dozens of shimmering balls floated up and eastward on the light breeze.

"My whole big, overwhelming family loves you already," Dustin said quietly.

Her heart pulsed hard. "Then we've got a good chance of the *maybe we're in love* thing sticking."

"Maybe." Dustin spun her, out, then back into his arms, gilding them into a smooth two-step as he danced them toward the children. "I'm betting on it."

Charity let the whirlwind that was Dustin twirl her around and around as bubbles shimmered in the air around them like a thousand moments of joy.

24

---

*D*ustin had a new level of respect for his brothers. How the hell had they been crawling out of bed every morning these past years, leaving their women behind, all warm and sexy as sin?

He nuzzled Charity's neck, reluctant to start his day without her. "Wake up enough to kiss me before I go," he ordered.

"Can I kiss you and stay asleep?" she muttered.

"Nope. I need full consent."

"Fine." She rolled unexpectedly and he ended up under her. The pouf of hair poking from her high ponytail bounced as she nodded happily. "Well, now. Look what I found in my bed."

"*Our* bed." Dustin curled his arms around her and kissed her long and deep, just because he could.

When he was done, Charity was flushed and breathing hard. "So much for sleeping in," she complained. "Now I'm hot and bothered."

"I'd do something about that, but Caleb will kick my butt if I'm late."

"Oh, I can take care of it myself." She waggled her brows.

The image of her stroking herself to a climax nearly killed him. "You're an evil wench. Which means you go right ahead. Imagining you with your hands between your legs will make for a great daydream."

Firm hands cupped his face. She swallowed hard then smiled like the sun. "I love you."

A shot of adrenaline raced up his spine like an explosive. "Holy shit. Really? Now I'm totally going to be late."

Her laugh was swallowed up by his kiss.

If it had been up to him, he'd have said screw it to work. But a moment later Charity was off the bed, shaking a finger at him when he would have hauled her back to the mattress. "Yes, I decided enough dithering with *maybes* and *falling*. I. Love. You. Now, go to work so your brothers don't make you stay late."

Dustin stood and held up a hand with a raised finger. "One, your timing sucks. Just saying."

She grinned.

"Two, meet me at the arena at four, and we'll go for a ride."

"Sure. Sounds great."

He wasn't done. He held up one more finger. "My brothers had better appreciate that I'm on time today in spite of number three."

She raised a brow.

Dustin spoke quietly. "I love you, too."

Charity pressed her hands to her face. "Go to work, right now, before we make unwise choices," she ordered.

"Going."

He kissed her again, though. Soft. Slow. Pulling back to say it again. "I love you, Tee. See you this afternoon."

The warmth of her words carried him all the way to the barn. Hell, he doubted his feet hit the ground the entire trip.

Fortunately, Dustin beat Caleb to the stalls by all of thirty seconds, which gave him time to at least try to wipe what he assumed was a goofy grin off his face.

Didn't work. His brother still raised a brow en route to saddling his horse. "Interesting."

Nope. Dustin wasn't about to apologize for being on cloud nine. "I'm in love," he blurted out.

Sudden silence fell in the stall next to him.

Dustin stepped to the side and glanced in to discover his usually staid and solid brother grinning at the ceiling.

"What?" Dustin demanded.

Caleb shrugged. "I just noticed your shadow isn't with you. Your dog, who's usually underfoot, is still somewhere else. That's all I was talking about."

Dammit. Still wasn't going to apologize. Dustin lifted his chin. "Well, Patchwork Annie loves Tee, too."

If anything, Caleb's grin got wider. "I'm happy for you. Is it safe to assume she feels the same?"

"Absolutely. Tee definitely loves Annie."

At that one, Caleb hooted out loud. Then he stepped over and caught Dustin up in a huge hug. "You're such a smart-ass. Glad for you, little bro. Now stop mooning over your woman and get your tail in gear."

"You're the one manhandling me," Dustin grumbled, getting in a few back pats of his own before returning to the task of getting ready for the day. He'd been flying so high he hadn't even noticed that Patchwork Annie had remained back on the porch. Which was amazing and special in an entirely different way.

He totally loved Charity enough to share his dog with her.

He and Caleb were out on the trail shortly, headed to check the grazing land in one of the farther fields.

"You guys plan to stay at the cottage?" Caleb asked after a while.

"I guess. If that's okay with Dare and the family."

Caleb lifted his shoulders in an easy shrug. "Everyone else has settled into their new homes. Seems the place is a good fit for you two if she's happy there."

"I'll ask, but I'm pretty sure it is." Dustin thought of another thing. "You okay with her working the office?"

His brother snorted then cleared his throat. "Not a problem. Family works the ranch. Some indoors, some out."

Dustin eyed him with suspicion. "What was that about?"

"Nothing." Caleb pointed ahead of them. "Wild sage is taking over this section. We'll need to do some careful burning to stop it from spreading to the grain fields."

Total avoidance of his question, but Dustin didn't care. Having Caleb share ideas for the coming year and ask Dustin's opinion—it was another layer of family. Another part of finding a solid foundation for himself and Charity to set down their own roots.

He and Caleb stopped at noon and sat on the ground, staring out over Silver Stone land as they ate sandwiches from their panniers and drank wicked-strong coffee. Caleb left him after lunch, grimacing as he patted Dustin's shoulder. "Have fun finishing up this afternoon. I have paperwork to deal with."

"Better you than me," Dustin teased before offering his brother a hand. "Thanks for the great morning."

Caleb shook it firmly. "You mean thanks for not teasing the hell out of you for being in *lurve*." He said the word the way his daughters would have, twenty letters long and full of sparkling heart eyes.

"Such an ass," Dustin muttered, but he smiled.

Riding northward, his head was full of Charity and the ranch. So many things he wanted to show her, so many things she still had to share with him. Dustin had to keep pulling his attention back to the checks he needed to do of the fences, the shelters, the gates.

A thin line of smoke circled upward from the north, and he swore. Unexpected smoke was always a danger on the ranch.

His good mood vanishing, Dustin sat upright in the saddle and edged his heels into Molasses's flanks to make her go a little faster.

He wasn't really surprised when the smoke led him to the small shelter where he and Luke had discovered signs of earlier trespassers. He still didn't believe it was a great spot for teens to hang out, though. Was it someone homeless? Someone lingering after the media crush in the hopes of more story?

If it was the first, the ranch had long ago put a system in place to help squatters get back on their feet and off the land. If it was the second, the trespassers were about to find out Silver Stone had a powerful legal team in place to take care of the assholes who didn't understand boundary lines.

No flames were visible, but it could be a smoldering cigarette butt. Sliding off Molasses, Dustin ground tethered her, then patted her neck. "Be right back."

He approached quietly, but there was no hint of sound ahead of him. No teenage voices or music playing, and the darkness inside the shelter was broken only by a soft yellow glow.

Dustin pulled out his phone and hit the flashlight button. Pacing forward, he stepped into the shelter.

A sleeping bag was tossed in the corner. A small cook set rested on one of the stumps he'd seen earlier. The smoke escaping through a crack in the roof came from a tiki torch attached to the wall. It was extinguished but still smoldering, tar black smoke drifting upward.

"The hell?"

He stepped forward to put it out just as something moved in the corner of his vision. Pain struck the back of his head, and he threw out his hands to break his fall.

Then...darkness.

25

Charity patted Beach's nose for the twentieth time. "Soon, sweetie. I know, you're ready to roll, aren't you?"

She paced forward, leading the horse in another circle around the arena in the hopes that he'd settle down. They'd walked so many loops by now that Patchwork Annie had lost interest. The dog lay sprawled beside the gate, waiting for something more exciting to happen.

"What's up with you?" Kelli asked, rounding the corner with Shim at her side. "You forget the part where riding a horse involves being on his back?"

"I'm not that much of a newbie," Charity complained. She checked her watch again. "Dustin said he'd meet me at four. He's running late, but Beach doesn't like that excuse very much."

Shim frowned, checking the time as well. "Dustin didn't call?"

Charity shook her head.

"That's not like him." Kelli hauled out her phone and hit a button.

"I didn't want to interrupt if he's busy with something," Charity complained.

Shim raised a brow. "If he's busy, he won't answer the phone."

"I guess." She checked the time again, glancing down the path Dustin should be returning on.

Kelli pushed her phone back into her pocket. "He's not answering. Plus, he's over forty-five minutes late, which is not like him. He's usually a five minute, *sorry I got distracted* type of late."

Shim tilted his head toward the office. "Easy to see if he's on his way home."

Kelli took the reins as Charity hurried toward the computer, Patchwork Annie once again underfoot. "I can't believe I didn't think to use the *Finder* app," Charity complained.

"You were expecting him to show up any moment," Shim pointed out. "Fire her up."

Charity restarted the computer, waiting impatiently as the program re-opened. "Dustin is..." She leaned forward. "He's going to be more than late. That's a long ride from here."

Shim peeked over her shoulder, concern rising on his face. "Click real time. It's too data hungry to run all the time, but right now, it'll help pinpoint his movements."

Charity made the adjustments, and they waited for the program to shift. Instead of an update every five minutes, this version could follow the GPS location live.

Two minutes later the cold spot in Charity's gut grew even larger as the icon showing Dustin's position didn't change at all.

"He's not moving." She glanced up at Shim and then at a

frowning Caleb who now stood in the doorway. "Dustin's not moving."

Caleb stepped into the room. "Who's the closest to him right now?"

Charity made the adjustments to the program, but shook her head as worry continued to rise. "No one. All of us—all the hands are en route back for dinner."

Curses hit the air, then Caleb called out orders. "Shim, you stay here and keep in touch if anything changes. See if you can find out who last talked to Dustin, and when."

"Yes, sir." Shim settled behind the desk.

Charity followed hard on Caleb's heels.

"Kelli. Call Luke and let him know Dustin is missing."

"Already called, and he's on his way. He'll grab an ATV and gear and join us." Kelli was tightening the clinch on Caleb's horse. "Lacey is nearly ready."

"I want to come with you." Charity spoke loudly to get their attention, her heart pounding in her throat.

Two worried glances darted her way then back to their tasks.

Caleb shook his head. "I have to ride fast, Tee. Dustin won't thank me if you get hurt."

"Kelli can ride with me, then. Beach is ready to go," Charity added. "Please. I need to be there. Just in case."

The look he gave her was full of understanding, his face still stern. Just when she had given up, he nodded briskly, motioning for Kelli to join them. "Don't fall off, or Dustin will kill me."

Charity couldn't speak past the knot in her throat.

They were up in the saddle, Caleb already whirling toward the trail. Kelli patted Charity's fingers reassuringly. "Hold on tight, darling. We're going to fly."

Slowly at first—slowly enough Charity wanted to kick her

heels into Beach's flanks and get him moving. But Kelli was smart, increasing speed one notch at a time until they were all but flying up and past the edge of Big Sky lake. Out to the east where the rolling hills slowly flattened to the grazing fields. Patchwork Annie raced beside them, a bundle of muscles and blur of fur as she too flew.

The bright blue sky was wrong. The fresh scent of summer an insult considering the fear pounding in Charity's chest.

She knew the trip had to have taken at least thirty minutes, but when they arrived, she'd barely had time to catch her breath.

Spotting Dustin's horse grazing outside the small shelter raised her hopes. Caleb shot ahead of them. He dismounted and darted into the wooden shelter, stepping back into the sunlight before Kelli had pulled Beach to a standstill.

"He's not here," Caleb snapped. "What the hell is going on?"

Kelli had her phone out again, even as she and Charity dismounted. "Shim? Check the monitor. Is Dustin still in one spot? Yeah? Okay, tell me when I'm near the marker. Hot if I'm headed the right direction, cold if I'm farther away."

After that ride, her legs were rubbery, but Charity somehow kept her balance and paced forward, Patchwork Annie by her side. They crossed into the shelter and Annie yipped, frantically digging in the hay.

"Nearly there? Damn, that means his phone is here, even though he isn't," Kelli said right as Annie barked, pawing at the ground.

Charity knelt and picked up the phone Annie had uncovered. "Dustin's." She glanced up at Caleb's stricken face. "We're not done yet."

"This is a dead end, Tee. The tracker app is set to our phones," Caleb reminded her softly, anguish in his voice.

"I know. But *she's* tuned in directly to Dustin." Charity knelt and called Patchwork Annie over. She held out the phone and let the dog sniff it, praying the order Dustin had given to guard could be reset. "Where's Dustin? Where is he?" She pulled the phone away then presented it to her again. "Where's Dustin?"

Annie whimpered, backing out of the shelter.

By the time Charity got to her feet, Patchwork Annie was sniffing the ground in ever widening circles.

"Come on," Kelli called, swinging herself back into the saddle. "Mount up, because if this works, we'll need to stay close."

One quick step forward, and Caleb was beside her. He leaned over, hands clasped into a loop for Charity to step into. With more grace than she felt, she was up behind Kelli a moment later, whistling for Annie.

The dog pulled up sharply and looked at her intently.

"Find Dustin," Charity ordered.

Annie raced ahead, and Kelli urged Beach after her. Thankfully, the dog constantly looked back to make sure Charity remained in sight. Caleb rode beside them, his gaze darting over the land as if hoping to spot Dustin out for a casual stroll.

They were on a part of the ranch Charity had never been to before. "Do you know where we are?" she shouted in Kelli's ear. "What's nearby?"

"We'll eventually hit the highway, but there are some landmarks coming up." Kelli leaned forward, urging Beach to go faster.

Time had no meaning. Tears streaked Charity's face as her eyes watered from the sharp wind. Her fingers gripping Kelli were rigid, and her entire body felt shaken through and through. None of the discomfort mattered, though.

Dustin. Where was he?

Annie veered sharply to the right.

Kelli slowed and pulled to a stop. Caleb switched from riding to running without a pause, racing to where Annie was scratching at a broken board laying sideways across the base of a wide culvert.

An instant later Kelli was helping Caleb lift the wood. Charity crowded in as well, the rough slab biting into her palms, splinters breaking off as they heaved it sideways.

He was beneath the board, half sunk into the mud. Dustin lay face up, his skin pale and a trickle of blood running down his temple. Charity dropped to her knees beside him, pressing her fingers to his pulse.

When a solid thump struck, she could have wept for joy. "He's alive."

"Thank God." Caleb crouched beside her, one arm around her shoulders. He touched his knuckles to his brother's cheek. "We won't move him yet. Kelli is calling in our location for a medivac." He squeezed her shoulders tightly.

Instinctively, Charity reassured him. "Dustin's going to be okay."

Caleb took a deep breath, shrugging out of his coat and covering Dustin the best he could. "He is."

"He has to be." Charity lifted Dustin's fingers to her lips and kissed them. "You hear that, Dustin? You're going to be okay."

Patchwork Annie slipped under her arm on the opposite side, whining because her favourite person wasn't petting her. Charity gave her a hug instead. "You are the best and smartest pupper ever."

The dog settled beside Dustin, staring at him with concern.

Charity held on tight and fought to be brave. "I love you," she whispered, suddenly glad that it wasn't the first time she'd said it. "I love you," she repeated, louder this time. "Now you need to get better so you can tell me you love me too. Because that was our deal."

Caleb was back, and Kelli was there, all of them crowded around to try to warm Dustin as they waited for the rescue team to arrive.

Inside her heart, a warm glow burned steady, and Charity put all her effort into holding Dustin there with the strength of her love.

26

———

*D*ustin's head hurt. Come to think of it, his butt hurt, his back hurt, and his mouth felt like trash. Small beeping sounds echoed from his right, and his hands couldn't move.

What the hell had he been doing?

"You're awake." Charity whispered the words.

He twisted his head toward her, and a spike of pain shot through his skull. "Ouch. What...?" A rush of memories arrived. The smoke by the shelter. Being hit. "Damn it. Someone clocked me."

She stood beside him now, fingers linked with his. "Yeah, they did. But you're okay."

"You're lucky you have a very hard head." Luke this time, stepping up behind Charity. His expression held more relief than amusement. "Like I've always told you."

Dustin didn't have the energy, but some things were sacred. "Picture me flipping you off right now."

He clearly was in a hospital room. The nondescript grey-white walls and the scent would have been enough of a clue.

But the bed railings and the IV sticking into the back of his hand were unavoidable proof.

Caleb now stood shoulder to shoulder with Luke, both towering over Charity who refused to let go of his hand. "You scared the hell out of us," Caleb said.

"I'll apologize after I find out what happened." Dustin lifted his free hand and gingerly touched his head. "Bandages?"

His oldest brother said something over his shoulder, and Luke stepped away. Caleb turned back and answered the question. "You might have a tough head, but even rocks get broken when smacked with tire irons."

Crap. Nasty shit. "Who was it?"

A second's pause. Charity made a face. "Well, you know how you said we didn't have to worry about your stalker anymore?"

"You're kidding me. It was Patty?" Dustin met Caleb's gaze. "You called the RCMP."

"I did. And they went and talked to her. She's been in town for the past month, living at the Heart Falls motel. They warned her to stay away—which appears to have set her off." Caleb tapped his head. "Not to excuse her behavior, but she's one sick woman. Like literally, she's not well."

"She nearly killed Dustin." The anger in Charity's voice was ice cold. "She can get treatment for her illness somewhere far away from Heart Falls."

"Agreed." Caleb rested a calming hand on her shoulder. "Dustin. Tell us what you know, and we'll fill in the blanks."

"I saw smoke coming from the shelter. Hopped off Molasses—" His horse. "She okay?"

"She's fine. When we hit the shelter, she hadn't moved more than five feet from where you dropped the reins," Caleb shared.

"You train animals well, bro." Luke was back, his smirk suspicious as all get-out.

Dustin ignored that mystery for a minute. "I had my phone in my hand so I could use the flashlight. Walked around the corner of the shelter and *bam*. Patty must have been waiting for me." He frowned. "How is that possible? She was way the hell out on the back of Silver Stone land just waiting for me?"

Caleb sighed. "Turns out, yeah. Seems word has gotten around about your favourite route. She told the RCMP she was certain that if she could just get you alone, you'd remember you were madly in love with her."

"And nothing says true love more than a tire iron at close range," Luke added.

"She had an ATV and somehow hauled you onto it. At some point, she realized that while she might be able to get away with driving illegally through town to her motel room, she was going to have a hard time explaining your unconscious body," Charity said dryly.

Dustin glanced around the room. "I'm guessing she didn't take me back to the ranch and apologize."

Luke shook his head. "She dumped you and tried to hide the evidence. The only reason we found you was Charity's quick thinking."

Charity shook her head. "Here's who rescued you."

She whistled. Suddenly, paws appeared at the edge of the bed. Patchwork Annie's low whine sounded as her nose barely made it to the top of the high mattress.

"Breaking all the rules here, bro," Luke warned, but he scooped the dog up and lifted her close enough Dustin could pet her. "Best purchase ever the day you brought her home."

"You don't buy friends." Dustin ruffled the top of Annie's head. "Good girl."

Annie snuck in a lick before Luke carried her off to hide her in the corner of the room.

It was all unreal. "Thanks for saving me."

"Thanks for being one tough bastard," Caleb said. "I don't ever want to have to do that again."

"I don't plan to have more stalkers." Dustin paused, worry rising. "Tee. You stay with Tamara and Caleb tonight. Don't go to the cottage by yourself—"

"It's okay." Charity squeezed his hand. "They caught Patty, remember? She's under arrest."

His head spun with relief. "Right. Good. How'd they catch her?"

"She came into town to pack up her stuff from the motel. Stopped at Buns and Roses, if you can believe it, looking all cocky. Only Shim had called Fern to tell her you were missing, and Fern got suspicious, so when Patty went to the bathroom, Fern locked her in until the RCMP arrived."

Shock hit, then amusement. "Only Fern. What if Patty had been innocent?"

Charity shrugged. "Fern said if she was wrong, she'd take the punishment, but she was ninety-nine point nine percent sure Patty was involved."

Which put the last puzzle piece into place. "I've got the best friends and family."

"You really do." Luke winked. "Glad you're okay, bro. Charity is going to stay with you. We're headed back to the ranch for a while."

"You need anything, you call," Caleb ordered Charity. "We'll be back in a couple hours. Or some of us will be back."

Charity released Dustin's fingers, rising from her chair to give both Caleb and Luke big hugs. "I'll take care of him," she promised.

"I know you will." Caleb kissed her forehead. He pointed a finger at Dustin. "Rest. Need you back at Silver Stone."

"Prefer to be there than here," Dustin assured him. He waved goodbye, the move taking more energy than expected.

The room grew quiet. Just the monitors with the faint noises and the low buzz of the overhead lights. Charity slipped back to his side, staring down at him as if memorizing for a test.

"Do I look like hell?" Dustin asked.

She nodded. "And yet I'll take you beat-up and bruised any day over what you looked like when we found you." Her voice broke. "I was so scared you were dead."

He opened his arms. "Damn it, Tee. You can't cry when I can't make it better."

She curled up against him, head resting on his chest, hands clutching his torso. With her body half in the bed, half off, Dustin held her as she wept quietly.

God, he hurt inside and out, listening to her cry.

"I'm still here." Dustin soothed. "And I still remember that this morning you told me you loved me. Whatever bullshit we dealt with today, that's the part I want to talk about. Loving you. Not just today, but tomorrow and the day after." He kissed the top of her head, stroking the curls away from her face. "We're going to go for horseback rides and swim in the lake. We're going to turn the cottage into our home, with pictures of family and friends. We're going to do all those things together."

Charity hiccupped, her shaky breathing slowing. Growing steadier. She wiggled upright, wiping tears from her face. "Okay."

Laughter tickled inside. Such a Charity statement. "What are you saying okay to?"

"All of it. Riding and swimming and decorating and time with friends." She lifted his fingers to her lips and kissed them. "But most of all to loving you each and every day."

Even stuck in a hospital bed, bumped and bruised, Dustin couldn't have been happier. "Love you, Tee."

"Love you, Dus," she offered, a hint of a smile breaking through.

A soft *woof* rose from by her feet.

She glanced down, then at the door of his hospital room. "Since you're already where you're not supposed to be, I may as well go into full-trouble mode."

A moment later, Patchwork Annie was on the bed, sniffing Dustin vigorously. He petted her then pointed to his feet. "Lay down."

Annie turned, sighing contentedly as she settled beside his legs.

Dustin eyed the remaining room on the bed. It would be tight, but he could do it. He wiggled slightly to the left then patted the space he'd created. "Now your turn."

He thought she'd protest, but Charity carefully lifted herself into place, curling up beside him. He stretched his arm over her, careful not to tangle the IV cord, and all the aches and pains faded.

"I love you," he whispered again.

She stroked his fingers gently. "Okay."

Dustin fell asleep still smiling.

EPILOGUE

August, Silver Stone ranch

Charity finished placing a potholder on the table next to a bright yellow present tied with pink ribbons. Harper's horse-themed birthday party was being held at Silver Stone with all the family in attendance. The fact that excited Charity instead of scaring her meant everything.

It had taken a little time. Time for Dustin to recover from his attack, and time for Charity to fully embrace being a part of the Stone whirlwind. She still liked the one-on-one time the best because that's when she found out more. Like how Kelli had found her way to the ranch, and what Sasha hoped for the future.

But the Stones continued to prove they were a family she could count on, and that knowledge was priceless.

"Sorry I'm late. Caleb was driving." Dustin rushed into the

cottage and past Charity. "I just need to get changed. I can be ready to go in five minutes."

"You can have thirty. Ivy called to say they're running late. Carter *accidentally* fell into the mudpies Chloe and Harper were making." Charity's amusement flashed bright. "There are pre-birthday party baths happening right now."

Dustin slowed his mad dash. "I'm sure they were mud *cakes*, being as it's a birthday and all."

"Probably. I'm sure the kids will tell us all about it when they get here." Charity followed him into the bedroom, watching with appreciation as he stripped off the dress jacket he wore. "I like how you look in your cowboy gear, but can I just tell you... In a suit? You are devastatingly handsome."

"The *hashtag silver stone stud* had to put on another good show for the media." Dustin slid into his usual jeans with a contented sigh. "I'm glad I only have a few more of these lined up to do, though. You were there when I did the first interview. You saw how fancy they did everything up."

"I did." She dropped to the bed, enjoying the current show as he stripped off the tie and shirt. "I also saw your Uncle Frank act like an entirely new man after you and Caleb insisted he be a part of the interview. Making that first story about both Silver Stone and Crooked Creek, and the family connection between them, was brilliant."

"It let us give the media the story we wanted to tell, about the horses and the operation. Kept their noses out of private lives and our pocketbooks."

"Mostly. I'm still *hashtag the silver princess*." Charity rolled her eyes at the latest social media tag to have shown up. She didn't want to waste time watching the drama, so Fern kept an eye out for any changes for them. "Which is better than people talking about your cock or stud services."

"Tons better. By the way, Uncle Frank was there today," Dustin shared.

Charity blinked. "Really?"

"Yup. Showed up in the parking lot and insisted on coming with us. He told me he'd listen closely to make sure none of our pre-arranged *out of bounds* topics slipped into the conversation."

Her amusement was bigger than her shock. "Go, Uncle Frank."

"I still can't get over the change in the man. I mean, he's still a cranky bastard at times, but he's turned a completely new leaf when it comes to the family. I told him we'd come visit later this month."

"Good."

"And Walker decided he'll come with me for the next interview. And I think Kelli is doing the final one. It's aimed at the breeding community, so she'll be brilliant."

Charity rose and strolled over, the roses on her skirt flashing as she walked. "You are all brilliant, how you've managed to take the whole media circus and turn it into a positive thing for Silver Stone. And Crooked Creek."

"We all have different talents. It's helped." He followed her into the kitchen and leaned against the counter beside her, looking thoughtful. "There's something... I can almost remember it."

She opened the pot and gave the soup they were bringing to the party one final stir.

Dustin snapped his fingers. "That's it. Stone soup."

Charity paused and frowned into the pot. "What? It's tortilla."

He stepped behind her, hands settling on her waist. "Not what you're cooking. What my family does. It's a story I was told a long time ago. About how even though we're stones, we're not just immobile lumps."

"*Ahhh.*" She nodded with amusement. "You're rolling stones." She wiggled from under his fingers and shook the soup spoon at him. "No tickling."

"We're resilient. And resourceful. Stones by birth or Stones by choice. He put the spoon aside. "Even when it feels as if there's no solution, we put on a pot of water and all chip in. Anything we've got. Some put in more, some less. Some days more, some days less, but we all do what we can. And in the end, we have enough to support the entire family. Enough—"

"Love," she interrupted before kissing him. The truth shone bright and clear. "You have enough love for an entire family because you *are* a family. Through and through. Even if you don't always do things the same way. Even if you like different things, you're always supportive of each other. That's love—we both know it."

The way he looked at her then was as if she had hung the moon.

"God, you're brilliant and beautiful, and I should wait and do this up special on your birthday next week like I'd planned, but I can't." He pulled a ring from his pocket. It was silver with pale blue stones set in the shape of a flower. "You know that bit I just said about being a Stone by choice?"

Charity's jaw dropped. "Dustin Stone. Tell me you did not just pull an engagement ring from your pocket."

"Not going to lie." He dropped to one knee. "Since we have mudpies baking, there's more than enough time to let you know that I'm one hundred percent certain. I'm in love with you, Tee. You make me want to do everything I can to make you smile. You make me want to sit still and listen to your heart beat. You make me want to climb mountains and shout your name to the moon."

She pressed her fingers to her lips, gaze darting between his eyes and the ring. This was really happening. Her heart overflowed with happiness, and she wasn't sure her feet were still touching the floor.

He spoke softer. "You make me hard, but while I'm glad we enjoy that part of our time together, this isn't just about sex. Because you make me want to be soft, too. To learn how to give to you, and be there for you, from now to eternity."

This was all right, and all wrong. Charity didn't want the traditional parts—she wanted him. A moment later, she was down on the floor next to him. Fingers wrapped around his.

Amusement bubbled inside along with joy. "One, your timing sucks."

He laughed. "I hope I know where this is going."

She held up a second finger. "Two, I promised we'd go riding with Emma and Sasha after the little girls go home."

"Beach and Annie will enjoy that." Dustin lifted her fingers to his lips and kissed them. "And three?"

"I love you." Charity shook her head in amusement. "Germs and all."

His expression softened. "So, you going to marry me?"

She raised a brow. "Did you ask?"

Dustin considered for a moment. "Maybe I missed that part."

Charity leaned her forehead on his. "Maybe you did. Although the ring was a big clue."

Dustin cleared his throat. "Tee, I really want you to marry me. So make me the happiest guy in the world and say my favourite word."

"Chores?"

He caught her against him. "*Tee*."

His eyes were shining, and she couldn't wait another second. She nodded. "No more teasing. Okay."

Dustin raised a brow. "Okay...*what?*"

She spoke softly. "Okay, I'll marry you."

"That's *hashtag one hitched cowboy*," he joked before turning serious. He slipped the ring on her finger, his hands trembling. "I do love you. I'm stoked to spend the rest of my life showing you how much."

Charity lifted her hand and admired the ring. "It's beautiful. But I'm hiding it until after the cake is served so we don't upstage Harper's big day."

She kissed him then, fingers entwined around his biceps. Stroking down his sides, pouring her love into the gesture.

"If we don't stop now, we're going to be really late for the party," he warned when she untucked his shirt from his pants and slid her hands over his bare skin.

"We'll be quick," she promised.

Quick, enthusiastic, and very satisfying. Charity couldn't have found a better way to celebrate being engaged to Dustin. To being exactly where she was supposed to be.

In love.

DUSTIN WAS GRINNING way too hard when they finally made it across the yard to the main ranch house. Somehow they walked in less than ten minutes after Walker's family had arrived, so the noise and confusion were still high enough no one noticed the just-had-sex glow on Charity's face.

Well, maybe one person saw. Tamara gave Charity a long look before turning to Dustin and rolling her eyes.

Dustin put the soup pot on the counter with a grin, not one bit ashamed.

He pressed a kiss to Charity's cheek. "Which part of the mayhem are you diving into?"

She leaned into his side as she glanced around the room. Dustin looked too, and another type of satisfaction rolled him up tight.

Family. Everywhere.

Ginny was curled up in her favourite spot on the couch with Demi nestled in her arms enjoying an early supper. Tucker stood behind the couch, supposedly talking to Ivy, who stood in the quietest corner of the room, but his gaze was fixed on his daughter.

Ivy wore an understanding smile as she tucked a strand of hair behind her ear then bent to answer her daughter's question. Harper pointed across the room, and Ivy nodded.

The little girl raced across the living room and crawled up on one of the mismatched dining table chairs. She tucked her fingers behind her back and stared intently at her birthday cake that rested in the middle of the table in a place of honour. The green icing top held a barn, fences, and three plastic horses.

It was the crown jewels based on Harper's expression.

Walker was working on something in the kitchen, Emma beside him. Tamara was visiting with Kelli, speaking quietly at the island. Kelli and Luke had announced her pregnancy the previous week. Luke's ear-to-ear grin hadn't faded one bit since.

Luke and Caleb chatted outside the open door while holding Carter and Tyler upside down by their ankles. The boys were screeching with laughter as they swayed like monkeys.

Chloe and Sasha sat on the floor in the laundry room, playing jacks.

"Everyone seems happy." Charity tucked her fingers into Dustin's beltloop. "I think I'll just stay here by you for a bit."

He nuzzled his nose against her neck. "Good by me."

Eventually the party slipped forward, triggered by Harper. She stood on her chair, finger bouncing as she counted everyone in the room. Her lips moved silently, but she nodded firmly when she reached the end then pointed at herself. "Daddy," she called loud enough to get Walker's attention. "All the Stones are here."

"Damn right they are," Dustin murmured in Charity's ear.

Walker flashed him a warning glance but laughed. "Yes, sweet pea. All the Stones are here."

She thrust her hands in the air. "Then it's time for my birfday."

Food, games, singing, and presents all followed. A happy mix of moments of contentment and wild flashes of energy.

They were walking out to the barn for the riding portion of the party when Dustin found himself next to Tucker.

Ginny wore Demi in a baby carrier on her chest. She was talking with Charity, who held Carter's hand in hers. The four of them were half a pace behind Dustin and Tucker, but Tucker's gaze kept darting back to his wife and child as if he couldn't help himself.

"You're going to trip," Dustin warned, amused as all get-out.

"Wait until you're in my boots. Then you'll get it."

Dustin nearly stumbled over his own feet before he realized he was staring at Charity. He snickered then elbowed Tucker. "I've already got the mooning over the woman I love part down pat."

Tucker laughed. "You two make a good couple."

"Thanks for hiring Charity when you did," Dustin returned. "Made for the perfect timing."

Tucker shook his head. "Can't take the credit for that one. I mean, I had it in mind to ask for help, but Caleb basically told me to get my act in gear. I think he called her in for the first interview."

"Not you?"

The man shrugged. "I can't remember the details, but I can say Caleb is the main reason Charity got hired."

Son of a gun. Dustin glanced over at his oldest brother. Had he really organized that? Hell of a good thing in the end, but...

Now ahead of him, Charity was held fast in Carter's grasp. It wasn't until they'd reached the arena that he let her go. Carter skipped up to Walker's side, tugging on his dad's sleeve frantically.

Walker lifted his son beside Chloe who was already balanced on the railing, and the two of them *oohed* and *aahed* as Ashton led a horse into the arena that held his beaming great-granddaughter, Harper, on its back.

Dustin clapped along with the others, but his gaze went right back to his oldest brother.

Charity curled her hand around Dustin's arm. "Why are you staring at Caleb as if he might explode at any moment?"

"I think Caleb might have set us up."

She paused, blinked, then smiled brightly. "If so, I'm very, very grateful. Also impressed. How on earth?"

"I have no idea. Wait—" Dustin ticked off the things he knew for certain. "He sent you to Crooked Creek with me. He agreed we should go to the bachelor auction together. When I brought you home to the cottage, he said he'd go to bat for me."

"He called in early June and asked if I was still looking for an office job." Charity considered hard, trying to remember. "The next call was from Tucker, but now that I think back on it, yeah. Caleb was the one who contacted me first and told me he thought I'd be perfect for the..." She stalled out. "Oh my God."

"What?" Dustin demanded.

She turned to face him. "He said I'd be a perfect addition to the Silver Stone family. I remember the wording because it sounded oddly old-fashioned but made sense. Because of course working at the ranch is like being a part of a family."

Dustin's heart pounded.

The entire time it had been Caleb.

So many emotions, so many memories. Caleb had always been there for the family, every step of the way. Even now, Dustin was still being guided by his brother.

Across the yard from where Dustin and Charity stood, Caleb leaned on the railing next to Tamara, his hand resting on her hip. The two of them comfortable yet connected as always. That's what Dustin hoped to look like years from now with Charity.

Caleb's gaze met his, and suddenly Dustin knew exactly what came next.

He caught Charity's hand, turning her to face him. "You have the ring in your pocket?"

Charity nodded, reaching in to pull it out. She opened her hand to show it lying in her palm. "Need something?"

"For you to put it on. The party can handle a little more celebrating at this point." He slipped the pale blue stone back where it belonged, kissed her knuckles, and stared into her eyes. "I love you, Tee. Thanks for agreeing to be mine. I promise you'll never regret saying yes."

He didn't need to do anything else. His family had already spotted the ring.

Cheers and handshaking and back-patting and laughter ensued. The children raced in circles with Patchwork Annie barking excitedly. All the ladies had to see the ring. All his brothers had to pat him enthusiastically on the back.

After offering a firm embrace, Caleb stepped back and dipped his chin at Dustin in approval. He pulled Charity in for a hug.

"Welcome to the family," he said when he let her go.

She had tears in her eyes as she took Dustin's hand again, leaning into him as she took in the happy chaos around them.

That night as they lay in bed and made plans, Dustin promised himself that he'd never forget what this felt like. Being in love. Being cared for. Caring for and loving Charity.

She cupped his cheek in her hand and smiled into his eyes. "I love you."

"Forever," Dustin vowed with all his heart.

New York Times Bestselling Author Vivian Arend
invites you to Heart Falls. These contemporary ranchers live in
a tiny town in central Alberta, tucked into the rolling foothills.
Enjoy the ride as they each find their happily-ever-afters.

The Stones of Heart Falls
A Rancher's Heart
A Rancher's Song
A Rancher's Bride
A Rancher's Love
A Rancher's Vow

Holidays in Heart Falls
A Firefighter's Christmas Gift
A Soldier's Christmas Wish
A Hero's Christmas Hope
A Cowboy's Christmas List
A Rancher's Christmas Kiss

The Coleman's of Heart Falls
The Cowgirl's Forever Love
The Cowgirl's Secret Love
The Cowgirl's Chosen Love

ABOUT THE AUTHOR

New York Times and *USA Today* bestselling author Vivian Arend loves to share the products of her over-active imagination with her readers. She writes contemporary, western, and light-hearted paranormal romances. The stories are humorous yet emotional, usually with a large cast of family or friends, and a guaranteed happily-ever-after. Vivian lives in British Columbia, Canada, with her husband of many years—her inspiration for every hero and a willing companion for all sorts of adventures.

www.vivianarend.com

www.ingramcontent.com/pod-product-compliance
Lightning Source LLC
Chambersburg PA
CBHW030758210726

48290CB00002B/322